THE FIRE

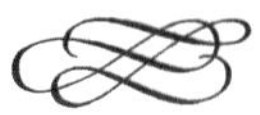

NANCY JACKSON

Hardback ISBN: 978-0-578562-84-1
Paperback ISBN: 978-1-655105-44-9
eBook ISBN: 978-1-393660-11-8

Published in the United States
Wild Ideas Press
Edmond, Oklahoma

Book Cover Design by
Angela Westerman of
AK Organic Abstracts
AKOrganicAbstracts.com

As always I must dedicate my work to my family. Being a wife, mother, grandmother, and great-grandmother has been the greatest pleasure of my life.

I want to dedicate this book as well to my editor Agho Armoudian. I am so blessed to have found you. Your work in editing my books has made me a better writer.

To Angela Westerman who creates my original book covers and graphics. Thank you for 'getting me'! Look her up and hire her for yourself at AKOrganicAbstracts.com

CONTENTS

CHAPTER 1

As unconsciousness gave way to awareness, suddenly adrenaline surged through her body. Panic seized her as she realized flames were licking at her feet. She struggled to pull free, but heavy rope wound around each wrist and secured her tightly. She tried to draw her feet up away from the fire, but they too, would not move.

How had she gotten to this place? This place of torment and fear? She was suspended on a large cross type structure, sturdy and solid. Surrounding the base of the structure was a circle of fire that was growing more ferocious by the moment.

The night was black and the only sound she could hear was the crackling of the fire. She screamed for help, but heard no response. There was no one there. There was no one to save her.

Sweat dripped into her eyes and stung as her body

convulsed with wracking sobs. She jerked her hands and feet in an attempt to pull free from the tightly wound rope. Whoever had tied her had taken the time to ensure it securely anchored her to the post. The rope was thick and rough and gouged into her skin.

I have to think clearly. I have to calm down. I have to figure a way out of this. She took a deep breath, closed her eyes, and mentally offered a prayer of panicked desperation.

Almost immediately, she felt a soothing calm blanket her, but it was not a calming assurance that she would be rescued, but one resigning her to her fate. She would die here today.

CHAPTER 2

Seven days earlier…

Monday morning Lainey stood before Carrie with flushed cheeks and a broad smile. She had just jerked her stocking cap off of her dark mane and it danced around her head in dark feathery wisps.

"Don't you just love Christmas time?" asked Lainey Tate, Carrie's partner at the Oklahoma State Bureau of Investigation.

Carrie was trying not to laugh at her partner and the result was a twisted grin on her face. It was hard not to love everything about Lainey. Her energy and positive attitude encouraged and enlivened everyone she came in contact with, even in the most difficult situations.

"Yes, Lainey, I've always loved Christmas," said Gerald, a seasoned OSBI agent who was standing nearby.

Carrie sat silent. She had loved Christmas when she was a child, but when her parents had both died in a fatal car crash while in her twenties, she had lost the will to live. Happy memories, holidays, and friendships had all died along with them.

Recently though, thanks in part to Lainey, Carrie had laid down toxic emotions and begun to move forward. Lainey had showed her that her parents, who had always been her champions, would want their love and encouragement to continue even though they were gone.

Carrie realized that wallowing in her pain only produced a destructive lifestyle. One that was rapidly taking her down a dark, emotional hole and bringing dishonor to her parents and the great job they had done raising her. So, she focused on their love which would never die. It had been a slow process, but the heavy burden she had carried for over eight years was nearly gone.

"I think this year Lainey, I will enjoy it," said Carrie as her smile widened across her face.

Lainey noticed Carrie's attempt to hide amusement and reached up to touch her hair. "It's sticking up everywhere, isn't it?" she asked as she attempted to smooth down her floating mane with both hands.

Carrie burst out laughing. Each attempt Lainey made to corral her hair only resulted in producing more static and therefore a growing black halo.

Suddenly Lainey stopped trying and was overcome by laughter, realizing her attempts were futile. She plopped down in her desk chair and both she and Carrie laughed until tears rolled down their cheeks.

Gerald stood and simply looked back and forth between the two. He had a wife and three daughters so this was common behavior to him. Finally, when he thought the worst of the hilarity had stopped, he said, "Okay, so Randy wanted me to talk with you two about this case. He was here earlier but he had to leave, so he asked me to pass it on to you two."

A new case caused the ladies to shift gears mentally and focus on the file Gerald held in his hands. That folder represented someone's pain and suffering, criminals causing destruction, and work for the agents. Both ladies stood and flanked Gerald, one on each side, and peered at the contents of the folder.

"There has been a series of deaths in the Robbers Cave area down in the southeastern part of the state," began Gerald.

Carrie reached up and took the file from Gerald and flipped through the pages. What she saw horrified her. She looked up at Gerald. "These people were all burned alive?"

"The coroner in Latimer County is inexperienced, but yes, she feels they were," responded Gerald. "There was smoke inhalation in each one.

"There have been animal deaths, burnings, in the same area recently. There were no autopsies on those, but they could have been burned alive as well, or not. Maybe the killer began with the animals and then escalated to humans." Gerald paused to let the gravity of it all sink in.

Lainey had been standing silently by listening. Her focus had been on Gerald and Carrie as they discussed what was in the file. She had been in law enforcement for several years with the Oklahoma City Police Department before being accepted to the OSBI.

Immediately upon arrival, she had been inserted into the middle of an ongoing investigation regarding human trafficking and murdered prostitutes. That had been horrific, but this seemed far worse.

"Randy wants you two down there ASAP. You are to meet with the county sheriff of Latimer County. Her name is Wanda Markum. She's the one who reached out for our help. Get on the road. I'll make arrangements for a hotel for you in Wilberton. You may be there a while."

CARRIE KEPT a go-bag for just such occasions, but she knew for a possible extended stay, she would need to add to it. Lainey hadn't thought to keep a go-bag, so she needed to prepare one. They agreed to go home and pack, and Carrie would pick Lainey up at her home in exactly one hour.

Wilburton, Oklahoma was two-and-a-half hours, east and then south, from Oklahoma City, that is with a normal person abiding by the speed limit laws. Carrie always tried to follow the speed limit, since she was in law enforcement, but today her foot was heavy.

Lainey's naturally happy demeanor was dampened. She had spent the first part of their journey reading the file Gerald had given them. It was enough to dampen anyone's spirit.

There had been three people die from fire. In the file

there were notations of at least six animal deaths in the last six months. Whether they had died in a fire or been burned afterwards, they didn't know.

Apparently, the animal deaths related to fire come and go depending on the time of year. Local law enforcement had been battling with those for years. But they had never had human deaths by fire until now.

Reading the text thoroughly was unsettling enough for Lainey, but when she saw the crime scene photos, she felt intense empathy for the victims. She could not imagine the horror of dying in a fire. She was glad she had not eaten breakfast, because it had tied her stomach in knots and she felt nauseous.

"Have you had to work a fire crime scene before?" Lainey asked.

"Yes. It was my first case with the OSBI. It was a bad deal. I saw things I never thought I'd see in Oklahoma."

"I can't imagine the horror of being in a fire. There's just something about it that terrifies me. Of all the ways to die, I think that is the one most horrific," said Lainey.

She turned her head and gazed out at the countryside as Carrie drove. Going east on I-40 from Oklahoma City, the landscape quickly changed from rolling hills and prairie to dense wooded areas. Being December though, the trees were gray and brown, hiding out until spring when they would once again come to life.

As Lainey watched the dreary landscape speed by, she felt a deep sense of foreboding inside. She had only felt that heavy warning once before. When she was only fourteen years old, she had been raped. She had felt that same feeling then, that she felt now.

"Are you okay?" Carrie asked. Lainey had gotten quiet and the atmosphere in the SUV seemed heavy.

Lainey turned to look at Carrie and gave her a reassuring smile. "I'm good." She didn't want to share her sudden concern with Carrie, after all it might be nothing at all. Sharing this particular feeling might give Carrie pause and cause her to wonder if she could trust Lainey to put her emotions in check in order to focus on the case.

The sun was trying to peak through the clouds as they pulled into Wilburton. The wind pushed against the SUV in random gusts. Carrie was glad that she would have a chance to pull over and stop fighting the wind. It had fought her the entire trip and was causing her to feel cranky.

"Lainey, text Sheriff Markum and let her know we're in town, but will stop and get a bite to eat before we head on over to their station," said Carrie.

Lainey sent the Sheriff a text. "Done. Wait, she already texted back and asked where we would eat. She said she would meet us there and have lunch with us." Lainey looked up at Carrie for instruction.

"Ask her where she recommends. I'm sure there is a local place that beats the chains."

Lainey looked back down at her phone. Her fingers flew, and a response was quickly received. "She said we can meet her at the station and ride with her, or just meet her at Riley's Eats. It's on Main Street downtown."

"Let's meet her there," said Carrie.

They were just one block from Riley's, so it only made sense to Carrie to meet there. She also didn't want to be without her vehicle.

At eleven thirty on a Monday morning Riley's was almost empty. The morning breakfast crowd had come and gone and the lunch crowd was just trickling in. Carrie and Lainey located a table where they could watch the front door and out the front windows.

Sheriff Markum soon arrived. Carrie's first reaction was, *I hope I still look that good at the sheriff's age; and after life and the job has taken its toll on me.* She chided herself for expecting a frumpy middle-aged woman.

Wanda was lean and attractive, classy even. Her dark hair was pulled neatly into a bun at the nape of her neck. No visible signs of aging made it difficult for Carrie to guess exactly how old she was.

Carrie stood and shook Sheriff Markum's outstretched hand and looked her firmly in the eye. "Thank you both so much for coming down here. We appreciate it."

Her sincerity was clear and Carrie responded. "We're happy to help. I'm Carrie Border and this is Lainey Tate."

"As you know, I'm the Sheriff of Latimer County. I was elected fifteen years ago after working for the Wilburton Police Department for twenty years. I've lived in this area all my life."

Carrie quickly did the math. This lady had to be at least fifty-five years old. She was also very well spoken. This part of the state often had a reputation for being backwoods and uneducated, but if the Sheriff was any indication of the rest of the population, those rumors were unfounded.

"Please call me Wanda. We're casual around here."

"You can address us by either our first or last names. We hear both and answer to most." Carrie smiled.

They all ordered lunch and got right down to business while they were waiting for their orders to arrive.

"As I said, I've lived around here most of my life and never in my thirty-five years of law enforcement have I ever witnessed anything so horrific. The coroner has determined that all three were alive when the fire started."

Lainey thought she might be ill. As the bubbly waitress sat their meals in front of them, Lainey's stomach lurched and she shut her eyes. But the smell continued to penetrate her body.

"I'll be right back. I need the restroom before I eat." Lainey stood and quickly left the table.

"Maybe we should put work aside while we eat," said the sheriff.

Carrie nodded as she looked to where Lainey had disappeared behind the restroom door. "I think that would be best. Sometimes I forget that Lainey doesn't yet have the constitution to discuss the gore of this job while eating."

Sheriff Markum nodded as she dipped two French fries in ketchup. "Honestly, this is enough to make me nauseous as well. I don't think I will ever forget the smell of those crime scenes."

Lainey was soon back, and they shifted the conversation to lighter topics. Wanda gave a little history of the area, particularly Robber's Cave which was in proximity to where the crimes had occurred.

It was difficult to grow up in Oklahoma and not hear at least some folklore about the cave being the hideout for thieves and outlaws. But Carrie and Lainey still sat transfixed as Wanda told tales of the area and the cave.

The cave is located in the Sans Bois Mountains. Rugged cliffs and dense woods made the area the perfect spot to hide from law enforcement. Criminals could live inside the many caves which were tucked back into the jagged cliffs for a long time. But usually their greed for more money would draw them back out.

Soon, after making quick work of their meals, they bundled back up to face the winter wind outside. Upon exiting the diner, the wind slammed hard against the three women. Carrie surveyed the sky. Dark swirling clouds were fighting the sun for control.

"It looks like we may get a winter storm. Have you heard the latest weather report?" Carrie asked.

The sheriff was nodding as she zipped her heavy jacket. "This morning they said that we had a winter storm moving in and there was a strong probability of snow. It won't make our job any easier, but maybe it will slow down the killer."

"Fire and ice," said Lainey. Her voice had been barely audible and the Sheriff and Carrie both looked at her.

Lainey turned to look at the other two and said, "I said fire and ice," Lainey repeated. Her brow furrowed.

Carrie looked at Sheriff Markum and nodded. "Let's go."

~

"GET YOUR LAZY ASSES UP!" Yelled Doc. He kicked the dirt next to Jimmy's feet. Both Jimmy and Bud had fallen asleep out by the old fire pit. They were supposed to be cooking, not taking a break.

"Don't tell me you're out here smokin' a joint when you are supposed to be cookin'." Doc was so mad he wanted to beat the two of them to a pulp, but they were all he had to help him, and after all, they were family.

Startled, Jimmy jerked and his chair tipped over backwards and landed hard on the ground. "Hey man!" Jimmy cried out. "What did you go and do that for?"

Bud scurried out of his chair before Doc could grab hold of him. "We're just takin' a break. The stuff's fine," said Bud.

"You can't be smokin' and cookin'. You have got to keep your heads clear!" Doc stomped off towards the cooking trailer where they continued to produce a steady flow of meth for Latimer and the surrounding counties.

He was pissed that those two were high as two pot heads could be, and they were not done with the product for the day. He would have to finish it himself to make sure they didn't all get blown sky high.

Bud and Jimmy followed at a reasonable distance behind Doc. They both knew Doc was smarter than they were, but he didn't have to rub it in their faces. Neither Bud nor Jimmy had even graduated from high school, but Doc had gone to college.

After college, he had even worked in Oklahoma City for

several years after getting his degree in chemistry. But when their mother had died, he had come home to check on things and never left again. He resented being pulled back into this cesspool, and he especially resented having to babysit these two morons.

There was no use for his degree down in these backwoods except to cook meth. It was also the only thing that would provide them a reasonable income. They were so far back in the mountains that it would be hard to locate them and certainly no one would stumble onto them by accident, so their operation was safe in that respect.

When Doc realized that those two were following him, he whirled around. "Go back to the house. I don't need your addle brains here to blow us all up. I'll handle it and finish the job. Go back to the house and clean up that nasty mess of a house."

Bud and Jimmy just stood dumfounded at Doc's tirade, then burst out laughing. They laughed so hard they doubled over and fell to the ground. Soon they were rolling around like two little kids in a pile of dry leaves on the forest floor.

Doc turned and continued to the cook trailer grinding his teeth. When he got to the trailer, the door was standing wide open and inside was a raccoon scrambling through the cupboards.

He chased after the varmint, well aware that the raccoon could hit the wrong thing at any moment and blow them both up. He grabbed a broom by the door and whopped the coon as hard as he could on the head. It stopped stunned, just long enough for Doc to grab it and throw it out the trailer door.

It felt like the top of his head would blow off from fury. Not only had they left the trailer, they had left the door wide open. His blood pressure was enough to put him under.

He donned his mask and coveralls and proceeded into the cook area. All looked well and appeared that they had at least kept a cool head while cooking. Nothing was packaged though, and Joe was coming in just a couple of hours to get the entire batch. He would have to work quickly to get it all done in time.

As he packaged the product, he dreamed of going back to a normal life and a normal job. Growing up, he had worked hard to make good grades in school so he could get a scholarship and get out of this hellhole.

College life was an adjustment at first, but Doc had found a part-time job and worked hard on both his studies and the job. On graduation day there had been no one there to see his accomplishment. Momma was too ill to travel and their daddy had left them all behind a decade or two earlier.

Jimmy and Bud couldn't find their way out of a paper bag, much less to the OU campus in Norman. And honestly, Doc hadn't wanted those two to come, anyway. They would have only embarrassed him.

A sharp rap on the trailer door startled Doc out of his past, just as he was finishing the last package. He went to answer the door, knowing it would be Joe Billings.

"Just finished. Let me help you carry it to the truck." Joe

was no nonsense and Doc was relieved that he had gotten it all ready by the time he had arrived.

Joe was meaner than a rattlesnake. He didn't suffer fools or anyone that threatened his operation. Doc wasn't sure he had ever seen Joe smile and that long jagged scar down his cheek added further intimidation.

He was in it to grow a large and powerful operation. He may have realized that he already had that power since no one in this area would dare challenge him. However, that is the thing about power; if you want it, you never have enough. Not being on time would have been cause for Joe to end their working relationship, and maybe their lives.

Doc needed the money. He was putting a nice nest egg back, more determined than ever before to get out of there. He would do whatever he had to do to get out of this backwoods pit and he would not let those two idiot brothers of his destroy his plan.

He watched Joe drive off down the narrow wooded trail that led away from their home. It was just a small clearing deep in the forest and the road was so narrow that few ever ventured down it.

Doc shivered and pulled his coat tighter. He looked up at the sky with a frown. There was a storm coming and coming soon. He was glad the shipment was out of the way before the storm. He could kick back for a while and not have to worry about getting another shipment to Joe soon.

He walked the path to the house and looked around. This was such a beautiful area, but his mother had lived on a small disability check which didn't afford means beyond the bare necessities, and his two brothers were so lazy that they did nothing to keep the place up. Junk lay everywhere disturbing the natural beauty of the forest.

The thought had crossed his mind several times that his two brothers would not, could not survive without him. But he still had to go. He couldn't live like this for much longer.

Icy raindrops fell just as Doc reached the rickety front porch. They felt like shards of glass hitting the back of his neck. Inside, a counter assault of heat met him when he opened the front door.

Those two idiots had over stoked the wood-burning stove and then fallen asleep. Doc left the front door slightly ajar to vent out the excess heat. As he surveyed the dirty dishes and trash lining the kitchen counter, his resolve to get out of there only increased. He would check his stash as soon as possible. Maybe, just maybe, he could leave sooner than he thought.

CARRIE AND LAINEY pulled up in front of the white stucco building. The clouds were winning the battle in the sky and it was now much darker. Once inside the headquarters for the Latimer County Sheriff's Department, Carrie and Lainey quickly shed their heavy coats and gloves. Someone had cranked up the heat, and it felt almost tropical inside.

Sheriff Markum had parked in the rear parking lot and entered from the rear door. She entered the front reception area quickly from the rear of the building and retrieved the agents, leading them to her office.

"Here are the files we have so far," she said as she

handed Carrie the three files. "Also, here is a file I've created with our findings so far on any animal burnings in the last six months. I can always go back further if you need them. We don't pursue them like crimes perpetrated on humans so the files are thin.

"There may not even be any connection, but I didn't want to assume there wasn't one."

Carrie handed the animal file to Lainey while she thumbed through the murder files. Victim number one was Beau Johnson a male age twenty-six, white. They found him on the ground in a clearing on what appeared to have been a pile of brush.

Victim number two was Corey Stiles a white male age twenty-two. His body had been found in a shed which had burned completely to the ground.

And victim number three was a female, Amanda Lee age twenty-one. She had been found tied to a cross type structure inside a barn. The front of the barn had been completely burned, but had spared some cross area and the back wall of the barn.

Carrie frowned as she studied the files. All three victims were white, but two were males and one female. Also, they were all burned, but in different scenarios.

"Do you have a room set up for us to lay this all out?" Carrie asked.

"Yes," Sheriff Markum was moving before Carrie had even finished her sentence. She led them through a maze of hallways. "Sorry this is so far back here, but it is closer to the back door so it will be easy for you to come and go. I'll get you each a pass card to get in."

She opened the door to an almost bare room. There was one long table in the center with two metal folding chairs. One white board stood off to the side.

"Sorry that it isn't much. We can get you a computer in here as well."

"It will work." Carrie gave the Sheriff a smile. She was used to the lack of equipment in smaller rural areas. She had brought a laptop from the OSBI should they need it. "What about a large area map?"

"Yes, anything else you can think of?"

Carrie shook her head, and the Sheriff left to retrieve the map. Lainey had been quietly studying the file of animal burnings.

"Anything stand out to you in there?" Carrie asked Lainey.

"I'm not sure yet." She looked up at Carrie. "Can I look through this some more?"

"Sure. But remember our primary focus is on these murders. That is mainly for preliminary information. They may not even be linked."

Lainey nodded. "I have a thought, but it could be nothing. I just want to look through them more thoroughly." Lainey sat down on a cold metal folding chair and laid the open folder on the table. She retrieved her notepad and pen while still focused on the file.

The door opened and in came the Sheriff unfurling a large map of the area. With Carrie's help she pinned it to the back wall.

I'll put red pins where we found the three murder

victims, and if you want, I'll put blue pins where we found the animals.

Lainey continued to study the file before her. There was something about these animal burnings that triggered a memory. She just couldn't quite put her finger on it.

Soon, the Sheriff had all the pins on the map. Carrie had watched while she had worked. It appeared to her as if there was no pattern.

"Does there appear to be a pattern to you?" she asked Sheriff Markum.

The Sheriff stood studying the map, shaking her head. "No. They are so random."

"Tell me about the area where these pins are."

The sheriff looked at Carrie. "Dense forest and mountainous areas with lots of rocky outcrops. And, of course multiple caves."

The task ahead of them settled in with Carrie. Searching in that area could be time consuming and counterproductive. They would have to work smart on this.

"I've got it!" Lainey chimed out. Both the Sheriff and Carrie swiveled around to look where Lainey sat at the table.

"These are satanic animal sacrifices. Well, most of them are. I did a detailed study on this in college." She stood up taking the photos and laying them out, side by side on the table. "See here." Lainey pointed to three of the photos showing faint markings in the ground. They were almost unrecognizable, but when you knew what to look for, you could see what had once been the outline of a pentagram.

"They tried to obliterate it, but didn't get it all. Also, the way the animal is laying and the deep cut to the throat of the animal. Even though they were burned, it appeared that there was no hesitation in cutting the line deep into the animal's throat."

Lainey paused and looked up at the sheriff and Carrie. Both were looking back with skepticism.

"Okay, look here," Lainey proceeded. "There is almost no blood on the ground. They catch the blood and use it in their rituals." She looked back at the women.

"You're right. The ground is almost completely void of blood," said Carrie. She looked at Sherif Markum with a questioning look.

Finally, the sheriff slowly nodded her head. "We've had reports. Some, well most were just rumors, but there were some very credible reports from people who said they had witnessed these rituals. I don't think any of us wanted to actually admit this was going on in our county."

"Do you think they are related to the murders?" asked Carrie.

Sheriff Markum stood staring at the photos slowly shaking her head. "I'm not sure. I would like to say no, but then we should probably keep that as a consideration."

"What do you think, Lainey?" Sheriff Markum asked.

"I haven't studied those photos. Let me see them." Lainey took the stack of crime scene photos and studied each one. She pushed the animal photos to the center of the table and laid out each of the crime scene photos side by side underneath.

Lainey was deep in thought and almost forgot that the other two officers were there in the room with her. "I'm not even sure the same persons did them all. If they did, I think they were trying to hide that fact and make it look like multiple perpetrators. I don't think human sacrifices by a satanic cult would care if we found them or not. They feel they are too powerful to be caught.

"Also, none of our victims have their throats cut like the animals." She reached down to pick up one photo in particular. "There is a faint outline of a pentagram here, but that could have been placed there to throw us off." Lainey handed the photo across the table to the other two.

"Sheriff which murder was first?" Lainey asked. The Sheriff helped Lainey arrange them by date of execution.

"The first murder was Beau Johnson. He was found, as I said earlier in a clearing on a pile of brush. There didn't appear to be any signs of restraint. The fire had curled the body into the fetal position so there was no way to know how he had been laying when the fire started. He was not dead and not restrained."

"He could have been drugged or knocked unconscious." Carrie flipped through the file to find the coroner's report. "It says here there were slight skull fractures, but they were at the back of the skull and could have been from a fall." Carrie continued to look through the file searching for a tox panel, but there was none.

"I'm sure there is a tox screen being done." Carrie said.

"Yes, but we have none of the three back yet," said Sheriff Markum.

Carrie walked over to the whiteboard and put the headshot of Beau they had pulled from his driver's license on the board. Underneath, she wrote age and the basic details of the case.

She then did the same for the next two. "Where did these three live? In Wilberton or in rural areas?" Carrie asked.

Sheriff Markum pulled out clear pushpins and after looking at their home addresses, she put the pins on the map. All three lived in rural areas, but none lived close to each other. More randomness.

Lainey was looking over the files for the three human victims. "Sheriff Markum, their throats weren't cut, but were there any other injuries that could have been used to collect their blood?

"Cutting a throat is almost instant death. If the killer had wanted to collect their blood, but keep them alive, they might have wounded them to begin a slow collection of blood, then leave them alive enough to experience the horror of the fire. Or maybe they were not quite dead yet, and were still breathing when the fire was started."

The sheriff stood looking at Lainey thinking. "I think we need to get with the medical examiner. The bodies were in such a horrific shape from the burning, she may not have seen that type of wound once she saw they had inhaled smoke. They did die from the fire, but there may have been additional wounds prior, which may have been covered up by the fire. I will have her take a second look."

"It seems that we have gleaned all we can from these files. I think it is time to go out and visit the crime scenes," said Carrie.

Sheriff Markum nodded. "We have them cordoned off to

keep them intact as much as possible. Hopefully, the wildlife haven't destroyed too much. Have you brought your winter gear? We could get caught out there when the storm comes."

"We did. Personal clothing, gloves and such, but not much else," said Carrie. She was chiding herself for not checking the weather before leaving and planning ahead. Winter storms were rare in Oklahoma. They would come and then quickly go. Some winters would get a pass all together, so thinking to plan for such a rare occurrence had skipped Carrie's mind.

"We have extra winter kits. I'll get a couple for your ride and put extra in mine. There are lanterns, sleeping bags, a battery operated mobile charger, meal bars, and several other items."

"You expect we'll get stranded out in the snow?" Lainey asked.

"You're in the country now. We have to plan for every contingency here. In some areas out there you could be twenty miles from the nearest town. The mountain roads can become impassable. You'll be glad you planned ahead," concluded Sheriff Markum as she led them to their gear and tactical room.

Just then, a deputy came in and handed Carrie and Lainey each a laminated key card. "These are for entrance into our station. They are visitor passes and only temporary," he said. They each slid them into their badge wallet behind their official OSBI identification.

"Ready?" Sheriff Markum asked. Both Carrie and Lainey nodded, so they headed out the door. Lainey had a knot in her stomach as big as Texas. It didn't help that she hated the cold. She had never even liked the snow as a kid. Now they were tasked with finding a killer in the shadow of a potential winter storm. There was nothing about this that Lainey liked.

CHAPTER 3

The little cabin sat deep into the woods on a tiny clearing. The woods were so dense there that had there been any sun, it would have hardly been noticed. Inside sat three young men in their early twenties. The darkness wasn't only on the outside of the cabin, but also on the inside.

River Billings sat on an overstuffed old chair and stared into the fire that roared in the stone fireplace. His black hair was cut in an awkward, jagged pattern which left it short in the back, with jagged locks hanging forward in his face. He slowly brushed those locks mindlessly to the side and continued to stare at the fire.

"River we've got a bad storm coming. We need to get out of here and back home before we get trapped here," said Blaine Barlow. He was standing in the center of the room, half afraid of disturbing River, yet equally concerned about getting snowed in so deep into the forest.

When River did not respond, Harley Atlee rose from the sofa and stood beside Blaine. "Blaine's right. We've got to get out of here soon." He shifted nervously from side to side, concerned about River's reaction to their suggestions to leave.

River continued to stare at the fire as if neither Blaine nor Harley had said a word. The fire fascinated him. It was fluid and intangible. It could harm you and grow out of control quickly without warning, and yet you needed its warmth to survive. It was a cruel game that the fire played. It had power over you. Power to keep you alive or to kill you.

Blaine was getting hot in his coat. He had put it on hoping they would leave, but River only sat silent. They had brought one vehicle, and it was River's.

"River, we've got to go!" Blaine came right up to the side of River's chair and slightly to the front so he could not be ignored, but River didn't move.

River terrified Harley, and he looked at Blaine with pleading eyes full of fear. He shook his head slightly to indicate that Blaine shouldn't push River too far. He had seen River at his worst and he didn't want to be on the receiving end of his rage.

Just then Blaine's cell phone pinged, and he looked down at it. It was his dad wondering where he was. It surprised him that the text had come through where they were. Calls certainly never made it through, but sometimes a text got lucky.

He responded that he was okay and would be home by evening. He didn't think anyone but the three of them knew about the cabin or it's whereabouts and they wanted to keep it that way.

When they had stumbled across it a couple of years ago, it was clear that no one had been here, much less lived here in ages. They had claimed it for their own and fixed it up, making a vow to never tell another living soul about it. So far they had kept their word.

Blaine leaned over and got in River's face. "We have got to go. There's a huge winter storm coming and we will be trapped here. We don't have enough supplies for that. My dad has already sent a message asking where I am."

River's jaw clenched and relaxed. "Then go," he said looking past Blaine to the fire.

"Go! How? That's your ride out there man!" Said Blaine completely exasperated.

"If you have to go, then walk," River said with cold quiet nonchalance.

Blaine stood back up and paced the floor. Harley stood wringing his hands looking back and forth from Blaine to River. After what seemed like hours, but was more like minutes, River swiveled the chair around and looked at his two companions with cold lifeless eyes.

"I want to stay," said River.

"We can't stay!" Said Blaine. He ran his hand through his sandy blond hair and continued to pace. Suddenly he jerked his coat off and slammed it onto the sofa. At that, River swiveled the chair back around to look at the fire, pleased that he had won.

A low wavering whine emerged from Harley. The fear he felt was coursing through his entire body. He couldn't think what to do. Why did he even hang out with these two? He knew better. He wasn't built for this.

River stood up and walked straight over to Harley and slapped him hard on the side of his face. "Shut the hell up and grow some, you weak snot."

Harley's head had snapped to the side and his cheek burned like fire where River's hand had made contact. He covered it with his hand and turned to slip away from River.

"Hey man, there was no need to do that," said Blaine. "We need to get home. I need to get home." Blaine and River had been friends since before kindergarten and they knew everything there was to know about each other. They had endured a lot as friends, but Blaine had seen his friend change through the last several months and it concerned him. He had become somewhat wary of him and his unpredictable behavior.

River looked at Blaine and repeated himself, "Then.. go.. home.." His voice was cold and deliberate.

Blaine knew that the harder he pushed, the more obstinate River would get. *Do we try to walk out,* he wondered. *If we leave, will River leave too and catch up to us in the jeep? Maybe we can walk to the road and catch a ride.*

Blaine knew he had to think about Harley too. For whatever reason, River had grown increasingly mean to Harley. He had to make sure Harley got home safe. If they started out and River didn't follow, they could get caught in the storm.

"Harley get your coat on. We're leaving." Blaine reached down, grabbed his coat and shoved his arms in it. Harley scrambled to grab his coat off of the hook by the door. He didn't like the idea of walking out of there, but he didn't want to be left alone with River.

River continued to stand in the center of the room and watched them leave. Then he sat back down and swiveled his chair to once again stare at the fire.

It only took about ten minutes to get from the Latimer County Sheriff's department to the turnoff to Robber's Cave. The wind had buffeted the sheriff's SUV the entire trip. There had even been slight fits of rain from time to time as they drove.

When they turned east and headed further into the forest, they were somewhat sheltered so the wind could no longer rock the SUV with such force. The road became much narrower and winding, and they had to slow down for safety's sake which prolonged the trip.

As they drove, Sheriff Markum went over what she knew of each of the three victim's personal and home lives.

Corey worked over in McAlester at a chain home improvement store. He had graduated four years earlier and had no interest in college. His supervisor said he worked hard and rarely missed work. He could see Corey getting promoted had he stuck with it.

Both of Corey's parents were still alive and lived close to a small town to the east of Wilburton called Red Oak. They had a small ranch about three miles north of there. It barely fed the two, much less Corey and his sister.

Amanda Lee was a year younger than Corey at twenty-one years of age. She was beautiful and popular in school. She had made good grades at Wilburton High School. She had then gone away to college for a year, but her parents soon realized that Amanda hadn't been able to seriously buckle down and work at getting a degree.

Extra money was slim, so rather than pay for her to squander it on a half attempt at an education, they made her come home. She had worked at the local drugstore in Wilburton ever since.

She had a boyfriend named Matthew Bradford, twenty-two. They had dated for the last year. There was talk of getting married but no official engagement. Her father was a coach at the high school, and her mother was a nurse for a home health agency.

Beau Johnson was twenty-six, a few years older than the other two. He had gone to college and come back after only two years. The classwork had been difficult, and he hadn't found the discipline to keep up.

He had floated from job to job for the last three years. His previous employers had said he lacked focus and initiative. There had also been reports that he often hung out with a few local dope heads who sold their drugs around the county. His only parent was a single mom who worked at a chain burger joint in Wilburton.

Carrie was absorbing the facts of the victims as quickly as Sheriff Markum could generate them. "As far as I can see, the only commonalities are that they are all in their mid to low twenties. They didn't go to the same high school, two went to college and one didn't, two male and one female. Can you see any common threads I'm missing?" Carrie asked Sheriff Markum.

The sheriff shook her head. "They didn't attend the same church, or have common friends. As far as we can tell, their parents didn't even know each other." The sheriff looked over at Carrie and then back to the road ahead.

Lainey heard the conversation between Carrie and Sheriff Markum in the front seat but her attention was fixed to the forest cowering underneath the dark swirling clouds. Rivulets of water were being pushed vertically on her door window as they drove. Lainey shivered as the foreboding grew.

"Maybe that's on purpose," said Lainey. "Maybe the killer is purposely choosing victims they know aren't connected." She remained looking out her side door window as she spoke.

They all sat and thought about Lainey's comment as they drove. It could be. The lack of connectivity could be the connection.

The SUV slowed and turned onto a gravel road that wound further up the mountain. The gravel crunched and shifted from the weight of the vehicle. The pine trees were so close on each side that one could almost touch them through an open window.

After another five minutes, they came to a spot in the road where a footpath began. They all bundled and Sheriff Markum grabbed her flashlight. The three checked to make sure their weapons were ready. It was unlikely that the killer was anywhere around, but they knew to be ready.

The footpath only allowed walking single file. As the

sheriff led, she pushed aside low-hanging branches which rained down water on them when disturbed.

Lainey knew that it was only about one in the afternoon, but with the dark cloud cover and the dense forest, it felt more like early evening.

"Lainey are you okay?" Asked Carrie. "You've been awfully quiet."

Just then, before Lainey could answer, the sheriff stopped. The clearing they had come to, barely accommodated the three. They all stood and looked where a pile of brush and limbs had been piled to make a large bonfire upon which Beau Johnson had been burned alive.

Carrie looked around. "There's nothing out here. No cabins, buildings, roads, nothing. How on earth did you find him out here?"

"A hunter. He lives about a mile to the north and likes to hunt for deer around here in season. He stumbled upon him. It was quite a shock as you can imagine."

Both Carrie and Lainey turned and surveyed their surroundings hoping for anything that could help them learn more about who would do this and why. But there was nothing but dense pines.

Sheriff Markum watched them and allowed them to look. She hoped, prayed, they might find something she and her team had missed. "Our forensics team combed pretty well, but they are not as practiced as your teams are. They were shocked by what they saw and I'm afraid it made it hard for them to focus."

Lainey had her pad and pen out and drew what she saw, which was little. A small clearing with a burned brush pile surrounded by pine trees. Then she noticed the faint outline of what she thought was a pentagram. She walked over and squatted down.

"Do you see this?" She asked.

Both Carrie and the sheriff came and squatted down on each side of her. Someone had drawn a thin straight line into the dirt. It might have been unnoticeable, but when you looked around the fire, there were other bits and pieces of lines. Lainey was sure if you connected them they would form a complete pentagram.

"I see it," said Carrie, and she looked over at the sheriff.

Sheriff Markum nodded. "I see it too. Let's take more pictures with our cell phones. Maybe we will capture something the forensic photographer missed."

They all three used their phones to photograph various angles. By the time they were heading back to the SUV, snowflakes were lightly falling.

There was a sense of urgency as the three got back into the SUV. The weather was growing worse, and they had not seen the other two crime scenes.

The Sheriff's radio chirped, and she responded. A short dialog between her and her deputy resolved the issue, and she started the engine. "We have two more crime scenes to see, but the weather doesn't seem to be blowing over. If we wait until tomorrow, it might be even worse. I'll leave it up to you. This is a four-wheel drive so I'm not afraid of getting stranded out here."

Carrie looked back at Lainey. "I'm fine," said Lainey. "I would just as soon try to see them today and get that part out of the way." Carrie nodded and said, "If you are good, then let's go ahead and try to view the other two today."

It was six miles to the next stop, but the difficult gravel roads made the trip seem like twenty more miles. "The next stop is where Corey Stiles was found burned in the shed. There used to be a trailer house there, but the owners had moved it and left the shed."

The small dirt road stopped at the edge of a small clearing surrounded by forest. "They moved the trailer several years ago. When they lived here they kept the clearing cleaned out, and it was a much larger area. Since they left, the forest has been steadily creeping back in."

The rain and random snowflakes had temporarily stopped. The wind couldn't penetrate down into the clearing and it felt almost peaceful. Lainey noticed the sounds of birds and something rustling in the brush. She smiled to think the wildlife were keeping an eye on them.

At the far side of the clearing away from where the sheriff had parked, there was a pile of ash where a small shed had once stood. "I'm surprised that the dilapidated shed hasn't fallen down long before now," said the sheriff.

Carrie gently moved partially burned boards to the side being careful not to disturb potential evidence. She knew the Latimer county crime techs took as much evidence as they had found, but she was hopeful they would find more.

As Carrie moved rubble, Lainey sketched. "Stop!" Said Lainey suddenly.

Carrie stopped midway from pulling a board up and looked at Lainey who was walking towards her. "The end of the board is disturbing the dirt. Look." Lainey pointed and then reached down to lift the end of the board straight up. Underneath lay the faint outline of the point of a pentagram. The end of the board was gouging into it and might have completely obliterated it had Lainey not stopped Carrie.

As they each sat squatting down looking at the marking, no one said a word. They were each lost in their own personal thoughts and scenarios.

"So we know from the picture there is a pentagram at the next scene. So, can we relate them to the animal sacrifices?" Asked Sheriff Markum.

"It would appear so, but are they just making the marks to throw us off?" Carrie asked. "I would like to think this helps us, but we have to find out if this is genuine or something done as a distraction."

"Sheriff do you know of anyone we could talk to who would know if this is genuine? Have you interviewed or connected anyone in the area to witchcraft? Anyone who is reliable for us to talk to, that is," said Lainey.

Sheriff Markum was deep in thought. There were a lot of crazies in her county and some she knew practiced the dark arts of witchcraft, but they lived deep in the forest and kept to themselves. She was trying to think of one that might talk to them.

"I think there is one that might talk to us. We don't just want one that will talk to us, but one that will give us a straight answer willingly."

They continued gently moving the remaining debris away, and they could see more faint lines of the outline.

Photos were taken and soon they were headed back down the narrow road.

"Lainey you haven't been yourself this entire trip. I mentioned it earlier, but you didn't respond. What's up?" Carrie had to know and didn't want to wait any longer. She didn't care if the sheriff heard her ask.

Lainey turned her head from the window to look at Carrie. She glanced at the sheriff and then back. "Carrie, I'll be honest. Since the moment we headed down here and discussed this case, I felt this heaviness fall on me and it won't go away. I keep trying to readjust my mind, I've even prayed about it. But it is like something unnatural. I can't shake it."

Carrie looked over at Sheriff Markum. "Lainey, I know what you're feeling. Since this whole thing hit our county, I've felt the same thing," said the sheriff.

Carrie turned to look out the front window again. She pondered what the two had said and did a mental evaluation of what she herself was sensing. "I think I know what you mean. I often get a heaviness when in the middle of a horrific case so I just passed it off as more of that, but this does somehow seem different."

Eight miles later, they pulled up to a place on the side of the mountain that looked out to the surrounding valley and mountains beyond. The burned barn sat just ahead of them.

As the three stood and took in the site's majesty before them, Carrie said, "Oh my, how on earth are we ever going to find a killer in this?" Miles and miles of dense forest lay before them, taunting them.

Lainey turned and headed towards the barn. It had not

burned down completely, but the fire had destroyed what had once been the double door entrance. Someone had removed enough burned out boards and debris to get to the back of the barn that still partially stood.

Looking up, Lainey clearly saw the outline of a pentagram. Someone had drawn it with chalk on the back wall behind where the cross stood. Her skin rippled with fear as she stood unable to move.

Blaine and Harley had hit the road walking fast. They scrunched their heads down into their coat collars and shoved their hands into their pockets. The nearest gravel road was four miles down the small dirt path that was barely wide enough for a vehicle to travel on.

The wind was brutal. The dense forest gave them some shelter, but then the path would take a turn just right and the wind would cut down straight into them. They didn't talk. Their focus was entirely on walking hard and fast.

Harley thought his face was freezing solid. Every so often a few frozen raindrops would fall and hit his face. His cheeks were so numb that he could barely feel them.

He chided himself for the thousandth time for even continuing in this group, of… friends? Were they friends? Blaine was nice to him, but River terrified him.

Growing up in the small town of Wilburton had left him out in the cold. He was not athletic and therefore not included in that crowd. He also was not smart, so those who were, had nothing to do with him. He didn't do drugs or go to church so those groups didn't include him either.

When he had first met Blaine, he had been nice to Harley. He wasn't sure why, but he didn't question it. Then he had met River. He saw Blaine's lack of fear towards River so he had assumed that River was fine. But he soon found out that wasn't the case.

If he stopped hanging out with these two, he would be alone again. Blaine was almost always with River. If he left River, then he left Blaine too. But, he had just about decided that it wasn't worth it.

It took them two hours to march down the winding dirt path before they reached the narrow gravel road. Blaine had been wrong about River following them in the SUV. He had figured, hoped really, that once they had left, River would follow.

When they reached the gravel road, Blaine pulled Harley aside into the woods. "I've got to stop for a minute. We're freezing. Let's build a fire and get warm."

They gathered what they could find of small kindling and dry leaves that had been sheltered from the damp. Working together, they were eventually able to get a small fire going. Both hunkered down with their hands above the small flame.

"Blaine, River scares me. I don't know how you can stand being around him. Doesn't he terrify you?" Harley asked.

Blaine thought for a moment before answering. He gazed into the small fire before them, remembering all the fun times they had had growing up. Both their parents were wealthy ranchers, and they had access to as many toys as two young boys could ask for. They had motorcycles, hunting rifles, bows, trucks, clothes, actually anything they wanted, they had.

He wasn't sure what had happened to River. The change has been slight and slow growing. It was as if one day Blaine just looked at his friend and suddenly noticed he was not the same person.

"I guess I remember how he used to be." Blaine looked up at Harley. "He wasn't always like this. We used to have so much fun. I guess I just thought it was a phase or something he was going through."

Harley's legs felt numb sitting in a squat for so long, so he stood. "You got any cell service?" He asked.

Blaine stood and walked a few paces to the road. "I have one bar."

"Can we call someone to come pick us up?" Asked Harley.

Blaine looked back at Harley. "We made a pact to not tell anyone about the cabin."

"We don't have to tell them about the cabin. We're miles from there."

Blaine thought about who he could call that wouldn't ask a dozen questions about why he and Harley were so far out without a car.

"What do we tell them about why we are out here?"

Harley squatted back down by the fire and thought. "I don't know. All I know is that I'm tired and cold and I don't want to get stranded out here."

Blaine agreed, but he wasn't ready to call anyone just

yet. River could still show up at anytime. He hated the power that River had over him. He hadn't seen it that way at first. They had just been friends, equals. But over the past year or so things had shifted. He had felt that he was at River's mercy, somehow under his control. And… he knew that River got off on power. He had seen it too many times.

They both continued to warm by the fire for the next thirty minutes. Then without ceremony, Blaine stood, took his booted foot and rubbed out the small fire. They had kept it small so scattering it and making sure it was out, was a simple task. "Let's go."

The narrow gravel road wasn't any easier to walk on. The gravel shifted underfoot and was slow going. The direction put them head on with the wind.

Harley's nose began to run and every few seconds he was pulling his hand from his pocket to take a swipe at it. "I don't know how much more of this I can take," said Harley.

Blaine pulled his phone from his pocket and looked. They were two more miles down the mountain and he now had two bars. Walking over to the side of the road to lean against a tree, he dialed his sister. She didn't answer. She rarely answered his calls.

"Of course," said Blaine to the blank screen. He looked up and surveyed the area where he was. Harley was hopping from one foot to the other next to him in an attempt to create some warmth.

"River isn't coming," said Blaine. "We need to keep walking. It's just another mile or so to the highway. We can make it."

Harley looked up at him with anguish, but he nodded.

What else could they do? Harley wasn't about to call one of his parents and he had no siblings. They readjusted their stocking caps, scarves, gloves, and jackets to make sure they were as tightly buttoned up as they could be. At least the road before them now was mostly downhill.

After another hour, the highway suddenly loomed before them and it felt like they had reached paradise. Even though the off and on fits of rain had sliced through them like icy needles, they had made good time.

"If we have to walk all the way back to the town where my truck is, we have five more miles to go," Blaine said. Harley knew this, but he knew Blaine felt protective of him and therefore felt a need to explain.

Blaine's mind was searching for an answer to what was currently going on with River. He had seen his moods go up and down, but today was different. He was sure that River would quickly snap out of it and come down the mountain. But, he hadn't. Blaine was afraid for River. If he got caught up there in the cabin, he could die should a storm come.

The crunch of gravel on the shoulder of the road broke Blaine out of his deep thought. He whirled around to see Sheriff Markum's SUV pulling up behind them. He wasn't sure whether to be relieved or panicked.

Carrie watched from inside the cab as the sheriff exited the vehicle and approached the two young men. Their faces were chapped red from the icy wind. They looked utterly miserable out here in this weather. She couldn't hear what they were saying, but it seemed amicable enough and soon the sheriff was leading the men back to the SUV.

The backdoor opposite of Lainey opened, and the two slid in and nodded a greeting to her. It felt like the temperature dropped ten degrees once they were inside.

"This is Blaine Barlow and Harley Atlee. These are OSBI agents Carrie Border, and Lainey Tate," introduced the sheriff.

"Where's your truck?" The sheriff asked looking through her rearview mirror at Blaine.

"In town," said Blaine. The sheriff just continued to look at him thinking.

"If your truck is in town how did you get a way out here?"

"We were with River in his jeep," said Blaine.

"Where's River?" Sheriff Markum asked.

Blaine would not tell her about the cabin, but he had to tell a lie that was plausible, one that wouldn't be found out later. "Oh, Sheriff Markum you know River. He got in one of his moods and the next thing we knew, we were out on our ears." He hoped that sounded okay and would not illicit an urge to investigate from the sheriff.

Sheriff Markum smelled a rat, but they were good boys and she had seen River's mood swings over the last several months. Maybe it was just a spat between friends.

"Well, we'll get you to your truck and get you warm." The sheriff put the SUV in gear and moved out onto the highway. To Blaine's relief, there was little to no conversation on the ride to town. But the further away from the cabin and River they got, the larger the knot grew in his stomach.

CHAPTER 4

TUESDAY

Marissa McClain lay on the forest floor with her Canon EF 200mm zoom lens propped on a fallen log. She had been laying there for almost an hour watching and waiting. She lay on a sleeping bag which she had laid on the ground to protect her from the damp leaves, but the cold had seeped through and she felt almost numb.

The adrenaline that had initially surged through her body had long since dissipated. The only activity she had seen so far was when one man had left their trailer home to go out back to feed the dogs in the pen.

Concern that he would set them loose, clouded her thoughts for a moment. They might sniff her out and betray her presence. She had brought some treats to use should something like that happen, but she also knew that one reason they had the dogs was to alert them of trespassers.

The camera shutter hummed as it captured the motions of the man. His life stopped still in suspended motion, on the camera's hard drive. Routine, every day motion such as feeding the dogs. She would delete them later.

Her mind wandered to her dreams of notoriety as a journalist. She knew if she could capture a grand story and get it published in a notable publication, she would be famous.

Scrambling for the big story was exhausting. It seemed she was always late to the game and other seasoned investigative journalists who had paid ears to the ground, always got the goods first.

So, when she had heard of the growing drug enterprise here in the southeast part of Oklahoma, she knew she had something to write about. Not only write about, but what if she investigated and uncovered clues that would break the case wide open? It would note her as one of the elite and then she too could be privy to early leads.

She had little care for her safety. The need to gain the story, uncover the clues, and reach her goal far overshadowed any thought for her personal safety. She knew she was clever and felt she was far more clever than anyone associated with this mess would be.

Her smugness placed a smile on her face as she captured a few shots of the man going back into the trailer. These backwoods nobodies were no match for her.

Once he was back inside and out of sight, Marissa's thoughts floated back to the previous night. She had worn her sexiest blouse and tight jeans and had known exactly how to fix her hair and makeup to be enticing.

When she had entered the bar, she spotted her target instantly sitting alone chatting with the bartender. Casually walking in, and purposely paying no attention to the man, she sat two stools down from him.

She had felt his eyes on her, wanting her, but had held firm not returning his gaze. Then after ordering her second drink, he spoke to her.

"I don't think I've seen you here before," he said. "My name's Doc."

Marissa didn't turn to look at him immediately. She wanted him to want her and so she had to play disinterested and hard to get. After a second or two though, she turned to look at the man on the stool.

"Doc? Are you are a doctor?" Marissa asked.

Doc ducked his head and smiled. He looked back up at her and said, "Naw. I was just always good with science and chemistry. One day in high school a classmate just called me Doc teasing me, and it stuck."

He had swiveled his stool around to look at her. She was beautiful. Dark, full hair, and plump dark cheeks. She had large almond-shaped eyes that looked like pools of rich chocolate. He could feel himself staring.

Marissa turned her stool around as well so that they were facing each other. "So what do you do now Doc?"

The smile faded from Doc's face and he turned back around to face the bar. "I'm just home for awhile helping my brothers with our place." *This is part of the problem with living here, he thought.* He could have no semblance of a decent life. He couldn't get involved with a decent girl while he was cooking dope.

Marissa realized she had lost their connection for the moment, but she was only temporarily dismayed. This was a marathon, not a sprint. She would be patient and wait. She paid her tab and got up to leave.

"Well, it was nice to meet you Doc. Maybe I'll see you around again." And without waiting for him to reply, she walked out the door.

Laying on the cold forest floor was making her stiff. She sat up and stretched, pushing thoughts of the previous night from her mind. The sun had come out today. Yesterday they had promised blizzard conditions, but the morning had brought sunlight.

In Oklahoma you had a love-hate feeling regarding meteorologists. They rarely got it right. But it wasn't their fault, really. The weather here was erratic at best. All signs would point to one catastrophic weather pattern after another and then without a moment's notice, it would just dissipate into thin air. But then sometimes it came back the same way when it was least expected.

Today, the sun was out, and the air was crisp, but cold. The wind had died, and it was a beautiful day.

Marissa stood and walked around to pump some blood back into her legs. She was trying not to grow impatient. She knew investigating this story could take some time, but there was a limit to her patience.

The little trailer in the far back of the clearing was idle. There had been no one coming or going from it all morning. She suspected that was the cook shack. If it were not broad daylight, she might have been brave enough to get closer and take some pictures inside.

But, she could always come back. After she had left the bar last night, she had hung back until Doc had left, and had then followed him. She had followed on several gravel, then dirt roads, staying very far behind.

Then, when she was sure he had turned onto a road that could only lead to one place, she had driven on past. She marked the spot on her navigation system and had gone back to the motel for the night.

This morning she found it again. She had driven until she saw a trail that her jeep could traverse and pulled deep into the woods on the mountainside overlooking where Doc lived.

I could camp here. I don't think anyone would ever find or notice me here. That way I wouldn't miss anything, she thought to herself. She tabled that thought for another time. She hadn't driven out there prepared to camp right then.

Besides, if she stayed out here, then she couldn't accidentally run into Doc again. She smiled at the thought of that. He had been surprisingly handsome. She had not expected that.

Leaning back onto a tree, she let her thoughts drift to his rugged face and closely trimmed dark beard. His blue eyes stood out and sparkled next to his tanned skin. Soon, she had lost herself imagining how it would be to kiss that man and feel his hands caressing her.

Her eyes flew open as an engine roared to life. She hunkered down onto the sleeping bag and looked once again through the lens of her camera. Someone was leaving, but she hadn't seen who had walked from the trailer to the SUV.

She clicked multiple shots as the vehicle turned and left

the clearing. Hopefully she had gotten a glimpse of who was driving. *But, does it really matter,* she thought.

Standing, she put her camera in the bag and then pulled up the sleeping bag shaking the leaves and debris from it. She would head to town, get a good hot lunch, and then maybe do more research. She might even run into Doc again, relatively sure he was the one who had left.

She smiled at that thought as she put the jeep into gear and left her mountainside hideout.

SHERIFF MARKUM HAD DROPPED Carrie and Lainey off the night before at their SUV and had headed home. Both were exhausted from fighting the cold and wind and the extended miles spent traveling.

Their hotel was a modest chain on the north side of Wilburton. The lobby of the hotel was filled with the smell of fresh cookies and the noise of a television blaring. Their rooms were clean and warm on the third floor. Even though it seem like the elevator had taken them to the twenty-third floor as tired as they both were.

Once in her room, Lainey stripped down and climbed into a hot shower. She thought she had died and gone to heaven. The water warmed her frozen body. When her need to rest overwhelmed her need for warmth, she cranked the handles off and reached for a towel.

With barely the energy to dry herself, she left her long dark hair tumbling down her back and headed for the bed.

She threw back the covers and told herself she just wanted to rest for a moment before combing her hair and dressing.

She could feel her damp hair soaking her pillow, but the soft covers enveloped her and lulled her quickly to sleep. Soon, in her dream she was swatting at a mosquito, but when it refused to go away, she realized her phone was buzzing on the nightstand. It was Carrie and an hour after she had laid down.

"Are you hungry? I'm starving. That early lunch said goodbye a long time ago."

Lainey rolled over onto her back and tried to clear the fog of sleep from her brain. "You know, I am. I'm starved actually. I took a shower then laid down in my towel and fell asleep. What did you have in mind?" Lainey asked.

"We can order pizza in so we don't have to go back out into the cold," said Carrie.

"Sounds good to me. I'm sick and tired of the cold. Order whatever kind you want and I'll get up and get dressed."

In a little over thirty minutes Carrie was knocking on Lainey's door with a large supreme pizza. Lainey was ready with freshly combed hair and a warm pair of sweats.

Carrie smiled when Lainey opened the door. "Yeah, I know! My hair looks like a rat's nest! I knew better than to lie down with it damp. I brushed it out the best I could." Lainey's stomach begged for the pizza as soon as the smell hit her senses.

The two sat on the rumpled bed with the pizza box between them satiating their emptiness. Neither one spoke until there was almost no pizza left in the box. In the past six months since Carrie and Lainey had worked together they had developed a friendship.

It had concerned Carrie when her previous partner Randy had been promoted to Special Agent in Charge. They had worked together for eight years and had grown very close. It had been a low point in Carrie's life when the promotion had come and getting a new partner had terrified her.

But Lainey had been a breath of fresh air and a quick friend. She had even presented some words of wisdom to Carrie that issued a fatal blow to the emotional wall she had fortified for years.

Lainey had also showed herself to be a sharp and competent law enforcement professional. Their first case together had put them both in severe danger, but Lainey had handled herself skillfully, facilitating the killer's capture.

"I'd love to have a beer," said Carrie. "But I'm not going out in the cold to get one."

Since her parents' death nine years ago, Carrie had struggled with drinking. But when she had surrendered to God and allowed him to help her in her struggles, she had learned she didn't need alcohol to medicate from life. She could now drink a beer, or not. The freedom and self-control to say no was amazing.

"Not me. I want a hot cup of coffee, but I know it will keep me up even though I'm exhausted," said Lainey.

"So, what are your thoughts about the case after today? It was a tough day, first driving down here, taking a quick look at the files, and then heading out in the cold," Carrie asked.

Lainey frowned and studied the last piece of pizza in the box. "You want that last piece?" She asked.

Carrie grinned. "No, you can have it."

The pizza was quite cool at that point, but Lainey didn't care. One thing she and Carrie shared was their love of pizza in almost any condition. As she chewed, she looked at Carrie and thought.

"I have a lot of thoughts, but I'm not sure where to start." Another bite and more chewing ensued. "What do you think?"

Carrie was hoping Lainey would start the dialog, but since the conversation had been volleyed back to her, she began. "The first case I had with the OSBI reminds me of this case. Similar, but yet different. I wonder why there are different crime scene settings. I wonder why the killer is purposely changing it up. We have a pile of brush, an old shed and then a barn with a cross.

"Is it to throw us off, or is there a methodology to the madness?" Carrie paused to select the next thought. "I know we found signs of a pentagram at each scene, but was that on purpose to lead us in a specific direction or was it part of their ritual? And, do the animal sacrifices have anything to do with any of it?"

Carrie stopped and pulled two candy bars from her hoodie pocket and tossed one to Lainey. She ripped the paper off and took a big bite. Then she sat looking at Lainey waiting for her response.

"I might not have hogged the last piece of pizza had I

known you were hiding candy." A broad smile grew across Lainey's face as she reached down to pick up the candy.

Lainey chewed on the chocolate, caramel and nut candy and thought. "The crime scenes were pretty destroyed by the fire, but I couldn't see much sign of blood. The animal scenes had little to no blood because, as I said, I think that they were satanic rituals which caused them to collect the blood.

"If the human victims were also satanic rituals, it would stand to reason there would be no blood there either. But then dying in the fire with no wound, would produce no blood at all. Did their forensics' team take soil samples?" Lainey could feel herself getting sleepy. The warm shower, hot food, and warm sweats were lulling her into a cozy coma.

Carrie wadded up her candy wrapper and stood up. She reached down and collected the empty pizza box and trash. "Help me remember to ask Sheriff Markum in the morning. I'm ready for bed, and I can see you are too. Let's get a good nights sleep."

"Okay, I'll be ready by seven a.m. so we can go get breakfast. Text me when you're ready."

Carrie nodded as she left the room with the pizza box tucked under her arm. By the time the door clicked shut, Lainey was already drifting back to sleep.

SHERIFF MARKUM HAD BEEN at work for over an hour by the time Carrie and Lainey walked through the door Tuesday morning. She had known they were stopping by to get breakfast on their way to the station. On the other hand, she had opted for a drive-thru biscuit which she mindlessly ate on the rest of her drive.

Turmoil assaulted her heart and her mind. Until this case was over and in the books, she would have little desire to eat. Her deputies were afraid. She could see it in their eyes. It dampened their mood and even though laughter and camaraderie would still erupt from time to time, it quickly dissipated.

The three assembled in the crude war room. The gray walls were doing little to lighten their mood. Carrie released her coat to a metal folding chair. She walked over to the map pinned to the wall and stood assessing it with new eyes regarding what she had seen the day before.

"The enormity of this map takes on a whole new meaning when you drive it," said Carrie.

"It does. I'm glad you requested we go to the crime scenes yesterday. It puts it into perspective, but also because Lainey's quick perception noted the traces of pentagrams," said Sheriff Markum.

"That reminds me," said Lainey. "I wanted to ask if your forensics team took soil samples where the bodies were."

The sheriff's face showed concern as she thought. "I'm not sure. I'll look." She was already opening a file before she had finished answering. She flipped a few pages and then stopped to read. "I don't see that they did. They probably didn't think to. They picked up lots of debris that may or may not be related."

Sheriff Markum looked up at Lainey. "Are you thinking they need soil samples to check for blood?"

Lainey nodded. "Yes. If we can determine whether there was any blood captured for ritual or no sign of blood at all, that will help us know more about them. Even if they tried to capture the blood, there is almost always some spillage."

"We still need to talk to that contact you referred to yesterday who could give us some insight on local witchcraft activity," said Carrie.

"Yes, we do. How do the two of you feel about us collecting the soil samples ourselves on our way out to see Hattie? Not that our forensics techs aren't capable, but you know the old adage about wanting something done right. Also, the sun is out, and it is beautiful out there. We might see something else we didn't see yesterday."

Carrie and Lainey were both agreeable to her suggestion. The Sheriff collected a forensic kit and several soil sample containers and met the other two at her SUV.

The ride to the first crime scene seemed to go much quicker than the day before. The weather was the complete opposite of the previous day and it was a pleasure driving in the bright sun.

"How are you feeling today Lainey," Sheriff Markum asked. She was looking at Lainey in her rearview mirror.

"You know, I feel much better. I'm not completely comfortable, but the crushing heaviness is gone. Today I feel eager to get going and solve this case. The sooner we do, the sooner I think I'll feel completely at ease again."

Sheriff Markum nodded her head. "I know what you mean. We have all felt it at our station. I can see the fear in a few of my deputy's eyes. We have a constant battle with drug dealers back in the mountains, and of course, burglaries and assaults. We have even had a murder or two, but none of us have ever experienced anything like this."

"Can you tell us about this person we are going to go see?" Carrie asked.

"Yes. Her name is Hattie Bean. Everyone calls her Hattie B. She is about eighty years old and has lived in these mountains her entire life. Her parents were an odd couple. They rarely came to town, only for necessities.

"They had three children. Hattie is the only one left, and she never married. People refer to her as a healer." Sheriff Markum paused and looked over at Carrie before resuming. "Her formal education ended at the eighth grade in a local mountain school. But she has an extensive background on local plants and their healing properties.

"For the people who live so far out in the mountains, they go to her when they have an illness. But some say that her skills are not solely in relation to her knowledge and application of plants."

"You believe she practices witchcraft?" Carrie asked.

Sheriff Markum nodded her head. "That's the understanding."

Lainey felt a chill ripple up her spine and she pulled her arms around herself to ward off the unnatural chill.

"How do you know her?" Carrie asked.

"My grandmother's place was close to Hattie's. I would go out there and stay with her sometimes. The first time I saw her was when she was in the woods collecting plants. I was only seven and when I saw her I stood stone cold still. I had heard the rumors of an old witch living out there and it terrified me.

"She had seen me long before I saw her though, and she was kind to me and coaxed me over. I was still wary of her, though. I'd read the story of Hansel and Gretel." The three women chuckled at the thought of the old fairy tale.

"Through time, I saw her often in the woods and she would show me what she was gathering and tell me what the plants did. She allowed me to go with her as she gathered and I thought it was a grand adventure."

"Did you ever see any signs of witchcraft?" Lainey asked.

"After a while, I forgot all about the rumors of her being a witch. But then, one day we wound up back at her cabin. She asked me inside for a cup of tea. By then I was very comfortable with her, so I went in.

"It was strange to me. There were dried herbs hanging everywhere and multiple jars of mystery items that I did not understand. There were also beaded things and charms hanging around. As a little girl I thought they were pretty, but it is true, once inside the cabin I felt horribly uneasy and knew something wasn't right.

"As a child I only went to her house the one time. As an adult, I've gone by a few times for business reasons, looking for criminals of one kind or another. It was always a good excuse to stop in and check on her."

Lainey sat watching the forest fly by through her side window. The light in the SUV cab flickered through the windows as it shot through the tall pines lining the side of the road. It reminded Lainey of how the light from an old movie projector flickered.

Suddenly, Sheriff Markum slammed on her brakes thrusting them all forward against their seat belts. The sudden stop gripped Lainey as she flew hard against her restraint. She caught her breath as it jolted her from her daydreaming.

They all sat still, as a huge buck finished crossing the road. Then, just as they thought the coast was clear, a doe and two fawns pranced out behind him.

Lainey sat with her mouth half open as she leaned forward on her seat. "How stunning!"

"Beautiful!" Carrie said, almost breathless.

With the little family finally across the road, the sheriff removed her foot from the brake and accelerated. "We have a lot of wildlife here, and we have to be on the lookout when we drive. You never know when they will decide to cross the road. I hit a deer once, and it totaled my SUV."

They continued to their destination. Soon, the SUV slowed as they wound up the side of the mountain just as they had the day before. At the site, they gathered their gear and headed down the path with the sheriff in the lead.

"I'm so glad the wind isn't blowing like yesterday. I was miserable. Today there's hardly a wisp of a breeze. What a beautiful day," said Lainey looking around as she walked.

When they entered the small clearing, the three stopped. Someone had tampered with the scene. The burned brush had been scattered and there was no sign of a pentagram.

"Was this a person, or did the weather or animals do this?" Carrie asked.

Shaking her head, the sheriff said, "No. This was deliberate. It's too neatly done."

"They did it in less than twenty-four hours. Few knew we had been out here yesterday and no one could know that we would come back out here today. If they wanted to remove signs of the crime why did they not do it earlier?" Carrie asked.

Sheriff Markum pulled out her phone and was taking extensive pictures, even though she wasn't hopeful they would reveal anything. "We can still take soil samples. We have plenty of crime scene photos that can probably tell as much about it as there is to know."

Lainey sat the forensic kit on the ground and retrieved a few small glass jars. She used a scoop which looked much like a miniature garden trowel to dig a sample up and then place it in a jar.

They placed numbered cards that corresponded with each sample on the ground where they had been retrieved and then took an overall picture. This would help them know exactly where each sample had come from.

It was an hour later when they climbed back into the SUV. "I hope this was a one off and that the other two scenes are still intact," said Carrie.

"I know. Me too," said Sheriff Markum as she backed the SUV and then did a turnaround. "If they aren't, then we have the possibility that someone is following our movements and wanted to eliminate any further evidence before we came back out today.

"It may have alarmed them that the OSBI showed up to help us. They had probably underestimated our local law enforcement and panicked when they realized I called you in. But then that makes me wonder who told them you were here."

"HEY HARLEY!" Blaine yelled across the main room of the feed store where Harley worked.

Harley nearly dropped the sack of deer corn he was picking up when Blaine's voice came hurtling through.

"Hi there," replied Harley.

"You need more than the one? I'll help you."

"Yeah, I need two," said Harley.

They each threw one sack of the corn on their shoulders and headed to the front of the store and out the front door to the customer's truck.

"What time do you get off work?" Blaine asked Harley.

"Five."

"You want to come out to the ranch when you get off?"

Harley did, but he was still uneasy about River. "Did River ever come in from the cabin?" Harley asked.

"I don't know. I haven't heard from him. You going to stop hanging out with me because of River?"

They threw the two sacks into the bed of the truck and rested against it. The bed of the truck was warm from the sun and felt good against Blaine's back as he leaned on it. Harley was facing the bed of the truck with his forearms resting on the top of the bed. He kicked the tire of the truck, deep in thought.

Before Harley could answer, the owner of the truck

came out, and the two walked back to the feed store. Harley's eyebrows dipped, and he wasn't smiling.

"Here's the thing," Harley began once inside. "I love hanging out with you. I've never had a best friend like you. But honestly I'm not sure how much more of River I can take. I know you remember him and how he used to be. You guys have a special friendship. But he doesn't feel that way about me.

"I feel like sometimes all he wants from me is for someone to torment." Harley stood with his hands shoved deep into his jeans pockets looking at Blaine.

"I get it. I do. I don't know what's up with him. He has even begun to scare me. He won't be there tonight. I haven't even seen him and if I talk to him, I won't invite him or commit to anything with him."

Blaine stood watching Harley. He was tired of River and his poor little rich boy mentality. He liked Harley. He was genuine and a good friend. He worked for a living and was grounded. River had been spoiled his entire life and Blaine was sick of his attitude.

"Yeah, all right," Harley smiled and reached his hand out with Blaine promptly slapping it back playfully.

"Just come on over when you get off work. You can eat with us then we'll watch the game."

Harley had to get back to work, so Blaine jumped in his truck just as his cell phone rang. He looked at the screen only to see the name River. He hesitated. If he answered the phone, he knew River would try to manipulate him into doing something he didn't want to do or going back on his word to Harley.

In a quick decision, Blaine hit the big red button and cancelled the call. He shoved the gearshift into drive and gravel flew has he wheeled around and sped out of the feed store parking lot.

Blaine's dad had given him a list of things to do while in town. By mid-afternoon, he was done and heading home. Their ranch covered around six hundred and forty acres and was situated about twenty minutes outside of Wilburton to the north.

As Blaine turned the last curve of their winding driveway, he saw River standing outside next to his jeep. Blaine swore to himself as anxiety shot through him. *Am I really to the point of being afraid of River after all these years,* he wondered?

River's black hair was equal to his dark mood. "Where the hell have you been? Why didn't you answer my call?" River demanded.

Blaine stiffened as he unloaded supplies from his truck. He didn't answer immediately, attempting to formulate the appropriate response that wouldn't set River off.

With two armloads full, he headed towards the house. "You mind helping me?" Blaine came across much harsher than he had intended, but it was in direct correlation to his frustration at seeing River here at his home. *How am I going to get rid of him before Harley gets here,* Blaine wondered?

"I'm not your servant boy," River snapped, standing as he was, watching Blaine struggle with the front door.

Unable to get the door unlocked with both arms full, Blaine finally sat his load on the front porch. He unlocked the front door and disappeared inside as quickly as he could, taking the sacks he had sat down, with him.

When Blaine finally went back outside to get the remaining items, River was still standing where he had left him, with a look of defiance plastered on his face. When Blaine looked up and caught River's eyes, they pierced through him.

Fear and anger fought for primary notice inside Blaine. Now he knew just how Harley felt. Two years prior, River wouldn't even have had to be asked to help. He would have grabbed a load before Blaine could have even gotten one.

Blaine knew it was time to address this whether or not he wanted to. He retrieved the last items from his truck and headed back inside. No one was in the house, but him. His dad was likely out at the barn or in the pasture. He had no idea where his mom was.

When Blaine did not go back outside to where River stood, he finally came in. Having to come to Blaine infuriated River.

"I asked you why you didn't answer my call?" River delivered through gritted teeth.

"I didn't want to," Blaine spat out.

Blaine's response momentarily surprised River. The two of them stood in the middle of the great room and stared at each other. Disdain for each other had replaced years of friendship.

Finally, the hurt sank deep into River's heart, but he didn't want Blaine to see it, so he turned away. Without a word River headed towards the front door and then he was gone.

Blaine wanted to call after him, but didn't know what to say when he had felt only relief upon seeing him leave. Then guilt hit him full force, and he trotted to the front door and slung it open. But all there was to see was a cloud of dust as River's jeep left the ranch.

CHAPTER 5

Looking through the dozens of photos she had taken, Marissa carefully thought about the need for each one. In this digital age of photography it was easy to gather enormous amounts of useless photos, often the important ones getting lost in the mix.

She smiled as she looked at a great photo of Doc. He had stepped outside to go to his truck and had been walking straight towards her when she snapped several shots. With the telephoto lens, he was none the wiser.

Finally, she felt she had culled out the unnecessary ones, and then turned to write. Her fingers flew across her laptop keyboard as thoughts that had been ruminating inside her finally found permanence on the screen in front of her.

After an hour of feverish writing, she stopped. Rereading her prose, she sat back frowning. She needed so much more. This was all supposition and hearsay. She needed good solid proof. She needed more times, dates, names, and locations.

The Sheriff's department had been less than helpful, as had the Wilburton police. She felt swatted aside like a fly in summer. Nothing to be considered more than an annoyance.

There had to be someone at one of those law enforcement agencies that would give her information on the side, if not in an official capacity, she thought to herself. Getting up from the rickety old hotel room table, she paced the floor thinking.

Images of the personnel at the various stations came to mind one by one. She knew she had only seen a few, but was certain that there had to be at least one she could coerce into talking to her.

Grabbing her coat off the bed, she decided another visit to both agencies was called for. This time her main mission was a reconnaissance on personnel. Just as she had charmed Doc, she could surely charm someone from law enforcement.

The day was still crisp and sunny as Marissa stepped outside her hotel room door. *What a dump,* she thought as she looked around. The thought of having to stay in such a cheap rundown rathole almost ruined her happy disposition. Should she need to bring someone back to her hotel, dare she bring them here?

Her first stop was the Wilburton police station. She took her notepad and a pen, looking the part of an eager reporter.

There was no hustle and bustle inside. The terms cold

and lifeless would be much more descriptive. A long waist-high counter ran the width of the room, with a small swinging door as an entrance to the rest of the building.

A loud ding rang through the empty room as Marissa slapped her palm on the solitary bell sitting on the counter. She waited, but no one appeared. She slapped it again twice in a row.

"Hang on!" Came an irritated voice bellowing from the back. Soon a rotund officer came through a door at the back of the room. Marissa could tell from his movements he had been zipping his fly. She must have caught him in the restroom. Was there no one else to cover for him?

He stood on the other side of the half wall next to the long desk on his side. He wore readers that were shoved up on his forehead when looking at a distance. "Yep? What's the hurry?"

"I wasn't sure anyone was here," Marissa said applying her sweetest smile. If it was this old codger she had to charm, then so be it.

"So what can I help you with?"

This wasn't how Marissa had hoped this would go. She had hoped to see a room full of young strapping men she could make eye contact with and lure with her smile. Now that she was face to face with someone her father's, no grandfather's age, she wasn't sure if that was the path to take.

"Hi there officer…" She paused as she read his name badge. "…Dixon. My name is Marissa. I'm here for a short time from OU. I've been given an assignment in my journalism class to do a story from an area I'm unfamiliar with.

"So, I'm here and am completely unfamiliar with this area. My assignment..." she paused to look at her blank pad for dramatic effect. "... is on local drug traffic." Once done, she beamed at the officer and batted her eyes.

Officer Dixon wrinkled his mouth. He hadn't been born yesterday and hadn't he seen her in there a few days ago? He had just been leaving out the back to go to lunch so he hadn't really been looking, but there were so few young black women in that part of the state that she stood out.

"Weren't you in here the other day?"

Marissa dipped her head to appear chastened, then turned her eyes up to look at him. "I was. Everyone was so busy that no one had time to help me."

"Busy? Here?" Officer Dixon frowned down at the young lady.

Marissa nodded. "I just need a few details to write my report and then I'll get out of your hair."

"Lady it ain't ever busy here. I suspect whoever was here turned you away and now you are back hoping it will go different this time." The officer stood with his hands on his hips looking down at Marissa.

Once again, Marissa tried for an Oscar. She dipped her head and put on her best forlorn face. "Please help me. I'm serious. I have to get this assignment done or I won't pass the semester. I just need to ask you a few questions." She held her breath waiting for his reply.

He huffed and nodded his head. "Okay then, what questions you got?"

A huge smile crossed Marissa's face. She flipped the first blank page over on her notepad so he wouldn't see it had indeed been blank and readied her pen. "On a scale of one to ten, what would you say the level of drug trafficking is in this area?"

Officer Dixon pondered for a moment. What could he say that would make her feel like she had gotten some information while actually giving her none? "I'd say a five."

"A five," Marissa repeated his statement as she jotted the note down. "Would you say that most of the illegal drugs in this area come from locals or from larger cartels shipping it in?"

He didn't like these questions. He had expected generic non-specific questions he could easily answer. "I'd say some of both."

"How much of both?" Marissa was persistent.

"Look, I don't feel comfortable discussing those types of details with you."

"It isn't really details, more like demographics of the local drug culture." Marissa continued to focus her award-winning smile on him.

He narrowed his eyes and placing his hands on the desk, leaned towards her. "I don't think you are a college student working on assignment. I don't know what you are up to, but that notepad didn't have a word written on it until you wrote the number five on it."

Busted. She was busted. "Okay. I'm a journalist and I'm doing a story on drug traffic in this area. I heard that there had been a significant increase to alarming statistics. I wanted to find out why." She held his gaze firmly and didn't shrink back.

Officer Dixon didn't move for several moments. Then he

finally stood back up. "Look, rumors are always flying around. Drug use is up, drug use is down. One day it is one thing and the next it is another thing. I hate to burst your bubble, but there ain't no story here young lady."

He looked down at his desk and shuffled papers. It was his sign of dismissal. "Isn't there anything you can tell me?"

With one final glance up, Officer Dixon just silently shook his head.

DOC HAD ENJOYED a nice lunch at Riley's without his two dipshit brothers. He'd counted his hidden bankroll earlier that morning and was pleased with the amount he'd squirreled away. But he wasn't quite sure that was enough.

Then, there was the problem of how to exit. Joe wouldn't let him just quietly leave town. He could slip out and leave the business of cooking to his brothers, but they'd wind up dead the first time they didn't get Joe's order done on time and then Joe would come looking for him to do the same.

If he made enough money, he could leave the country all together, or go to another state with a new I.D. Either way, he still needed to do a few more batches until he felt he had enough.

The sunny day was enough to lift anyone's spirits and rather than drive to the local hardware store, Doc walked the block and a half.

As he came to the old wood and glass door and reached

for the handle, the door came thrusting out at him shoving him backward.

Just as curse words formed in his mouth, he saw the beautiful woman he had met at the bar the night before. The words stopped cold in his mouth.

"Oh, I'm so sorry," Marissa offered, wearing a concerned look on her face.

Doc smiled back at her and shook his head. "No worries miss. None at all."

The two stood awkwardly in front of the store for a few moments, both wondering how to continue a conversation.

"Well, I guess I had better get going," said Marissa.

Doc nodded, wanting to say something to keep her there longer. "Hey, I know this may be out of left field, but would you like to have dinner with me tonight?"

Marissa appeared to ponder the question with great deliberation, knowing all the while she would say yes. "I think that could be arranged." She gave him a wide smile with straight white teeth.

"Wonderful. Where can I pick you up?" Doc asked.

"Why don't I meet you at the restaurant?" Marissa asked in return.

Doc gave her instructions to the only decent restaurant in town, and they set the time to meet at six p.m. He only wondered for a second why she would prefer to meet, then realized she didn't know him and it was wise of her to not trust a stranger too soon.

She congratulated herself for only slightly stumbling when he asked where to pick her up. Changing hotel's suddenly became a priority.

Both still feeling awkward, said their goodbyes. Doc stood for a moment outside the hardware store and watched her walk down the street and get into a jeep. When she looked up and saw him still watching, she smiled and waved.

I've got him, she thought.

Marissa drove over to the Sheriff's department with a smile on her face. Even though she had been shut down at the city police department, she was hoping the basket of goodies she'd purchased from the bakery next door to the hardware store, would help to endear the deputies to her.

If she could just get them to relax and feel comfortable with her, then she was convinced that she could get information from them.

The Sheriff's department was only slightly busier than the police department. At the front desk, a man of about fifty-five sat answering calls. *Great. I hope this will not be a replay of earlier,* she thought.

The man looked up and Marissa gave him her most charming smile. *Honesty. This time I'll try honesty.*

"Hi. My name is Marissa McClain. I'm a journalist from Oklahoma City, and I was hoping I could ask your deputies some questions. I know it is a huge imposition, so I brought you all some goodies from Miss Mildred's Bakery Shop."

The smell was wafting through the area before the words had come out of her mouth. The deputy stood and looked over the counter at the large basket covered in a red-checked cloth, a clear sign that the goodies had come from Miss Mildred's.

The battle between his stomach and properly manning

the front desk quickly ensued and was won by his stomach. Miss Mildred's could make any stomach stand up and take notice.

He looked up at the charming young lady. What could it hurt to answer a few questions for her, he wondered.

"Well, it isn't proper protocol, but I think a few questions won't hurt." He moved to open the locked door, allowing her to enter the area where the deputies desks were. She confidently walked right in and sat the large basket down on the nearest empty desk.

"Hi everyone. I'm Marissa and I've brought you a little treat." She whipped the red-checkered cloth from the basket to reveal a large assortment of Miss Mildred's best. With the removal of the cloth, the smell filled the room, and all eyes turned to her.

Without another word, three deputies surrounded the desk grabbing up their favorites. Marissa didn't want to rush this process, so she allowed them plenty of time to enjoy the tasty delights. Besides, they couldn't talk while their mouths were full.

While she waited, she observed. There were two men probably in their thirties, and one young woman around twenty-five. One young man had a wedding ring on and the other didn't. He was the one Marissa poured her charm on.

"You know you chose my very favorite one! I just love the cream she puts in those." She looked straight at the unmarried deputy and smiled.

The young woman's comments caught Derek Lassiter off

guard. He'd been thoroughly engrossed in the buttery goodness of the flakey cream filled croissant when she'd spoken to him. When he met her eyes, he was engaged by their beauty.

"Hey there Derek, cat got your tongue." The other male deputy, Randy Turner poked a finger in Derek's ribs teasing him. Derek's face flushed red.

"Stop giving him a hard time," said Amelia Stone, the female deputy. Marissa ducked her head in mock embarrassment, still smiling.

It took about ten minutes for them to all get their fill, nearly emptying the basket. In total, there were four deputies on duty. The one from the front desk, Milford Barnes, and the other three younger ones.

When Derek pushed the last bite into his mouth, Marissa said, "I'm a journalist from Oklahoma City. I'm here writing a story on the challenges of law enforcement in rural areas. Would you mind answering a few questions for me?"

Unsure of what to do, Derek looked up at Milford, the senior deputy on duty. Milford shrugged and nodded his okay.

"Is there a conference room or somewhere we can sit down?" Marissa asked.

Derek nodded and led the way. He found a small interrogation room and left the door open. He couldn't imagine the ribbing he would get if he'd shut the door in order to be alone with her.

With Derek on one side of the table, and Marissa on the other side, she pulled her notepad out of her satchel and opened it up to a page where she had written a few notes. She couldn't stand for him to see a blank page.

She hoped that by starting with a seemingly benign topic such as the challenges of law enforcement in a rural area, she could get him to talking about some specifics and then to her true topic of the drug trade.

With each question, Marissa poured on the charm without being too obvious. She could tell by the look in his eyes it was working.

The fourth question in, Marissa got to her point. "Would you say that drug enforcement is your greatest challenge in the area?"

Derek had answered the other questions easily. They had seemed harmless enough. He supposed this one was too.

"Yeah, I guess." Derek's eyebrows were dipping in concentration.

"You seem hesitant about that, Derek." Marissa said, making sure to use his first name as often as naturally possible.

"Well, we have a challenging county to police. The mountains and forest. It seems a natural place for criminals to come to hide away."

"Yeah, I've heard the stories." Marissa grinned.

Derek chuckled. "Well, yeah, the old stories, for sure. But they still do in the backwoods." Derek was becoming animated. "We have people so far back in the mountains cooking meth that we may never find them."

"So, would you say the drug traffic in this area has grown?" Marissa slid out.

"I would say so. Actually," Derek stopped, catching himself. "Well, I probably shouldn't say anything else."

Marissa nodded, giving him an understanding gaze. "Sure, I get it."

"What are some other challenges you face as law enforcement in a rural area?" Marissa hoped redirecting back would get him to open up more.

Derek sat frowning, looking down at his hands in his lap. "You seem troubled by something Derek. What's wrong?" Marissa asked.

He tilted his head over and back then looked at her. She saw fear in his eyes. "I shouldn't say anything," he said glancing away.

"Is it a secret?" Marissa asked.

Derek looked out the window and then back. "No, not really."

"Then what is it?" Marissa was internally on the edge of her seat.

"We've had some murders here lately. We have the drug trade and it grows every year, but it is nothing like what we have going on now." Derek's eyes pleaded with Marissa. He wanted to talk.

"Derek! Time to get back to work," Milford shouted from the other room.

Marissa reached out and laid her hand over Derek's which he had placed back on the table. "Derek, can we get together later for a drink?"

"I… uh… well…," Derek stuttered. "Sure, I guess."

Marissa pulled off a sheet of paper and wrote her cell phone number and email address down and handed it to him as he rose from his chair. She was pleased. She could get so much more out of him outside of here with a few drinks in him.

"I have a dinner meeting, but can you call me later? Say around 8:30 or 9:00?"

Derek nodded as he folded the paper and slid it into his rear pocket.

As Marissa exited the station, she grabbed the basket and waved goodbye. She was elated. She had come in hoping to find out about the local drug trade and was leaving hoping to investigate a series of murders. Her day was looking up!

THE SCENE at the shed was the same. Wiped out. Brushed clean. They stood disheartened at the sight.

"Well, here's my thought," began Carrie, "They may have wiped out evidence from before, but may have inadvertently left us new clues. Let's approach this as if it were a brand new crime scene."

Sheriff Markum and Lainey looked at Carrie considering what she had just said. As they did, they both nodded in agreement.

With fresh new eyes, the three worked the crime scene as if seeing it for the first time. They took photos, collected debris samples, and soil samples. This time though, they widened the search. There was a huge possibility someone had watched them from the woods when working the crime scene before. If so, then they may have left evidence there.

Lainey was in the forest to the north of the small clearing. She had walked about fifteen feet in and then looked back as if she had been observing it herself. *What would they have seen? Where would they have positioned themselves for the best view while staying hidden?*

To her right and down the hill about three feet was a large boulder sticking up out of the ground. As she walked over to it, she could see where the fallen leaves had been disturbed. *Could be an animal laid here,* she thought.

As she squatted down, she noticed a partial footprint in the small patch of dirt exposed between the leaves. She used her phone to take several pictures from several angles. Then with a small stick, she gently lifted the leaves one at a time to expose the footprint fully without disturbing it.

Once done, she had approximately three-fourths of a man's work boot print. She once again took pictures from several angles, then rose to call for the other two.

Sheriff Markum sat down her forensic kit and opened it. She pulled on blue gloves and opened a sealed packet of plaster which she gently poured into the print for a mold. As soon as she finished, she looked up at Lainey. "Great job!"

Carrie patted Lainey on the back and smiled. "Excellent job!"

"Whoever this was, could have easily hidden behind this boulder and had a full line of sight to what we were doing at the burn site," said Sheriff Markum.

Lainey sat squatting, still looking and thinking about the boot print. "The size would indicate a man, unless the woman had unusually large feet. But that boot print looks quite common." Lainey stood up, facing the other two.

"It's something. We keep digging. You know how it is, a step at a time," said Carrie.

When the plaster set, Sheriff Markum removed the print and placed it in a sealed bag.

Finally, when they had exhausted searching every area they could think of, they took once last look around and left the scene; on to the next one.

At the scene of the barn, it was the same. Although it had not been outside on fresh dirt, the barn floor had been swept clean and the burned wood removed. They had however, left the burned cross. The chalked outline of a pentagram remained on the back wall, as well.

"I guess they assumed that we wouldn't get any information off of the cross or back wall. So that is where I'll start," said Carrie.

Sheriff Markum began by taking photos. Lainey once again ventured outside to the edge of the woods. Since they had found something out there once, why not twice?

This area was much rockier, with steep rock crevasses. Lainey climbed on several, thinking they would make a good outlook, but soon realized most were treacherous. Whoever was watching would want a simple outlook.

After another hour of circumventing a widened perimeter of the clearing, Lainey found another area where the leaves had been disturbed. After getting down close to look for clues, she spotted a glint of metal when standing.

Just as before, she took photos, then used a small stick to gently uncover the metal. It was a girl's hair clip, about three inches long. It was an oval tortoise shell plastic disc. Inexpensive and one generally used to pull your hair back at the nape of the neck. It had been nearly buried in the dirt with only the end of the clasp protruding.

Before bagging, she once again called for Sheriff Markum and Carrie. They were all encouraged. It was coming together.

Carrie had found a small stub of white chalk nearly hidden in the crack of the barn floor where it had met the wall, just underneath where the pentagram had been drawn. It was such a small piece that Carrie thought it could have just broken off while in use. But she hoped that there still might be a partial fingerprint or some other trace on it.

Leaning with her face against the barn wall, Carrie looked at the area where the pentagram had been drawn. She noticed a small shiny spot about the height where someone might rest their hand while drawing. She smiled and called the Sheriff over.

"Our team took tons of fingerprints, but there was no way they could have seen that if they hadn't looked from that angle."

"We may not get a print, but there was some type of residue there that could have possibly come from the killer's hand," said Carrie as she delicately coaxed the residue from the wall into a small glass jar like the ones they were using to collect soil samples.

"One thing is clear though, there was little blood on the floor of the barn. It hasn't been scrubbed, only swept. I noticed just a tiny amount in one area. Had there been a large amount, it would have shown once the burned boards and debris were removed," said Sheriff Markum.

Loading up the SUV with their latest finds, Lainey realized just how hungry she had become. She had never before thought ahead about eating when working, since there was always food close by. But where on earth would they eat way out here? They still had to go see Hattie B.

Just then, Sheriff Markum slid a large cooler out to the edge of the back of her SUV. She reached in and retrieved three folding chair bags and handed them to Carrie. "I know you guys must be starving. I know I am. I made sure I had food packed. You have to prepare when working way out here."

Inside the cooler there were six roast beef sandwiches, apples, grapes, bananas, chips, and various kinds of meal and candy bars. To Lainey it looked like heaven.

"I'm starving!" Lainey gushed. "I'm so used to working in the city where the only food crisis is deciding where to go eat."

Carrie set the three chairs up in a semi-circle and the sheriff sat the cooler down in the center and went to get three large bottles of water.

"Water is all I've got. I hope that is all right."

"That's awesome," said Carrie right before downing half her bottle in one gulp.

As the three sat and satisfied their hunger, they talked about the case.

"I'm thrilled we have new clues. Actually, any clues!" Sheriff Markum exclaimed. "We gathered a lot of stuff before, but who knows if it will give us anything of use."

"I know we have taken soil samples and need to wait on a report, but I don't think there was much blood, if any. Maybe some, but not like you would see if someone killed the body with no thought to capturing the blood," said Lainey.

"So do we think it is indeed a satanic cult?" Carrie asked.

Lainey sat thinking as the other two watched her. She seemed to be the expert, and they deferred to her opinion. "I'm still not sure. What if it was someone who wanted us to think that? Someone who knew that capturing the blood was part of their ceremony. How much have you delved into the personal lives of the three victims?"

It was Sheriff Markum's turn to contemplate. "We did with the first victim Beau Johnson. Since it was the only murder we had at the time, was on an open brush pile, and didn't notice the pentagram, we felt it had to be personal.

"Then two weeks later, when we found Corey Stiles in the shed, we knew they were linked. Or we felt sure they were. But then one of my deputies suggested that it could be a single targeted murder and one or the other a decoy to throw us off."

Sheriff Markum shifted in her seat and stared at the ground deep in thought. "The third victim came one week later. The pentagram was noticeable, and it was a woman this time. We had to keep readjusting theories." She looked up at Carrie and Lainey.

"They are escalating," said Carrie. "First two weeks in between and then one week in between. Exactly how long has it been since the last one?"

"The day before we contacted you. Someone found her Sunday evening and by Monday morning you two were here."

"Do we feel you found her the day it happened? What did the medical examiner say about time of death?" Carrie asked.

"They confirmed that it had been done on Sunday."

With barely a minute of silence rolling by, they simultaneously got up to load and leave. What they didn't know, was that they were being watched.

It was three in the afternoon when Sheriff Markum pulled her SUV down the rough dirt driveway to Hattie B's small home. The sun continued to shine, but they knew the days were short and with the mountains towering over them, the light would fade soon.

"Stay here for just a bit. I want to greet her first and let her know I have you with me. I don't want to spook her with all three of us standing on her porch."

The sheriff gently shut her door and walked to the front porch looking around and taking in as much as she possibly could. Not much had changed through the years that she could see.

She tapped on the old front door, hearing nothing from the inside. "Hattie, it's Wanda Markum. Are you there?" The sheriff waited, straining to listen. When she still heard nothing, she tapped and spoke louder.

Then out of the corner of her eye she noticed the curtain

in the window next to the door move slightly. The latch scratched open, and the knob turned.

"Wanda?" Came a scratchy old voice through the crack in the door.

"It is. May I come in?"

The door slowly swung further open, and the sheriff stepped onto the threshold. I have two other ladies with me, may I wave them in?"

A thin woman with white-gray hair rolled into a bun at the nape of her neck, stood before the Sheriff. She stood barely five feet tall. Slow to respond, she finally nodded.

Sheriff Markum turned and waved for the other two to come in. The SUV doors slammed shut startling a flock of birds in a nearby tree.

Lainey was wary of meeting Hattie, and her nerves were taut. Carrie stepped in first with Lainey behind her, shutting Hattie's door. The little house was old, but tidy. The front room was so small that the crowd of four filled it.

Hattie walked to an old wooden rocker and motioned for the three to take a seat where they could. There was a small loveseat that Carrie and Lainey occupied underneath the front window and Sheriff Markum pulled a chair from the adjoining kitchen table and sat close to Hattie.

"Child, I know why you are here," said Hattie. "I been expecting you." Her rheumy eyes were sad and her mouth down-turned.

Sheriff Markum reached out and patted Hattie's hand which rested on the arm of the rocker. "I'm sorry I haven't come out sooner to check on you. It seems the only time I do is when there is a tragedy of some sort to discuss with you." The sheriff looked at Hattie with fondness.

"It's okay darlin'. I know you are busy. Old Hattie is fine." The old woman coaxed a thin smile from somewhere deep inside.

"You're right though. I've come to talk to you about the three burned bodies we've found. These two ladies are from Oklahoma City from the Oklahoma State Bureau of Investigation. They have come to help me. This is Carrie Border and Lainey Tate.

Hattie nodded and offered them the same thin smile, but her gaze lingered on Lainey. In response, Lainey gave the frail old woman her warmest smile, a smile that betrayed the cold hard fear she felt inside. Finally, Hattie looked away and back at Sheriff Markum.

"Do you know anything Hattie? Have you heard anything?"

Hattie sat back in her rocker, breathed deeply, pulling herself straighter up in her chair. Looking at the far corner of the room, she seemed to have drifted off somewhere the other three couldn't go.

Then the rocker creaked and Hattie began, "I'm not sure what I know, but I will tell you all that I do know. There is evil in those woods out there. I know that everyone has called me a witch since I was a young girl, but that is merely their opinion.

My momma taught me how to gather medicinal herbs from the woods. My daddy would buy me books from time to time when he would have to go into town. Books on herbs and natural medicines. I loved reading about the plants, and I learned.

Being so far out here there is no way a person could get to a doctor back then, so they would come see my momma and she would treat them the best she knew how, and a far site better than most doctors could do." Hattie used her boney index finger and pointed at the sheriff for emphasis.

Lost again in the faraway land beyond the corner of the room, Hattie grew silent again. "I learned from my momma. But times changed and rumors began that healers were witches. If you didn't go to the doctor, then you was a witch. We weren't no witches. But, the good earth provided and for that I was thankful."

Lainey felt uncomfortable, and as the old woman spoke she wondered if she knew God and thanked him for the plants he provided, or if she worshiped the earth, which was just his creation.

Hattie's gaze found Lainey and rested there once more. Lainey squirmed in her seat and looked down at the floor unable to hold Hattie's gaze.

"Girl you got a dark cloud following you." Hattie pointed that boney finger at Lainey. "It ain't you that is dark. You got a light inside you, but it be after you."

Lainey almost stopped breathing. Panic set in and that foreboding feeling fully engulfed her. Her mind darted about and vertigo set the objects in the room adrift visually.

She quickly stood up and searched for a way out. In a surreal mental fog, she grabbed the door handle and exited the small house. Once outside, she doubled over and fought to hold consciousness. Her breath came in short staccato bursts.

Lainey jumped when Carrie's hand touched her back. "You okay?"

"No, I'm not okay," said Lainey as she stood upright. The ground seemed to spin and suddenly moved out from underneath her. Carrie reached to grab her before she could fall to the ground.

"Here, sit for a bit." Carrie eased Lainey onto a weathered bench on the front porch. Lainey sat with her head in her hands, staring at the ground beyond the porch. *What is wrong with me? What is tormenting me?*

For the first time in her life, Lainey felt something coming against her that she didn't know how to fight. It was invisible and yet it seemed stronger than any enemy she had ever faced.

Even when she had been raped, she knew she had to overcome the fear and shame that was thrust upon her, and move forward. A loving family and friends had surrounded her. All had spoken encouraging and loving words of wisdom to her. It was a slow process, but she had not only survived, but came out the other side stronger.

But how did she fight something she couldn't see, something she couldn't define? She couldn't focus her mind and find a foothold to think rationally. It felt as though her entire being was spinning out of control and that she was powerless to stop it.

"I think I will call Randy and see if he is good with me sending you back. Gerald can come help me. This is not good for you, Lainey."

Lainey sat unresponsive to Carrie's comment. She had to overcome this. She wouldn't back down. "No. I'm not going home. I have to fight through this."

The door to the little house opened and Sheriff Markum stepped out. She bent down and hugged the little woman, offering promises to come see her more often. Turning to Lainey, her concern was evident.

She squatted down in front of Lainey. "You okay?"

Lainey looked at the sheriff with trepidation. "Not yet, but I will be." Her eyes locked with the sheriff's. Lainey thought the sheriff wanted to say something more, but was holding back. Then just like that, the sheriff stood and turned, and walked toward the SUV.

She knows something, thought Lainey. *I have to find out what. I will find out what, somehow, someway. She knows something that can help me. She knows what is tormenting me and how to fight it.*

CHAPTER 6

Harley's old pickup truck rumbled down the driveway to Blaine's house. He had to admit that he had a knot in his stomach half expecting to see River's jeep in the drive when he pulled up.

He knew Blaine had sworn that River wouldn't be there, but they were almost always together. Blaine couldn't control River and if he showed up, Harley doubted that Blaine could ask him to leave.

But when the ranch home came into view, River's jeep was not there. A rush of relief washed over Harley. Of course that didn't mean that River wouldn't show up later. But tonight he had his own vehicle and he could leave at any time.

As Harley stood on the porch after knocking, he looked around and noticed the beautiful setting. Even in the dead of winter the lush pine trees added color. He shivered and turned back to the front door when he heard it open.

"Hey man. Mom's got dinner just about ready. Come on in," Blaine was genuinely glad to see Harley. He had had concerns that Harley would back out of his promise to come.

Harley walked into the large great room with its vaulted ceiling rich with wood beams. He looked to the corner of the room next to the huge stone fireplace where a very large ten-foot Christmas tree stood beautifully adorned and lighted. Wrapped presents spilled out from underneath.

"I keep forgetting how close it is to Christmas. I've got to get some shopping done," remarked Harley.

"Here, give me your coat," said Blaine reaching for Harley's coat. "Well, that's all mom's doing. I still need to do my shopping too. I always put it off until the last minute."

Harley looked towards the kitchen. The smell of baked bread and something else he couldn't quite put his finger on, wafted through the house and made his stomach yearn for it.

"Smells good," commented Harley, hoping they would call them to the table soon.

"Yeah, mom's a great cook. Let's go into the den and wait until she's done. I have the television on the sports channel where the game will be." Blaine led Harley down a short hallway to a large room with leather sofas, a round game table next to a large window that overlooked the pasture. A fire roared in the fireplace.

They sank into the sofa directly in front of the television. "I half thought you might back out," said Blaine.

Harley didn't respond right away. He wanted to say

what he felt, but then he never was good at putting words to what he was feeling. "I'll admit that it concerned me that River would be here. Not that you would invite him, but that he would just impose himself on the situation and not leave."

"He tried. But we had words, and he left. That was right after I came home this afternoon."

Harley looked over at Blaine a little surprised that he had stood up to River. Without comment, he turned back to the television and the bank of commentators sitting behind a wood desk.

"I think something abnormal is going on in River's life. I think something has caused him to tilt off center this way," said Blaine. "I'm not making excuses for him, but there seems to be anger, maybe even rage over something that has happened. I don't know if something has happened at home or with his family, or somewhere else."

Harley just sat watching the television. He didn't know River enough to have an opinion. He just knew he didn't want to be involved with him the way he was.

"Blaine, it's time to eat." The boys jumped to their feet the moment they heard Blaine's mom call to them.

The rest of the evening was any guy's dream. A huge home-cooked meal and hours spent watching sports by a cozy fire. For Harley, the evening was over way too soon. For the first time, he felt free to relax and enjoy his friendship with Blaine. He had never realized before the true extent of pressure and tension River had inserted into his time with him.

The sky was bright, and the stars were out as Harley

stepped out of the house. It was super cold, and the air was crisp. Surprisingly, there was no wind. He stood for just a moment zipping up his coat soaking in the night sky, feeling good about life.

The old vinyl seats of his truck were ice cold, and it quickly bled through his jeans. The starter didn't take hold until he had cranked it twice. He then sat for a few minutes waiting for the engine to heat before taking off.

It was eleven at night. Not too bad for a work night. He could still get plenty of sleep and get to work on time.

He put the truck in gear and headed back down the winding drive, going slow to maneuver the sharp turns. He was still wallowing in the pleasant evening with Blaine and his family, when suddenly his rear passenger tire blew.

Surprised, he struggled to maintain control of the truck. As it finally slammed to a halt, the gravel from the drive threw dust in a gray cloud around the cab.

What the hell happened, Harley thought. He reached for his gloves and shoved them on. Just as he was opening the door, someone jerked it outward pulling him out and down to the ground.

Before he could grasp what was happening, a boot plowed into his ribs shoving him over, then plowed into him again. Sharp pain shot through his body. He moaned and rolled over on his other side.

The night stars did not provide enough light to see more than a silhouette standing before him. But he knew. He knew it was River, and he curled up in fear and pain waiting for the next onslaught.

It never came. At retreating boots crunching on the

gravel, Harley opened his eyes to see the silhouette disappear into the forest edge. He shut his eyes from the sharp pains that came with each breath. He had to get up and see about his tire.

With determination, he held his ribs with one hand and pushed himself up with the other. Standing upright, he thought he might lose that wonderful home cooked meal. Nausea and dizziness came in waves.

Gritting his teeth and shutting his eyes, he told himself that he was stronger than this. He would push through.

The lever easily flipped his truck seat forward, and he groped for a flashlight. The cab light had burned out, and he cursed at himself for not taking care of it sooner. Pulling the flashlight out, he prayed the batteries were still good.

As the button flipped to the on position, the light fluttered and then went out. Harley shook it and the light returned with a steady beam. Turning it to the ground in front of him, he saw imprints of the boots that had just assaulted him.

Gingerly, he squatted down by the tire. It had blown, but Harley could tell that the cause had been a bullet. River had shot out his tire! *That sorry…*, thought Harley.

Anger surged a rush of adrenaline through Harley's body and fueled him to remove the tire. He had found his jack and raised the truck. He then removed the wheel corralling the lug nuts so he wouldn't lose them.

The work had been an ordeal. With each movement, sharp pain surged through his body and took his breath away. He would stop for only a second to regroup and then continue on.

Finally, he reached for his spare tire and pulled it towards him. As he did, he could tell that the tire was not as hard as it should be. The rubber gave way underneath his hand. The spare was flat!

Harley stood and leaned against the open tailgate of his truck. The adrenaline that had fueled him drained out in an instant. *What was he going to do now?*

Leaving everything as it was, he walked back to the cab of the truck and crawled inside. He pulled out his phone and dialed Blaine's number.

"Hey man, did you make it home okay," Blaine asked.

"No, I didn't. I'm still on your drive, nearly to the road. I need some help." Harley's words were short and breathless. Talking hurt more than breathing and breathing was almost unbearable.

"Sure man. What's up? That old truck of yours give out?" Blaine was good-naturedly teasing his friend.

"Just come get me, Blaine." Then Harley ended the call. He couldn't talk any more.

In about five minutes two headlights illuminated the cab of Harley's truck causing him to open his eyes. He had been sitting as still as possible holding his broken ribs. He opened the cab and slid out of the seat.

When he turned to face Blaine walking toward him, Blaine stopped short "What the hell? What happened to you?"

Harley told Blaine everything. He couldn't swear it was River, but who else would it be? Blaine's fist pounded on the bed of Harley's truck. He was fuming. Did River now hate them so much that he would hide out in the woods and then attack Harley? Blaine just shook his head in fury.

"Okay, well, let's just get you back to the house." Blaine walked beside Harley holding the flashlight and then opened his passenger door for him. He jumped in the driver's side and turned back toward the ranch.

"Do you need to go to the doctor," Blaine asked.

"Man, I don't know. I hurt like a son-of-a...," Harley's words trailed off. River had kicked hard, twice maybe more. "I know he broke my ribs, but they can't set those, anyway."

At the house, Blaine helped Harley into the house and back into the den where they had earlier enjoyed a great evening. The soft leather sofa felt good, but the plushness of it pushed against the ribs, causing Harley to catch his breath.

"Sit here. I'll go get my mom."

"No. Blaine don't. I don't want to bother her." But Blaine had already left the room.

Lights began to flip on through the house and soon Blaine's mom and dad were standing before Harley. The story was once again told, this time by Blaine.

MARISSA CHECKED out of the flea-ridden motel she had been staying in. She didn't know what the night would hold, but didn't want to be staying in a place that she couldn't bring someone back to.

She was set to meet Derek after her dinner with Doc, so she wouldn't be bringing Doc back tonight, but you never knew about Derek. The thought didn't thrill her. She was not attracted to him in the least, but maybe she could ply him with alcohol and get more out of him then let him pass out.

Now Doc was another story. He was fantastic looking and Marissa thought she would enjoy bringing him back to her room. But, having a meeting with Derek after her and Doc's dinner would force her to take things slower. She needed to take her time with Doc.

After calling around town for over thirty minutes, Marissa had found one reputable chain hotel that had surprisingly low weekly rates. If she worked her money smartly, she would have enough for a while.

The restaurant where they would meet was a casual local dining spot, so Marissa knew she would look terribly out of place if she dressed up. But she had some sexy tops that would look great with jeans.

She took her time applying makeup. Once done, she took a long look in the mirror and smiled. She was thankful that she had been blessed with beautiful features and skin. Knowing how to apply her makeup expertly to accentuate those features even further was a bonus.

She added a bit of jewelry and her high heeled black boots. Checking her phone for the time, she realized she would be right on time.

Doc had arrived a little early at the restaurant. He was as nervous as if this had been his first high school date. He'd not even considered dating anyone since he had moved back home. He didn't want to get tied down here and honestly, no one around here interested him.

He knew that Marissa was not from around here, and he hoped that she wouldn't want to stay. Since meeting her the night before at the bar, he hadn't been able to get her out of his mind.

When she stepped inside the restaurant and slid her coat from her shoulders, several sets of eyes turned to stare at her. There were very few young black women in Wilburton, but one this stunningly beautiful was rare anywhere.

Doc did a half stand and motioned her to the table. As she walked she moved gracefully as if she were a model on a runway. She knew all eyes were on her.

As Doc slid her chair out to assist her, he smelled her perfume and it stirred something deep in his loins. Her loose gold top slid gently to one side of her shoulder, and he had to force himself not to reach out and touch the bare flesh.

"Thank you," said Marissa. "There aren't many gentlemen these days." She sat casually back in her chair and crossed her long legs. She smiled softly at Doc and studied his face.

Embarrassed, Doc cleared his throat. "They have wine here. Would you like a bottle? The selection isn't great, but they have a few to choose from."

"That would be nice. You choose."

Doc chose a cabernet, and they reviewed their menus. "Do you recommend anything in particular," Marissa asked.

"I usually eat steak. But I think all their dishes have a good reputation."

The waiter came and went, taking their orders. Without the activity of searching the menu's distracting them, it now forced them to conduct face-to-face conversation. Doc's palms were sweaty, and he rubbed them on his jeans.

Marissa could see his nervousness and it amused her, but she refused to let it show. "So now Doc, before you moved back to help your brothers, where did you live?" She wanted to skim right over what had made him shift gears the night before.

"I lived in Oklahoma City. I went to OU for college and then stayed. I worked for an oil and gas company for several years. My mom passed away recently and so I came home to help my brothers get through that and take care of some things." His gaze shifted away from Marissa and she knew she was on the verge of losing him again.

"I'm from Oklahoma City too. I work as a freelance journalist." She took another sip of her wine.

Doc studied her face. A journalist. *What could she possibly be writing about way down here,* he wondered?

The waiter brought a basket of fresh-baked rolls and whipped butter. Doc reached out and picked up the basket offering Marissa a roll. She took one and then he did the same. He was thankful for a natural pause to their conversation.

"What are you writing about that brings you down here?"

Marissa smiled. She would never tell him that the rise in local drug activity had brought her here. Now she had another excuse. She leaned across the table and in a conspiratorial tone whispered. "Have you heard about the local murders?"

Doc nodded, and she leaned back and buttered her role. She wanted to ply him for information on what he knew, but settled into the rhythm and flow of the process. Slow and steady wins the race.

Doc reached into the basket to retrieve another roll and asked, "So, what have you learned so far?"

Not much yet, she thought. "Well, I just got into town and have just begun my research. I stopped by both the local police station and the county sheriff's office. Neither are very forthcoming as you can guess."

"What have you heard?" She looked up at him with a coquettish smile.

Doc smiled back, taking in her beauty yet again. "Not much. Three bodies found, all burned, alive I think."

Marissa's eyes grew wide. "Burned alive?"

"Yeah, it was awful, well what I heard anyway. Three local kids in their twenties. I think they were all murdered differently and at different times, but all were burned."

Marissa focused on her glass of wine for a moment. She was trying to comprehend the enormity of what was happening.

The waiter brought their meals and both Marissa and Doc refocused on enjoying their feast. The food was genuinely good and they both ate and enjoyed.

During their meal, the conversation centered on lighter fare. Marissa talked about how she had always wanted to write and investigate and had never wavered as she was growing up the way some kids did, wanting to be something new each week.

They discovered they had both gone to the University of Oklahoma at about the same time and discussed the irony. Marissa asked about his work with the oil and gas company, at which Doc seemed to light up. She could tell he had loved his work there, so why had he come back to cook meth, she wondered.

They both passed on dessert but sat lingering at the table, neither one wanting to end the evening. Finally, about seven-thirty, Marissa reached across the table and laid her hand on Doc's.

"I've had a great evening, and I hate to end it, but I absolutely have to go back to the hotel and get some work done." She smiled and let her eyes linger on his, drawing him in.

"Could we do this again?" Doc asked.

"I would love that," Marissa said, giving him a glowing smile.

The check paid, Doc helped her on with her coat. Walking to the door of the restaurant he rested his hand against the small of her back protectively.

The bright night sky greeted them once they were outside. He walked her to her jeep and bent down to kiss her. She welcomed his soft lips and languished in his arms that held her tight.

ONCE AGAIN THE long hard day had been tough on the three. Sheriff Markum dropped Carrie and Lainey off at their hotel; she was exhausted both physically and mentally.

They had walked and climbed for a good part of the day. But the genuinely taxing part, was the constant assessing her mind did at each thing she saw and heard. Did it fit, did it mean anything, what to do next? Those and many more thoughts rolled through her mind all day long.

The pressure of urgency never let up. If Carrie's assessment was true, the killer was escalating and they could find another body any day. They didn't have the luxury of time.

Her husband's truck was in the driveway and the lights were on in the kitchen. The sheriff smiled, appreciating her loving husband. She knew he would have dinner waiting for her yet again.

Shep greeted his wife with a peck on the cheek. "Dinner's ready."

She grabbed Shep's lapels and pulled him closer. "Have I told you recently just how much I appreciate you?" Studying his light blue eyes. She had been looking into and loving those eyes for the last twenty-five years.

Shep gathered her up into a huge bear hug, picked her up off the floor, and swung her around. "Yes, my dear you have. But don't stop." He sat her back down and gave her a proper kiss.

"Now come eat." He had laid the table out with two place settings, a basket of cornbread, and a small vase with a single rose in it. Shep grabbed a large pot off of the stove with potholders and sat it on the table. Lifting the lid, the savory aroma of beef stew escaped.

"Have I died and gone to heaven?" she asked, already filling her bowl.

With their bowls full and their cornbread buttered, Shep said, "You look tired sweetheart." He worried about her, but she had done this job since before he knew her and he knew she was more than capable. This case was different though. He could see something different on her face besides the fatigue.

She considered what to say before she answered. "I am tired. We have been physically doing a lot, but mentally this case is wearing on me." Wanda stopped and thought about Lainey.

"And there is something else, isn't there?"

She looked at the man she loved with her whole heart. He was the man that was also her best friend and confidant. She knew she could tell him anything and he would understand.

Nodding she said, "Yes. Lainey, the young OSBI agent that came to help us, is struggling. I feel like, well I am almost certain, that she is suffering under some kind of demonic attack.

"First, she talked about how she was feeling a foreboding feeling since taking on this case. I've watched her. It will ease up and I see her bubbly personality, and that she is a precious child of God. She genuinely shines his light. But then a darkness comes over her, and I can see the oppression she feels."

She stopped to butter another piece of cornbread and refill her stew bowl. Shep sat thinking about what she had just said.

"You know, most of the world doesn't understand those oppressive feelings. They ascribe it all to some mental state. But from what you've just said, that is not normal for Lainey. Why do you believe she is feeling this now?"

"Lainey is young and innocent. I know she has had some life challenges, but there is a sweetness about her. I've seen pure joy radiate out from her. Wouldn't it be just like the enemy to target the one with the most joy?" She asked.

"What about the other one, Carrie isn't it?"

She thought about Carrie. "She is solid. I'm not sure exactly how to describe her, but I think about anything could happen and it wouldn't topple her. She's strong inside. I don't know what she has experienced through life, but I know that now she is incredibly capable and has an amazing mind with law enforcement."

"Today we were out at Hattie B.'s and the old lady looked at Lainey and flat out told her she had a dark cloud following her. It wrecked Lainey. She fled the room and nearly passed out when she got to the porch. Something supernatural is going on."

"You know the solution," said Shep.

"I do. But I can't just blurt out what I know. It has to be the right time and when she is ready. In the meantime, I'll pray earnestly for her."

"How about the case? Are you gaining any ground?"

"Very little it seems. Today when we went back to the crime scenes, someone had dismantled and wiped them clean. We just looked at that as a secondary crime and approached them in that manner.

"Lainey actually found a few clues. Carrie too."

"Is it a satanic cult as you were thinking?" Shep asked.

"That's the confounding thing. We can't tell yet if it truly is or if someone is just setting it up to look like one to throw us off."

"So, what did Hattie B. say?"

"She was rather tight-lipped until Lainey fled the room and Carrie followed to check on her. When it was just she and I, she said that she believes the opposite. That it is a satanic cult trying to make it look like regular murders that someone is trying to throw back on a cult."

"Pretty clever if you ask me," said Shep.

"I think that's one reason for Lainey's foreboding feeling. She's very sensitive to God's joy which can, if unprepared, make her sensitive to all activity in the spirit realm. The enemy is using it to take her down; to get her to back off."

"What about the animal sacrifices?" Shep asked.

Wanda dropped her spoon into her empty bowl and stood. "I think they are all tied together somehow. I personally think the cult is escalating, but don't want to get caught, and Hattie B. is right. They are trying to throw us off."

"Was she able to point you in a direction?"

"Not yet. I think I will go back out there by myself and talk to her again. I think with her it will be a step at a time. She will get to thinking about our conversation today and putting things together. She may have more for me later."

"Do you have the luxury of 'later'?"

"No. But what choice do I have?"

Shep walked over to his tired wife and slid his arms

around her. "I'll pray too. You know that with the blessing of the Lord we can chase our enemies far away. We'll put the whole mess of evil spirits to flight!" Shep grinned and gave her another kiss.

"Now, let's head to bed so I can hold you close," said Shep.

She felt such peace. She did not understand how she had been so blessed with such an amazing man. How could she have ever done this job without him by her side?

One by one they flicked the lights off inside, while outside the darkness took note.

CHAPTER 7

WEDNESDAY

As the sun peeked over the valley horizon on the Barlow ranch, Harley sensed the room lighten. He opened his eyes and his mind groped to remember where he was and why he was there. Then as he went to roll over, it all came back as the pain pierced through his body.

Harley gently laid himself back down and ran through the evening before when leaving Blaine's house. He would like to say he knew for certain it had been River who had assaulted him, but he couldn't.

Blaine peeked into the room. Seeing that Harley was awake, he came in and sat down. "I would ask how you are feeling, but I can see it written all over your face."

"I appreciate your family helping me out last night. Your mom did a great job of wrapping me up with that ace bandage. I don't know how I'll be able to work today though. I've got to call Mr. Watson and tell him."

"My dad wanted to call the Sheriff, but when I told him it might be River, he wanted to wait until today."

"Why?" Harley asked.

"He wanted to give it some time to see what you wanted to do."

"What do you think I should do?" Harley searched Blaine's face. He was furious at River, and he wondered if Blaine was too.

"I think you should call them. If it was River, this has gone too far. If it wasn't, then whoever it was needs to be dealt with."

Harley had to admit, Blaine's response somewhat surprised him. "I'm glad, because I agree. I can't say for sure it was River, but my gut tells me it was."

Just then, Blaine's dad, Charles Barlow came into the room dialing his cell phone. "Good. You're awake. I'm calling Sheriff Markum now."

"Sheriff this is Charles Barlow. I'm sorry to call you so early, but we've had an incident out at the ranch."

Sheriff Markum's stomach knotted up. Was it another burned body, she wondered? "That's fine Charles. What's happened?" She asked while pulling on her coat and kissing Shep goodbye.

"Well, it actually happened last night, but it was so late I hated to bother you then. Harley Atlee came out and spent the evening with Blaine. He left about eleven to go home and near the end of our drive, someone shot out his tire then assaulted him."

"Did he get a look at who did it?" Sheriff Markum asked.

"No, it was too late and too dark."

They ended the call with a promise from the sheriff that she would be there soon. She didn't need this right now. If it wasn't so early, she would send a deputy, but six a.m. was a little early for her bunch. She felt sure she would have this buttoned up and be back at the office before they even arrived.

Harley made calls all around. He knew it would worry his parents that he hadn't come home. He was an adult, and they didn't hover, but since he was still living at their house, they would worry when he didn't come in. He also got in touch with Mr. Watson and explained to him.

Soon, the sheriff's SUV pulled up outside. Once inside, they led her to the den where Harley now sat rather than lay.

The sheriff sat on the edge of the sofa next to Harley facing him. "Did you call your mom?"

"Yep, does Uncle Shep know?"

"He does. He was standing there when Charles called me. That's why I wanted to make sure you called your mom, because I knew he would call her. I wanted you to let her know first." The sheriff chuckled. Her husband Shep and Harley's mom Janet were brother and sister, and they were close.

"Are you okay?" Sheriff Markum said as she pulled out a pad and pen to take notes.

Harley nodded. He didn't want to talk any more than necessary. He realized now that if he had gone to the doctor, he would have at least been given some pain pills. He could sure use one now.

The sheriff had Harley walk her step by step through the events of the previous evening. When Harley began to glaze over something, she would pull him back seeking more details.

Finally, she closed her pad and rose to leave. "You feel like going to the truck with me?"

"If you will help me up and help me get dressed." Harley had a huge grin on his face.

The ride to the truck was excruciating. Harley had forgotten just how rough Blain's driveway was. Each tiny piece of gravel that the sheriff's tires spat out behind them, felt to Harley like they had just climbed and then dropped over a boulder.

"Why do you feel so strongly that it was River?" Sheriff Markum asked.

Harley thought before speaking. How much should he tell her? If he went too far, he might reveal about the cabin. Not even Blaine would be happy about that.

Harley told her what she generally needed to know rather than details and specifics. Telling her how River had become increasingly moody and his behavior had grown erratic, dark even.

He also told her about the spat that River and Blaine had had earlier the previous day. "Maybe River is jealous of Blaine spending time with me."

As Harley talked, Sheriff Markum was becoming increasingly concerned. Her mind kept dragging her to the murders, but she kept regrouping, telling herself that River couldn't have anything to do with them.

Back at his truck, Harley once again went over every

detail of the event, this time showing the sheriff where it happened. The boot prints were now vague. After Blaine had picked him up, his prints had nearly wiped all others out.

Sheriff Markum knelt beside the tire. Someone had blown it out with a bullet, but could she find it? The side of the road next to the truck was thick with tall dead grass.

She felt inside the damaged tire and moved it to see if the bullet was still inside. It was likely that when Harley had removed the tire, the bullet had fallen out. She searched on her hands and knees from the truck to just beyond where Harley had laid the tire.

It took several minutes, but she finally found the bullet and placed it in an evidence bag. Now she was hoping to find the casing. She would have to determine exactly where the truck was when it had been hit and then try to determine the trajectory of the bullet.

Harley took her to where he thought he had been, and soon they decided where the shooter had probably been standing.

After instructing Harley to get back into her SUV to rest, Sheriff Markum walked to the edge of the woods and began searching. As dark as it was last night she doubted the shooter would have been able to police their own casing.

Soon, a glint caught her eye. It was the casing. She smiled and slid it into an evidence bag with her gloved hands. She held the bag up to the light to see it better.

Growing up in this area with brothers and a father who loved guns, then being in law enforcement for so many years, one thing she knew was guns. She was almost positive that had come from a modified AK-47. In the US, the fully automatic version was illegal, so any AK-47 here would have been modified to semi-automatic. It would have been the perfect rifle for shooting a tire out at close range.

Now she just had to find the rifle. In her county that wouldn't be easy. No one around here owned just one gun. If someone owned a gun, they likely owned a dozen or more.

As she stepped out of the edge of the woods, Dan Atlee, Harley's father pulled up alongside her SUV. The sheriff stood next to his driver's side window that he had rolled down. His face was pinched with concern for Harley.

"Harley's okay. He's in my SUV. I think you should go ahead and take him to get looked at," said the sheriff.

"Do you know who did this?" Dan Atlee asked.

The sheriff shook her head. "No, but I have the bullet that blew out his tire and the casing too." The sheriff smiled.

Feeling she had done all she could right then, she left Harley to his father and headed back to town. She had heard the rumors about River from other sources. After all, it was a small town. He had been a carefree and fun kid; a good kid growing up. *I wonder what changed,* the sheriff thought.

Then on her way back to town, she made a sudden decision and turned around. She would go straight to River's home. She might as well confront this right then. Hopefully, it would still be early enough that his parents would also still be there. She would get the truth out of him somehow.

She really didn't need this on top of the murders, and she hoped that River's accelerated bad behavior had nothing to do with anything other than a bad mood.

But when she arrived at the Billings ranch, her doubts only increased.

DOC WOKE early and began cleaning their filthy trailer house. He had tolerated it long enough. He knew he couldn't bring Marissa back here - clean or dirty, so what was the point? The point was that he was better than this. He couldn't get out of here fast enough.

His brothers were eight and ten years younger than he was. He had loved them like any brother had growing up, but when he had left for OU, Jimmy had only been ten and Bud twelve. He hadn't been around while they were going through high school.

There had been no positive male influence in their lives, and momma had been sickly. They weren't the smartest two on the planet and school had been hard for them. Soon, they were hanging out with the doped up drugged out kids. Nothing had changed since.

Once again, he was tormented as he furiously cleaned. What would happen to them when he went back to the city? He felt like leaving them would issue their death warrants.

I could take them with me, he mused. That thought made him sick to his stomach. What would he do with them there? He would just be taking care of two grown baby men.

They knew how to cook meth. They would have money to live on as long as they didn't infuriate Joe. But, how long would that last? Again, guilt rose at the thought of leaving them to fend off Joe. It would be a different type of death sentence.

Jimmy stumbled into the living room half dressed and his hair tousled on top of his head like a wild man of Borneo. "Hey Doc, what's all the ruckus? I'm tryin' to sleep."

Doc slammed down the pan he held onto the kitchen counter. Jimmy jolted and stood still. Doc had gotten his attention.

He left the pan where it was and walked over to Jimmy like a raging bull. "You worthless, lazy, no account idiot! Don't you ever get sick and tired of living like this?" Doc raged at Jimmy until the hurt in Jimmy's eyes finally pierced through Doc's rage.

Doc stopped yelling and looked at his brother. He looked like a lost little boy. He knew nothing else. No one had been there to love him and show him he could live differently. What had Doc expected?

"Hey look man, I'm sorry. I just get sick and tired of living in this filth. What do you say you help me clean it up?" Doc patted Jimmy's bare shoulder and pulled him to himself in a side hug.

Quietly, Jimmy nodded and agreed to help. "Can I get me a bowl of cereal first?" Jimmy asked unsure of whether to make eye contact with Doc.

"Of course you can. But you promised to help."

"I will. I promise."

Doc tasked Jimmy with cleaning their bathroom and he headed down the hall. Soon, Bud came in yawning. "What you and Jimmy bellowing about?"

Doc just shook his head and continued to clean. "We're cleaning this house today. All of us."

Just as Bud started to complain, he saw the look on Doc's face and stopped. "Okay man, I'll help too."

With Doc giving specific directions on who cleaned what and then double-checking their work, it still took five hours for them to get everything cleaned to Doc's standard. He wouldn't let them stop half way. They changed the sheets, trash was collected, and dishes all done. Doc even cleaned out the refrigerator and oven, which had never been cleaned.

Then, once they had finally finished everything they could think to do, the three of them sat exhausted in the living room.

"Doc why did you make us do all that today?" Bud asked.

Doc took a deep breath. He didn't want to rail at them again, saying bad things about them. He wanted to see if this could be a teachable moment.

"I'm concerned about you guys." Jimmy and Bud started to laugh and blow it off, but the serious look on Doc's face stopped them.

"I came home to get everything situated after momma's death. Once I got here, I felt I had to stay and take care of the two of you. But you are adults now. You need to get yourselves together so you can take care of yourselves.

"I'll go back to the city when I can." He let that sink in before continuing. He had never said he would stay. He always felt they understood that, but to his brothers 'someday' was too far away to think about.

Bud got mad. "We don't need anyone to take care of us. You just go on back. Leave us here. We're fine without you." Bud started to get up and Doc motioned for him to sit back down. Jimmy just sat quietly.

"Maybe you can take care of yourselves. You're adults. You should be able to. But to do that, you have got to take life seriously. You have to stop smoking so much dope.

"If you keep cooking meth when I'm gone, you have to get serious or Joe will kill the both of you. You have to be clear headed to fill his orders on time. Can you do that?"

Bud took a deep breath. "Sure Doc, we can do that."

"You understand the consequences if you don't?" Doc asked.

"Why do you have to leave?" Bud asked, still angry.

"I left to get a college degree in science. I wound up getting a master's degree. I spent six years in college and then I got a great job that I loved. I want to go back and do that great job again. I don't want to stay here, live in this dirty trailer and cook meth." Doc was trying not to get angry all over again.

He was also trying not to be condescending. His two brothers knew nothing of life outside of these mountains. He doubted they had been further than McAllister.

As he sat, he searched to see if he could remember them

ever talking about having dreams about bigger things when they were young. All he could remember was that all they wanted to do was play. Momma was always getting after them. It seems like nothing had changed.

"Have either of you ever had dreams or goals? Anything? Any kind of job you wanted to have? Did anything ever interest you?"

Bud snorted. "Yeah, gettin' high." He laughed and looked over at Jimmy and grew quiet.

"I did," said Jimmy.

It suddenly surprised Doc. He hadn't expected either of them to admit to that.

"Tell me about it," Doc said.

Jimmy looked down at his hands and played with his fingers, deep in thought. His forehead furrowed and just about the time Doc thought he would not speak, he did.

"I wanted to build houses." Jimmy's eyes darted away as if ashamed to admit that to his brothers.

Doc was both stunned and amazed. "That's a wonderful dream Jimmy. You can do that. I'm sorry about all the stuff I say when I'm angry. You're not stupid. You can learn to do that."

"I don't know how. How do I do that Doc?" Jimmy's pain ridden eyes finally met Doc's. He was broken, afraid, and ashamed.

Doc's heart broke for his brother and he wanted to take back all the hurtful things he had ever said to him. "Well, you start out small. There are two ways. You can go to trade school and learn carpentry, or you can start out working for a builder and learn from them.

"You could learn a little at a time, then someday you could be a builder yourself." It thrilled Doc to see a tiny glimmer of hope in Jimmy's eyes. "But you have to make some changes to do that. Anytime you have a dream or a goal, make sure you do what you have to do to get there."

"What do you mean," asked Jimmy.

"I'm not saying you can never smoke dope again, but you have to decide you will only do it in the evenings after work or on weekends. And not so much of it any more.

"Get into a routine and get up on time every morning and get to work or to school. You can't get lazy and miss. You'll get fired or kicked out of school. Keep telling yourself that your dream is worth it. It is up to you to improve your life, to make it what you want it to be."

Jimmy seemed encouraged and Doc could tell that his words had landed and were being considered. He looked over at Bud who sat slumped down into the sofa with his arms crossed in anger.

"What about you Bud? You ever have any dreams or goals?"

Bud wouldn't look at Doc. Finally after several moments, Bud turned to look at Doc. "You come back home with your highfalutin' college degree and you think you are so much smarter than we are. You yell and scream and boss us around, telling us just how lazy and stupid we are and now you are tellin' us we should have dreams and goals and go for it." Bud spat the words at Doc.

They stung, but he was right. "You're right Bud. I was wrong. I was angry for having to leave my job and come back home and I took it out on the two of you."

As Doc's apology hung in the air, all three sat lost in their own personal thoughts. Doc searched for the right words to say to help his brothers. Even if he got Jimmy started on a good path before he left, he felt certain that Bud's lifestyle would suck Jimmy back down again once he was gone.

"Thank you two for all your help today getting the house cleaned. It feels good, doesn't it?" Doc asked. "What do you say that we get cleaned up and go to town and I'll buy us all a steak dinner?"

Jimmy smiled big at Doc, but Bud just sat on the sofa still brooding. Doc reached over and put his hand on his brother's knee. "Bud, I'm genuinely sorry for all the things I said. You're my brother and I love you. Let me take you out and buy you a nice dinner."

Bud looked up at Doc and studied his face. He admired his brother and resented him too. It had hurt him deeply when Doc had gone away to college, rarely coming home. He felt abandoned by the one person he had truly looked up to.

Bud nodded and got up and headed down the hall. "I'll shower first."

"Don't mess up that bathroom I just cleaned," Jimmy called after his brother laughing.

When Doc and Jimmy were alone, Jimmy looked at Doc. "Do you really think I could do what you say I can?"

"Yes Jimmy, I do."

"I don't even know where to start." Jimmy rubbed his hand over his face overwhelmed.

Doc wanted to make promises to help Jimmy. He

wanted to do what he could, but he also didn't want to make more promises he wouldn't be able to keep.

"We'll talk about it more. I'll help as much as I can, but the hard work will be up to you."

Jimmy studied Doc's face. "Can I go with you to the city when you go?" Jimmy asked.

Doc's stomach churned. He wanted to help his brother, but did that mean taking him back to the city with him? He wanted a good life for his brothers, but he wanted a good life for himself too. He asked himself if he was willing to make personal sacrifices for his brothers, beyond what he had already done. Wasn't coming back here enough of a sacrifice? How much more would he be required to do?

"We'll talk about it later, Jimmy," said Doc hoping to give himself more time.

"I can't make it here if I can't." Jimmy's eyes pleaded with Doc. "I can't resist this life if I don't go. I'll die here Doc."

Doc simply nodded his head. "I know Jimmy. I know."`

Carrie and Lainey arrived at the Sheriff's Department before Sheriff Markum. She had called them earlier to apprise them of the call to the Atlee's home and to let them know she would be there shortly.

Lainey stood looking at the whiteboard. "We don't have any suspects on this board, none. Doesn't that strike you as odd?" She turned to look at Carrie who was checking email.

Carrie looked back at Lainey. "It does. You would

think as well as the sheriff knows this county and the people in it, she would have some strong suspects by now."

"What if they aren't from here? What if they are targeting this area because of the terrain and their anonymity is shielding them? It may well be someone the sheriff has never met and no one but the victims have ever seen," said Lainey.

"How strongly do you feel that this is a satanic cult?" Carrie asked now standing beside Lainey looking at the whiteboard.

Lainey stood for a moment before answering. "My gut tells me it isn't. My gut tells me it is an imposter trying to misdirect us. But, I don't want to just assume that."

Carrie walked back over to the computer to finish checking her email. "Henry Bloom came down to the morgue here to review the bodies for a second opinion. I have the three official autopsy reports here."

Carrie scanned them searching for similarities or something that could help lead them in a specific direction. She printed all three for the files and sat reading them. "Lainey let's make a list from these reports on the whiteboard," said Carrie.

"One, all had smoke in their lungs. Died from the fire, not before. Two, no sign of accelerant was used. Three, no jewelry found on the victims. Four, there were no other obvious injuries perimortum."

"That's odd. How did the killer get them tied up without resistance?" Lainey asked.

"Here's something else odd. There were no shoes found

on the victims or at the crime scenes. They were all barefoot," said Carrie.

Going back to her email to scan for correspondence from the lab, Carrie found what she had been searching for and clicked the email. "The tox screen found a high alcohol content in all three victims." She paused and looked up at Lainey.

"So, let's think about this. If someone would do this, first they would have to have the burn site set. They would have had to decide where it would be and then gather brush and wood to burn. In the barn's case with the cross, they would have had to construct the cross.

"Then, they would have, what, gotten the victim drunk and then carried them to where they wanted to burn them? These weren't particularly small victims. It would have taken a very large or strong person to have carried them to the spot."

Lainey thought about the shoes. "Where are their shoes? If they weren't wearing any, and they weren't found at the crime scenes, then they may still be with the killer. Were they removed for practical reasons, or were they trophies?" Lainey asked. "What about socks? Did they have socks on?"

Carrie scanned back through the reports to the list of clothing articles. "No socks either." She looked at Lainey. Both were deep in thought attempting to formulate the reason a killer would remove both socks and shoes.

"It's winter. Removing their socks and shoes could keep them from running off or escaping, or at least slow them down," said Carrie. She glanced again at the clothing list. "There were no coats found either. Keeping their coats, socks, and shoes would be a deterrent from them escaping."

"If we could find where they were keeping them prior to killing them, we might also find those items."

"We should check with their friends and family to see if they could give us an idea what those items most likely looked like. I know we all have several pairs of shoes and different coats, but everyone has their favorites," said Carrie as she began making a list of things to do.

"Also, we need to get a tighter timeline of each victim before they were killed. We need to track their movements in as much detail as we can. Who they talked to. Where they went. I'm sure they came in contact with the killer and someone saw them, and didn't realize it," said Lainey.

Carrie shuffled through the file and pulled out the one for the first victim, Beau Johnson. I don't see a current job listed here. We should go talk to his mom again. Carrie made a note of his mother's name and address.

The next victim, Corey Stiles worked in McAlister at a chain home improvement store. "We can go talk to Corey's supervisor and his parents. Also, he had his own apartment.

"Amanda Lee lived at home, but worked locally here at a drugstore. We could go there and to her parents," said Carrie continuing to make notes on her to-do list.

"What are the most important questions we need to make sure we ask," Lainey asked.

"We need to know what outer clothing they most likely were wearing. We need to know their movements as closely as possible on the day they disappeared. We also need a list of friends and local hangouts that they frequented. Someone at those places may have seen something."

Lainey sat nodding and thinking. "We also need to ask if anything changed recently in their behavior or routines. You know, if they started hanging out with new people or going to different places than normal."

Carrie sat looking at Lainey thoughtfully for a moment. Her focus shifted from the case to Lainey herself. "We haven't talked about what happened at Hattie B.'s." Carrie waited to see Lainey's response.

"I know. I don't really want to talk about it." Lainey's gaze back at Carrie was pointed and stern.

"How are you now?"

"You don't need to worry. You don't need to send me home."

"Okay, but that's not why I'm asking. I really want to know if you are all right."

Lainey looked away, swallowing. Her eyes darted around while she attempted to assess herself in order to give Carrie a response. With determination, she looked back at Carrie and said, "I'm fine. I'm tough. Nothing, seen or unseen will take me down."

The look in Lainey's eyes was one of steeled determination. Carrie knew that Lainey was tough. That was good enough for her. She herself had worked for years with her own personal demons plaguing her daily and yet her work was stellar. There was no reason to think Lainey could do less.

"Okay then. Good enough for me." Carrie stood up and began organizing the files. "But you do know, or I hope you know, that you can talk to me anytime. Don't be afraid that I'll send you home.

"I worked for years with Randy. He knew my struggles, and I knew he always had my back, both in the field and personally. If it hadn't been for him, I know there were times I wouldn't have made it. I want you to feel the same about me. Sometimes we all have to talk."

Lainey nodded. "Thank you. I appreciate it. But honestly I don't know what I would say if I could verbalize it. There's just this unnatural anxiety that seems to well up inside me from time to time. I sometimes feel like a huge weight is pressing in on me. Other than that, I have no idea what to say about it."

Carrie stood looking at Lainey. She was the most vibrant and happy person Carrie had ever met. She was beautiful too. Her long dark hair framed a lovely face, but it was the abnormal light which radiated out from her, that enhanced her beauty uniquely. Today, Carrie could see that whatever Lainey was dealing with was taking its toll on her.

Lainey's eyes looked sunken, and she'd taken little time to fix her hair and makeup. The constant beaming smile was gone, and there seemed to be fine lines around her mouth now.

"Okay, but let me stress one more time, I'm here."

Just then Sheriff Markum came rushing into the war room. We have to go, now!

BEFORE SHERIFF MARKUM even arrived at the Billing's ranch she could see smoke rising in the distance. She pushed away thoughts of the murders, choosing to believe the fire was from a thousand other things.

But when she pulled up to the ranch house and barns, she could see an old smoke house a ways back behind the house on fire. No one seemed to be present on the property.

She immediately called the fire department and rushed to the house. No one answered. Forcing herself to calm down and think rationally, she searched for a water hose. Realizing they had all been stored, and the faucets winterized, she prayed for an idea.

Looking up, she saw an old well with a pump handle just outside and behind the smokehouse. Running as hard as she could, she reached the pump and began pumping. The pump sat slightly uphill from the smokehouse so even without a hose any water pumped out would run straight down to the smokehouse.

The smoke house had not been entirely engulfed in flames when she'd arrived, but that was rapidly changing. Had there been anyone inside, she wouldn't have been able to rescue them. She pumped as hard as she could for several strokes with no results. *I hope this isn't a dry well. God please bring water up.*

At first there was only a tiny gurgle, then finally the water rushed out. The sheriff kept pumping. Her arms began to burn as her muscles rebelled from the sudden over exertion, but she kept pumping.

The water rolled down the slight hill to the base of the smokehouse. As it hit the base of the burning back wall, it sizzled and steam rose. As she continued to pump, the water seemed to fight back against the fire. It rolled in through the holes the fire had created and across the floor.

It looked like it was making a slight difference. Sweat dripped into her eyes and her muscles burned. Smoke had invaded the fresh air she was breathing. The fire had finally completely engulfed the structure, but then slowly the water seemed to cover what remained of the floor and the rising steam helped to suffocate more of the flames.

She hoped that if nothing else, at least it would keep the fire from jumping to the cedar trees that were dangerously close. The sap in those trees always caused them to act like a torch that would flare up in a second, decimating the tree and then jumping to the next one.

After fifteen minutes of solid pumping, Sheriff Markum eased up. The small smokehouse was a smoldering pile of boards and ash. Steam continued to rise from the water and heat.

She collapsed to the ground to catch her breath. Still, no one had come from any of the buildings or the house. In the distance she could hear the faint piercing siren of the fire truck. Soon, the red flash of color parted the gray dormant trees lining the ranch's drive.

Gathering strength, she stood and waved as if they wouldn't see the towering pillar of smoke rising from the hillside. She had opened a gate and left it open when running to the smokehouse. The firetruck drove through and up to the fire.

Three men jumped out and two began unreeling a hose. Grady Daniels, the head of the fire station, walked up to the sheriff. She had called him to the three murder scenes because of his expertise in fires, even though the fires were no longer burning.

"Is this what I think it is?" Grady asked.

"I honestly don't know. When I got here it was completely engulfed and I have no idea if we will find a body inside or not."

Grady turned and looked at the smoldering smokehouse. He held up his hand to the other two firemen. "Hey boys, hold off on that hose. It looks like the fire is under control. That hose could obliterate evidence. Stand by just in case we get a flareup.

Grady tossed the sheriff a pair of heat proof gloves and they walked over to the smoldering pile. The building had been about fifteen feet by fifteen feet and now lay in a smoldering pile of rubble.

When the ranch had first been homesteaded, the owners had built the smokehouse to smoke meat. It had been strategically placed back away from the main structures in case of a fire. The Billings hadn't used the smokehouse to smoke meat in for decades and only contained remnants of an old smoker and other various tools used for that purpose. Before them lay the remains of the roof which had caved in. Steam still rose randomly in small shafts.

The sheriff looked at Grady. "One board at a time?"

"One board at a time."

They began carefully removing the top layer of boards and shingles that had been the roof. After about an hour of removal, Sheriff Markum looked down and saw a blackened and curled fist. Her heart sank. She had hoped that this had only been a random fire.

"I have to go get my team and supplies. Would you and your men continue to gently remove only the top layer of debris? Don't go down past the body. I want as many clues as possible. Also, if you don't have another call to make, please stay until I get back. Someone tampered with all three other crimes scenes after the fact.

Grady agreed and gave his men strict instructions in how to remove the debris to preserve any evidence that might have survived.

Sheriff Markum ran to her SUV and soon she was rushing to town trying to push down the growing anxiety and dread which refused to go away.

CHAPTER 8

The night before had gone as planned. Marissa had enticed Derek, and it had been him that had suggested they go back to her hotel.

The next morning, Marissa made sure Derek woke early to make it to work on time. She had gotten a good bit of information the night before and didn't want him hanging around the next morning.

Their pillow talk discussions had given her the basics of not only the fire murders, but also the name of Joe Billings. A local who had grown up in the area on a large ranch on the north side of Wilburton next to the National Park.

Derek had shared the highlights of what they knew of Joe's life and criminal activity. But the details of what, why, and where he did not know. He knew Joe was under constant surveillance of the DEA and FBI. He also knew that he had locals scattered over several counties cooking for him.

What he did not share, because he did not know, was that ranch life had not suited Joe. His twin brother Jeff was however, more than happy to take over for their father. Even though he knew he didn't want to ranch, he wasn't in a hurry to move away from the ranch.

Their mother had passed away when they were in their twenties, and their father when they were only thirty. He had made it clear in his will that since Jeff loved the land and ranching, he would get the ranch, while he would give Joe a cash inheritance.

Oil wells on the ranch subsidized the ranch income and both Joe and Jeff shared the royalty equally. Neither one lacked a livable income.

Being twins, everyone always assumed they were the same. But they weren't. Jeff was a cowboy through and through. He was a good-hearted man and loved the land.

Joe on the other hand, had always loved the adventure, or misadventure rather, that a more nefarious life brought. He had not hung around his brother's friends in high school. While his brother had been the star quarterback, he had been out riding motorcycles and hanging out with a local biker gang.

After high school, he had considered pledging to the motorcycle club, but needed more independence than that life would provide, so he gradually weened himself away from them.

He took drugs some during high school and afterwards, but his desire to be in control of his faculties gave him the self-control to leave them alone. He was however, drawn to the large sums of cash that selling them created.

Joe had always been a smooth talker and soon realized he had a shrewd business acumen. With the inheritance his father had left him, he could have made a legitimate fortune in any of a dozen business ventures, but instead he chose the illegal world of drug dealing.

At forty-five, Joe was now the largest drug lord in the southeastern Oklahoma, southwestern Arkansas, northwestern Louisiana, and northeastern Texas areas. It was a full-time job just to create or find new businesses to launder the money.

He had bought a local gas station early on and as far as most people knew in the area, that was what he did. He had purchased additional gas stations as needed and was known as a successful entrepreneur. He had worked hard to build this credible front and to keep his true business operations a secret.

Everything had worked fine. Not even Jeff knew until about six months ago when his nephew River stumbled into his drug operation. Joe had denied it to his nephew, but River was smart. Apparently he had had his suspicions for some time and had watched his uncle, to confirm those suspicions. Then one day, he caught Joe red handed at one of his warehouses, making a trade.

River had been inconsolable. Joe knew River had always idolized him. He had never taken to ranch life either and loved hanging out with his uncle. But unlike Joe, River had been a good kid in school. He and Blaine Barlow were always competing at sports and in their studies.

Marissa sat and looked at all that she had written. Notes really, just extensive notes trying to get everything down that Derek had told her. There was so much back story that she just did not know and needed to find out.

The sheriff's department only covered Latimer County and Joe's business stretched across state lines so the DEA had the lead on him. The sheriff's department cooperated as needed, but did not have the full scope of leads and information.

Marissa made notes of family members of Joe Billings. She wanted to talk to them if possible and watch to see which ones were also involved in Joe's operation.

Was it unrealistic to think she could bust both the drug cartel and the murders wide open? Would she be stretched so thin attempting to do both, that she would bungle both stories? Picking one to focus on made more sense, but when did she ever shrink back from a challenge?

Derek had given her much less information on the murders. The investigation was turning up few leads, and they were struggling to put it all together. He was not working directly with the two OSBI agents who assisted the sheriff, therefore was not directly in on new information.

But with her connection to Doc, she was well in and could use this new information about Joe to get a great story there. Although, Doc was the kind of man who would not brag about cooking meth. And, he had said he was planning on moving back to the city soon, so it made Marissa wonder just how involved he really was.

She shut her laptop and looked out the window. The wind was picking up and the crisp cold of the previous day seemed to fade fast. The sun still shone brightly, but that wind chill dropped the temperature by ten degrees.

Marissa shuddered and moved away from the window, plotting how to connect with Doc again. She could go back to her surveillance spot and take more pictures. Just as she was debating what to do, her cell phone rang.

Seeing Doc in bold letters on her screen made her smile. *Hmmm… Looks like I was on someone's mind.*

"Hello," said Marissa in her most sultry voice.

"Hi. It's Doc."

Marissa smiled. "Hi there. How's your day going?"

"Been cleaning. Just stopped for a moment. I keep thinking about you and last night and wanted to call and tell you what a wonderful time I had."

"Oh, me too," Marissa coo'd.

"I want to get together again, but I'm going to take my brothers out for a steak tonight. I just want to treat them. I would ask you to come, but I just want to do something nice for them."

"I understand. Maybe soon." Marissa tried to hide her disappointment.

"Well, I should get back to what I was doing before I lose momentum. It was good to hear your voice. I'll call you again soon," said Doc.

"I look forward to it."

As Marissa heard the phone go silent, she sighed. *Shoot. I was hoping to see him today.* If they were just cleaning the house, then they won't be cooking, so there won't be any transactions going on either. Pointless to go out and take pictures of nothing.

Derek had not given her the names of the murder victims. Maybe for today, she could switch tracks and work on that story. She would make a trip to the local newspaper and chat them up, see what she could glean from them.

She stuffed her laptop in its case, pulled on her coat, and grabbed her purse. As she stepped out the glass door of the hotel, the icy wind nearly pulled it from her grasp. Cursing, she pulled up her hood and ran to her car.

The entire local newspaper office was the size of the office of the editor of the Daily Oklahoman in Oklahoma City. Marissa chuckled at the vast difference.

There was a front desk reminiscent of the one at the police station. Then, there were six desks she could see in the main room. Two had occupants sitting in front of computer screens.

The cold wind that had entered with Marissa made both, one man and one woman, look up to see who had walked in. The man got up and came to the front counter.

"Hi. How may I help you?" he asked.

Marissa had thought about how to approach the newspaper office. She had wondered if she should just tell them she was a freelance reporter and offer to work with them to get the story, or to just lie. In the end, she thought it best to work together, even if it meant sharing a byline.

"I'm Marissa McClain and I am a freelance reporter from Oklahoma City. I have been doing some research and investigating on two local stories. Could I ask you or one of your colleagues some questions?"

The man turned to look back at the lady. Her curiosity was piqued, and she was now walking towards the desk.

"Our editor is not in today," the lady said.

"I'm not looking to publish in your local paper. That

would be up to you. I have my sights set on a much larger venue. We could work on your off time if you feel your editor wouldn't approve."

They looked at each other, smiled and nodded. The man opened the swinging door to allow Marissa access to the back room.

"I'm Brian Davis." Brian stuck out his hand to shake hers. They shook and Marissa smiled.

"I'm Mandy Reese. Our editor will be out all week. We are free to talk here if that is okay with you," said Mandy.

Marissa agreed and soon they were in their conference room with Marissa laying out the two stories she had been working on. Maybe with two additional reporters she could get both stories done.

As Marissa spoke, she had both Brian and Mandy's rapt attention. They made notes as all good reporters do and sat transfixed to her story.

Then when Marissa finished, they gave her the backstory as they knew it. The backstory that Derek could not give her.

SHERIFF MARKUM'S face was flushed, and she was nearly out of breath when she rushed into the war room. In a few succinct movements, she had filled Carrie and Lainey in on the fire.

They grabbed gear and forensic kits and headed back out to the SUV. The sheriff instructed deputies Derek Lassiter and Amelia Stone to come as well in their vehicle. She made a call to the county medical examiner.

During the ride out to the Billings ranch, Sheriff Markum filled them in on the details of her morning call.

"Do you believe the assailant was River?" Carrie asked.

"I think Harley and Blaine believe it was, but since they are in some kind of feud with him I think they have tunnel vision. I honestly don't know who it is or why."

"Was anything stolen from Harley?" Lainey asked.

"No. And they were lying in wait for him. It was someone who knew he would be at Blaine's and was willing to wait patiently until he left. I found the casing from a 7.62x39 round. I'm hoping we can get a fingerprint off of it. Those are common around here so without a print it will be anyone's guess whose it is.

"I also got a spent round out of the tire weld and we can have forensic's get rifling marks to compare it to, but unless we have a suspect and know which rifle to compare it to, that won't help us."

"So, do you think it is a coincidence that they are accusing River and then there is a fire and a body at his home the morning after?" Carrie asked.

Sheriff Markum had been trying to determine all morning if they were connected and had yet to decide. "I just don't know. I think there is a lot we don't know and cannot make any kind of educated guess until we do."

"Is it unusual for no one to be home at the Billings ranch? Do they work outside the home? Does River work somewhere?" Lainey asked.

"To me it seems unusual. However May, River's mom,

does a lot of volunteer work and she may be in town for that reason. Jeff, River's dad, may have gone into town or he may be on the backside of their property.

"River's older brother Jessie helps work the ranch. He may be with their dad wherever he is. I don't know that River has a job. Honestly, I think he does stuff around the ranch but doesn't work at it too much. I don't think he ever really enjoyed working on the ranch."

As the sheriff turned the SUV onto the long drive heading to the Billing's ranch, a large gust of wind slammed against the side of the SUV rocking it hard. The bright blue sky was once again fighting gray clouds for prominence, and it seemed like the dark clouds were winning.

"Looks like the weather is changing again. I knew the beautiful crisp calm day we had yesterday wouldn't last," said Sheriff Markum glancing up at the sky.

As they pulled up to the remains of the old smokehouse, they could see that the firemen had done a great job of clearing the debris from off of the corpse. They had only removed as much as necessary to reveal the body, waiting on further instructions from the sheriff.

"Thank you guys. I really appreciate it."

"We can move more if and when you want us too. I also took several pictures before we moved too much, and also along the way each time we removed a little more. I didn't know if there would be something in there that would help you," said Grady.

"Have you seen any sign of the family while you've been out here?" Sheriff Markum asked.

Grady was already shaking his head. "Not a sign of anyone."

As Derek and Amelia pulled up, the sheriff met them and spoke through the driver's side window. I need you two to locate May or Jeff Billings. No one out here has seen them on the farm. Call dispatch and see if you can get a number for one of them. When you do, let me know."

Lainey was squatting as close to the body as she could while still staying outside the perimeter of the smokehouse. She had moved and looked several times to glimpse any sign of markings. Her pad was out, and she had already made a few small sketches.

"What do you think?" Carrie asked Lainey as a strong gust of wind pounded them, attempting to take Carrie's cap with it. She snugged it down tight on her head and squatted down next to Lainey.

"I don't see a pentagram or any signs that there was one. Of course, it could have been destroyed by fire. If they had put chalk on the floor there might be some residual chalk, but then the water rushing over the floor might have removed it. I don't think we will know until we have the floor completely uncovered."

"The medical examiner is on her way. Have either of you noticed anything that stands out to you?" Sheriff Markum asked.

"Could be the lack of a pentagram. I don't see one now, not that there wasn't one, but I don't see signs of one," said Lainey. "Also, no coat, shoes, or socks, that I can see."

"Why don't we work the exterior of the smokehouse like

we did yesterday until the medical examiner gets here?" Carrie said.

They immediately got to work just as before. Lainey searched the woods that backed nearly up to the smokehouse. Had the killer come from this way, waited and watched, or just brought the victim here from another route?

After thirty minutes of searching, Lainey had nothing. Sheriff Markum had a few boot prints, that may or may not be related. Carrie had taken fingerprints off of the old steel lock and latch on the door. The medical examiner arrived, and they gave her room to work.

With a very preliminary exam, she determined that it was death by fire, but they would have to wait to know for certain until she could review in an autopsy. Once she was done, her assistant helped to carefully transfer the body to the body bag waiting on the gurney.

Lainey stood and studied the void left by the body. Was she trying too hard to envision a pentagram? Trying too hard to see something that wasn't there?

"I have Mr. Billings on the phone," said Derek as he handed Sheriff Markum his phone.

"What the hell is going on out there on my ranch, sheriff?" Jeff Billings demanded.

"Jeff there has been an incident. I was coming to talk to River this morning and saw your smokehouse on fire. There is no one here at the ranch. Where are you?"

"I came to McAlister to get a new piece of equipment."

"Where's May?" Sheriff Markum asked.

"She went to her sister's yesterday. She has a bad case of

the flu and May went to stay with her for a few days and help."

"And the boys?"

"I don't have a clue where they are. I don't even know if they were home when I left. I just assumed they were in bed asleep. I'm about twenty minutes out. I'm on my way."

"Jeff, one more thing," Sheriff Markum took a deep breath. She hated to say this on the phone, but once the medical examiner's van left, it would be all over town. She needed to tell him now. "There was a body in the smokehouse."

MARISSA SAT LOOKING at the vast amount of notes she had taken while Brian and Mandy told her all they knew about Joe and his drug dealings. Why hadn't she come to them first? Back in the city no reporter would have ever divulged this much information, especially to another reporter, but Brian and Mandy couldn't wait to share all they knew.

"How do you know all of this? Can any of it be verified?" Marissa asked.

Brian and Mandy looked at each other with conspiratorial glances. Finally Brian said, "If you mean verified as in tape recordings or documents stating facts, then no. But, this is a small town and we've lived here all our lives. We know because we just know."

Marissa understood, but you can't write a story on hearsay. "If I'm going to investigate these stories, I need actual proof. Are you two willing to help me do this? I promise bylines."

They readily agreed. Brian knew more about the drug cartels and those involved so they decided that he would work that angle and Mandy would work on what she could find out about the murders. She had already been writing small articles on what she knew, but now she was suddenly motivated to dig deeper. The thought of a byline on a big city newspaper or even a magazine article was huge.

The police scanner crackled in the other room and all three went to listen. There had been another fire and the sheriff's department was on the scene. It was out at the Billings ranch.

"I grew up with Jessie Billings. He and I were in the same class and we still hang out together. That's why I know so much about Joe Billings," said Brian.

"About six months ago he came over. He wanted to get out of the house because his brother River had gone off the rails, yelling and screaming at his dad. Apparently River had discovered Joe at one of his warehouses and had caught him in a drug transaction.

"River was furious. He had always been an easy-going guy. He and Blaine loved sports and hanging out fishing and stuff in the mountains. He had been a good student, and he was happy. After that incident, every time I've seen River, he looked angry like a dark cloud is consuming him. He's scary to be around now," said Brian.

Marissa sat and thought for a moment. The ranch where the brother of the largest drug lord in this area, had just had a fire and maybe a body. Her two stories had just possibly merged.

Mandy and Brian stood with bated breath waiting for Marissa to give them instructions. They never thought they would get the opportunity in this small town to do anything so literary worthy and were waiting for marching orders.

Let's go out to the Billings ranch. The worst they can do is make us leave. But we may get something more than we have now.

A ripple of fear ran down Mandy's spine. She had never been much of a daredevil. "I don't want to get in trouble." Her uncertainty made her hesitate.

"Come on Mandy. We can't do great things by just sitting back, afraid," Brian urged. "I'm going even if you don't."

"I'll go," said Mandy nervously nodding her head.

Being in such a small town, they easily locked the newspaper front door, stuck a note on it, and climbed into Marissa's jeep.

They took the time to get to know each other better on the drive.

"I just graduated with a degree in journalism last year and then came home. I'm still living at home with my parents. It's not really what I had envisioned, but coming back here at our newspaper at least has given me some experience for my resume," said Mandy.

"I never finished my degree. I had to come home for financial reasons, but because I had done a lot of journalism in high school, the editor hired me. I've been here two years," said Brian.

"I graduated from OU five years ago. I worked for the Daily Oklahoman for three years and then received an inheritance from my father's estate when he passed last year. It wasn't huge, but was equal to a couple of year's salary at the paper. I thought about it for a long time and then decided that I would take some time off and try my hand at freelance investigative journalism.

"I did a ton of research while still at the paper to see what might be a great first story to get in the game and make a large enough impact that I could keep going. I wouldn't mind going back to the paper, but my heart really wants to be an investigative journalist, traveling the world." Marissa had a faraway look on her face caught up in her vision of her future.

"But, we have to get this story right. If we all work hard, I won't be the only one benefitting," said Marissa.

"Do you think the fire is related to the recent murders?" Mandy asked.

"I don't know, but if it is, then the two stories have become one huge story!" Marissa was so excited she couldn't hide her growing smile as she turned the jeep onto the Billings drive.

About a mile ahead of them, they could see wisps of smoke still rising faintly in the distance. About halfway up the road they passed the medical examiner's van leaving the ranch.

"There was a body all right," said Marissa.

Brian got a huge knot in his stomach. "I hope it wasn't

Jessie." Fear for his friend had now replaced excitement. They had been close friends for a very long time and he hated to lose his best friend.

Mandy reached over and patted Brian's hand. Her sympathetic look did little to comfort him. His mind raced to think of any information he could contribute to the investigation. All he kept coming back to was River's recent dark behavior.

Ahead was a pile of rubble and the remains of an old smokehouse. They had removed a sizable amount of debris and piled it to one side. There was the local firetruck, three firemen, Sheriff Markum, two of her deputies, the two OSBI agents, and the local police chief. Even though this wasn't his jurisdiction, he came to assist however he could.

As the three reporters got out of the jeep, they quietly closed their doors. They hoped to ease into the crowd of personnel and blend in to get inside information before anyone realized they were there.

They had parked in front of the ranch house and walked to the far side of the fire truck opposite of the smokehouse. They moved quietly around the front of the truck and stood behind the three firemen listening.

Marissa had her phone open to a voice recording app. Mandy was taking extensive notes, and Brian was snapping pictures with his phone. There was no longer a body as suggested by the medical examiner leaving, but there was a void on the floor of the smokehouse where the body had lain.

The two OSBI agents were squatting close to that void engaged in deep discussion. The sheriff was on the phone and looked distressed. The police chief was standing to the side and front of the sheriff talking to the two deputies. The firemen stood waiting for further instructions.

One fireman, Hunter Clark sensed a presence behind him and turned to look over his shoulder. "What the hell are you doing here," he whispered, seeing his former classmate Mandy.

Immediately, Mandy placed a single finger on her lips showing him to be quiet. She was met with a disgruntled look on Hunter's face, but he turned back around to look at the smokehouse not saying a word.

Sheriff Markum, now off of her call, squatted down next to the OSBI agents. "Well, anything at all?"

"Nothing that I can tell. I had hoped that underneath the body would be signs of a pentagram, but I see nothing," said Lainey.

"The fire has caused so much damage this time and the water washed away what remained," said Carrie.

"Why did the barn not burn to the ground at the other crime scene?" Lainey asked the other two, searching their faces. "It was as old and as dry as this smokehouse. It should have been consumed like the old shed and this structure, but it wasn't."

Neither the sheriff nor Carrie said anything in response to Lainey. She was right, why hadn't it been consumed by the fire? Something had stopped it.

Sheriff Markum stood and looked at Grady. "What do you think stopped the fire at the barn? It should have been consumed just like this structure and the shed. But it wasn't."

Grady frowned at the sheriff, thinking back to the scene at the barn. They had placed the cross in the center of the barn where the roof was at its peak. The old barn had a considerable amount of boards gone, including most of the roof. The floor was concrete.

"Sheriff, didn't it rain that night? Not a huge deluge, but there was a light rain for about an hour or so here. If it rained there, it might have been enough to put the fire out before it consumed the barn."

Sheriff Markum stood thinking about what Grady had said. Then nodding, she said, "I think you're right. It wasn't a hard enough rain that it washed away the markings on the back barn wall though. But a light rain just might have been enough to smother the fire. The roof had large holes in is as did the walls."

The police chief had been listening to the conversation. "Sheriff, what can my department do to help you with this investigation?"

"None of the bodies had shoes, socks, or coats. We believe that they were held somewhere else prior to their deaths. It is a possibility that removing those items was a deterrent to keep them from running away in this frigid weather. We need to find where they were being held.

"We will conduct further inquiries with the victims' families and employers. We want to find out what their most likely outer clothing and shoes would have been and tighten down their last movements prior to their disappearances. If you would, could you talk to their employers again? I'll send you the list we have."

The police chief nodded. "I'll get started now."

At that, the three reporters quietly retreated to Marissa's jeep. No one but Hunter had seen them. Once in the jeep, Brian asked, "What's next?"

"We go to the medical examiner, but wait to go inside until the sheriff has left." Marissa put her jeep in gear and headed out from the ranch. Back on the main road she found a spot and pulled over. It was not uncommon for vehicles to pull over there to look at the view. From there they would wait and watch for the Sheriff to go by.

At the smokehouse, Sheriff Markum stood looking at Lainey and Carrie. "We'll head to the medical examiner's office as soon as Jeff arrives. I don't want to leave that to my deputies."

The OSBI agents nodded and they all three headed to the sheriff's SUV to get in out of the cold. They were all feeling the same gravity regarding their situation. So many bodies in so little time.

"This killer isn't giving us enough room in between to even catch our breaths. We have to get ahead of them instead of merely reacting. Something has to shift. We have to get a lead somewhere, somehow," said Carrie.

"Maybe this body will give us one," said Sheriff Markum. "As soon as we find out who it is."

JEFF BILLINGS roared onto his ranch with his truck spitting gravel and blowing dust. He pulled up beside the sheriff's SUV, shoved it in park, and slung his door wide open. In a split second, he was standing outside the Sheriff's door with a grief-stricken face.

Sheriff Markum opened her door and stepped out of her vehicle. She faced this man she had known her entire life.

"What's going on?" Jeff Billings asked the sheriff. His hands shoved deep into his jean pockets, and his shoulders hunched against the cold. The wind was attempting to rip his winter Stetson from his head. But all Sheriff Markum saw was the pain in his eyes.

"I came to talk to River this morning. His friend Harley Atlee was attacked last night, and I just wanted to talk to River. When I got here, I saw the smokehouse on fire. I knocked on the door and no one answered." The sheriff continued to give Jeff the details as she knew them.

"The body, was it one of my boys?" Jeff was terrified of the answer, but he had to know. His mind had already created the worst possible scenario after hearing the news.

"There was a body, but we don't know yet who it was. I'm going to the medical examiner's office now to see how they are progressing. In the meantime, call around and see if you can locate Jessie and River. When you find them, let me know."

Jeff nodded and looked down at the ground. Finally he said, "Okay sheriff, I'll let you know." He stood watching the sheriff leave as a tear rolled down his cheek.

CHAPTER 9

The Latimer County medical examiner's office was a fraction of the size that Oklahoma County's was where Henry Bloom worked. The medical examiner in Latimer County was Sharon Pine. She had graduated with honors in pathology after receiving her medical degree. Somewhere along the way she knew she would rather help solve the mysteries that ended life, rather than solve the mysteries that were trying to take it.

Sharon was bent over the last body, attempting to remove bits of charred clothing with a pair of stainless tweezers. She barely looked up as the three entered the cutting room while still gloving up.

"Hi Sharon," began Sheriff Markum. "How's it going?"

Standing, after pulling a swath of what had been a red plaid flannel shirt from the victim, Sharon smiled at the sheriff. "Fine, but slow going. I'm being careful to remove these bits so hopefully there will still be some trace of the killer." She pulled a bag from the side table and slid the fragment of cloth inside.

She nodded to Lainey and Carrie. "I'm Sharon Pine, medical examiner for Latimer County. Welcome to my cutting room." Lainey and Carrie nodded and smiled.

"As you may know, I've only been an independent medical examiner for three years. I worked under Henry Bloom in Oklahoma County for one year and when this position came open, I applied. With Henry's glowing letter of recommendation, I got the job. The year with Henry was the most valuable year in my education.

"I feel sorely inexperienced for what we are dealing with now. That is one reason I called Henry the other day and he came down to add assistance. He had to return yesterday to get back to his duties. We had no idea we would have another body so soon.

"However, while he was here he continued to teach me while reviewing the previous bodies. A horrible thing to have to learn from the deaths of others, but I do feel somewhat better equipped with this one than the others."

"Have you found anything yet that might give us any indication of who this is?" Sheriff Markum asked.

Sharon shook her head. "Not yet. I wanted to remove any debris or outer clothing first to preserve evidence. Once I've complete that, I will take x-rays to find a dental match."

Carrie picked up the evidence bag that Sharon has just sealed. "Can we take this? It might help us. We could show it to the Billings and see if they recognize it."

Sharon agreed, and the Sheriff signed the chain of

evidence log. "Please call me the moment you know anything for sure."

"You know I will Sheriff," said Sharon once again leaning back over the charred body to tease yet another scrap of flannel from the body.

Dark gray sky greeted the three as they stepped outside. The wind had increased and they had to push against it to walk back to the SUV.

"The weather is getting worse," said Carrie. "What's the forecast?"

"They've issued another winter storm warning. I only hope it's another false alarm like earlier in the week," replied Sheriff Markum.

"So where are we at, and what do we need to do next?" Lainey asked.

"Chief Branch will assist us by contacting the employers of the previous victims. I explained to him we need to know what type of outer clothing they were likely wearing and to narrow down their final movements. That will be a great help to us."

"So we still need to interview family as well," said Carrie.

"Yes we do," replied the sheriff.

"Are you feeling slightly overwhelmed with all we need to do with this last body?" Lainey asked.

"Yes, I am. I felt a sense of urgency before, but now urgency is an understatement," said the sheriff. "I'm thinking we may need to split up to get more done."

"Sounds fine to us," said Carrie.

"I could give Chief Branch the family interviews, but I

would prefer that we did those. I just feel that we have more instincts regarding when to shift gears and push forward. Not that he isn't competent, but..."

"We get it," said Carrie. "How do you want to handle them?"

"How would you feel about us each taking a different victim's family? I have a secondary SUV back at the station that one of you could take. It's older and not decked out the way this one is, but it is serviceable. We could each go our separate ways and cover much more ground."

Carrie thought about that. They rarely ever went solo when investigating for safety's sake. But the sheriff was right, time was of the essence. "I think that would be okay. What do you think Lainey?"

That feeling of dark foreboding was back and as strong as ever, but Lainey knew she had to do the job and work the crime. "Yeah, I'm fine with that. I'll probably need a map to find my way though." She then snorted as she thought of the vast wilderness surrounding them.

"You'll have whatever you need," confirmed the sheriff.

Just then the sheriff's phone rang, and she answered, "This is Sheriff Markum."

"Sheriff this is Jeff Billings. I reached Jessie. He had left early to go out and fix some fence on the north side of our place like I had asked him to do today. He knew that bad weather was coming in and went out there early."

"Have you heard from River?" Sheriff Markum asked.

"No sheriff, I haven't." Jeff's heart and voice was heavy. "I called May and told her over the phone what had happened. I was hoping that she had heard from River, but she hasn't.

"Why did you want to speak with him this morning sheriff?" Jeff asked.

Sheriff Markum took a deep breath. Should she tell him everything, she wondered? "Last night when Harley Atlee was leaving Blaine's house at about eleven o'clock, someone shot his tire out and then assaulted him."

"Yes, you said that. What does that have to do with River?"

"River and Blaine had an argument earlier in the day. There seems to have been some jealousy between the three friends. Harley said he thinks it was River who attacked him." The sheriff stopped speaking, hoping that this news was not misery compounding misery.

Jeff thought about what the sheriff had just said. His first instinct was to just brush it off, but he had to admit he had seen a huge change in River over the past several months. He himself had had more than one raging argument with his oldest son.

The silence that greeted Sheriff Markum from Jeff's side of the line surprised her. She fully expected Jeff to quickly come to River's defense. "What do you know Jeff that we don't?"

"I don't think River would attack Harley, or Blaine for that matter. But he hasn't been himself lately, that's for sure."

The sheriff could hear the heaviness in Jeff's voice. She had three adult children and could easily understand how horrible it would be to be in Jeff's shoes right then.

"Do you know why River's behavior has changed so drastically?"

There was no way Jeff wanted to tell the sheriff about his twin brother Joe's drug business. He was still reeling from the news himself. He had argued with River, adamant that Joe would never do such a thing. But, when he had confronted Joe himself and learned it was true, the truth had devastated him. He'd never felt such shame in his entire life.

"I'm not entirely sure, sheriff," Jeff finally said.

"Well, hopefully it's just a passing phase." The sheriff was attempting to provide some emotional relief to this terrified parent. "I'll keep you apprised if we find anything regarding River and if you hear from him, call me immediately."

"I only pray that I do hear from him again," said Jeff, fully aware that it might just be River's body that lay charred on the county medical examiner's table. "I hope I do, sheriff."

BACK AT THE sheriff's office, Sheriff Markum pulled out the files of each individual victim and gave one to each of the OSBI agents.

"I'll take Corey Stiles. His parents live the furthest away on a small ranch east of Wilburton. The other two victims families live in the country too, but closer to town."

"Lainey here are the keys to the SUV. It's fully stocked with winter gear.

"Carrie, let's keep in touch on what we find. Follow any leads that the two of you come across. I know you know what you are doing, so just run with anything you find. We've got to gain some ground somewhere."

Carrie took Beau Johnson, victim number one who had been burned on the pile of brush. His mother was a single mom who worked at a local burger chain.

Lainey had victim number three, Amanda Lee's family. Both parents worked. She decided to go to their home first, then if no one was there she would go to their individual places of work.

They each headed out and to their respective assignments. Carrie soon pulled up at the burger chain where Mildred Johnson worked. It was two o'clock in the afternoon and there were only a few cars in the parking lot.

The light glowed from the inside and she could see various workers scurrying about tending to the customers. It was the slowest part of the day for fast food, but she still hated pulling Beau's mom out from her shift.

As she was exiting the SUV, bits of icy rain began to blow down, feeling like needles on her bare cheeks. She wrestled the door away from the force of the wind and got it securely shut.

She zipped her coat up to her neck and pulled her collar up as high as it would go. The wind entered the burger place with her and the diners looked up to see who had entered. When they realized it was a law enforcement individual, fear crossed their faces. Carrie wondered just how much more bad news this little community could stand.

She walked over to the counter and stood behind the

teenager placing an order. The employee taking his order looked to be about the age that Beau's mother could be. When it was her turn, she stepped up to the counter.

"Excuse me for the interruption, but my name is Carrie Border and I'm with the Oklahoma State Bureau of Investigation. I need to speak to Mildred Johnson if she's available." Carrie watched as the lady looked down at the credentials Carrie had held up for her to read, then back up.

Was it Carrie's imagination or did the lady age another ten years in those few seconds? The charm she had intentionally put on to serve her customers had vanished and sorrow filled the void.

"I'm Mildred Johnson."

"Ma'am I know you are on your shift, but if I could pull you away for just a bit to ask you some questions, it would help me greatly."

Mildred nodded and looked around nervously to the other employees. Finding the one she was looking for, she walked over to him and they spoke in hushed tones. He nodded and looked up at Carrie. He patted Mildred on the shoulder attempting to assure her it was okay.

Mildred directed Carrie to a hard plastic booth in the corner of the dining area the farthest away from the other occupants.

"Do you have any news on who hurt my boy?" Mildred asked. Carrie knew she had used the word hurt rather than face the reality the word killed brought with it. People grieved in different ways and at their own pace.

"No ma'am. We are working hard though to find any clues that will help us. That is why I've come to talk with you today. I have some specific questions that I need to ask, but I would also like you to tell me some about Beau. What his life was like, what he liked to do and where he liked to go. Also, who he liked to hang out with."

Carrie remembered she wouldn't have Lainey to take notes for her and had thought to bring her own pad and pen. She felt at a disadvantage because she knew she actually absorbed what people were saying better if she focused on them rather than writing it all down.

"Well, there isn't much to tell other than what I told Sheriff Markum." Mildred sat looking at the table gently wringing her hands. "Beau was always a good kid. He made pretty good grades, but not all A's or anything like that. When he graduated he went to community college because his friends did. He only lasted a few semesters.

"He never could seem to find where he belonged. He tried a few jobs, but he never would stick with them. He kept saying they just didn't fit him. I don't think he liked someone telling him what to do. His daddy left when he was real young and with me working all the time, he never had the firm hand to keep him in line the way he should have."

Carrie had abandoned the notepad and just focused on Mildred. "Who did Beau hang out with the most?"

Mildred gave Carrie a few names that she wrote down and where she thought some of them worked. "But honestly, he was hanging out with some guys that he never brought around. I think they were doing drugs." Mildred's last words were barely a whisper uttered in shame. She couldn't make eye contact with Carrie and there was moisture lining the rims of her eyes.

"Did he ever mention any of their names, even a first name?"

Mildred thought for a few moments then shook her head. "No, sorry."

"When was the last time you saw Beau?"

Mildred swallowed as she thought. "I… I… guess about two days before they found him."

"Can you tell me about that day?"

"He doesn't live at home anymore. Well, sometimes he stops in and spends the night, but mostly he doesn't come home. He had stopped by and went to his room. He was looking around for something. Opening drawers and digging around.

"That was unusual for him to be searching for something that way. So, I followed him to his room and watched. Then I asked him what was he looking for. He mumbled something and then when I didn't leave, he snapped at me and told me to leave him alone, that he was fine." A tear slid down Mildred's cheek and she swiped it away.

"Did you ever find out what he was searching so frantically for?"

Mildred shook her head. "He wouldn't tell me."

"Do you think he found what he was looking for?"

"I don't know. He searched for a good long time and then just suddenly stopped and stormed out. I called after him and asked where he was going, but he never responded."

"Do you remember what he was wearing when he left?"

Mildred sat picturing the last time she had seen her son. "I think he had on a brown t-shirt and jeans." She looked back up at Carrie.

"What else? What kind of coat and shoes?"

"He just had an old jean jacket with one of those sheep collars on it. He always wore boots. Round toe not cowboy. Why?"

"When Beau was found he didn't have a coat or shoes on. We wanted to know so if we came across them, we might find clues with them. Is there anything else you might think of? Anything, any little thing no matter how insignificant might help us," Carrie softly pleaded with Mildred.

"They never mentioned finding his old truck. It was a 1977 blue and white Chevy truck. Pretty beat up, but he kept it running. No one has ever mentioned seeing it since."

Mildred looked at Carrie with an ounce of hope that what she had just said might help. Carrie gave Mildred a huge smile and nodded. She reached out and covered Mildred's hands with hers.

"I promise you I will work hard on this case to find out who did this. I can't promise you we will find the perpetrator, but I promise I won't quit trying to find out who it was."

"If you don't find the killer, will he keep killing others? You have to stop him Miss Carrie. You have to stop him so he will stop killing."

~

LAINEY PULLED over to the side of the road to check the directions again. This SUV had no navigation system and her phone's map program did not have the Lee's address on there. It was a county road that had recently changed when the postal system updated its carrier routes.

Another gust of wind slammed against the side of the SUV and Lainey shivered. The vehicle was warm inside, but it was hard to not feel chilled from the weather surrounding her.

The Lee's had just lost their daughter. Amanda had been the third death and the one that had occurred the day before Lainey and Carrie came to Wilburton. The body had not yet been released, so they had no closure and were still grieving in a holding pattern.

Lainey laid the instructions in the passenger seat, believing she now had her bearings and put the SUV in gear. She was on the north side of Wilburton, on a road she had traveled several times over the last few days. But she was about to turn off on a road she was unfamiliar with.

The Lee's worked in town, but lived deep into the mountainous area to the northeast of Wilburton. The roads wound through the dense forest and Lainey drove slowly not knowing what would be around the next curve. It set her nerves on edge.

After forty-five minutes of her uncertain and cautious driving, she found the Lee's home. She had made a few wrong turns and had to backtrack each time. Relief washed over her when she saw the name on the mailbox.

There were several cars in front of the modest home. Since it was so close to finding Amanda's body, she was certain the parents were still in shock and most likely at home. The other cars were probably friends and family who were there to help in whatever way they could.

As Lainey exited the SUV, she thought the wind had subsided somewhat. She stood and looked at the sky which had been dark and ominous just a few minutes before. It appeared that the clouds and storm might head to the south of where she was.

On the front porch, she took a deep breath and prayed for knowledge on what to ask and sensitivity to their grief. Soon after her knock, the door opened and a lady of about forty years old opened the door.

"May I help you?"

"I'm Lainey Tate with the Oklahoma State Bureau of Investigation. I would like to speak with Mr. and Mrs. Lee."

The lady turned to look back into the room, nodded to whoever she was deferring to and then opened the door for Lainey to walk in.

The living area was large and open. The house was probably a century old, but the interior had been recently updated and was very welcoming. Lainey stood just inside the door as a man came to great her.

"I'm Amanda's father, Griffin Lee." He held out his hand to the agent. Lainey smiled and shook his hand. She always struggled with the family of the deceased. Her naturally optimistic outlook and deep faith compelled her to offer hope from her perspective, but it was often the right thing to say at the wrong time. She had learned that listening was often the best thing to do.

"I'm sorry for your loss Mr. Lee. I know this is hard, but

I need to speak with you and your wife. I need to get more information to help our search to find out who did this."

Griffin nodded and motioned for Lainey to come further into the room. He continued into the kitchen where his wife was putting dishes in the cabinets. He whispered into her ear, a shadow fell over her eyes, and she glanced at Lainey. Her presence was a grim reminder of the tragedy that had occurred to their family just days before.

"If you can come back here to the den, we will have more privacy." Griffin exited the kitchen through a door on the other side and Beth motioned for Lainey to follow him.

The room was small but cozy. There was a fireplace with a small fire going, and several overstuffed chairs surrounding it. She took a seat and pulled out her pad and pen.

Looking at Amanda's mother, Lainey said, "Mrs. Lee, I am so sorry for your loss." It was a rote sentence that every law enforcement personnel had uttered countless times. But there was no other way to express that they truly were sorry for that person's loss.

"I know Sheriff Markum has been out to see you, but as we have been working on the case, it occurred to us that we need to ask you a few more questions."

Both Griffin and Beth nodded.

"I didn't know your daughter. Can you tell me a little about her? What she liked to do, about her personality, just anything that can help paint a picture in my mind of who she was."

Beth looked over at Griffin. The effort it took to talk about Amanda felt comparable to pushing a boulder uphill.

Griffin coughed and leaned forward in his chair. "Amanda was an easy child to raise. She was vibrant and full of life. She always made very good grades and in high school she was a cheerleader. I suppose you could say she ran with the popular kids in school.

"She wasn't perfect. We weren't naïve about that. She rebelled some in high school, but it was just the normal stuff, missing curfew, not doing chores, and stuff like that." Griffin looked away towards the window. The sun had actually peeked through the clouds and was shining a thin sharp ray into the room.

"Did she have any hobbies or activities outside of school that she liked to do?" Lainey asked.

Lainey's words drew Griffin back to the conversation, and he sat and thought for a moment before answering. "When she was young she played sports, but in high school she said cheerleading was enough of a sport for her. She spent a lot of time with her friends going to movies, and stuff. There isn't a lot of variety for kids around here."

"My file said she went to college after high school, correct?" Lainey knew it was correct, but used the questions as a segue to her life after high school.

"Yes, she got a scholarship to college because of her good grades, but when she got away from home, she didn't seem to have the discipline to stop playing and having fun long enough to study. In high school I think her grades came easy to her. In college where she had to work harder at it, she didn't know how to, or didn't want to.

"After two years, we had her come home when her grades were consistently reporting C's and D's. The scholarship had run out, and we were having to pay at that point. She didn't know what she wanted to be. One day it was a nurse, the next day a teacher, and then something else another day.

"We thought if we had her come home, and she had to work for a while, then she would decide what she really wanted to do. We could send her back if that is what she wanted. We just felt she needed to mature a little more in order to take school more seriously."

Lainey nodded. She had seen that time and time again. For so many it was a hard transition from high school to college. "After she came home, she was working at the Blanchette Pharmacy, correct?"

"Yes, she worked in fast food when she first came back, but then an opening at the pharmacy came open and she applied there. She seemed to like it. Steve Blanchette was a great boss, and Amanda seemed to work hard for him."

"Can you tell me the last time you saw Amanda?"

Beth sucked in a sharp breath at the thought she had actually seen Amanda for the last time. Fresh tears ran down her face and across the hand that covered her mouth. Lainey paused to allow her a moment to recover.

Griffin, fully aware that his wife was not capable of contributing to the inquiry continued. "Amanda was here on Sunday. She slept late, got up, and had lunch with us. She laid around most of the afternoon, but about three, she got dressed and went to town. She said Matt was taking her to a movie. That was the last time."

"Matt. Is that her boyfriend?"

"Yes."

"Was it unusual for her to meet Matt in town? If they were going on a date why did he not come to pick her up?"

"It was just easier. If he came to pick her up, it was a lengthy round trip. They just decided a long time ago that it was quicker and easier for them to meet in town. They didn't always. Matt spent a lot of time out here. He would even pick her up, but they had been together so long and were so casual with their relationship that at some point they just thought it was easier for both of them to meet from time to time."

Lainey thought that made sense. "When Amanda left Sunday afternoon, what was she wearing?"

Griffin tried to remember, but then looked to his wife. He rarely remembered those kinds of details. Beth took a deep breath to garner the strength to talk. "She was wearing a navy blue sweater. It was one of those bulky ones that pullover, and jeans."

"Could you tell me what her coat and shoes looked like?"

Beth looked at Lainey suspiciously. "She had a dark gray wool coat. Double-breasted that was about thigh length. She was wearing a pair of black boots."

She continued to look at Lainey wondering why, but only her eyes inquired.

Griffin however, did. "Why do you ask about her coat and shoes?"

"When we found her, she did not have a coat or shoes on." Lainey's words were delivered softly to soften the blow.

Beth burst into wracking sobs at the thought of her

sweet girl being out in the cold without her coat and shoes. Griffin moved over to her chair and wrapped his arms around her.

Lainey gave them a few moments. She still needed to get a list of friends to interview and to ask about favorite hangouts and such. The parents had done well to have given her this much information. They were still in the early stages of grief and shock. Just how much more dare she try to get from them today?

When Beth couldn't seem to regain her composure, Lainey rose. "I have more questions, but I will come back tomorrow. I know this is a lot to handle. I appreciate you speaking with me today. I'll show myself out."

Lainey made her way back through the house and out to the front yard. The grief this family was feeling affected her greatly. From deep inside she felt a firm resolve to push past her own struggles with this case and find this killer.

As she zipped her coat up, she glanced to the far edge of the clearing. Was she seeing things, or had a glint of something flashed in the edge of the woods. She watched for a while but saw nothing else.

She shivered as she stepped into the SUV, but it wasn't from the cold.

SHERIFF MARKUM HEADED EAST of Wilburton to the small town of Red Oak, then turned north into the mountains. The drive from Wilburton to the small Stiles ranch took her about forty-five minutes. She was used to the winding roads doubling the time it took to get anywhere.

As she pulled onto the ranch, it was quiet except for the howling wind through the trees. It was three o'clock in the afternoon and almost as dark as evening. The clouds were the color of dark charcoal black.

The ranch home was a modest frame home with white siding. Sheriff Markum knocked on the front door and waited. A frisky puppy, a brown lab came bounding around the corner of the house and onto the porch. She had to laugh at his exuberance.

She squatted down to pet the pup and was met with a wet tongue licking her face. It made her laugh out loud. The creak of the screen door reminded her of where she was and what she was there for.

As she stood and turned, she saw Corey's mother, Linda, holding the screen door open. "Hello, Linda. May I come in?"

Linda Stiles nodded and led the sheriff into their front room. It was small but warm and cozy. Sheriff Markum sat on the edge of a worn blue plaid sofa and Linda took a blue chair directly across.

Corey's mom didn't ask why she was there. There was no worse news she could deliver and what did it even matter at this point if they found who did it? It wouldn't bring her boy back. So Linda just sat and waited for the sheriff to get to the point.

"Linda, I know you have answered what seems like an endless amount of questions, but would you mind if I asked you a few more?"

Linda nodded agreement. Sheriff Markum noticed that she had barely brushed her hair and the clothes she wore looked to be a few days old. How hard it must be to recover from such a tragedy. To even get up and get dressed at all must take all the strength a person could garner.

"Can you tell me exactly the last time you saw Corey?"

"He came by the Sunday before... before..." Linda stopped. She couldn't bring herself to say before he was killed.

"Was it in the morning, afternoon..." Urged the sheriff.

"He came by that evening after work. He got off at four that afternoon and came over and had dinner with us. He left here about nine to go back to his apartment in McAllister."

"Did you notice anything different or if he was upset about anything?"

Linda's eye narrowed. "What are you getting at sheriff? Do you think whoever did this knew Corey?"

"We honestly don't know yet. I'm trying to get some details that may help us establish a timeline and his frame of mind."

"He didn't seem any different at all. Actually, he was in a great mood. He was being considered for a promotion at work. It thrilled him." Linda looked away. It didn't take much effort to hold back tears, because she had already cried them all out.

"Do you remember what he was wearing?"

Linda looked back at the sheriff. "Just a shirt and jeans." She paused for a moment trying to remember the shirt. "I think it was a blue-checked shirt."

"What kind of coat was he wearing, and shoes?"

"He had his Carhart coat and his brown cowboy boots on."

"Okay, that's good Linda," said Sheriff Markum as she wrote it all down.

"I know that Corey had moved to McAllister, but did he have the same friends or do you know who he hung out with lately?"

"You think one of them did it?"

"No, no. I'm just trying to get a list of anyone I should interview that might help me get a better idea of where he was right up to when the event happened. It may help us track down the assailant."

Linda shifted in her chair and pulled her worn sweater tighter around her shoulders. She thoughtfully gave the sheriff a list of names and what she knew of where they might work.

"Is your husband at work? I'd like to talk to him as well. Sometimes what one parent doesn't notice or know, the other one might."

"He went back to work this morning. It doesn't seem right to be going back to life as normal when it is the furthest thing from it. The ranch doesn't provide enough income any more, so he took a job at the gas station in town. The one on Phillips Street that Joe Billings owns. It's not much, but it helps."

"Is he there now?"

Linda nodded, and the sheriff got up to leave. "Linda, we've known each other a long time so you know when I say that I'm here for you, I mean it."

The sheriff reached out and hugged Linda. She felt her bones through her thin sweater and Sheriff Markum knew Linda hadn't been eating. She made a mental note to pray for her.

The wind hadn't let up, and the sky was growing even darker if that was even possible. She would head back to town and go talk to Bill Stiles before calling it a night and going home.

It was challenging to hold the SUV steady as she drove. The constant battling of the wind and weather, the stress of this case, worry that she couldn't stop this killer, and overall fatigue, caused Sheriff Markum to just want to go home.

She longed for their cozy fireplace and the arms of her loving husband. He was steady and solid and was always, no matter what, there for her when she needed him. But tonight she wouldn't be seeing him anytime soon, and she sighed.

The drive back to town was uneventful, even fighting the wind. As she pulled into the gas station where Bill Stiles worked, she noticed the station was nearly empty except for the one vehicle which she assumed was Bill's.

This was one of the original gas stations in Wilburton. It was the original type that serviced cars and pumped gas. It could barely compete with the newer convenience store types, except here they actually serviced vehicles, changed oil, and made repairs. That was the only thing keeping it afloat. Not that Joe Billings needed it to succeed; he owned at least three other stations with convenience stores in town.

The warmth of the building welcomed the sheriff, but the smell of grease and solvent assaulted her nose. Bill came through the door from the garage wiping his hands on a red shop rag. "Hi sheriff. What can I do for you?"

Was it Sheriff Markum's imagination or had he suddenly gotten completely gray headed overnight? His aged appearance since she had seen him last week stunned her.

"Hi Bill. Can we sit and talk for a bit?"

Bill nodded and motioned toward a chair in the waiting area. It was old, rickety, and the sheriff felt like she was sitting on remnants of oil and grease that had made their way from the garage. Bill pulled up a rolling chair from behind the counter.

"Bill, how are you doing?"

The face that looked back at her was broken. Pain had etched lines deep in his face and she wasn't sure he would ever recover.

"Sheriff, I guess I'm doing as well as I can be. Just trying to make it through a day at a time. This is my first day back at work. I thought the work might distract me, but it hasn't."

"I need to ask you more questions. I'm working hard to sort this out and catch who is doing this, but I'm struggling. I've called in the OSBI to help. We are working almost around the clock. So, I want to ask you a few more questions. I know memories often sharpen after the initial shock."

"I know you are doing all you can. I just can't imagine who would want to kill my boy." A sob escaped with Bill's last word and he put his hand over his mouth as if to hide it.

"I just came from visiting with Linda. She hasn't been eating, Bill. You need to encourage her to eat. Grief will take a toll on her health if she doesn't fight back. You still have a daughter to live for, to parent, and to love."

Bill was nodding as tears were sliding down his face. "I know this has been hard on Traci. You're right, we've been so caught up in our own pain I feel like she's slipped through the cracks. We need to get better at comforting her. Life just seems so hard right now."

"I know."

"What did you need to ask me?"

"Well, I got from Linda what Corey was wearing. He did not have a coat or shoes on when he was found. We hope that if we find those items it can link someone to the assailant.

"Linda said the last time she saw him was the Sunday night before he disappeared. Did you see him after he left your house that night?"

"No. He was going back to McAllister. He had to be at work early the next morning and so did Linda and I."

"Linda also gave me a few names of old friends, but she didn't know any new ones he might have since moving to McAllister. Can you think of anyone he might have mentioned?"

Bill sat with his hands on his knees staring at the floor. He was trying hard to remember passing moments that had come and gone without notice. He was trying to pull out simple conversations they had had in passing, ones that he had barely heard or given thought to.

"He mentioned one person. He worked with another

guy… James, or Jack or Jimmy. I can't quite remember. I think they were friends and did things together. You know, hung out and stuff. Other than that, I can't remember Sheriff."

Bill looked at Sheriff Markum ashamed that he knew so little about his son's life and ashamed that he couldn't do more to help the sheriff bring to justice the person that had killed his boy.

"Bill, that is a huge help. Really, it is. If you think of anything or anyone, please let me know, no matter how seemingly insignificant." She patted Bill's shoulder and turned to leave.

"Sheriff, why would anyone want to kill my boy?"

She turned to look back at Bill, wishing she had an answer, as if an answer would fix it all. "I don't know Bill. I just don't know."

CHAPTER 10

THURSDAY

The sheriff, Carrie, and Lainey had met back at the sheriff's station the previous night and compared notes. Lainey explained that she needed to go back out and continue the interview with the Lee's the next day.

Both the sheriff and Carrie had collected a long list of people to interview from their day out, so they agreed that they would once again split up to cover more ground.

The next day, the wind had blown through, and it relieved Lainey. It was almost pleasant driving through the forest in the morning sunlight. She still had to stop and check her directions several times. *I just don't know if I will ever get familiar with any of this forest,* she thought.

It all seemed to look the same to her and each dirt or gravel road looked just like all the others. It was incredibly hard for her to keep her bearings. She was never completely sure which direction she was going or if she was winding up or down the mountain.

The route to the Lee's house was a challenging one for someone who was familiar to the area. With Lainey, it took her much longer, but she was finally able to arrive with only three wrong turns.

Seated back in the den with Griffin and Beth Lee, she could see that the additional day had helped them get just a bit closer to recovery, if only in the slightest.

"Thank you for meeting me again this morning."

Both parents nodded at Lainey.

"I need to get a list of Amanda's friends and any contact info you might have, phone numbers, emails, etc. I also need to talk to Matt. It seems he may have been the last one to see her that evening so I need to talk to him."

"You don't think he had anything to do with this do you?" Griffin looked at Lainey with a horrified look on his face.

"No sir, I am just trying to get the tightest timeline down, so we can try to track when exactly she might have been taken and from where. I think he is probably in the best position now to help with that."

Relief washed over Griffin's face. "He's a good boy. We really thought he might be our son-in-law one day, and we were pleased with the thought."

Lainey spent the next thirty minutes taking notes and getting as much contact information that she could. She also took notes on places Amanda liked to hang out.

Back in the SUV, Lainey looked at the list and tried to devise a plan to route sensibly so she wasn't driving back and forth. She soon realized she would need help to do that since she didn't know the area. So, she focused on finding Matt Bradford first. He really was key in this interrogation.

Lainey backed and turned to head back down the narrow road. After about ten minutes the rough road jostled her phone into the floor and it wedged itself underneath the accelerator peddle.

She removed her foot and tried to drag it out with her heel, but it was awkward and kept sliding back down. Finally after several attempts, she leaned down to reach for the phone while attempting to see over the dash and steer with her left hand.

Her reach was not quite long enough, so she stretched to grab the phone in a quick movement. For just a brief second she lost site of the road, but it was the worst possible moment for that to happen. As she reached for the phone, her left hand jerked the wheel slightly to the right.

The SUV had been critically close to the right side of the gravel road which dropped downward to more forest and mountainside below. Just as Lainey lost sight and moved the wheel, the right front tire rolled across a large rock which started shifting and sliding down the hill.

Unable to maintain control of the SUV as she would have with both hands on the wheel, Lainey felt the gravel shifting and the SUV begin to slide downward sideways. She'd gotten the phone, but it had come at a cost.

Panic seized her as she attempted to compensate for the shifting gravel. The SUV had all wheel drive and was proving a solid defense against it. But after fishtailing a few times, the sideward momentum took over, and the SUV began to pick up speed sliding down the hill.

It didn't go far however, before the passenger side slammed into the first forest pines. It jolted Lainey to the side and popped her neck. Her phone went flying across the cab and cracked against the passenger door window.

Gravel dust, dirt, and dry leaves were flying in a large thick cloud around her. She was hanging from her seatbelt with her driver's side door pointed towards the sky. The forest had stopped her downhill plummet before it was too late.

Her first thought was concern over the stability of the SUV. It was bouncing slightly in the trees as they responded to the weight. Was it stuck in the trees and stable? If she tried to get out, would it set it off balance and continue down the side of the mountain?

The dust settled somewhat, and she looked out the windows. From what she could tell, the SUV was firmly wedged in the trees. The rocking had stopped, and she rolled down her passenger side window. Residual gravel dust fell in and choked her.

A coughing fit ensued. Finally, when she could breathe well again, her thought was to climb out the window. She didn't think she could open the door, hold it open, and climb out all at the same time.

She reached over and unbuckled her seatbelt. Instantly her body fell to the passenger side where her feet and legs already hung. She was now literally standing inside the SUV with her feet on the passenger door. She was careful to not jar the SUV with any uncertain movement.

She reached up grabbing hold of the bottom of the open window and pulled herself out of the SUV. It wasn't as easy as the thought had played out in her head, but soon she was standing next to the undercarriage of the SUV on a small pile of fallen logs. Relief was short lived though, because she soon realized she had left her phone inside.

Carefully she climbed back on top and dropped her feet inside, gently lowering herself back into the cab. Squatting down, she reached for her phone. Just as she did, the SUV began to shift, the trees moaned, and Lainey reached out to steady herself. The SUV shuddered and then rested firmly back into place.

She shut her eyes and breathed a sigh of relief. It felt as though she could feel each nerve ending bristling on her skin.

The shift had only been minor though and was quickly over. She looked at her phone only to see a shattered screen. It wasn't just cracked. It was shattered. *Can this get any worse,* she thought?

They outfitted the SUV with the sheriff's department radio, but now as she contemplated it, she realized it had been silent the entire trip. Maybe it just hadn't been turned on.

She reached out and turned on the radio and clicked the mic. "This is Lainey Tate. Can anyone hear me?" There was only intense static coming through. She tried again to reach someone on the other end. After several minutes and many attempts to contact someone, she realized she was on her own.

It seemed to take all her effort to once again climb back

out of the cab. Standing on the fallen logs, she looked up to the edge of the road where the slide had began. She chided herself for grumbling. This could have been so much worse. The embankment was critically steep and had those trees not stopped her fall, she would be dead now. She was suddenly thankful to God for the dense thick forest being so close to the edge of the road.

By the time she had clawed her way up the side of the mountain, her fingernails were split and broken and her hands were severely abraded. She was exhausted from the climb and sat on the side of the road trying to catch her breath. Even though it was cold, she was covered in sweat.

Now what? I'm not even sure where I am, she thought. She had no idea where her directions or her notebook were. Probably underneath the seat somewhere, but she wasn't going back down there. Surely she could find her way out. Just keep winding down the mountain long enough for someone to come along and find her.

Sitting on the side of the road, she attempted to revive her phone. The screen finally lit up, but was unresponsive. When she tried to delicately slide her finger across the shattered screen, all she succeeded in doing was slicing a cut across the pad of her finger.

She shut her eyes, took a deep breath, and told herself to adjust her bad attitude, all while praying for help to do just that, oh, and for rescue too.

The first part of the walk down the mountain was almost enjoyable. The forest really was beautiful, and the day was clear and clean. The wind had taken a holiday and Lainey thought she was making good time.

After approximately twenty minutes of walking though, the road began to go up steeply. *So much for walking down the mountain,* Lainey thought. She was trying to remember the part of the road she was now on from her drive out, but it all seemed so different walking than when driving.

At the top of the steep incline, she looked around to try and gain her bearings. She stood in the middle of the road and all around there was only dense forest. She couldn't tell where she was or see any landmarks. Not only that, but the road split. She now had two choices, and neither one looked familiar.

She needed to take a break, so she walked to the side of the road and sat down. Her thirst rose for the first time and she realized just how much she needed a drink of water.

The SUV had been fully equipped with everything she needed, but all those supplies, including a case of bottled water was resting on the side of the mountain at least thirty minutes behind her. It had never even occurred to her to get a few supplies to take with her.

Nothing to do but keep going. She stood and decided, for no particular reason, to take the road on the right. Soon, an unexpected gust of wind hit her full on and felt like ice cutting through her. It froze her sweat laden brow and her body shuddered from the cold.

The beautiful clear sky was now gray, but not as dark as it had been the day before. But as she walked she realized it was growing a little darker with each step. The gust of wind had not come alone and others quickly followed, pounding her, one after the other.

Suck it up buttercup! She yelled at herself internally. *Do what you have to do to get out of here.*

But no matter what she said to herself all she wanted to do was cry.

HARLEY AND BLAINE were no longer angry at River. They too feared that the body was his. No one had seen or heard from him since he had stormed off of the Barlow ranch after the blowup with Blaine.

Blaine and Harley were still keeping a tight lip about the old cabin, but they thought he might be there, if that wasn't him that had been found in the smokehouse fire.

"Harley do you feel like going to the cabin with me to see if we can find River?" Blaine asked.

The doctor had given Harley only a few pain meds to get him through the worst of it, but he still didn't know if he could withstand the bouncing around that the rough roads would inflict on him. "I don't know. I want to go with you, but I don't know if I can take the ride."

Blaine nodded. He understood. "Do you think under the circumstance we should just tell someone about the cabin?" Harley asked.

He had considered that. They had made the promise before all this turmoil and chaos. "You're probably right. Things will never go back the way they were, even if River is still alive and just up at the cabin. Even if he was not the one who assaulted you, I don't think I can be friends with him anymore," said Blaine.

"Will you go with me to talk to the sheriff?" Blaine asked.

Harley nodded, and soon both were walking in the front door of the Latimer County Sheriff Department. It was a frantic hive of activity. They now had four murders, and someone who had shot out Harley's tire and then assaulted him. And so far, there was no sign of River and no ID on the body.

It seemed like it had been days, but it had only been the previous day when the fourth body had been found. Sheriff Markum didn't want to get impatient with Sharon Pine, but she wanted an ID. Jeff and May Billings were beside themselves with grief and worry.

She looked up to see both Blaine and Harley standing at the front counter. She knew they would be anxious also to find out who had assaulted Harley, and to find out if it was their friend in the smokehouse.

"Hey guys, I know you are eager for information, but I have nothing new for you right now." Sheriff Markum was more brusque than she had intended to be. Her frustration at the interruption was showing.

"We know you're busy, we may have some information for you. Well, we do have some information for you." Blaine was hem-hawing around, still uncomfortable with what he was about to disclose.

She swung the door open and allowed the two into the main bull-pen area. "Come with me," she said and began walking towards her office.

"Sit down." She motioned towards the two chairs in front of her desk.

She plopped down into her own chair, releasing a whoosh of trapped air from the cushion. The wheels creaked as she leaned back to look at the boys. She sat as calmly as she could with her hands folded across her waist.

Harley and Blaine looked back and forth at each other indecisively. Finally, Blaine blurted out, "We think we might know where River is, that is, if it isn't him you found in the smokehouse." Blaine felt a mixture of relief and new anxiety.

Sheriff Markum leaned forward placing her forearms on her desk. She frowned at Blaine. "Where do you think he is?" Her words had lost all patience and were quite pointed.

"Well, there is this old cabin up on the mountain we found. We found it a long time ago. No one had lived there for years and it was falling apart, so we cleaned it up and we go there sometimes," Blaine rambled out.

The sheriff's eyebrows rose to indicate that he should continue.

"We only went there some. We would hunt and hike and just hang out, but since River has been in such a mood the past few months, he has spent a lot of time up there." Blaine dipped his head and stared at the floor.

"That's where we were coming from on Monday when you picked us up on the road. We didn't want to get trapped up there by the storm and River wouldn't come with us. So… we walked." Blaine's words trailed off.

Sheriff Markum shut her eyes. She didn't need this. It would take precious time to see if River was indeed there, but if he was, she needed to know.

"We would go see, but Harley doesn't feel up to the ride.

We talked about it and thought we should just tell you," said Blaine.

"You did the right thing. Blaine, if I send you with one of my deputies, can you show him the way to the cabin? I believe it's best for you to not go alone under the circumstances."

"Sure," replied Blaine.

Sheriff Markum got up and went to her door. She motioned for Derek Lassiter to come over. "I need you to take Blaine up the mountain. He thinks he may know a place where River could be." She spoke in hushed tones in order to not disseminate unfounded information. "Keep this between us for now."

Derek nodded and motioned for Blaine to follow out back where he was parked. Harley stood next to the sheriff and watched them go.

"What if he's not there sheriff?" Harley asked.

"Then he's not there."

LAINEY WASN'T sure how much more of this frigid cold she could stand. She had never liked the cold and being out here traipsing through the forest just made it worse. She had always been a city girl. An occasional jaunt to the country for a weekend or canoe trip had been fine with her as long as they got back to the conveniences of home pretty quick.

In police training they had equipped her for hand-to-hand combat, critical thinking, surveillance, and a host of other special skills for the job, but she had not had wilderness survival training. She was trying to be strong, but the cold was getting to her.

The road she was on appeared to be heading down the mountain which was good, but appeared to be rarely traveled. She didn't think she was on the road she had driven in on, but it seemed to go down the mountain which is what she wanted, so she continued on.

The damp piles of leaves made the ground spongy and difficult to walk on. She had almost twisted her angle at one point when she stepped onto a rock hidden underneath. Her foot shifted to the side, and she had to quickly regain her balance. It felt slightly sprained, but nothing that she couldn't walk out.

Her frame of mind needed to change. She was not herself. The ominous feeling would not leave her and only created an onslaught of thoughts she knew she needed to overcome. She knew she must control her thoughts and push out the negative ones, but it seemed impossible here and now in this situation.

Suddenly, while lost deep in her negative thoughts, she felt her body start to fall. She had been so distracted that her concentration had not been on the terrain. A pile of leaves underfoot had shifted and took her foot with them.

Panic seized Lainey once again, as she fell hard against the ground; both feet out from underneath her. She was sliding down the mountainside. Her hands flailed about looking for anything to grab hold of, anything at all. The dirt and leaves suddenly ended, and she was now hurtling down a sheer rock face.

Her broken and chipped fingernails grabbed frantically at the rock, searching for even the slightest hold. Suddenly, her right hand found a slim sapling growing from a crevice in the rock. It halted her fall, but it was only a slim reed and Lainey could feel it trying to slip through her hand.

Her heart was pounding, and she squeezed her hand as tight as she could around it. Sobs sucked gulps of air into her lungs.

Her left hand was swiping the rock underneath it, feeling for anything to grab onto. Then, she finally felt a small divot in the rock face about three fingers width wide. Holding on with her fingertips, she could take a small bit of pressure off the sapling.

A moment of relief took her heartbeat down, she rested her forehead on the rock face, and took a deep breath.

With her movement temporarily halted, she began searching with her feet to push herself up. But to her horror, she quickly realized there was nothing there. She was dangling from the side of the cliff. With both arms out to her side, her coat was pushed up and she could not see how far down the fall would be.

She had to think, but she couldn't. Terror took over and sobs broke free from deep inside. Then suddenly, she felt the sapling begin to slowly slip through her hand.

CARRIE WAS MAKING her way quickly through her list of Beau's friends and coworkers. Since he had come back from college, his former friends no longer hung out with him. As for coworkers, he hadn't been able to hold a job down and was currently unemployed.

She had asked the sheriff about his truck and found, as she had expected, they had put out an APB soon after they had found the body. No one had seen it yet.

The wind began to pick up again and rocked her SUV as she sat and tried to review her pathetic notes. She had relied on Randy for years and now Lainey, who were both excellent and fastidious note takers.

She preferred and excelled at maintaining her focus on the individual speaking and committing not only their words, but facial expressions to memory.

However, when names and dates, even times were involved, it was good to have it written down somewhere.

One of the old friends she had talked to mentioned a bar he used to hang out at and felt strongly that he still did. Carrie found the note and read the name, Buster's. She Googled and Buster's did not come up. *Hmmm, I bet they don't have a Yelp review either,* Carrie thought comically to herself.

Her phone rang as she waited for Sheriff Markum to pick up. Finally, on the last ring, "Hello."

"You sound frustrated," replied Carrie.

"I am." The sheriff relayed the entire visit from Harley and Blaine to Carrie.

"If River is at the cabin, then he isn't the victim, but could he still be the perpetrator?"

"As much as I hate to say it, yes he could. That is one of many reasons I sent Blaine with my deputy. I didn't want Blaine going alone and I'm not sure he wanted to, anyway."

"I don't feel like I'm gaining much ground, but someone mentioned that Beau often visited a bar named Buster's. I'm going over there now, but have no idea where it is."

Sheriff Markum gave Carrie the address and directions and ended the call. It wasn't hard to find. When she arrived, there was only one car off to the side. At least she could question the owner without the distraction of customers.

Stepping into the bar brought back a flood of old emotions. It wasn't that long ago that she spent most of her nights after work in a bar just like this. That old familiar tug began to pull on her.

Then in a flash, she remembered all that God had brought her through and with that, she had the strength to resist and push back. She didn't need this or anything that it offered. She was free, and it felt good.

"Hello," Carrie called out. The bar was dim, and she didn't see the occupant of the lonely car in the lot.

A man about her age finally came through the door from the back and nodded. "We aren't open yet."

"I'm Carrie Border with the Oklahoma State Bureau of Investigation. I need to ask you a few questions. Is this a good time?"

He eyed her suspiciously, but acquiesced. Nodding toward a table on the far side, he led the way.

Carrie pulled out her pad and pen like a good little agent and smiled to herself. "Could I get your name?"

"Dan Blankenship".

"I'm here to find friends or associates of Beau Johnson. When was the last time you remember seeing him in here?"

Dan had rested his forearms on the table. He looked out

into the bar area as if it held the answers to her questions. "I'm not sure."

Carrie watched Dan as he looked away and then back at her. She was very good at reading people, but wasn't quite sure yet if he was lying or not. "Does he come in here frequently?"

Dan nodded. "Well, he used to."

"When was the last time you remember him coming in here?"

He dipped his head and looked at his hands clasped on the table. Carrie could tell he was thinking, but was he thinking of a good lie or for the truth? "I think it was a Saturday night about three or four weeks ago."

"Who was he here with?"

Dan shrugged his shoulders. "I don't know."

Carrie sat quietly for awhile looking at Dan. Her partner Randy had always been an expert at the quiet torture that could weaken the most difficult. There was something about the silence that made one uncomfortable.

She, on the other hand had always been one to rapid fire one question right after the other. They had been a good balance and the way they had worked together was an art form. She genuinely missed him since he had been promoted to Special Agent in Charge.

Dan rubbed his hands together and sat back in the booth, crossing his arms over his midsection. "Look, he hangs out with some pretty rough people these days. I don't want to get all up in their business, ya know?"

Carrie remained silent, waiting. Dan huffed. "Okay. So

he runs with a crowd of locals that are supposed to be dealing drugs."

"Supposed to be…" Carrie let it trail off, encouraging him to continue.

"I don't know for sure. But I've heard rumors."

"Tell me about these rumors. And, I want names."

Dan knew he was beat and that they would be here until the bar opened and closed if he didn't tell her what she wanted to know.

"I don't do drugs."

"But, if you did…"

"If I did, I would go to these guys." Dan shook his head in surrender. "J.C. Manley, Poke Hoffman, and Lenny Grimes."

"Poke?" Carrie looked up when writing the name down, unsure if she had heard him right.

"Yeah, Poke. Nickname but I don't know what his real name is."

"Do you know where I might find these fine upstanding citizens you are so afraid of?"

Dan frowned. "I ain't afraid of no one."

Carrie smiled. "Sure you are. Now where can I find them?"

She wrote down all that Dan knew about where she could find the three men.

"Can you tell me anything else about Beau Johnson that might help me find his killer?"

Dan shook his head.

"Can you tell me what he was wearing that last night

you saw him? What kind of coat or boots he might have been wearing?"

Dan's eyes roamed as he was watching the reel behind his eyes trying to replay that night back in his mind.

Looking up at Carrie he said, "I think he had on a light brown puffy down kind of coat. Looked old. Had some darker brown knit at the collar and cuffs."

"Boots or shoes?"

Dan went back to the screen behind his eyes. After a few moments he shook his head. "Nope. Got nothin' there."

Carrie pulled out her business card and slid it across the table. "Will you call me if you hear anything that might help us with any of the killings? You hear things here in this bar. I'm not looking to jam you up. I just need to catch this killer. Who knows, it might be you next."

Carrie had locked eyes with Dan and he nodded. "I will. I promise." And he slipped the card from the table.

THE NIGHT before with his brothers had been a great time. Doc really enjoyed being with them and taking them out to eat. If it could just always be that way, he thought.

It was afternoon though, and after getting word from Joe that he was expecting another shipment soon, he got cooking early. It seemed to Doc that the orders were coming more and more frequently. That was both good and bad.

It was good because he could put more money aside and get out of here sooner, but bad because it seemed Joe was becoming more and more dependent on them to produce, which made stopping not an option.

The three of them spent the day working to produce as much as they could. Doc was glad that they had a limited supply of raw ingredients. It was the perfect excuse to be done and to stop for a while.

He stepped out of the trailer and pulled his mask up, resting it on top of his head. The winter storm had passed over them once again and it was another crisp, clear day. He unzipped the white jumpsuit he wore and walked toward their house.

Jimmy and Bud were supposed to be finishing up the packaging and cleaning up. They appeared to be clear headed this morning so Doc didn't worry that they would screw up.

He pulled a beer out of the fridge and plopped on the sofa. It was good to be in a clean house. He hoped he could impress on his brothers to keep it that way.

Just as he was taking a large swig of his beer, his cell phone rang. The name said Marissa in big bold white letters. He got up and went to his bedroom and shut the door. The need for privacy was strong, and who knew where this conversation might go.

"Hello," Doc answered.

"Hi there," came Marissa's voice across in a sultry tone.

Doc decided that privacy had indeed been the right choice. He lay on his bed and they talked for almost an hour. He wasn't sure what it was about this lady but she stirred something in him on a level he had never felt before. He wondered if she felt the same.

After about an hour, they made arrangements to meet in town again at the same bar where they had initially met.

"Oh, and Doc..."

"Yes?"

"Plan to stay in town tonight."

CHAPTER 11

Lainey braced for impact. How far above ground was she and what was below her? Would she fall on brush or sharp rocks?

Just then, she collided full on with flat ground. The air exited her lungs with force and her breathing stopped. Then without notice, her body took over and began its routine once again. Her lungs burned as they refilled with air.

Laying prone on her back, she could see where the sapling stuck awkwardly out from the rock. She had only fallen about twelve feet, but it was enough to have severely injured or paralyzed her.

I'm okay. I can just get up and walk away, she thought. But as she attempted to move, sharp pain shot through her entire body. As she gently lay her head back down, colored lights shot behind her eyelids like fireworks.

The pain had been so intense it caused her to feel nauseous. When she opened her eyes, it seemed as if the world above her was swirling. The ravine she lay in was about thirty to forty feet deep on both sides. The floor where she lay was about eight to ten feet wide. She couldn't raise her head to see how far the ravine ran, but her guess was that it went on forever.

She screamed out at the top of her lungs, "Help me!"

Only silence rang through the forest. *No one is around. There is no one to hear me or help me.*

Taking a deep breath to steady her nerves and focus her mind, she knew she had to gain rationality and think her way out of this. She began to take an inventory of her body. She could wiggle her toes. That was good. It meant she was not paralyzed.

Next, she tried to move her ankles. Sharp pain shot through her right leg. Okay, so something is wrong with my right ankle. Then she tried moving her left leg. It wouldn't move. The pain was so horrific that she knew she must have broken it in at least one place if not more.

Tears slid from the corners of her eyes as she realized she would not be walking out of the ravine. *God, help me, please.*

CARRIE FOUND the nest of vipers that Dan Blankenship had described. They were at J.C.'s small house on the edge of town. The exterior was sorely unkept to the point that the painted siding was nearly down to bare wood.

Junk of all kinds lay strewn about. Rusted metal, empty beer bottles and cans, and random trash. Tall dead grass had grown up around it all in warmer months, and no one had bothered to cut it down. Amid it all sat three broken old webbed lawn chairs with several straps hanging loose and waving in the wind.

Carrie checked her pad, pen, badge, and gun. All were ready. She opened the SUV door and stepped out. The neighborhood appeared quiet, and she anticipated no surprises. She shut the door quietly. Not that she wanted to sneak up on these men, but she also didn't want to startle them either.

She had tugged on her stocking cap and pulled it down tight. Her coat was zipped up, but she still shivered. The first two attempts at knocking on the door went unanswered. The third time she noticed movement in the window to the right of the door.

She waited and when there was no response, she knocked again. "This is Carrie Border with the OSBI. I know you are in there, so you need to open the door or I'll call for backup."

Moments later the front door opened and there stood a man in his mid-thirties with disheveled hair as if he had just woken up. He stepped back to allow her entrance into the room.

Carrie stepped through the doorway with one hand near her gun. She monitored her situation and the interior of the house. All seemed to be fine, but the hesitation to open the door had aroused her suspicions.

The man who had opened the door had turned and made his way across the room. He plopped into an old recliner that had seen much better days. His head bobbed to the side to indicate Carrie should sit.

"As I said, I'm Carrie Border. What is your name?"

"Poke. Poke Hoffman." The man said. His backwoods accent was strong. He had several missing teeth that may have contributed to his nearly inarticulate speech.

"I was under the impression that this was J.C. Manley's home."

Poke nodded. "It is him home. I stays with him."

Carrie wondered if his mispronounced words were tied to a speech impediment, mental deficiency or lack of education. "I'm here in Wilburton investigating the recent murders. Right now I am running down leads for Beau Johnson. Did you know him?"

Poke once again nodded his head.

"Did you hang out with Beau, was he part of your crew?" Carrie hoped by using the word crew it would wedge a door open.

"Crew?" Poke asked with a questioning look on his face.

"You know, does he work with you guys?"

Poke's brows furrowed. He was having trouble understanding what Carrie was asking.

"That's okay. When was the last time you saw Beau?"

Poke's face relaxed, and he sat thinking for a moment. "Awhile ago."

"Where were you when you saw him last?"

"We'ze here."

"You and Beau and who else?"

"Lenny and J.C. and me. We'ze all here."

"Do you remember what day of the week it was?"

Suddenly Poke stood and stormed out of the room. The movement startled Carrie, and she stood. "Lenny. Lenny, get up. There's a lady here askin' me questions. Get up."

Carrie could hear Poke yelling at someone, Lenny presumably. Soon, Poke came back in. "Lenny's comin'. He'd tell you. I ain't good with that stuff." Carrie nodded.

As Poke reclaimed his spot in the old recliner, Carrie relaxed but continued to stand. There were shuffling noises coming from the back, the creak of bedsprings, footfalls on the wood floor, and a cigarette lighter clicking.

As the sounds grew closer, Carrie turned to see a man in his late thirties standing in the doorway to the hall. He had sleek black hair and dark eyes. A lit cigarette hung from his lip. He was leaning up against the door facing and had squinted his eyes, watching Carrie. His arms were crossed over a tank type undershirt commonly know as a 'wife beater'. Horrible name, but sexy as hell, well on the right person that is. And, he was the right person.

Carrie coughed and regained her composure. "I'm Carrie…"

Lenny stopped her with a wave of his hand. "I know who you are. I heard you and Poke in here. Woke me up." Lenny came on into the room and took a chair on the other side of the room across from the sofa that Carrie had been sitting on.

The wife beater stretched across ripped abs as Lenny sat back in the overstuffed chair. Carrie realized she was still standing in the middle of the floor. Both men sat looking up at her to explain why she was there in their house.

She sat back down on the edge of the sofa. "I'm here

investigating Beau Johnson's death. I understand you were friends. When was the last time you saw him?"

Lenny took a long drag from his cigarette and exhaled, controlling the smoke as it funneled upwards into the room. "I think it was a day or so before he died."

Poke fidgeted in the recliner. It's springs squeaked, begging for grease or relief, one or the other. "Do you remember the day of the week? Was it a Saturday or a Sunday?"

Another puff of smoke and Lenny looked Carrie up and down. "You here all by yourself?" A chill rippled up Carrie's spine realizing she was in a two against one situation.

Today I am, but not normally. We are trying to cover more ground. "Look, I just want to find who killed Beau. You should want the same thing since he was your friend. I'm asking everyone that might have come in contact with him when they last saw him so I can get an accurate time-line of where he was and when. It will help me figure out where he was when he was taken, therefore helping us get closer to who took him."

It frustrated her. She was used to being out of town and being treated as an outsider. But today they needed to make ground on this case, and the delay tactics were only hindering her.

Lenny nodded and leaned forward. He'd reached the end of his cigarette and stubbed it out in an ashtray sitting next to him. He sat looking at her with his elbows on his knees and his clasp hands underneath his chin. His dark eyes were focused on Carrie and she swallowed. Could he see the tension he was causing her, she wondered.

"It was about two weeks ago. We were all at Buster's drinking and playing pool."

"Do you remember when he left? Was anyone with him?"

"He left by himself. I'm not sure what time, but it was well before closing. If I had to guess I would say about midnight or one in the morning."

"Did you see him or talk to him at all the next day, Sunday?"

Lenny shook his head and a dark lock of hair tumbled onto his forehead. "Nope. I stayed in bed most of the day and then hung around here. It was cold and since I didn't have anywhere I had to go, I didn't."

Carrie nodded and wrote a few notes down. "Can you think of anything that might help point me in the right direction? Anyone who might want to hurt him? Anywhere he might have gone after you saw him? Did he have a girlfriend?"

She was back to her old habits of rapid firing questions. *Slow down, let them process,* she told herself.

Poke's chair creaked again. She was making him nervous and looked over at him. "Are you okay, Poke?"

His eyes darted to Lenny, and he continued to squirm. "Naw. I'ze fine." He got up and went into the back of the house where Lenny had been.

"As far as I know, he doesn't have a girlfriend."

"Do you know where he worked?"

"He wasn't working right now that I knew of."

Carrie nodded, watching Lenny. The initial reaction to seeing him was fading, and she wanted some answers.

"Where do you work, Lenny?"

"I'm what you would call an entrepreneur." Lenny smiled with white straight teeth and lit another cigarette.

LAINEY WASN'T sure just how long she had been out. Whether it had been the pain or sheer exhaustion, she didn't know, but she had passed out. She was cold to the bone and shivering. It was the pain that had woken her. As she opened her eyes, she was greeted by a white sky and large flakes of falling snow. They stuck to her lashes and stung her eyes.

What am I going to do? She no longer felt panic. Despair had replaced it. She closed her eyes and drifted back to sleep. The quiet of the snow was peaceful and she let it envelope her.

Lainey drifted in and out for what seemed like hours. This time when she woke, she was blanketed in a layer of snow about an inch deep. A very faint sound had woke her, and she remained with her eyes closed as she tried to determine what the noise was. It could be help, or an animal.

She heard footsteps; quiet footsteps crunching the snow. Looking up, she saw a man towering above her dressed in a long wool coat and a wide brimmed felt hat that had seen better days. His hair was long and straggly. Was he friend or foe, Lainey wondered.

"Hello. Can you help me? My leg is broken and I don't

know what else is wrong. I can't walk," Lainey pleaded with the man. He did not speak, only stood looking down at her. Then without a word, he turned and walked away.

"Wait, don't go. Please come back." Even raising her voice to call after the man sent shock waves of pain through her body. "Please don't go."

The man quickly returned with long straight branches about nine feet long. He removed an old blanket which had been rolled up on top of the pack on his back. He laid the branches about two foot apart on the ground and worked to fasten the blanket to them. He worked quickly, quietly, and with skill.

"Thank you for coming back," said Lainey. But the man only worked and never spoke or acknowledged that Lainey had spoken to him. *Maybe he's deaf,* thought Lainey. *Or, maybe he can't speak.*

Abruptly, Lainey felt pain once again shoot through her body as she was being drug backwards. Large strong hands had gripped her underneath her armpits and pulled. The pain was excruciating, but necessary to get her to safety.

Once on the blanket, the man gently laid her down. He took off his wool coat and laid it on top of Lainey. She thought he had several layers of flannel shirts and thermals on. She hoped it would be enough to keep him warm.

The makeshift gurney started with a jerk as the man lifted the ends and began walking. Facing behind, Lainey couldn't see where they were going, but she hoped it would be a short journey. She wouldn't know though, because she had soon once again passed out again from the pain.

~

CARRIE MET Sheriff Markum back at the sheriff's department. The weather had turned, and the long-promised winter storm had arrived.

The warmth inside felt good. As Carrie sat down in the chair in front of the sheriff's desk, she felt worn out. She just sat looking at the sheriff for several seconds. The sheriff looked as tired as she felt.

Then Carrie realized that she didn't see Lainey. "Has Lainey come back?"

Just realizing for the first time that she hadn't thought of Lainey all morning, the sheriff became alert. "No, I haven't. I haven't heard from her all day, have you?"

Carrie was suddenly alarmed. "No, I haven't. I've been bogged down in trying to pry information out of shady men who didn't want to talk."

Her phone was ringing against her ear as she waited for Lainey to answer. No answer. "Lainey call me." She tapped the red button closing the call. A gnawing feeling of dread was growing inside her.

"She should have been back by now, right?" Carrie asked.

"Yes, I would think." The sheriff was dialing the Lee's home from her land line. When Mrs. Lee answered, she said, "Beth, this is Sheriff Markum. Did an agent named Lainey Tate come visit you this morning?"

"Yes, she did. Sweet lady."

"She hasn't made it back and we're concerned."

"Oh, my. I think she left here by about ten this morning.

Well, let me talk to Griffin and see if we can get down the road. It's been snowing pretty heavy here for a while, how about in town?"

"Just started here about thirty minutes ago."

"It has been snowing for about two hours here. We probably have a foot or two of snow by now."

"Beth, if Griffin can travel at all, that would be great but I don't want you putting him in peril. However, if he does, please let me know what he finds."

"Will do, sheriff."

Sheriff Markum looked at Carrie. "She left the Lee's around ten this morning. She should have been back hours ago, unless she went to follow more leads." The Sheriff was standing pulling on her coat.

In the bull-pen she said, "Has anyone here heard from agent Tate? What about over the radio?" Everyone just looked at her and shook their heads. "What about Derek and Blaine?" The sheriff was irritated that she had lost track of time mired in paperwork and hadn't realize that neither party was back.

"We need to go out and find her," said Carrie standing beside the sheriff.

"We do, but we need to know where to look. If we drive all the way out to the Lee's and then find she made it back to town and was interviewing someone else, that is precious time wasted."

The sheriff went back in her office and redialed the Lee's phone. "Yes?" Beth Lee's voice came once again over the phone.

"Beth, what names did you give agent Tate that she would go interview?"

"Well, she was mainly interested in Amanda's boyfriend Matt, that's Matthew Bradford."

The sheriff got each name that Lainey had discussed with the Lee's. Most lived in town or near town. If they spoke with those and Lainey had not been there, then they would know she never made it back from the Lee's.

The sheriff split up the list and handed each deputy and Carrie someone to call. In just fifteen short minutes on the phones, they determined that Lainey had never made it back from the Lee's. No one had seen or spoken to her.

The radio buzzed and the sheriff spoke, "Derek, where are you at?"

No response. Panic was growing inside the sheriff. She felt like she was in a shit storm of trouble. An agent missing, a deputy missing, the murders wouldn't stop. Then, "Go sheriff, it's Derek."

Sheriff Markum breathed a huge sigh of relief. "Where are you guys? Did you make it to the cabin and find River?"

"We made it to the cabin, but there wasn't anyone there. We're trying to get back but the roads are getting real bad, real quick. It's slow going."

She knew that the road to the Lee's was in an entirely different part of the forest from where Derek and Blaine were, so it was no use to hope they might run across Lainey on their way back. Maybe Griffin Lee would run across her. Maybe she just had a flat tire or vehicle trouble. The radio hardly worked on that section of the mountain. But she would have her cell phone, that is, if she got reception that far out.

Carrie was standing alert waiting for the sheriff to give direction. She wanted to just head on out and look for her, but the sheriff knew this area best and would know what to do.

The sheriff scrolled through the contacts on her phone. Finding the one she wanted she dialed.

"Barry, this is Sheriff Markum. I have a situation."

"Another murder?" Barry Yates was the head of forestry division for this area. He was well aware of the murders and was on high alert.

"Yes, but that isn't what I'm calling about. There was a murder yesterday at the Billings ranch, but I've got an OSBI agent who hasn't reported back in."

"Where were they last?"

"At the Lee's home."

"Griffin and Beth Lee?"

"Yes." The sheriff's stomach was in a knot.

"Roads are bad out there sheriff. I'll go out and see what I can find."

"Thanks Barry."

Sheriff Markum turned to look at Carrie. Her mind was engaged in mental gymnastics attempting to push aside her emotions with rational thinking.

"I want to go find her," said Carrie who had locked eyes with the sheriff.

"I know. I do too, but we risk getting stuck ourselves. Then we would be no good to anyone."

"Isn't there anyone who has a vehicle that would get us

where we need to search?"

Sheriff Markum thought of the roads from here to the Lee's. Some areas were so narrow that large vehicles would have a hard time making their way through.

"Barry, our forester for this area is out. He has a vehicle built to navigate the forest. He's headed toward the Lee's and Griffin Lee was going to try to head this way. He also has a heavy duty four-wheel drive he uses to get in and out with.

"As hard as it may sound, I think we should stay put and stay in contact with them."

Carrie bristled. She didn't want to stay put. Feeling responsible for Lainey, the need to rescue her was overwhelming. "I'm not staying here. I'm going to go find her."

Sheriff Markum placed her hands on each of Carrie's arms. "It would be best for Lainey if you stayed here. If you get stranded out there and she needs you, how will that help her?"

Carrie knew the sheriff was right, and she hated it. She turned and paced the bull-pen. The deputies felt the tension in the room and knew they had nothing to add, so remained quiet.

"Damn!" Carrie slammed her hand on the nearest desk. She leaned forward with her hands supporting her weight and stared down at the desk. Suddenly the urge to drown her fear and frustration in a bottle of Jack Daniels hit her like a tidal wave. It came unexpectedly, and she felt unable and unwilling to resist it.

Her mind locked tight like a vise and she shut out all rational thought. Anger surged through her and she stormed out of the room. She headed straight for the back door and to her SUV.

Once inside, she slammed the door and turned the key. The tug to find a bar was winning over the reminder of the freedom she had found in sobriety. The turmoil was almost more than she could handle. And right then, she couldn't handle it. She wanted to drink, more than she wanted to be free.

The SUV fishtailed as she left the parking lot. The snow was getting deeper by the moment, and in an instant, she made the decision to rebel against what she had come to know as right for her.

IT COULD HAVE BEEN miles from where Lainey had fallen to the man's cabin. She didn't know since she had slept the entire time. Despite the man having covered her in his coat, she was so cold that her extremities felt numb. Sleep was preferred though over the pain that tormented her while awake.

They had arrived at a small clearing surrounded by dense tall pine trees. The canopy was so tall and close together that Lainey could barely see the sky. The snow was still falling and was now about a foot deep.

She tried to twist her neck around to see more of her surroundings, but every movement, no matter how slight, shot unbearable pain through her entire body. She shut her eyes and was once again hit with sparks of light.

The man had laid the poles down and Lainey was now

laying flat on the ground, the snow still working to cover her. She had heard a door creak; she thought. Then, once again the man picked up the gurney and pulled.

She felt it rise and bump along as if he were pulling her over a very uneven surface. She realized as they passed through a doorway that had been the front porch. They were now inside.

A faint glimmer of light rose from the stone fireplace. The man crouched in front of it adding kindling. The fire caught, and the flames shot upward. He stood gazing at the fire for a moment, then reached to the side for a log which he laid on the fire.

The man mesmerized Lainey. He had still not spoken a word. Even now he stood gazing silently at the fire before him. She knew he didn't mean her harm or he wouldn't have gone to such lengths to rescue her from the ravine. But what if he wanted to kidnap her and keep her for unsavory acts, thought Lainey?

Then as the man turned and looked toward where Lainey lay on the floor of the cabin, they locked eyes. There was comfort in his eyes. Lainey no longer felt afraid, for she now knew this man was not a danger to her.

"Thank you," said Lainey while the man looked at her. Hopefully, he could at least read her lips if he could not hear her words. But there was no response from the man.

He turned and walked out of her sight and Lainey shut her eyes. She could feel the warmth of the fire drift her way and slowly it began to sooth her. The numbness in her limbs was stubborn though, as she tried to wriggle her fingers and toes.

She could hear movement in the other room as if furniture was being moved. The man's footfalls were heavy and rough against the old wooden floor.

"We've got to get you warm," said the man.

Lainey's eyes shot open. He could speak. He was once again towering over her. She only nodded.

He lifted the end of the gurney and drug it close to the fireplace. Lainey could feel that something soft was underneath her now. He had gotten a thin mattress, from his bed possibly, and laid in on the floor in front of the fire to lay her on.

The old wool coat came off with a whoosh and Lainey lay exposed. Snow was still resting on top of her underneath the man's coat that had covered her. The man brushed it away. "You got to git warm," he said once again.

"Ye.. Yes, I do," Lainey shuttered from the cold.

He removed Lainey's gloves and began to rub her hands between his. They were rough and felt like sandpaper against her skin, but the friction began to bring back the feeling.

Once he had worked on both hands, he untied her boots. When he began to pull on her right boot though, her ankle rebelled and Lainey cried out. The man stopped and looked at her.

Gently, he spread her boot laces as far apart as they would go, pulled the tongue forward and gently eased the boot off. Daggers stabbed at the ankle as the blood shot back through.

When he attempted to do the same for her left leg, she screamed in agony. Her leg was definitely broken, and broken badly. The gentle tug of the wide open boot was more than she could bear.

Finally, both socks were gently peeled off and hung to dry by the fire. In their place, the man slid on a pair of dark olive colored wool socks.

"I… I think I broke my leg bad." Lainey motioned with her left hand to her left leg. "I need a doctor."

"No doctor," the man grunted.

Lainey tried to sit up, but the wind sucked out of her once again from the pain. She realized her ribs were broken too. She did however, manage to get slightly up on one elbow and look down at her leg. It looked straight enough through her pants leg, but what lay underneath was anyone's guess.

"You must set it," she said to the man looking straight at him. Their eyes connected and he gave her a nod.

She laid herself gently back down and undid her pants so he could pull them off. The man gently pulled the bottoms of both pant legs. Lainey held her breath. *I have to endure this. I have to do what I need to do to get through this.*

She looked down to see her once pale white legs now colored in large swaths of dark blue and deep purple. She could see two spots on her lower left leg that she knew were broken. But they had not broken through the skin however, which she was instantly thankful for. She knew what she needed him to do, but she wasn't sure she could endure it.

"Do you have any whiskey?" she asked the man.

He nodded and rose. A large jug and a tin cup were in his hands when he returned. He poured a generous portion into the cup and Lainey once again endured the pain of rising up on one elbow. She took the cup and swallowed the whiskey down.

The burn took her breath away, and she winced, handing the cup back to the man to refill. He did so and once again she downed the whiskey. After three cup fulls, she felt she was as ready as she could be.

Once again, she gently lowered herself back onto the mat and looked at the man. "Grab hold of my left foot and pull to straighten it out so the bones will be lined up and able to heal correctly." She watched his face for understanding. He understood and nodded.

He rose and came back with a leather strap and held it to her mouth. Lainey knew he had provided her something to bite down on. She opened her mouth, and he slid the leather in. She bit down, closed her eyes, and nodded.

He moved to her foot and squatted down. Carefully with rough hands, he took her heel in his left-hand and held the top of her foot in his right. Then with a sudden steady jerk, he popped her leg back into place.

Lainey passed out. Her mouth opened and the leather strap slipped to the side. The man took a long straight strip of wood and placed it alongside her newly set leg. He worked quickly to tear bed sheets into strips and used them to strap her leg to the wood.

He finished her care by wrapping her right ankle with leftover rags and resting it on a small folded bundle of flannel shirts. He laid several woolen blankets on her, tucking them in on each side. The fire rose in the fireplace and Lainey rested.

CHAPTER 12

Doc knew a storm was coming and left home early to head to town. He wanted to see Marissa and wanted to beat the storm. There wasn't much to do in town, so he went to Riley's for some coffee and pie and to wait.

He'd brought his iPad, which was useless out at their place. He had missed the technology he enjoyed living in the city.

After hours of coffee, pie, and social media, he thought he might call Marissa and see about arranging an earlier dinner date.

"Marissa, it's Doc."

Marissa's first thought was that Doc must be calling to cancel because of the storm. "Hey Doc."

"I came into town early so I wouldn't get stuck out at the farm. I've been hanging out at Riley's and thought maybe we could get together earlier."

A huge smile grew across Marissa's face. "Of course Doc. In fact, why don't you come on over here and we can be in from the snow. There is a restaurant next door so we can walk over and get a bite when we get hungry."

They agreed, and Marissa flew into a frenzy picking up previously worn clothing and toiletries she had scattered through the room. Soon there was a knock on her door.

Seeing each other through the open door once again confirmed the magnetism that existed between them. It wasn't something they had imagined. It was real and tangible.

Two hours later, after falling asleep in each other's arms, Marissa eased out of the bed and slipped quietly into the bathroom. Being a light sleeper, the movement woke Doc, and he heard the shower suddenly come to life in the next room.

Wow, I didn't expect that, he thought to himself. *But how wonderful it was*! He sat for a few minutes thinking about the events that had quickly transpired upon seeing Marissa again.

The room was chilly, so he threw back the covers and dressed quickly. He sat at the small table in the room where Marissa had her work station set up, bumping the table as he sat down caused her laptop to spring to life.

He leaned back in the chair and glanced at it. Not wanting to pry, he looked away. But as he did, he noticed in her document, wording regarding drug trade in Wilburton. He turned back towards the laptop and leaned forward.

It was a story she had been working on. His pulse began to quicken as he read details of the story that could quickly lead to him and incrimination. There were names and dates. She knew all about Joe Billings and his other legitimate businesses.

The document was lengthy and cited several instances of trade in the area. It stopped just short of naming Joe's product sources of which Doc was one.

He was seething. But the story contained nothing about him or his part in the operation. There was nothing in there that incriminated him. But he knew if she kept digging, she would find it.

He knew he had to sever ties with her, but not let her know why. Could he pull it off? He glanced out the window to see mounds of snow that had fallen while he had been all cozy in bed with a potential enemy.

The shower shut off in the other room and just as the bathroom door opened, Doc stood up and looked at Marissa. Fury replaced the previous magnetism. But he did his best to hide it.

Marissa frowned. "What's wrong?" She instantly knew something was wrong. Doc was standing by the table with her laptop showing the article she had been writing.

"I thought you were writing an article on the murders?"

"I am."

For several moments there was only silence in the room. Marissa did not know what to say. Normally she would spin a ton of lies and half-truths to manipulate the situation, but she was falling in love with Doc and had no idea what to say.

Doc had suspicions about why Marissa had befriended him. Did she already know Doc's part in the drug trade and was using him to get info? She'd never asked him one question about it, though. As he stood looking at the face he was falling in love with, he no longer knew the truth or what to do.

"I'm actually writing two stories. I originally started on the drug problem here in this area. But once I got here, I learned of the murders. It seemed I was suddenly given two big stories. I didn't know which one to follow or if I could actually do both.

"I met Brian Davis and Mandy Reese at the newspaper office and they were willing to collaborate, so I thought maybe between the three of us we could do both." Marissa had spoken honestly and sincerely.

Doc watched as she spoke. He felt her sincerity, but was he being fooled? If he wasn't involved, then it shouldn't matter to him which story she was working on. He had to play this off casually.

"I see. I just felt like you had lied to me about what story you were doing. Made me feel funny." He smiled at Marissa and the longing to be rid of his part in Joe's operation increased.

Marissa smiled back, and she walked over to Doc and slid her arms around his waist. "I didn't intentionally lie to you."

Doc nodded, still not completely convinced. It just seemed too big a coincidence that a journalist writing a story on drug trade had conveniently come into his life. But, it was hard to not get lost in those beautiful dark eyes. He slipped his arms around her and bent to kiss those supple lips, knowing he was playing with fire.

~

CARRIE WALKED into Buster's trying to push away the guilt she felt. Her actions seemed familiar, but her feelings were different. There was a turmoil that she was working hard to suppress.

She wondered if the owner, Dan, would remember her from earlier in the morning. Shoving that thought out of her mind, telling herself she didn't care, she walked up to the bar and ordered her usual, a whiskey neat.

The familiar buzz hit her harder than it used to. It had been months since she'd had one sip of whiskey. Yes, she had a beer or two from time to time, but had lost the desire to drink anything stronger. She went from completely sober to well on the way to intoxication in half the normal time.

She tapped the bar indicating she wanted another, and it quickly appeared in front of her. Out of sheer defiance she threw it back in two gulps. The room was off-kilter. And she felt as though the barstool was moving underneath her.

Sliding off the stool carefully, she concentrated on making her way to the nearest vacant booth. If she was going to get drunk, she would need a nice stable place to do so.

The waitress brought another drink, but Carrie decided to slow down a bit. The current buzz felt good, and she wanted to maintain and enjoy it. She nursed the drinks, stretching them out to keep her buzz right where she wanted it. The only problem was, the intoxication made it impossible to know how drunk she really was. It was all so deceptive and always had been.

The snow riddled sky darkened early as Carrie sat watching the bar fill up. It was a small bar and filled quickly with customers who didn't want to spend the evening in the quiet of their home. Lonely people ready for a party. Lonely people trying to escape their loneliness.

Carrie knew them all, because for years she had been one of them. Tonight though, she didn't want a party. Tonight she was angry and afraid. She felt guilty for letting Lainey go out alone. She felt cowardice for not going out after her. And if she was honest, the drinking wasn't washing those feelings away.

It must have been about five-drink-thirty when a man slid into the booth across from her. She looked at him through semi blurry vision. Blinking her eyes, she tried to remember him. She thought she should, but she couldn't. She was drunk, and she knew it.

Lenny Grimes sat smiling at a drunk version of the OSBI agent that had been in his living room earlier that very morning. He was quite amused.

"Hello there," said Lenny.

Carrie said nothing, only looked at the man who she felt some attraction to, but didn't understand why.

When the waitress came to check on her, Carrie waved her away. She knew she needed to sober up. Memories of a year ago when she had overridden her gut feeling cautioned her. She had nearly died then, and was in no mood to repeat that mistake.

Lenny sat making small talk as Carrie listened and began to slowly sober up. She couldn't remember yet where she knew him from, but she remembered the visceral physical reaction he generated within her. But the more she sobered, the more her gut said no.

But it had been a long time since she had had a man to hold her. Her old routine had been one, two punch of drunkenness and sex. She had left all that behind when the grace and mercy of God had delivered her with His overwhelming love.

So why was she back here in this place? Guilt once again rushed in. Why am I doing this? The old familiar battle between not wanting to do this anymore and the inability to stop, engaged.

Remembrance of the morning and interviewing Lenny came back to her as she began to sober. She remembered the attraction she had felt seeing him half dressed, his cut physique, and handsome features.

Feeling shut off and alone, she tried to muster the self-control within herself to do what she knew she should do. She knew she needed to get up from the table and go to her hotel room. The excuse of being drunk and unable to legally and safely drive conveniently surfaced in her mind.

The door to the bar suddenly opened and the harsh cold wind ushered in a small snow flurry. Carrie looked up and there stood Sheriff Markum. Lenny followed Carrie's gaze and when he saw the sheriff, he suddenly got up. "Oh shit," was all Carrie remembered of his exit.

Soon, Sheriff Markum was sitting where Lenny had been, and seeing her face, Carrie began to cry.

~

As soon as Carrie and the sheriff had stepped outside of Buster's, the cold wind aided her sobriety. But the walk to the sheriff's SUV was still challenging and as Carrie reached for the door, she bent over and threw up. Her head was pounding, and she felt like death warmed over.

Still bent over, she hung to the door handle while attempting to recover from the sickness. Fresh waves of guilt raged through her. "I'm so sorry. I'm so sorry," kept rolling out of her.

The sheriff came around to the passenger side and stood next to Carrie.

"I'm so sorry. I'm so sorry." Carrie couldn't help but to keep repeating it through her sobbing.

"I know. I know. Let's get you out of the cold." The sheriff helped navigate Carrie around the putrid snow pile and into her passenger seat.

Carrie buckled her seatbelt and once that nearly insurmountable task was done, she shut her eyes and laid her head back on the headrest. The pounding in her head wouldn't subside.

She didn't even know where the sheriff was taking her and she didn't care. Feelings of failure and brokenness brought her back to the point of despair she thought she had left behind months ago.

They rode in silence for several minutes.

"Did you find Lainey?" Carrie asked.

"No, not yet. Griffin went as far down the road as he could, which was quite a way and there was no sign of her. Barry could get all the way to Griffin's house from the highway end and he saw no sign of her either. We've got every agency looking as much as they can, but no one has seen her yet. The local news is even posting a notice that if anyone has seen her they are to call our office immediately."

Fresh tears flushed Carrie's face. "I should have been out looking for her!"

"No, you shouldn't have. You don't know these mountains. I would have had two agents lost.

"We'll find her. We will find her," confirmed the sheriff.

Soon, Carrie realized that they were pulling up to an attractive home tucked into the trees. She didn't recognize it, but assumed since it wasn't her hotel, that it was the sheriff's home. The lights were on inside and it looked warm and inviting.

"Why didn't you take me to the hotel?" Carrie asked.

"You don't need to be alone tonight."

The sheriff was right, but she felt ashamed that the sheriff had felt the need to rescue her. But, in all honestly, she was glad she had.

As they stepped through the backdoor to the mud room adjoining the kitchen, the smell of savory food met her. Her empty stomach lurched and urged her to investigate. Emptying her stomach earlier, had ridden her body of much of the alcohol and had helped her to sober. She was starving now, and the food smelled good.

An attractive man with graying hair and a short beard was bustling around the kitchen. He had set the table with three plates.

"Hi there!" Shep greeted Carrie with a big smile on his

face. He seemed… so joyful, Carrie realized. She liked him instantly.

"I feel like I'm intruding," said Carrie.

"Nonsense," Shep immediately responded. "We're thrilled that you're here."

Sheriff Markum motioned for Carrie to hand over her coat and she hung it on one of the hooks on the wall.

"I made this huge roast and we need help eating it. Besides, it has to be tough so far from home. You need a good home cooked meal," Shep said.

"You cooked it?" Carrie asked before realizing how it sounded. "I didn't mean that you couldn't cook, or shouldn't cook. I've just never met a man who wanted to cook. Sorry."

Both the sheriff and Shep were laughing. "It is one of many reasons I married him. Who can turn down a man who can cook this good and likes to?"

Carrie took a seat at the table and looked at the huge roast, carrots, and potatoes. Just as she sat down, Shep sat a steaming boat of gravy and a plate of large fluffy biscuits on the table.

Shep sat down at the head of the table with the sheriff across from Carrie. He reached out to the two ladies, and they took his hands. "Father God we are so thankful for all that you do. Bless this food and find our friend Lainey. Thank you, Lord."

Carrie heaped her plate, then sat looking at it. "It feels wrong to be eating like this when Lainey may be cold and hungry."

The sheriff looked at the pain in Carrie's eyes. "We have

to stay strong and eat so we can be strong enough and sharp enough to know how to help Lainey. If it were the other way around, you would want her to eat, and to enjoy it."

Carrie nodded and the need to eat took over and she cleaned her plate.

THE WIND HOWLING around the cabin woke Lainey some time in the night. Her first awareness was of pain. She felt so enveloped in it that it was as if her entire body was broken.

As she lay there, she realized she needed to go to the restroom. She knew she could not move however, and looked around for the man. The fire had died down but the burning coals still emanated a comforting heat. The dim light made it difficult to see.

Lainey gently rolled her head to the side searching for any sign of the man. Then suddenly, he was there at her side. He had noticed her movement and quickly responded.

"I'm sorry, but I have to use the restroom. But I can't move." Lainey's face was pinched in concern. She felt so vulnerable and apologetic for being such a burden to the man.

Without a word, he left and brought back a shallow round pan. Lainey was embarrassed, but had no other choice. Her jeans had been removed earlier when she had first arrived. Somehow knowing what she was feeling, the man held the blankets so they would not slip down while she worked to slide her underwear down. Then she pushed down with her hands to raise herself and the man blindly helped slide the pan underneath her.

Once done, he slid the pan out and left to dispose of the waste. Lainey was grateful for her caretaker and humbled by her vulnerability.

He was soon back, adding logs to the fire and kneeling down beside her with a container of water to drink. She knew she had to drink, but it was almost more effort than she could exert.

She did her best to drink all that the glass offered. When she finished, he sat it aside and then sat down beside her, watching her. She thought she saw concern on his face.

The man then smiled and soon, Lainey drifted back to sleep.

SITTING across from each other at the restaurant next door, Doc and Marissa waited for their food.

Doc wanted to confess to Marissa and come clean about his role in the drug trade. He knew it was the exact opposite of what he should do, but the urge wouldn't go away.

"Tell me about how you got into journalism?" Doc asked.

Marissa told the tale of her life and path to journalism. She wanted to come clean about knowing he was involved with Joe, but her fear of his anger kept her from it.

"Doc, what's keeping you here in Wilburton? You seem to love the city and your job there. I know you came to help after your mom died, but what is keeping you here now?"

Doc said nothing, only looked at Marissa. If this was just a fling, then what did it matter if he told her, except it could land him in jail. If there was more to their relationship, then he would have to tell her at some point, or she would find out on her own.

He took a deep breath and looked out into the restaurant. There were only a few tables occupied. The snow had kept people away.

Before Doc could answer, Marissa said, "I think I may know why. Are your brothers involved in Joe Billings business? Are you here to help them get out?" Marissa thought that would be a subtle way of half way telling him she knew more than she did.

Startled, Doc looked at Marissa. Her questions had been soft spoken with a caring inflection. He sighed and leaned back in the booth. "They aren't the sharpest two crayons in the box, but I love them. I feel guilty for leaving them with momma. She wasn't able to take care of them the way they needed and with daddy gone there wasn't a man around. They looked up to me and I left.

"They weren't good at school. They don't have a trade. There were so many factors that caused them to wind up cooking meth. It was the only way they saw to make money."

"So you help them. Cook meth, that is?"

"I am right now. It's a wonder they haven't blown themselves up. Only problem is that Joe really likes the product

I've been producing. I've done my job way too well, and now he wants more and more.

"My goal was to make enough to get Bud and Jimmy set straight and then put some cash back for me to get back to the city. I'd go tomorrow if it weren't for my bothers. Honestly, I'm afraid if, well, when I leave, Joe will kill them both. They won't be able to keep up with Joe's demands. I feel stuck."

"Take them back to the city with you."

"I've thought of that. Jimmy would go with me in a heartbeat and I think he would do well in a vocational school or in construction or something like that. But Bud doesn't want any part of it. He's angry at me for leaving them behind. He wants the fast money of the drug trade."

Marissa was becoming emotionally involved in not just Doc, but this story. She felt compassion for Doc and his brothers and their dilemma.

"If you stop and leave, Joe's wrath will come down. What's saying he won't follow you to the city?"

"Nothing. He could get so furious that he would track me and my brothers down wherever we were." Their food came, and both stopped to converse with the waitress and then taste their food.

"Have you thought about going to the DEA and turning state's witness on Joe?" Marissa's questions hit Doc hard. It would incriminate his brothers.

"I can't do that to my brothers."

"It might save their lives, and yours."

It was a thought. Doc mulled it over as he chewed. "Bud

wants to stay here and cook. He would turn against me in a flash and you think Joe can't get to me behind bars?"

Marissa knew Doc was right. "So what's your plan?"

Doc shook his head. "I have no idea. I've been asking myself that same question the whole time."

They ate their meal and talked about other lighter topics. There seemed to be nothing else to say about the drug matter.

On their walk back to the hotel, Doc held Marissa's hand. "Thank you for listening."

"Doc, I have an idea."

He looked down at her. Snowflakes were swirling between them and they sparkled from the streetlight.

"What if you helped me with my story and it was enough to take down Joe? We could do it so he would never ever know it was you. And we could do it in such a way that it would never incriminate your brothers either."

Doc wondered if that would be possible. It sounded like a good plan, but one wrong move, one wrong turn of events, and it could take them all down.

He leaned over and kissed her, oblivious to the cold and snow.

SHEP RESISTED any effort on the women's part to help clean up. He knew that Wanda had brought Carrie here so they could have some time alone. Cleaning up would keep him in the kitchen and give them some privacy.

Both he and Wanda had been praying for Carrie and he

prayed even now that God would give Wanda the words she needed to say.

The sheriff led the way into their great room. It was warm and inviting with a roaring fire in the fireplace. There were a few lamps lit which bathed the room in low warm light.

Carrie sank into the soft leather sofa and stared at the fire. It was mesmerizing. Soothing yet erratic and spontaneous at the same time.

"I'm a good listener, if you want to talk," the sheriff began.

Carrie didn't know where to start. Not that she didn't want to talk, but where did she start? She respected the sheriff and if she were to choose a close friend, she would want them to be just like her. But there was so much in her past she didn't want to dredge up and how could anyone understand what she was going through now, without knowing the past?

But, soon she began anyway. It had seemed like so much to tell, but when Carrie began it all came out succinctly and easily.

"God gave me a new lease on life. I felt him that day that I read Pride's letter. I know it was written by God's inspiration. While reading it, I felt something break that had been holding me hostage for years. He delivered me from the destructive lifestyle I was living.

"I couldn't do it myself. I kept trying to do it myself. But he did in an instant what I had been fighting to do for years. I felt so fresh and clean and the old desires were suddenly just gone. I have even been able to drink a beer or two and never even want another. I haven't even felt I needed them.

"I've stopped wanting sex as a substitute for loneliness. I'm not even lonely anymore. But tonight, something happened. I was so angry. I felt so guilty that I let Lainey go out alone. I felt like I had abandoned her by not going out after her. I think I was even a little angry at God for letting Lainey get lost.

"It felt like I was going back to doing what I knew I shouldn't do, as an act of defiance. I can't believe I would do that after all that God has done for me." Carrie stopped. Tears dripped one by one as she sat still looking at the fire.

The sheriff got up and threw another log on the dying fire. She didn't want to speak too soon. The verse that said, *be slow to speak*, came to her mind.

"Once in there, I couldn't stop. At first I didn't want to stop. Then when I did, I tried, but I couldn't stop and the longer I failed, the guiltier I felt.

"Now I'am terrified. Terrified that I am back to where I was, doing the old stuff. You know, I thought I was good to go, fixed for good. I felt… I felt confident in where I was.

"I don't want to go back to that. I don't want to fight this battle all over again. I don't know what to do." Her words ended in the rising pitch of panic.

Carrie looked over at the sheriff and she hoped, prayed that God would give her the words she needed. Sheriff Markum leaned forward placing her arms on her legs. "Carrie, God never expected us to fight these battles on our own. He doesn't expect perfection because he knows none of us can be perfect. We all fail and we all screw up, but that doesn't change God's love for us and it doesn't change his desire to help us.

"And we can never get cocky about where we are. First, it was God's deliverance that freed you to begin with, and it can only be God's grace that keeps you free. When we become confident in where we are, we become susceptible to temptation. We must cling to our relationship with God, nurture it, thank him for what he has done in our lives. Pray as Jesus directed us, to deliver us from temptation."

"He understands. He knows your pain. If we ever feel guilt, that's not from God. He does not cause us to feel guilty about anything ever. It says in the bible, *there is therefore now no condemnation to those who are in Christ Jesus.* It's the enemy that comes to accuse us with guilt.

"The guiltier we feel, the further away from God we run and the enemy knows that. God corrects us, but it's always with love. He can correct us with a single word that will bring restoration, pulling us back to him in an instant.

"I know the pain you feel over Lainey. I felt like if I had not asked us to split up, this would never have happened, but beating ourselves up will never fix this. God reminded me he is with her even if we are not. Wherever she is, she is not alone."

They both sat in silence for a few moments. The sheriff felt she should allow the words to resonate and sink in. And Carrie thought about them. She felt so selfish for running to the bar because she was angry and afraid, but her selfishness only hurt her.

"Is that what happened tonight? God delivered me from temptation by sending you to the bar?"

"I think so. I was about to head home. I'd been praying for you and Lainey while I finished some paperwork. Then I had this overwhelming urge to get up and go to the bar. Without questioning it, I got up and went."

"Thank you. I was about to slip further into my old habits and jump in bed with a man I didn't know or care about. As bad as the regret is right now, I don't know that I could have come back from that." Carrie leaned forward and rested her forehead on her knees and sobbed.

The sheriff let the room remain silent for several more minutes. "With God we can come back from anything, but he rescued you. Your anger led you to sin. It led you to rebel, to go get drunk. Not just have a drink, but to get drunk. You were on a mission of defiance fueled with anger, but God still rescued you."

Carrie sunk down into the sofa and rested her head back. "What do you think has happened to her?" Carrie asked the sheriff as her eyes searched the sheriff's face for hope.

"Carrie, I honestly don't know."

"Do you think the killer has her?"

Sheriff Markum shut her eyes. "I pray he doesn't."

"I can't imagine where she is if he doesn't."

"She could have had car trouble and started walking."

"But then she could be stranded out in the cold."

"Carrie we have to believe the best. We have to hope and pray for the best. God is watching over her and he will lead her to a house or to shelter."

Carrie shut her eyes and quietly prayed for God to take

care of Lainey. The shadow of guilt still loomed heavily over her.

Both the sheriff and Carrie sat in the room's comfort for the next thirty minutes. Shep had finished cleaning and had gone upstairs to bed via the back staircase, not wanting to disturb the women.

"We need to get some rest," said the sheriff. "Carrie, can I pray with you before we head to bed?"

"Yes." Carrie felt relieved the sheriff asked. "I'm still new at all this. I need all the prayer I can get."

The sheriff leaned forward and took Carrie's hands in hers and bowed her head. "God, we are so concerned about Lainey. We know wherever she is you are watching out for her, but we need to feel your comfort and we need to know that you are comforting Lainey. I also pray that you will wash your joy and comfort over Carrie. Let her feel your forgiveness just as strongly as she did the very first time. We love you father and choose to trust you. Amen."

Carrie broke down crying once again. Sheriff Markum got down on her knees next to Carrie and held her in her arms. "She'll be okay Carrie, and so will you."

CHAPTER 13

FRIDAY

All who had hoped that the winter storm would quickly blow over and the day would awake crisp, clear, and clean were sorely disappointed. It had been decades since a winter storm this intense had hit Latimer County. Sunrise brought dark gray skies still sifting snow onto the already mountainous drifts.

The smell of frying bacon woke Carrie the next morning and for a moment the events of the previous night did not invade her thoughts. When they did, she sank against her pillow in despair.

I love you Carrie, as much as I ever did. You are free, walk in that freedom.

Carrie's breath caught. She knew that voice. It was her Father God's voice. It soothed her like no other. It was one thing to hear the sheriff's reassurances. They brought comfort, but his voice brought wholeness once again.

She threw her covers back and stood. "Thank you

Father. Thank you for, for, for everything." Carrie felt refreshed and new. The reminder of her behavior the previous night kept trying to come back and overtake her thoughts, but she kept pushing them back and with determination, focused on where God had brought her from.

Downstairs the sheriff was at the stove. "I thought Shep did all the cooking around here."

Sheriff Markum turned and saw Carrie's smiling face. "You look better this morning."

"I feel better. The thoughts won't go away about what I did wrong, but I know they are just thoughts."

Carrie walked over to the stove and asked if she could help. The sheriff pointed her towards the coffee and instructed her to just sit.

Watching the sheriff, it reminded Carrie of the first time she had seen the sheriff. She wanted to talk about a strong intuition she had right then, but wasn't sure what to say.

"Thank you," said Carrie.

The sheriff turned and smiled. "Of course, you would have done the same for me."

"I don't know that I would have. I don't know that I would have known to."

Carrie fidgeted with her warm coffee cup.

"This may sound far-fetched, but something happened the first time I saw you. It was strangely weird." Carrie moved in her chair. She knew the moment she tried to explain, she would sound ridiculous, but she had to know what was going on.

The sheriff turned off the burner and sat the bacon and two plates with eggs on the table. She pulled out the chair across from Carrie and waited. "Don't worry. Just say it." The sheriff smiled at Carrie.

"The very first time we met, Lainey and I were sitting in Riley's when you walked in. I looked up and inside I immediately sensed in my heart 'she's a Christian'. It was almost audible. I could see something different about you. You were radiant.

"I'm a Christian. Lainey's a Christian, and I'm sure there were others in the diner with us who were as well. But there was something different about you. I don't know what the difference is, but I want whatever it is that you have." Carrie looked directly into the sheriff's eyes.

And the sheriff looked back, but said nothing for quite a while. She was silently praying, trying to decide what to say and how to say it. She pulled two strips of bacon off of the platter and took a slice of toast.

"I understand what you're saying. It's a discussion that I want to have with you, but not one I feel that I can just quickly have. It's true that everyone who professes Jesus as their Lord is a Christian. At that moment we are exchanging our old sinful selves for a new and righteous us. That only happens because of the sacrifice that Jesus made on the cross.

"It has nothing to do with behavior. You were just as righteous sitting in the bar last night drunk and ready to have sex with an unknown man as you are this morning. In fact, it is because of Jesus' unfailing righteousness which we have received, that causes us to feel remorse and regret over our sin, therefore keeping us from continuing to sin."

Carrie hung on every word. She knew what the sheriff

was saying was true. She'd been fortunate to find a church that taught that very thing, but it still didn't answer her question.

"In most ways I am no different from you."

"But there is something different. I want whatever it is."

The sheriff nodded and smiled. She could see Carrie's eagerness. "Okay, but let's eat breakfast first."

The door in the back hallway opened and in blew a flurry of snow and cold air. Shep was in the center of it. His cheeks were rosy red, and he was swathed from head to toe. He had a pair of heavy overalls on, a stocking cap, and sheep lined leather work gloves.

He stripped down the outerwear and leaned over to kiss Wanda who was getting up. "I've got you a plate ready," she said.

Shep poured the last cup of coffee and started another pot. "That sounds great. I went out and checked on all the animals. I had to break the ice in the water tank. It was an inch thick."

Turning to Carrie, he smiled. "How are you this morning?"

Carrie was thoroughly embarrassed and couldn't look Shep in the eye. "I'm fine. Thank you."

"I'm glad Wanda brought you out here. I would hate to be trapped in a blizzard in a hotel room."

The words that Shep had spoken took a moment to sink in with Carrie. "Trapped in a blizzard? You mean we can't get out?" Fresh panic set in as she realized they wouldn't be able to go look for Lainey again today.

Carrie looked over at the sheriff. "I've already contacted

the forestry department and they have a search and rescue team able to traverse the snow coming in to search for her. I set it up yesterday. Since it was already dark, they couldn't begin until this morning. But, it gave them time to prep their gear and get here."

"We're going, aren't we?" Carrie's eyes pleaded with the sheriff.

"We will try. If we can't get out on our own, I'll call Barry and see if they can spare someone to come get us and take us to their base camp."

It was still very early, and the sun had just risen. Carrie sat and wondered what that meant for Lainey. Was she buried in snow, frozen, or had God done just what they had hoped and protected her through the night.

"I'll put the blade on the old tractor after breakfast and see if I can't grade our driveway. Maybe the highway will be passable." Shep said as he forked in a pile of eggs and bit off a hunk of bacon.

"Carrie, eat. You'll need all the food your body can hold once we are out in the cold," said Sheriff Markum.

"Can we take some food with us for when we find Lainey? I don't want her to be hungry and cold one moment longer than necessary."

Sheriff Markum nodded. "We will Carrie. We will."

SHEP HAD BEEN successful in using the old tractor equipped with a grader blade to clear their driveway of huge snow-drifts. It hadn't been easy, but after two passes, he could get enough of a clearing for the sheriff's SUV to maneuver down the drive.

The state vehicles were out and the highway to Wilburton was passable even though the snow kept falling. The continuous heavy snowfall made visibility difficult.

Both Carrie and Sheriff Markum breathed a sigh of relief upon arriving at the sheriff's department. No one had attempted to clear the back parking lot, so the sheriff parked alongside the curb out front, making sure to not get caught in the deep drifts.

Inside, they were the first to arrive and flipped lights on and turned on the heat. Just as they finished, deputy Milford Barnes arrived.

"Good snowy morning," Milford called out a greeting.

"I'm glad you moved to town last year, just so you could make it to work in the middle of a blizzard," the sheriff winked.

"Got to do what you got to do, right?" Milford loved working for the sheriff. Sitting at home during a blizzard would not be an option for him as long as there was a missing agent and a murderer on the loose.

Milford started the large department coffee pot and looked for any overnight fax's or other correspondence that had come in. It was rare that a fax would ever come in with scanning and email's so prevalent and easy these days, but one never knew, so he made it his routine to check.

"Barry, this is Wanda Markum. Have you got anything for me?" Sheriff Markum asked after dialing the forester's number.

"Not yet sheriff. Search and Rescue started early this

morning, at first light, but we are working to just clear the roads before we can even get in to search. The helicopter is grounded because of the blizzard. We were hoping we could fly over to find her vehicle or some other sign of her, but that idea is on hold for now."

"Right. What can we do here?"

"Work the cases as best you can and find that killer. We'll keep you posted. If you hear of any information that might help us find the agent, let me know."

The sheriff sat down at her desk and began going through emails. In the back room where they had set up a temporary war room, Carrie was dialing Randy's number.

Upon hearing him answer her call, Carrie said, "It is good to hear your voice."

"How's it going? I feel powerless here."

"I feel powerless here. It took the sheriff's husband grading the snow from their drive just to get us to a highway that was only marginally clear. We've heard nothing from Lainey. The search and rescue team is severely hindered by the snow. They are just trying to clear enough snow to get up the mountain. Helicopters are grounded."

Randy was pacing his office. The snow had hit the entire state of Oklahoma, but from what Carrie was saying, it seemed far worse where she was.

"They are telling us not to get out here, but I could get to work. We have a few other agents here as well," said Randy. "What can I do for you from here?"

"We need an ID on that last body. We also need a rush on trace. I know there was little to go on, but there has to be something in all that was collected." Carrie's frustration was clear as she spoke.

"I'll see if I can put pressure on the lab to get it set as a priority. The escalation of murders concerns me. There is barely time in between to investigate one before you have to work another one."

Their joint concern that Lainey would be the next victim hovered unspoken between them. "Do you think.." Carrie began with Randy quickly cutting her off.

"No! Don't even go there. We won't think about that. We'll just work the cases we have," said Randy.

"I feel responsible," said Carrie.

"I don't know that I would have handled anything differently. Time was of the essence and splitting up to gather more information was necessary."

It felt good to hear Randy's affirmation, at least somewhat. "Well, okay. I'll call you back as soon as I know anything different."

Just as Carrie hung up from the call with Randy, the sheriff walked into the room. "We have an ID on the last body that was found at the Billings ranch. It wasn't River. It was Erin Jenkins. She was a twenty-four-year-old white female.

"Tended bar at a small dive in Talihina called The Rusty Nail. Didn't leave home after high school. Parents are poor. Mom stayed home most of the time between house cleaning gigs and some waitressing. Father worked on various ranches from time to time doing odd jobs and handyman work."

Carrie sat and focused on what the sheriff said. "That is

four seemingly random victims. They seem to have absolutely nothing in common. We've got to get a clue from something, somewhere.

"What about River? Did he ever turn up?" Carrie asked.

"Not as far as I know."

"Okay, we have to start from the beginning and add in the new information we've learned. Maybe going over it all again, something will stand out," said Carrie.

They rearranged the white boards adding in timelines for each victim. I have tasked the local police chief in Talihina with notifying the parents of Erin Jenkins. The sheriff would have done it had the roads been in better shape, but he was local and knew the family.

Soon, the only common thing was that each of the first three victims left on their own in the evening before their death. Beau Johnson left the bar at around midnight. Corey Stiles left his parents' home around nine p.m. the evening before. And from Lainey's notes, Amanda left her parents' home to go meet Matt in town around 4 p.m. She was going to meet him to go to a movie.

"Do you know if anyone ever talked to Matt?" Carrie asked. "I wonder if they made it to the movie."

The sheriff dug through several of her notes from speaking to Matt after the incident. "They met and went to the movie. He said she went home right after because it was getting colder and it was late. Looks like the last time he saw her was around ten p.m. that evening."

"They all disappeared between nine and midnight the night before their deaths." Carrie said. She turned from the whiteboard and looked at the sheriff. "There is something to this, but I have no idea what it is. But let's keep digging."

Carrie pulled out each file and went through the entire list of items collected at each crime scene. The list was always extensive since they would always collect little bits of random debris. You never knew what would carry a clue to the killer. She felt thankful to live in an age where technology was so advanced.

She started with Beau Johnson, the first victim. They had just received an updated list with lab findings for each item. There was very little found. The burned wood was local from the trees surrounding the clearing.

Just as she was about to close his file, Carrie noticed a new addition to the list from the lab. Then, she quickly checked the bottom of each of the other lists and found the same addition, except for one.

"Sheriff," Carrie called out excited. "Come quick."

MARISSA AND DOC spent the better part of the night developing a plan to execute an article that would uncover and take down Joe's drug cartel. They made a list as far as Doc knew of every member and their role in the operation.

Doc hoped Marissa's plan would work the way they wanted it to, but he still had a heavy heart. He knew, barring a miracle, that Bud would refuse to leave the cartel and come to live with him in the city. He knew in his heart this plan would send his brother to prison, but it might just spare his life.

Marissa was initially excited about their plan, but knew that Joe wouldn't mess around should he find her attempting to write a story that would uncover his operation. There was a lot on the line with this story and part of it was her own life.

After a little sleep, the two woke to dark gray skies and blowing snow. "We aren't going anywhere today," said Marissa standing at the window. She had not seen one vehicle attempt to pass through the street in front of the hotel. It was heaped with so much snow that the drifts in the parking lot came almost to the roof of her car. "I've never seen snow like this."

Doc walked up to the window and stood beside her. "Me either. I would have never thought this would happen. We've had some bad snow storms, but they have always been temporary. Soon, the sun would always come out and it would melt away quickly."

Doc dialed his phone, attempting to reach the land line at their trailer. No answer. It was still early for those two, and if they weren't cooking, then they would still be in bed. No doubt they were stranded there.

Marissa reached Brian Davis on the second ring. "Good morning Brian. This is Marissa."

With the niceties out of the way, Marissa said, "There has been a new turn of events with the drug cartel story. Doc has agreed to help us pull it together, but there are conditions. No one can know that he was our source."

For the next hour, the three of them sat with Marissa's phone on speaker discussing a specific plan. Brian was close friends with Jessie Billings and he planned to use that friendship to get close to the Billings. He knew that River knew about Joe and his operation. Hopefully, he could get closer to River and find out exactly what he knew.

"Doc has given me a list of names, places, and some dates. I'm going to dig deeper and see what I can turn up here in town. Once Doc gets back out to his place, he will keep cooking, but be more engaged with Joe. He's never tried to foster that relationship, but will work on that now," said Marissa.

"We should all be taking as many pictures as we can, keep them organized with notes about where they were taken, who was involved, and what specifically is going on at the time they were taken.

"We need to work as quickly as possible. It will be better for us all if we don't allow this to drag out," said Marissa.

With their plan fleshed out, Marissa hung up the phone. "I think you need to make plans for a quick exit back to the city. Maybe rent an apartment there and start sending out your resume. When it is time to go, you'll need a place to go. You can also use it as a stash to keep the money you've saved."

Doc thought about what Marissa said and nodded. "Sounds like a good plan. I have most of my stuff in a storage unit there and can empty it. I can talk to Jimmy and tell him we are working our way out. He has very little of worth, so when we go, moving him will be quick and easy."

"Can you trust him to keep his mouth shut?" Marissa asked.

Doc thought for a moment. "I think so. I must impress on him that if he truly wants out, then he will have to keep it quiet. It will be tempting to tell Bud, but after his outburst the other day, I saw something change between the two of them."

"Emphasize to him that his silence truly is a matter of life and death. His and yours."

THE MORNING BROUGHT stiffness along with the pain. Lainey had laid in one position since becoming injured. She needed to move, but each effort was met with intense pain. Using the pan to relieve herself last night was horrific.

She gently turned her head to survey the room. The fire was full and vigorous, indicating that it had just been stoked. The windows revealed dark gray skies and more snow. Her heart sank.

There were quiet noises coming from the far side of the cabin and she smelled food. Her stomach growled in response, and she tried to remember the last time she had eaten a meal.

Now to the issue of moving. She knew she needed to move to heal. Moving her head and neck was less painful than it had been, so that was progress. She moved her right arm. Stiff and sore, but not painful.

She continued to move one limb and area of her body at a time to take inventory. Her arms seemed fine, but as she did, she felt sharp pains in her midsection. As she moved her arms, the muscles tugged on her broken ribs. She had no way of knowing how many, but she felt like there were several. She could feel at least a couple grind so she knew they were truly broken and not just cracked.

Despair overwhelmed her. Yes, she was thankful for the man, but her situation seemed insurmountable. She laid still knowing her ribs would need to be bound and rendered immobile if they were to heal properly. Tears rolled from each eye and puddled in her ears.

Sensing movement next to her, she opened her eyes to see the man squatting beside her with a bowl of food. In the dim daylight, she could see he was much younger than she had first thought.

He appeared to be in his late forties, maybe early fifties. He had gray hair, but it was only scattered like salt through his dark hair. His eyes were a bright and clear icy blue color.

"My ribs are broken. Each time I try to sit up, I feel them move. Can we wrap them?"

Immediately the man sat the bowl down and left to retrieve whatever he felt was needed. Lainey glanced over into the bowl and saw that it was a heaping bowl of oatmeal. There was a large lump of fresh butter melting on top. Remnants of undissolved honey also rested there. Her stomach tugged to get to it.

The man arrived with more ripped sheets. Lainey began unbuttoning her shirt, and the man turned away, which surprised Lainey. "I need help to get my shirt off. It's okay." Lainey had a sports bra on and it covered her modestly. It was also quite comfortable in her current situation.

The man gingerly turned back around trying his best to not look anywhere unnecessary. He took her right arm and bent it at the elbow and pulled the cuff of her shirt. It slipped up to come off of her arm.

He then moved around to the other side and repeated the process. Lainey took as deep a breath as she could and rolled to lean up on one elbow. The man made quick work of wrapping the strips tightly around her. After a few wraps he looked at her for affirmation that he was not wrapping too tight. All without a word.

The man had brought adequate strips and had done an excellent job of wrapping her entire midsection securely. He helped to gently lay Lainey back down and pulled a wool blanket to cover her.

"I'm so hungry and that oatmeal smells wonderful. But I'm exhausted and hurting after all that. Can you help me eat?" Lainey looked at the man with pleading eyes. He merely nodded and began to offer small spoonfuls to Lainey's lips. He didn't stop until the entire bowl was empty.

"That was so good. I don't know how long it has been since I ate," said Lainey.

The man offered a small smile and rose to take the bowl back to the kitchen. He soon returned with a steaming cup of tea. He helped Lainey raise her head and carefully tipped the tea to her lips. He'd made sure it wasn't scalding so it wouldn't burn her.

After several sips. He let her head rest back on the pillow he'd provided some time in the night. "I would be dead by now if you hadn't come to rescue me," said Lainey. "I'm so grateful to you."

The man nodded and looked away as if it embarrassed

him. "It looks like it snowed all night long. Is the snow really deep outside?" Lainey asked.

He nodded, then helped her to drink more tea.

"Is there a way I can call someone or radio out to someone?" Lainey asked.

The man shook his head. His eyes were sad.

"I know there are people worried about me. I want them to know I'm all right."

"I'll go soon," he said.

Lainey smiled at the man.

Once again seemingly embarrassed, he dipped his head and stood, taking the empty cup to the sink.

THE SHERIFF HURRIED into the war room with expectancy all over her face. "What did you find?"

"There are updated reports from the lab. In the pants pocket of the first three victims they found a silver coin. Now on the first one, the pocket was on the topside and the silver melted. It didn't preserve the emblem on the coin.

"On the second body, the coin was in the pocket laying between the body and the floor of the shed. It was protected, but still somewhat damaged. The markings or emblems were still very clear. The third body that was found on the cross, had remnants of melted silver lumped in what had been the bottom of the pocket.

"The fabric of the jeans that all three were wearing burned and melded into the silver and adhered to the burned skin of the bodies. It wasn't until the techs were combing thoroughly through the clothing that they noticed the intact coin. It was unique, so they searched for something similar in the other two.

"The fourth victim did not have a coin. The lab is sending us pictures of all the silver remnants they found."

The sheriff's mind focused on every word Carrie spoke. A coin. They almost all had a silver coin. Questions were forming as Carrie spoke, but the sheriff tabled them until she was done. "Are they sure the silver was all from the same type of coin?"

"Yes, they did an analysis and the alloy of silver was exactly the same."

"What type of coin was it?" The sheriff asked.

"Nothing they had ever seen. They felt it was a proprietary minting. Maybe not for expenditure, but something like AA has for reaching certain levels of accomplishment."

Carrie's email pinged, and the sheriff moved around to look at the screen of Carrie's laptop. The face of one side of the coin was on the screen. It showed a large urn with flames of fire reaching up. On that side, the urn filled nearly the entire face of the coin. A generic pattern of tiny ribs circled the edges of the coin.

The other side of the coin showed a smaller version of the urn resting on top of a tapered block or hill. Underneath in large letters were — ZDV — in Romanesque typeset.

The sheriff pulled out a chair and sat next to Carrie. "What on earth?" Sheriff Markum asked, not expecting an answer.

"The fire emblem on the coins cannot be a coincidence. There are fire victims with silver coins stamped with fire emblems on them. To me, this sounds like some type of cult, even though no one we talked to said anything that would lead us to look at that. It could even be that the cult targeted them for some reason," Carrie said.

"This changes everything. I was thinking deranged serial killer who was a pyromaniac. I wasn't expecting something like this. We need to do some research."

"I'll do an internet search for this symbol, but I'll also send it to a professor I know at OU. He is an expert on cults and ancient religions. Maybe he can help us," said Carrie, already typing an email to Dr. Franz.

The sheriff went to her office and shut the door. She sat behind her desk and rested her arms on the desk with her hands clasp and then rested her forehead down on her hands. She began to pray.

She began by praying what she was feeling in her heart, what she hoped would happen. She prayed for Lainey, for River, and for them to find the killer or killers. But her words seemed so inadequate and soon became repetitive, so she did what she knew was the perfect thing to do. She began to pray in the Spirit.

Thirty minutes later she was still praying, unaware of how much time had passed. The door to her office suddenly opened and Carrie walked in stopping suddenly upon hearing the sheriff's odd words. They were foreign to her, but there was a strong feeling of God's presence in the room. She stood reverently and quietly.

The words stopped, and the sheriff continued to rest her head on her hands. She knew Carrie had walked in, but longed to linger in the heavy, peaceful presence. The strong feeling of comfort the Spirit had brought lingered, and she was hesitant to disturb it.

Soon, the sheriff raised her head and looked at Carrie. Neither one spoke quickly. Soon Carrie's keen intuition took hold, and she asked, "Is that the difference? What were you doing? I want to pray like that. I felt the presence of God the second I walked into the room."

Sheriff Markum nodded to Carrie. Come home with me again this evening. We'll talk more.

An intense spiritual hunger rose up inside of Carrie. She suddenly felt an overwhelming desperation for more of God. "No!" Carrie turned and locked the sheriff's door so they wouldn't be disturbed. "Now. Pray with me now."

Carrie's urgency surprised the sheriff. She smiled and motioned for Carrie to sit on one of the two chairs in front of her desk, as she sat in the other.

The sheriff reached for her bible and turned to the scripture that would explain in the simplest way what Carrie had witnessed. As she read it, Carrie was barely listening.

"Okay, Okay, just pray with me. I know it was from God. I want all of God I can get. I can't live without it." Carrie's eyes pleaded with the sheriff.

So, the sheriff prayed with Carrie and the moment she began, the Spirit filled Carrie to overflowing and she too began to pray those strange words. And she didn't stop, but continued to pray uninterrupted for the next twenty minutes.

A knock on the door reminded Carrie that she was at work and in the sheriff's office. She stopped praying and rose to unlock the door.

"Hey sheriff," Milford began, "Search and rescue is on the radio."

"Okay, we'll be right there."

As the sheriff walked out of her office door, Carrie looked to the window. The sun was out, and the light was so bright, it nearly blinded her.

CHAPTER 14

"This is the sheriff, go," The sheriff said, as she clasped the radio in her hand.

"This is Dale with Search and Rescue. We found your agents SUV. It's hard to tell with all the snow why, but she went off the road and over the edge of the mountain. She was lucky though. The pine trees are thick here and it caught her vehicle and kept it from falling further down the mountain. It looks just like it was cradled in arms of pine boughs.

"The side slopes down just right here, so it was nearly impossible to see the vehicle from the road, and now with the snow, we almost missed it."

"What about Agent Tate? Is she there?"

"No ma'am. No one is in the vehicle. Snow has covered any possible tracks, too. But at least we now have a starting point. Just wanted you to know."

"Thank you, Dale." The sheriff rested the mic back on

the desk and turned to Carrie and smiled. "They are making progress."

"And, the sun has come out. Let's hope the snow melts fast now," Carrie felt radiant and filled with more hope than she had ever known.

Sheriff Markum smiled at Carrie and nodded. "Let's get to work finding out where those coins came from."

They both went back to the war room. "Had you found something when you came to my office earlier?" Sheriff Markum asked.

"Well, I'm not sure. I searched for 'coin with fire urn' and there were several returns. I scrolled through until I found this one. It's an ancient coin and somewhat different from the one we have, however, the urn and fire are almost exact. I don't think that can be a coincidence."

Carrie clicked on the image of the coin she found. It took her to a Wikipedia site for Fire Temple. She read aloud even though the sheriff was also reading the page.

A fire temple in Zoroastrianism is the place of worship for Zoroastrians, often called dar-e mehr or agiyari. In Zoroastrian religion, fire, together with clean water, are agents of ritual purity. Clean, white "ash for the purification ceremonies [is] regarded as the basis of ritual life", which "are essentially the rites proper to the tending of a domestic fire, for the temple [fire] is that of the hearth fire raised to a new solemnity". For, one "who sacrifices unto fire with fuel in his hand..., is given happiness".

Carrie stopped reading and sat back in her chair. Neither she nor the sheriff spoke. Both were trying to process what they had just read. "I've never heard of such a thing," the sheriff said. "We need to know more. Did your contact at OU ever get back with you?" Sheriff Markum asked.

"Let me look," Carrie said as she pulled up her email. "He did. I'm surprised, but being a snow day he probably had the time."

Carrie once again read out loud…

Carrie it is so good to hear from you. I hope you are doing well. The picture of the coin you sent is very interesting. It resembles the coins used by an ancient religion called Zoroastrianism. The coins they used were quite different, but the urn seems to be exactly the same.

I feel this must be an offshoot of this ancient religion. There are still areas of the world today that do continue to practice, but they are rare. Most have dwindled because they do not allow anyone to come into their religion that is outside of the familial ancestry. Some groups have deterred from that through the years and the numbers have increased in those areas.

The letters on the back ZDV are unfamiliar to me. I cannot find those letters in any of my texts. Therefore, I suspect, that it is a new offshoot from the original religion, and those letters are indicative of that splinter group. Another curious note, is that these burned bodies are associated with this particular religion. A Zoroastrian would never burn a body, even in cremation as they feel it is sacrilege.

One of the primary tenets of their religion is creation worship. They feel that creation itself is divine. Their belief is that when a person dies, they are to be offered back to creation in the simplest manner. When one dies, they are often left on a temple alter for the birds and vultures, or rather for creation, to reclaim the body.

Another strong tenet of their religion is that they adhere to a strong moral code. They believe the greatest way to honor or worship creation is by making sure that every single decision or choice a person makes is governed by the highest moral code. A human being's eternal destiny hinges entirely on whether they make correct moral choices throughout their life.

Of course I am oversimplifying this ancient religion. Ironically, the way they worship creation, the earth, and its animal inhabitants is very familiar to what I see growing in our current society. I have seen an awareness of our misuse of planet resources and concern for endangered species grow to an almost frenzied and abnormal type of creation worship in and of itself.

It may just be that you have a group that have these same idealogical beliefs and have stumbled into this ancient religion which has fueled and fostered this cult. Because, if they are burning bodies then they are off the path of Zoroastrianism and have entered into cult status.

Typing quickly, Carrie responded.

Thank you, Dr. Franz. If you happen to come across any additional information that might help us, please let me know. I owe you a steak dinner!

Carrie hit send and turned to look at the sheriff. "Now that we have some sort of name and icons to search for, I will do a search on our statewide database and even VICAP. There may be other cells of the cult in other parts of the US."

"Great thinking. I'm still trying to imagine how these victims play into this cult. It's true what the professor said, the younger generations seem to have grown more concerned with our planet and the animals than their fellow human beings.

"I agree that we are to live responsibly and not to unnecessarily damage our world. I also believe that to harm animals unnecessarily is wrong. But to take those ideas and push them to a frantic state of abnormality, and into a form of worship, is becoming the norm in many areas.

"Could it be that they lured these young victims into this cult by their desire to protect the earth? And, if they had innocently become part of it, why were they burned alive?" Sheriff Markum asked.

"I don't know, but I feel very encouraged that we're making headway. I think we need to re-interview their friends to see if we might find any others who also had the same beliefs and know about this cult," said Carrie.

"We have to be careful to not call it a cult though. That could turn followers off and panic others."

Carrie nodded her head. "There is already more than enough panic going around."

SHARMA PACED THE FLOOR. He was greatly disturbed. For decades he had grown increasingly concerned about their precious earth and the animals that occupied it. Mankind was destroying both.

When he had found like-minded people, they had become determined to do something about it. One day, about five years earlier, one of their group had brought a new person to their meeting who had studied ancient religions.

He talked about Zoroastrianism and Sharma felt as

though he had come alive. A true religion that worshiped creation just as he did. Creation, earth and the animals in it, were to be revered and worshiped. Yet humankind always elevated themselves above creation. To Sharma that was just incredibly wrong.

For the next several years he studied Zoroastrianism and found that it had been declining for several reasons. He secluded himself away for thirty days, renamed himself Sharma, which means protector, and fasted. Each day he endeavored to enter into a meditative trance, in order to hear from creation itself.

On the twenty-first day, weak and hungry from fasting, and enlightened from the drug cocktail he frequently partook of, he heard. On the twenty-first day as he began to meditate, a vision came to him. A vision of how Zoroastrianism should change to thrive; needed to change to thrive. It never occurred to him he was hallucinating because of lack of food and the drug cocktail he had become reliant on.

Energized from the vision, he quickly began to write down the tenets of the renewed Zoroastrian religion. The manifest was titled: Manifesto Zoroastrianism DeVito Variantia which meant DeVito's variant on Zoroastrianism.

The ancient religion had used temple gold coins with great urns of fire imprinted on them. Sharma decided that they should mint their own coins as well. They would use silver and use the urn that had previously been used, but on the back the letters ZDV, standing for Zoroastrianism DeVito Variantia, would be stamped. This would be a symbol of established worshipers into the group.

Unlike Zoroastrianism, they would allow anyone in who

bore concern for the environment. Only by banding together could they bring about real change. Only by banding together in creation worship, would creation then regain its divine power and flourish once again.

Things had gone well for the next several years. Then members came who worshiped creation, but strayed from the strong moral code established by Zoroastrianism. Each one must make perfect moral choices. If any one member strayed, it diluted their worship power and weakened creation.

They must get better at vetting new recruits. All recruits must understand how important living by a strict moral code was to their religion. Maybe that had been his biggest mistake, presenting them as a well meaning group, not a religion. He had initially felt that it would be easier to gain recruits if it was not presented as such.

But it had weakened the power of the whole. Quality over quantity must be the gauge. They must adhere to that. With each poor moral choice it weakens a human being, therefore weakening the whole.

Today as he paced, he pondered how to instill in the recruits the dire necessity of making perfect moral choices.

He'd seen struggle in the group through the years, but that was why the most devoted worshipers eventually lived together, so they could strengthen each other, and Sharma could monitor their behavior to ward off any impending deviation.

Maybe they should stop taking recruits unless those recruits showed that they understood the need to live within their group. Yes, that was where he had gone wrong, allowing new recruits to live as they normally did. They could attend meetings, but not belong until they were completely dedicated.

HARLEY WAS RECOVERING NICELY. Neither he nor Blaine had seen or heard from River and were both concerned.

"I know you and the deputy went to the cabin, but what if he was just not there at that moment, but came later?" Harley asked.

"Nah, the snow was getting too bad by then. I don't think he could have gotten there," said Blaine.

"But he has that jeep that can climb anything. If he wanted to get there bad enough, he would have tried and probably made it."

Blaine thought about what Harley had said. "He may be at his Uncle Joe's. I never thought to check with him."

Harley nodded. He'd heard the rumors about Joe Billings and wondered if that had anything to do with why River was the way he was. "Hey Blaine," Harley began, not sure how to complete his thought.

"Yeah?"

"Have you heard the rumors around town about Joe?" Harley held his breath.

"What rumors?" Blaine asked, even though he knew.

"The ones about him being in the drug trade."

Blaine looked at Harley for a moment. The rumors had only been wisps floating around him, no one had been bold enough to comment one way or the other in his presence;

because everyone knew how close he and River were, and they also knew how close River was to his Uncle Joe. "A little, but nothing really. What are they?"

Harley looked at Blaine with sympathy. "You know how people are. They talk bold behind a person's back, but never to their face or in their presence. Everyone knows how close you and River are. Like brothers more than friends. I'm sure they are all just rumors."

"Tell me what the rumors are. Often they have a little truth to them," Blaine wasn't sure he wanted to know the truth about River's Uncle Joe, but he knew he needed to know the truth.

So, Harley took as deep a breath as he could take with his broken ribs, and told Blaine every rumor he had ever heard about Joe Billings. He knew some had to be pure speculation and fantasy, but he himself didn't know which were true and which were not.

The look on Blaine's face said that he wasn't shocked by what Harley said. "I would say that most of those rumors ring true. It answers so many unanswered questions I've had through the years.

"River was always partial to his Uncle Joe because he didn't take to ranch life. River felt since Uncle Joe didn't enjoy ranching then it was okay for him to not like ranching. It caused friction between him and his dad.

"But something changed about six months ago. He suddenly stopped talking about Joe. Before, he was always talking about this or that thing that Joe thought or did, but then it all stopped. I wonder if River found out about Joe's involvement in drugs?"

Harley thought about what Blaine had just said and nodded. "You don't think Joe would hurt River if he found out and maybe threatened to talk?" Harley suddenly felt compassion for a guy he didn't even like.

"No, I don't. River is more like a son to Joe. I just can't see him hurting him."

"So where do you think River is?" Harley asked.

Blaine shook his head. "I have no idea."

MANDY WAS SO excited to be working on the murder story. She just wished she had more to go on. She and deputy Amelia Stone were friends, and Mandy had blatantly pumped her for all the information she could, but the truth was, they knew very little.

The snow was getting to Mandy, and she was restless. All this snow had to be a direct result of global warming. There could be no other excuse for it, and she fumed just thinking about it.

She plunked down in her desk chair and began typing. She had read every article on global warming, saving the planet, and animal protection she could find, but they wrote new ones every day.

Reading through her email she saw three more notices from blogs she was subscribed to. Each one proved to amp up her resolve to get more involved in saving the planet.

Her reading led from one blog post to another and then to a new post contributor she hadn't read before. From there it led her to a website and a blog that she spent the next hour reading through. The more she read, the more excited she became.

She eagerly filled out the contact form at the bottom of the home page asking for more information. While waiting for a response, which she hoped would come quickly, she typed the name of the website into Google to see what would come up.

The first page of Google was the website, Zoroastrianism DeVito Variantia, which she had just been on. Below it, were only posts regarding Zoroastrianism. She read each one, however none but the first website discussed the name in full.

When she grew tired of reading through Wikipedia, she flipped back over to her email and noticed a new one in her in-box. They had responded! She eagerly devoured every word. It appeared that pouring her enthusiasm into the comment form had encouraged them to respond quickly.

They had invited her to a group meeting they were having that very evening. With the weather as it was, she probably would not be able to attend. It was only about thirty-five miles south of Wilburton at Sardis Lake, but with the snow, it would seem like a million.

Mandy glanced outside. The sun had come out, but there were still huge snow drifts outside her house. *I wonder what the roads are like,* she thought.

She dialed Amelia's number and waited for her to answer. "Amelia, did you go into work today?" Mandy asked.

"Finally. Derek came and got me. The sun is out now and the snow is melting," said Amelia.

"Do you think the main roads will be passable by this evening?"

Amelia huffed and said, "I have no idea. Where are you wanting to go?"

"Well, there's a meeting at Sardis Lake this evening that I really want to go to."

"That's Highway 2. It could be okay. What kind of meeting is it?"

Mandy spent the next ten minutes telling Amelia all about ZVD, according to what she had read on the internet. "I would love for you to come with me."

Amelia's excitement was tempered with trepidation. "Why have we not heard of them until now and why isn't there more about them on the internet?" Amelia asked.

"According to their website, the founder, Sharma, has spent decades battling climate change. Five years ago he started ZVD attempting to unite those who are truly serious about our planet. It just takes time to grow these things. And you know that not everyone who mentions caring about it, truly cares. His name by the way, means protector. He feels he has been called to be 'protector of creation'."

"Let me check and see if I can find out about the roads. If they aren't completely clear, then when night falls, they will refreeze and be even worse than they are now. But if the roads seem to clear off, I'll go with you. I'd like to check all this out."

"Oh, that's awesome. Hey, have you found out anything new about the murders?" Mandy suddenly shifted gears in their conversation.

"The sheriff and Agent Border seem energized about

something, but they haven't told me anything. Oh, and the search and rescue team found Agent Tate's SUV. She wasn't in it, which is good. Hopefully, someone rescued her, and she is just waiting it out somewhere."

"Can you find out what they may have found that is getting them excited?" Mandy asked. She really hated using her friendship with Amelia for story fodder, but they had been friends since grade school. However, Amelia knew they would be friends with or without her providing information.

"I'll see what I can find out and let you know. Well, I better get back to doing something. I'll offer my services to Agent Border and see what I can find out."

"Thanks Amelia! You're the best."

By late afternoon Marissa and Doc had made great progress. Doc had given every bit of information that he personally knew about Joe Billing's drug trade. He gave names, dates, and addresses as best that he could.

Marissa was good to nudge his memory by asking pointed questions. Doc thought she really had what it took to be an excellent investigative journalist.

While Marissa worked to polish up what she had written, Doc began making calls to see about getting set up in Oklahoma City again. He called his old apartment complex to see what they had available. He'd always paid on time and had taken care of his apartment so he hoped it might facilitate the application process.

The thought to go to a different complex crossed his mind. Would he be making it too easy for Joe to find him by going back to an old address? But, if they did their job well, as they had planned, Joe would be spending his time with the feds. And if Joe really wanted to find Doc, he would no matter where he went.

Doc hoped to make it look like he took off to the city because of Joe's arrest rather than prior to. He wanted Joe to think he had fled to avoid arrest, not that he had caused the arrest.

"Hey, you're finally awake," Doc said to Jimmy when he answered.

"Yep. Where are you? Still in town?"

"It got too bad to come down our roads, and it was late."

"Sun's out now," Jimmy offered.

"I'll be home as soon as I can."

"Joe called. He wants more stuff. I'll have to cook."

Doc could tell by the sound of Jimmy's voice that he was not looking forward to it. After their talk, he could tell that Jimmy was growing disillusioned by his current situation.

"Where's Bud?" Doc asked.

"He's already out there."

"Jimmy, I want us to make an exit plan. We can't tell Bud. He'll turn us over to Joe. Can you keep this a secret?"

Doc heard hope in Jimmy's voice. "You mean, you and I leave here and go to the city?"

"Yes, but we have to do it in such a way that we don't alert Joe or Bud. I have a plan. You just have to be ready to go when I say go. And you have to keep your mouth shut in the meantime."

Jimmy huffed. "You don't have to tell me that twice. I'd be a dead man walking were I to say anything. You too."

"So you agree that you'll go with me?"

"You bet. I keep thinking about our discussion the other day. You'll help me won't you Doc? Help me get started on something new?"

"Yes, Jimmy, I will. I promise. No more cooking. And in the meantime, no more smoking weed and getting high. Your mouth flaps too much when you're high."

Jimmy felt relief wash over himself. "I promise. Imagine, no more cooking. That's great Doc. That's really great."

Doc hung up from talking with Jimmy to see and hear Marissa on her cell phone.

"Thanks Brian. I appreciate your hard work on all this."

She hung up her cell phone, turned and looked at Doc with a huge smile on her face. "Brian spoke with Jessie. Jessie is so rattled because of the body that was burned in the smokehouse and River missing, that he just rattled on and on to Brian.

"Jessie knew about Joe's drug trade. He just tried to stay as far away from it as he could. He'd heard the fight River had with their dad, but he had already heard the rumors around town.

"He was with River one night in town and River had him drive over to a part of town where there are several warehouses. Jessie had no idea what they were doing, but River wanted to just sit and wait. They did, and saw Joe trade a huge truck of drugs for cash. The drugs were in stacks of tires. They were stacked about four tires tall and wrapped in heavy plastic sheeting that had been shrink-wrapped around them.

"The men got in the truck, opened one stack, and looked in. Out came a brick of white powder. They put it back and resealed the small opening where they had opened the plastic sheeting.

"Jessie didn't know the men with the money, but he knew the men with Joe. He even remembered the truck and the logo on the side." Marissa stopped to take a breath and waited for Doc to respond.

Doc was deep in thought. "I spoke to Jimmy. He's ready. I have a two-bedroom apartment on hold from my previous apartment complex. I gave them my deposit over the phone with my debit card.

"We need to get eyes on that warehouse and take pictures." Doc paused for a moment and frowned. "This just all seems too easy, doesn't it? If all this information is so readily available to us, then why haven't the feds used it to shut Joe down? I feel like we won't be telling them anything they don't already know, or have evidence of."

"They may have some of it, but they don't have your first hand testimony. They are also probably wanting a bigger fish. My guess they want to nail whoever Joe's boss is."

"Then what makes us think they will do anything with what we give them?"

Marissa smiled. "They will do something with it because we are writing a story. They know that if we print a story before they make the arrests, then their cover is blown and they won't be able to then."

"What is to keep them from killing your story?"

"Freedom of press. I'll send a copy of my finished article to the FBI and the DEA at the same time I'll send a query letter to a list of magazine editors I have. They won't get the full story, but enough to make them want more. However the feds will get the whole story. I'll send it with a cover letter stating that I have already sent it to several publications. Their hand will be forced and they'll move quickly."

Doc sat and thought about what Marissa had said. It sounded iffy to him. Was it the right thing to do? Would it mess up the feds investigation if they forced their hand too soon?

He finally decided that he didn't care. Big fish or little fish, he wanted his life back, and he was ready to get on with the plan.

"Jimmy said that Joe had called and wanted another supply. I know we are not the only supplier. My guess is when he picks up from us he takes it to the warehouse and they pack it into the tires and he keeps picking up product until he has a truckload and then there is an exchange. It may take him a couple of days, a week, or a month. We have no idea when he will make another exchange."

"Well, we should watch the warehouse until there is one. Brian may be willing to trade off with us. We can also find Joe and take pictures of him in his day-to-day business. Maybe some of those are associates in on the drug trade."

"He has several gas stations and convenience stores. I'm sure they are ways to launder money. The first one he bought is an old-fashioned gas station and they make repairs, change oil, and… sell tires there."

Marissa's eye's lit up. "Then we should start there."

RIVER SAT in a dark closet in his Uncle Joe's warehouse. Some goon who worked for his uncle had shoved him in there. He'd been hovering around watching his uncle's operation when he'd been hit from behind. The next thing he knew, he had awoke in the closet.

There were no windows and only a few empty old metal shelves occupying the closet. They had thrown in a few old blankets soon after throwing him in the closet. That had been almost twenty-four hours ago.

They had brought him something to eat twice and gave him an empty five-gallon bucket for a toilet. He was already raging with anger at his uncle before this, but now he was exploding with anger.

He'd asked to speak with his uncle repeatedly and had been ignored. In the closet's dark, fear enveloped him. Then anger would wash back over him and he would beat the walls with his fists screaming for them to let him out. His screams were only met with silence.

The time in the dark closet gave him time to do only one thing, and that was to think. At first he wished he had one of his guns so he could defend himself against these men. He was angry enough he would have done it too.

But then when the fear had come, it tempered the anger and his thoughts went to his mom and dad, and brother

Jessie. He hadn't been home in a few days and he knew they would be worried about him.

After he had argued with Blaine, he wondered if Blaine would even miss him. Thinking of Blaine brought remorse over the way he had treated him the last few months. He had almost confided in his best friend about what he was going through, but the shame over what his uncle was doing tamped down his near confession.

So, he had kept it inside and brooded. The brooding had turned him sullen and irritable. The more irritable he had become, the more it had pushed Blaine away. Now he and Harley were spending time together the way they used to do, and that compounded River's rage.

It was his own fault, yet he felt powerless to change his behavior. It was probably good he didn't have his gun, because he would have used it on himself by now. The toxic cocktail of emotions; shame, anger, guilt, fear, and disappointment had dominated him completely the last few months and being held in this closet amplified them all. He was ready to end it all.

Suddenly the door opened and River shielded his eyes from the light. His eyes had grown accustom to the dark and the light coming through the door hurt.

"Get up," ordered a man who worked for his uncle. He was not the one who had thrown him in the closet, but he remembered seeing him before.

River slowly rose to his feet. He felt completely broken, and didn't care if there were repercussions, so he moved at his own pace. His young healthy body had grown stiff in the closet from the cold and lack of movement.

Once to his feet, the man grabbed River's shoulder and jerked him out into the warehouse. His Uncle Joe stood watching.

"River, what are you doing?" Joe asked.

River just stood looking at his uncle. The fire had gone out of him and he didn't even care enough anymore to respond.

Joe walked over to River and put his hands on top of Rivers shoulders. He stood looking intently at River's face as if studying it and him. River couldn't take the scrutiny and ducked his head.

"Let me go. I just want to go home," said River.

Joe removed his hands and stepped back a step, but only continued to watch River. "Why have you been lurking around here, watching?" Joe asked.

River looked up at his uncle. A tingle of the old anger rose up. "I used to look up to you. And then I find out you are a drug dealer." River spat the words out. He then shrugged and in a whisper said, "I don't even care anymore. Just let me go home."

Joe could see that River was tired and the look in his eyes said he was disillusioned. Disappointing River had never been a concern of Joe's. He knew his brother Jeff had never respected him, but then there was River.

"It's just business, River."

River shut his eyes. "I don't even care anymore. Just let me go home."

"And if I do let you go home, how will I know that this will stay between us?"

"I won't say anything. I have said nothing for months."

"What will you tell your family about where you have been?"

River looked at his uncle for a moment. "I'll tell them I went to the cabin I have up in the woods. Blaine knows about it. He can confirm."

"River I answer to people. People who don't care if you are my nephew. If you talk, then they will kill you. I don't want that to happen."

"Have others talked?" River asked with an edge of defiance.

"Yes River, others have talked. And they aren't around to talk anymore."

"You're threatening me?" River was incredulous that his own uncle would threaten him, but then what had he expected? Everything he had ever thought he had known about his uncle had been a lie.

"I'm not threatening you. I'm just saying, it isn't only up to me. I can only do so much to protect you."

Through gritted teeth, River said, "I won't talk."

Joe considered River for a moment longer and then with a nod of his head, indicated for him to go. He hoped that wasn't the last time he would ever see his nephew.

CHAPTER 15

Several phone re-interviews later, Sheriff Markum and Carrie sat in the war room to compare notes.

"From what I've gleaned, at least two were advocates for climate change. As far as religion, Corey attended the local Baptist church with his family almost every Sunday. Amanda had a somewhat steady church attendance as well.

"Beau on the other hand, never attended church. His friends laughed when I mentioned concern about climate change. His world consisted solely of drugs. He didn't care about anything but getting high. However, we know he had a coin in his pocket."

Sheriff Markum sat processing what Carrie had said. She got up and began to make notes on the whiteboard. When done, she turned and looked at Carrie. "One victim didn't have a coin or silver in her pocket. The last one, Erin Jenkins."

Carrie rifled back through the file to see if she had missed something from the lab. "No, nothing here."

"We have two victims into climate change, three with coins, and two into nefarious endeavors. Erin Jenkins tended bar and from all the interviews she was probably dealing from the bar."

"If Beau was not into climate change, why did he have a coin in his pocket?" Carrie asked. "The overlap makes little sense. I honestly thought we were getting somewhere with this cult."

"What if Erin had a coin, she just didn't have it with her?" Sheriff Markum asked.

Carrie thought about that. "Could be. But it still doesn't track that we have two who were probably not concerned with climate change or the cult."

Derek popped his head in the door. "Sheriff, Charles Barlow is on the phone for you."

Sheriff Markum took a deep breath and nodded. She reached for the phone and pressed the blinking light. "Hi there Charles."

"What have you found out about who was on my property shooting at Harley?"

"Honestly, nothing. I was headed to talk to River that morning that we found the fire and he has not surfaced. I have nothing else incriminating anyone. I haven't stopped investigating, but with the snow and the murders, I've not made the progress I had hoped I would."

"Sure, I understand. Is there anything I can do?"

"No, Charles, there isn't. If you see River again, you can let me know."

As she hung up the phone, her deputy Amelia knocked lightly on the door as she stuck her head in. "Sheriff, do you know how the roads are. The highways, that is."

Sheriff Markum looked at her deputy. "Where are you planning to go?"

"Nothing for work. I was just going to go with a friend to a meeting at Sardis Lake tonight and if the roads were still bad, we weren't going to go."

"Last I heard, the sun had melted most of the highways clear after the snow plows had gone through this morning. But you know as soon as it gets dark any moisture will freeze to solid ice."

"I do, but Mandy was really wanting me to go with her. I'm just concerned about the roads."

"I would hate to see you out there tonight Amelia, but you have good judgement, so if you go, just be careful."

"Thanks, sheriff," said Amelia.

The sheriff sat back in the metal folding chair and pinched the bridge of her nose. "Could it be possible that the drugs and the cult are intermingled? Could the cult members be involved with the drug dealing and use?" Sheriff Markum asked, looking up at Carrie.

"Maybe Corey and Amanda were part of the cult, but Beau and Erin were part of the drug side of things," said the sheriff.

"That's plausible," replied Carrie. She turned to her laptop and did a Google search on ZVD. Nothing came up. Then she searched for Zoroastrian VD. Nothing came up.

"If the 'Z' in ZVD stands for Zoroastrianism, then what on earth does the 'V' and the 'D' stand for?" Carrie typed in just Zoroastrian. Several Wikipedia articles popped up, all concerning the ancient religion.

Just then, Deputy Randy Turner came hurrying through the door, "Sheriff, I just saw River driving through town."

"Which way was he going?" Sheriff Markum asked.

"Looked like he was heading north to the ranch."

The Sheriff grabbed her coat off of the back of the chair, and looked at Carrie, "Let's go."

River's jeep made good time on the roads and he was in a hurry to get home. By the time Sheriff Markum caught up with him, they were on the drive to the ranch. The Sheriff followed him right up to the house and parked beside him.

River got out of his jeep and looked over at the sheriff. "He looks like hell!" Carrie said.

"He does. Let's see where he's been."

When River saw the sheriff and Carrie, his hands went up as if to ward off questions. He shut his eyes and shook his head. "Look sheriff, I'm tired and just want a shower and my bed."

"Where have you been River?" Sheriff Markum asked.

River drew a deep breath, dropped his hands, and let it out. "I've been up in the mountains at an old cabin. I got snowed in there."

"I'm having a hard time believing that. Blaine and Harley came in worried about you, so Blaine and Derek went up to look for you. Harley was in no shape to travel the rough road." She said that on purpose to see River's reaction. There was a slight flicker in River's eyes.

The front door opened and River's mom, May Billings,

stood there looking at River with concern on her face. She looked from River to the sheriff and back again.

The Sheriff nodded towards May, indicating that River should go in. He did, and they followed. May hugged her son tightly. "We were so worried about you." She searched River's face for answers that he didn't provide.

"May, we need to speak to River privately," Sheriff Markum said.

"Yes. Yes. I'll just be in the kitchen," said May, as she hurried off after giving River one last look.

"Have a seat River," said the sheriff, as she and Carrie sat opposite the chair closest to him.

"Now, let's start over. I'm more concerned about what you did to Harley then where you've been the last couple of days. I've put it together, so just tell me your version of events."

River sat with his forearms on his knees and his head slumped forward. He felt a hundred years old. Had it only been three days since he and Blaine had argued? And, what did he tell the sheriff? He had to avoid talking about Uncle Joe.

Carrie and the sheriff waited patiently for River to collect his thoughts. There was something entirely different about him. He had been like a powder keg about to explode. Now he appeared as if it had, and all that was left was the shell of who River had been.

"I guess I just got jealous of Blaine and Harley spending time together."

They sat and waited for more, but it never came. "River we know about Joe," Carrie volunteered.

River's head jerked up and his mouth hung open. In an attempt to recover, he dipped his gaze and said, "What do you mean?"

Carrie leaned forward to make eye contact. When she did, she said, "We know he has a major drug operation, and we know that you found out about six months ago, and have been furious ever since."

River leaned back in the chair laying his head back and putting his hand over his eyes. This was all too much. He'd promised Joe he wouldn't tell, but they knew. What was he going to do?

"There's nothing left to do River, but tell us everything. The quicker you do, the quicker you can get to that shower, and bed," said Sheriff Markum.

He felt so defeated, so he told them everything. It felt good to let it all out. He had no idea how holding it all in for so many months had affected him. When he finished, he looked at the sheriff. "If he finds out that I talked to you about this, I'll be a dead man."

"Has he killed others?" Carrie asked.

"Not him, but he said that he answers to someone else, I don't know who, but that he has killed and wouldn't think twice about killing me."

"Then we will do our best to protect you. But we still have the issue of assault on Harley."

Remorse flooded through River and it showed on his face. "I'm really sorry about that. I was just so angry about everything. Harley just got in the way." River sat quietly thinking for a moment, "What do I need to do to make it right, sheriff?"

~

"WE'RE ABOUT ready for the meeting tonight Sharma," said Jacob.

"How are the roads?" Sharma asked.

"Much better. The snow graders moved a ton of snow and then with the salt and sun, they are almost clear."

"Good. We may have some new people tonight."

Sharma was sitting behind his large desk. "Jacob, can you sit for a minute? I wanted to discuss something with you."

"Sure," said Jacob as he sat.

"As you know, our goal is to grow by recruiting large numbers of those interested in stopping climate change. We must increase in number to truly facilitate change. But we also must, absolutely must, be morally effective as well."

Jacob leaned forward and focused on every word from his mentor. He owed Sharma a great deal and would do anything to further their cause. "Yes, I agree."

"We have a dilemma here. We've been recruiting and our numbers are growing, however, the moral issues have not been addressed. In our last several meetings I've discussed the importance of making right moral choices, but the newer recruits don't seem to understand that to fight climate change we must also make right moral choices, that it empowers us and creation.

"Creation cannot regain its strength without our moral purity. As we worship creation through our right moral choices, creation itself will flourish. I fear that we have gained several recruits who will not under any circumstance, change their behavior."

"I wholeheartedly agree, Sharma. It angers me that we have so many who take our cause so lightly. Charlatans, all of them. We need them gone!" Jacobs face had grown red and revealed the anger he felt inside.

"Now, now, Jacob. We have to recruit, but we must be wiser about it. We cannot allow anyone who has not been truly vetted to join our inner group. They may attend the weekly meetings, but not become one of us until they are completely on board and have shown they will live with the utmost moral integrity."

Jacob rolled inside. He didn't feel that Sharma was being tough enough on those that said they love creation, but weren't willing to selflessly make right choices. He felt, no, he knew, they were doing more damage to creation than they were doing good.

"Yes, Sharma. Just tell me what I can do."

"Watch for me. Let me know those that are doing what they can. Those that are trying to adhere to the moral code versus those that take our cause too casually. Be my eyes and ears."

"Yes, Sharma. You can count on me." Jacob felt pleased that Sharma had chosen him for this task.

As Jacob left Sharma's office, he felt smug. He was convinced now more than ever, that he had been chosen to assist the greatest man the world had ever known, in order to restore creation to perfection. He knew that his devotion in creation worship far exceeded any other.

Just then, Emma came running up to Jacob. "Ava has lost her coin!"

Another flash of anger rose in Jacob. Yet another reason that only the most devoted should be given coins as a sign of passage to the inner circle, but Sharma disagreed. Forcing himself to remain calm on the surface, he said, "Where was the last place she saw her coin? Doesn't she know that we are to keep it on our person at all times?"

"Yes Jacob, she does." Emma suddenly embarrassed, ducked her head. "It was a few weeks ago. She had gone on a date. She hasn't seen it since."

"Can she go back where she was and look for the coin?"

"She's looking, but she's concerned."

"Why is she so concerned?"

"Well, they were at a bar and she thinks she may have lost it there."

Jacob thought he would explode with anger. "In… a… bar…"

"Yes." Emma could feel the anger radiate off of Jacob and was suddenly fearful for her friend.

"Does she think being in a bar is making a good moral choice?"

Emma looked at Jacob confused. "There isn't anything wrong with being in a bar is there?"

Jacob shut his eyes. How was he to get it through to these idiots! "Does your generation even know what is moral and what is not?"

Emma wrinkled her brow in thought. "Maybe Jacob, what is moral to one person isn't necessarily moral to anther one."

It took Jacob back. Of course. He realized now. He and Sharma must write down what the definition of moral was. They all needed a list of moral absolutes so they would know what to do and what not to do. They had not had a set of defined laws to follow, but now that he understood the need, he could fix that.

WITH THE SNOW beginning to melt, Doc felt it was imperative to head back out to the house. Marissa had a plan to watch Joe and get pictures. Doc was somewhat uneasy with Marissa's plan, but knew she was not a novice at surveillance and understood the gravity of the situation.

Earlier they had gone to the gas station slash tire shop that Joe owned. Bill Stiles greeted them and asked how he could help. Doc remembered that his son Corey had been a victim of the recent killings and lost a little steam.

He didn't want to do anything to add to Bill's grief and stress. Marissa on the other hand was thrilled to learn she had another potential in to the murders.

"Marissa, take it easy on Bill. I forgot he was even the one managing this place for Joe. Maybe it isn't such a good idea to interview him."

"Don't be silly. He won't even know he's being interviewed." Marissa punctuated that last statement with one of her devastatingly beautiful smiles.

So, they had gone in and talked with Bill. He hadn't been in the mood to talk, about any of it. He was tired and ready to close up and go home when they had arrived.

Coming up empty-handed, they regrouped. Doc would go home and check on his brothers and Marissa would do reconnaissance at the warehouse.

Armed with enough junk food to last a month, a heavy blanket, and her trusty camera, Marissa was ready. She would stay out all night watching if she had to. She had parked in a place behind another warehouse where her vehicle couldn't be seen, but had just enough vantage between the buildings that she could take adequate pictures.

For several hours straight, nothing of any note whatsoever happened. She was thankful for the full tank of gas, because ever so often she would have to start the engine to heat up.

The ringing of her phone was welcome when she looked down and saw Doc's name. "Hi there." Marissa greeted Doc in her most sultry voice.

Doc smiled. Her voice did something to him. "I'm just checking in on you. I wanted to make sure you were doing okay."

"Bored, but other than that, I'm okay."

"Seen anything yet?"

"No. No sign of anyone or anything. I had resolved to stay as long as necessary, but I didn't take into account that I would have to keep the jeep running so much. When my gas tank gets low, I'll have to go back to the hotel."

"How much gas do you have left?"

"About a half of a tank. I'll be here awhile still."

"Did you get done what you needed to do at home?"

Marissa knew her phone wasn't being tapped, but she still wanted to avoid discussing certain things while on the line.

"Yes. Doc already picked it up too. That was an hour ago. That is why I thought maybe you had seen him by now."

"Hmmm. Well, he must take it from your house to another site to package it differently. Or maybe store it there until they have enough from all the different pickups." Marissa's voice was questioning. She was trying to think out loud what the delay could be.

"Could be."

"So, how is it with Bud and Jimmy? Jimmy keeping his mouth shut?"

"He is. He's smart, and he's scared. Bud's been high since we finished cooking so he has been oblivious to us."

"That's good."

"Well, I just wanted to check in on you and see how you are. Call me if you need me, otherwise I'll talk to you in the morning."

Their goodbyes lingered, neither one wanting to end the call, but finally they did. By ten o'clock she was about to question her resolve. Could she really stay all night? Was that even necessary? She was cold and tired of fighting sleep.

At about ten-fifteen though, the large bay door of the warehouse started to go up. The light from inside caught Marissa's eye. She grabbed her camera and began to take pictures.

She soon realized that her vantage point while good

with the eye, was not such a great photo vantage point. She decided to get a closer look.

Taking only her camera and cell phone, she got out of her jeep, quietly shutting the door. She moved around the corner of the warehouse she had parked behind, being careful to reduce the crunch of snow under her boots. It seemed with the snow it was much quieter than normal and that sound carried further.

Once around the side of the other warehouse, she could see a truck was being pulled into the warehouse. It was the tire delivery truck that they had been told about. It was pitch dark out and with the only light coming from the inside of the warehouse, Marissa felt confident that the darkness of night would blanket her in secrecy.

She inched along one careful step at a time. When she was where she thought she could get a few good photos of the interior of the warehouse, the door started to go down.

Just as she was about to rush forward and attempt to sneak in underneath the door, everything went black.

"I'M SO glad that the roads cleared off enough for us to go to the meeting," said Mandy. She was elated that she had found this group and eager to get involved.

Amelia was slightly less enthusiastic. "What do you really know about this group, Mandy?"

"The thing that excites me the most, is that they are truly serious about stopping climate change."

Amelia thought about Mandy's comment. "But aren't there a lot of other groups out there just as serious?"

"Maybe. But as I read their website, I could feel their passion about the issue. They love our earth and to them preserving creation is not just something to yell and scream about, but something sacred."

Amelia looked at the glow on Mandy's face when she talked about ZDV. All she could think was that she hoped this was as serious a group as Mandy thought they were. But she couldn't deny that she was concerned about Mandy's sudden reverence for this group she knew virtually nothing about.

The drive took longer than the thirty-five minutes it would have normally taken. The directions to where the event was being held took them off of the highway about a mile. While the highway had cleared, the mile to the meeting place was still covered in deep snow.

There was a large building with a logo of an urn with a fire in it, then the letters ZDV just like on the website. Surrounding the building, there were several other smaller buildings that looked like small cabins or houses. In the dark, it was hard to see what they really were. They each had only one light over each front door.

Amelia noticed that in the parking lot, there were very few cars, maybe three or four. She assumed that the snow had kept many away.

They were greeted at the front door by a cheery faced young woman about their age. She handed them each a brochure and gestured for them to take a seat wherever they felt comfortable.

There was a table set up with coffee, tea, and water. There was also some homemade baked goods. Amelia was hungry and sampled the treats. She had a weakness for chocolate, so she took two of the rich dark brownies.

Mandy was too excited to eat, but got a cup of coffee. "Do you notice that there isn't any styrofoam cups or non-biodegradable items?" Mandy said excitedly to Amelia. "They really are serious."

Amelia nodded as she followed Mandy to a chair. The metal folding chair was cold against her clothing and she was glad she had also gotten a cup of coffee to go with her brownies.

The room had four rows of gray metal folding chairs with about six chairs in each row. Amelia quickly did the math, twenty-four chairs. She wondered why so few chairs. This group may not be nearly as large or as near a force as Mandy was hoping. Of those twenty-four chairs, only about ten were occupied.

At exactly seven o'clock a gong of some type sounded and in walked a man of about fifty, dressed in a long off-white linen robe. He had dark shoulder length hair, and a neatly kept beard. He walked in quietly with his head held high and his hands clasp in front of him.

"Welcome all who bear the concern of creation!"

For the next hour, Mandy and Amelia sat and listened to Sharma discuss the travesty of how mankind had decimated our plant earth. He listed all the ways we were destroying the very thing we had been entrusted to care for. His passion was undeniable.

"Wow," Mandy exclaimed when the meeting ended.

"Couldn't you just feel the call to do more? Couldn't you just hear his passion? What did you think?"

Amelia agreed that there was a lot of passion, but something didn't quite sit right with her. She couldn't put her finger on it. She agreed with everything that Sharma was saying, so she couldn't exactly tell Mandy what she felt was wrong. "Yes, he has a lot of passion," was all Amelia could say.

After the meeting, everyone stayed and mingled about. They were warm and inviting to Mandy and Amelia. Soon, Sharma made his way around to the two newcomers.

He took Mandy's hand in his and looked her warmly in the eyes. "Welcome."

"Thank you," replied Mandy. She was so drawn to Sharma it felt like a religious experience to her.

For the next twenty minutes, Amelia stood and listened to Sharma talk more about ZDV with Mandy. He looked her way from time to time and she nodded appropriately, but honestly, she was tired and ready to go home.

Finally, Mandy and Amelia crawled into Mandy's cold vehicle around ten p.m. Mandy was still bouncing with excitement from the high of hearing Sharma's words, but Amelia was bone tired.

"I'm coming back tomorrow," said Mandy.

Amelia jerked her head over to look at her friend. "What? What for?"

"Sharma asked me to. He could see how passionate I am about creation and he wanted to discuss greater involvement with me."

Amelia didn't say a word, even though she just didn't

feel right about it. She spent the rest of the ride home trying to decipher exactly what was wrong that she couldn't see, but felt. However, when Mandy pulled up to her house, she still hadn't come up with anything.

"Thanks for going with me!" Mandy said still full of excitement.

"I'm glad I went. It was a good meeting," was the best that Amelia could come up with. "Mandy…"

"Yes?"

Amelia just smiled at her friend. "Be careful tomorrow."

Mandy frowned at her friend's hesitation. "Of course. Amelia, I've finally found my passion. There is nothing to be careful about." Amelia nodded, and when her friend drove away, she still had a huge smile on her face.

MARISSA WOKE with a splitting headache in the same closet that River had been held captive in just hours earlier. Her phone and her camera were gone. So were her shoes, socks, and coat.

She shivered and scrambled to wrap herself in the blanket that was laying wadded underneath her.

Normally, she was very brave and even cocky about feeling fearless, but at that very moment, she was terrified. She had never been in such a dire situation before. It is one thing to imagine how bold you would be, but another to actually have to be bold in the face of danger.

Just outside the door, she could hear voices, but she couldn't distinguish what they were saying. She had lost all sense of time being in the dark closet. Being unconscious for a portion of that time, didn't help. She had no idea how long she had been out.

The door opened and a large man reached in and dragged her out. He threw her into the middle of the warehouse floor. The tire truck was gone, and they had parked her jeep inside. Maybe they would let her go after a stern warning.

There were three large men standing in the room with guns. They were Joe's soldiers standing at the ready. After about five minutes, Joe walked out casually. As cold as she was, the room seemed to take on a deeper chill.

Standing in front of her, he said, "I know you are a reporter. Who else is working with you?"

Marissa's mind flitted around to find the information he demanded. But fear had blocked her ability to think clearly so she stood saying nothing.

Joe strolled around Marissa as she stood shivering, clutching the blanket around herself. After one complete round, he stood in front of her once again. He looked her in the eyes and stood assessing her. Her hair was bedraggled and her makeup smeared. He could see the fear in her eyes.

"You were bold to be out taking pictures of us. Where is that boldness now?" Joe laughed. Then, darkness cloaked his face. "I said, who else is helping you. Who knows what you know?"

"No one. I'm a freelance reporter." Her words stumbled out insecurely.

"I don't believe you," Joe growled. "How did you know to come here?"

What should she say? She could hold firm, but she knew they would torture her for the information. She could give up Doc and Brian, but her heart sank at that prospect. This specific information had come from Jessie though. Yes, through Brian, but Joe wouldn't hurt Jessie.

Joe took the large knife he had been holding and rested the point under her chin, tilting her head back. "I… said… who… told… you… about… this… warehouse."

A tear escaped out of the corner of Marissa's eye and rolled down her cheek. "Jessie. Jessie Billings"

"Joe's head jerked at hearing Jessie's name. He had no idea his other nephew knew anything at all about this place. His eyes clouded over and he stepped back. It was one thing for River to know. He had always been Joe's shadow, but Jessie… He had stayed true to ranch life and his father. This news was unexpected.

A droplet of blood trickled down Marissa's neck where the point of the blade had pierced her skin, but she was too terrified to wipe it away. She shivered so violently that she didn't know if it was from the cold or from fear.

"How do you know Jessie?" Joe asked. He knew that something wasn't right. Jessie wouldn't be privy to this information independently.

"He came with River one night when River came to watch the warehouse." She hoped staying within the family would protect the boys and her true sources of information.

That made more sense to Joe. River's reconnaissance mission had been prior to capturing him the previous night. He didn't think he would have any more problem's out of River, and Jessie wouldn't talk. But, Jessie had talked.

This lady had to be taken care of. They would demand it of him. Doing so would hopefully deflect the target off of his nephew's backs.

Joe nodded toward the closet and the man who had drug her out threw her back in. They would keep her in the closet a little longer then take her to the woods and dispose of her.

Looking at his right-hand man, Joe said, "Get everything prepared and then come back and get her."

CARRIE ARRIVED at her hotel room around nine p.m. exhausted. She flopped down on her bed and lay looking at the ceiling. She had barely had time to process all that had happened during the day.

Foremost on her mind was Lainey. She didn't want to lose hope, but she had been missing since early the day before. Had it just been a spring or summer day, she could see how Lainey could adapt and survive, but this winter storm had been horrific and she knew Lainey wasn't up to navigating it.

Carrie shut her eyes and asked God to find Lainey. She asked him to watch over her and take care of her wherever she was. She didn't know what else to ask without repeating what she had just said.

The sheriff had said that when we don't know the words to pray, the Spirit does. That is a perfect time to pray in the Spirit. So, Carrie did. As she prayed, she began to feel energized. The fatigue of the day seemed to dissipate as fog exposed to the sun.

When she felt done, she rolled over on her side towards the hotel nightstand. She reached over and pulled open the top drawer. As she suspected, there was a Gideon bible. She hesitated before pulling it out.

Reading the bible had been a challenge for her most of the time. Even some of the most modern translations seemed to fall flat when she read them. She would find herself having to read verses repeatedly in an attempt to process what they were saying. Reading the King James Bible, had been impossible. But, she pulled it out of the drawer, anyway.

Sitting up, she leaned against the headboard and fanned through the pages casually with her thumb. She wanted to understand the bible the way so many that she went to church with did. Admitting that she had trouble with it, wasn't an option. She was too embarrassed to admit she didn't measure up.

Her heart stopped, and she opened the bible and looked down. The page open was at Acts 11. She began to read at the top of the page which was at verse four. As she read, she suddenly realized that she understood. Elation surged in her. The words were coming alive on the page.

She turned the bible over to read the front cover. Yes, it was a King James Bible. She went back to where she was reading and hungrily devoured every word. At verse fifteen, she read it twice. *This is what happened to me today with Sheriff Markum!*

The words she read, she profoundly understood. This

was a different kind of understanding, one she could not define. But the words satiated her in a way that she had longed to be filled. She felt as though she had been a dry and thirsty soul that was now being flooded with rivers of fresh clean water.

So, she read, and read, unable to put it down. She finished the book of Acts, then went to Romans, and then back to the gospels. Her heart yearned to read it all again and again, but her eyes grew heavy.

It was three in the morning when her eyes took control and closed, the bible laying open on her chest.

CHAPTER 16

SATURDAY

Lainey woke feeling somewhat better regarding pain, but if possible, she felt more lethargic. She still felt very constricted with the broken ribs and stiffly set broken leg, but had tried to move what she could to keep up her circulation.

Each time she became hungry, thirsty, or needed to use the restroom, the man was there beside her offering whatever she needed. Once the task was complete, he would disappear again to another part of the cabin out of Lainey's eyesight.

He kept the fire stoked, and she knew she was as comfortable as she thought she could be.

Yesterday when the sun broke through the dark clouds and it had stopped snowing, Lainey felt hopeful that she would soon be rescued. But no one had come. She knew in this deep tiny valley, the snow was piled deep. Even now, she could see snow drifts that reached just above the bottoms of the windows.

The man, apparently sensing she was awake, appeared at her side. He spent the next half an hour helping Lainey to use the pan, dispose of the contents, and provide her with another hot steaming bowl of oatmeal.

Once that was done, the man said, "You need to move."

Lainey knew what he said was true and had hoped that the little she had done was enough. The pain was still intense with no painkillers of any kind and the lethargy she felt further discouraged more movement.

She looked at the man with sorrowful eyes. "I know, but I don't think I can."

He nodded and reached over to the arm furthest from him, pulled her gently up, then tucked a soft bed pillow underneath her.

It had happened quickly and skillfully, but had still taken her breath away. For the rest of the day, each time the man came to tend to her, he also helped her to move, propping her in different positions. Once done, it felt good to have the pressure points changed and to be lying in a different position, but the horrific pain was almost unbearable.

Lainey was having trouble staying awake and alert. She wasn't sure if it was a blessing or a curse. At least asleep time would pass faster. And honestly her discouragement and pain had pushed her to the point of despondency.

After the third time the man had helped her move, and he had gone away, Lainey laid and let tears fall from her eyes. She just didn't know how much more of this she could bear.

~

THE BUZZER GOING off startled Carrie. She jumped and quickly sat up. She was still fully clothed, having rolled over and pulled the comforter over herself sometime in the night.

It was six o'clock. She had had only three hours sleep. She dropped back to the pillow and curled up once again under the comforter. Knowing she had to get up, she laid there with her eyes open, allowing her body to wake up naturally, recovering from the jolt of the alarm clock.

As she laid there, she thought of the previous night and the exhilaration she felt in reading the bible. She pondered it, realizing the only difference was that she had… what had Sheriff Markum called it… been baptized in the Holy Spirit. The new prayer words brought feelings of comfort, peace, and confidence in her prayers.

When reading the bible it was as if some veil or blockage had fallen from her eyes or her mind. She could suddenly understand with clarity what she had struggled merely hours before to even read.

She once again thought of Lainey and prayed a short prayer both with words she understood and words she did not, knowing that God understood.

Finally, she threw back the comforter and walked through the chilly room to turn on the shower. Once under the hot rushing water, she felt revived and ready to take on the day.

The contrast between staying up drinking all night and staying up reading her bible was not lost on her. Today she felt invigorated and alive, unlike the many times she had been recovering with a hangover.

Once outside, she noticed the skies were dark gray again. The wind whipped and tugged at her coat and she ducked her head down inside her collar. The sidewalks of the hotel had been sprinkled with ice melting salt and some felt like little ball bearings under her feet. She wasn't sure if it was any better than walking on ice.

As she pulled up to the sheriff's department, large flakes of snow began to fall once again. She resisted the urge to feel discouraged, reminding herself that it had been less than a week since they had arrived to help with this case. Had Lainey still been here by her side, she would feel encouraged by their progress.

Inside, Carrie found Sheriff Markum already at her desk and Deputy Milford manning the front desk.

"Good morning," Carrie greeted the sheriff with a smile.

"Good morning," Greeted Sheriff Markum, returning Carrie's smile.

"Anything new?"

"Well, I have River and Harley coming in later this morning. By all rights, Harley should press charges, but I want them to meet and talk it out. If he continues with charges, then I will book River and turn him over to the DA's office.

"If they can make amends to each other, then I will

suggest, unofficially of course, a course of community service for River to complete. I'm hoping that these guys can work it out."

Carrie sat thinking and nodded. This small town was run so differently from the big city. There would have been no doubt that charges would be filed there, but she saw the reasoning in what the sheriff was doing, and felt they would all be better off for it.

"No new news on the murders. I've gone over every single file one more time along with the updated lists from the tech team. They got a palm print off of the wall at the barn, but no match in the database. If we get someone, then we can use it to match to them.

"The hair barrette we found was void of DNA that was usable enough to get a match, and there were no fingerprints. The boot print is generic. It is a Redwing work boot size ten."

The sheriff stopped and waited for Carrie's response. "What about the coins? Was there any DNA or fingerprints that survived the one intact coin?"

"No. And the remains were too charred as was the clothing to find any other traces." The two sat deep in thought for a few moments.

"We have the cult and drugs. They seem to be two separate veins, but I suspect they are somehow intermingled. I don't know how or why, call it a hunch, but I just feel they are. However, we have to follow them separately and then see if they lead back to each other," said Carrie. Her strategic mind was clicking away.

"Tell me all that you know about the local drug trade

here," said Carrie. Her mind was alert, and she sat receptive, ready to catch every detail.

"I guess it all starts with Joe Billings. As you know, he is Jeff Billings brother and Jessie and River's uncle. Jessie loved the ranch life like his father, but River didn't and looked to his uncle Joe as a mentor.

"He first bought an old gas station in town after his father passed. It faired. Even though they did automotive repairs, and sold tires, the economy for small towns like Wilburton are tough.

"Ironically though, Joe began adding newer convenience stores to his list. It surprised the community at his success. He kept it quiet though and soon was buying additional stores in other small towns.

"It is believed that he uses local men to cook the meth. In the mountains and back deep in the forest, it is hard to monitor their activity. He collects the product, and ships it out in quantity.

"I've been in contact with the FBI and DEA. He is a much bigger fish than I want to fry and they are eager to get at him. However, they are really after who he answers to. There is a level between him and the top dog, Carlos Anterria. I've been told to stand down and not 'meddle' in any drug activity in my county."

Carrie sat and contemplated all that the Sheriff had said. They weren't to 'meddle' in the drug affairs, but now they had come to them. If the drug trade and the murders intertwined, Carrie wouldn't think twice about taking them down.

"So, if we pursue the drug angle, then we get hit hard by the big dogs. Seems we have no choice but to follow the cult lead. If it proves that it truly involves the drug angle, then we will not hesitate to pounce." The look in Carrie's eyes told the Sheriff she was on for a fight on whatever front it presented itself.

"We can assume that since the murders are happening in this area and all but one victim had this cult coin, it is a local cult. We need to get hard on the trail of any groups that are actively involved in climate change in this area," concluded Carrie.

"Okay, let's get a plan and divide up the duties with my deputies. The Wilburton police chief has agreed to help as well."

The sheriff called everyone together and told them the plan to track down any group associated with climate change that was active in the area. She also asked that they flag any climate change zealots.

Once the duties were assigned, Carrie and Sheriff Markum retreated to the war room. Just after closing the door, it reopened. Standing there was Amelia. By the look on her face she had something to tell, but didn't look forward to telling it.

"Come on in and shut the door," said Sheriff Markum.

Amelia came in and sat down at the table with Carrie and the sheriff. "Remember when I asked about the roads yesterday so I could go to a meeting with Mandy last night?"

"Yes," replied the sheriff.

"Mandy Reese works at the newspaper and we've been best friends since grade school." Amelia directed the explanation to Carrie, as the sheriff was already well aware of who Mandy was.

"She is also deep into climate change issues. When she was snowed in, I think she read through every new article out there. She stumbled across a group I've never heard of and that meets at Sardis Lake. They had a meeting last night and Mandy begged me to go."

"Go on, tell us everything," encouraged the sheriff.

"The name of the group is something really weird. I'm not sure I can even pronounce it. I have a brochure at home that I can go get. It was something starting with a Z."

Carrie looked at the Sheriff. A familiar surge of excitement rushed through her. It was that feeling she always felt when a case turned on a dime for the better.

The sheriff got up and went to the whiteboard, pulled off a photo they had attached, and brought it to Amelia. "Does this look like anything they had at the meeting?"

Amelia looked over the picture of the front and back of the silver coin and began to nod. "I didn't see a coin like that, but that urn with the fire, yes. And those letters, ZDV, they were the initials of the group name. Much easier to say than that long string of complicated words."

For the next hour they sat pumping Amelia for every tidbit of information that she could remember. Names, any dates, descriptions, and even the most minute detail they could pry out of her.

The result was a goldmine of information. Amelia did

well in law enforcement because she remembered the most minute details even when it was unnecessary.

"Mandy is going back out there today."

"Why?" Sheriff Markum asked.

"This Sharma guy asked her too. Something about a way to get more involved in their cause. Mandy was all over it in an instant."

"What is your honest take on this organization Amelia?" Carrie asked.

"At first I was all on board. But when we got there, something didn't feel right. I couldn't put my finger on it. I think one thing that bothers me the most is Mandy's response. She has gotten weird. It's like she has become consumed with Sharma and ZDV. I don't know. I can't describe it."

"Amelia, thank you. Go back out and work on what we gave you. Say nothing to anyone else about this. Carrie and I need to talk," said the Sheriff. "Oh, and Amelia, thanks for coming to us as soon as you did."

"Of course. I just hope Mandy is okay."

Once Amelia left the room, Carrie and the sheriff began to discuss options. If they forced their way in, they might lose valuable information and the group might shut down. They didn't even know for sure how the group was involved in the murders.

Another alternative was to encourage Amelia to increase her involvement with Mandy in order to feed them intel. Carrie knew firsthand just how dangerous undercover work can be, but sometimes it is the only course of action that makes sense.

They brought Amelia back in and discussed a plan for her. At first she was very reluctant. She didn't want to put herself in so much danger that she faced murder. But then she had signed up for law enforcement and all that it entailed. If nothing else, she would feel that she was keeping her friend Mandy safe.

"When do I start?" Amelia asked.

"Right now," Carrie and the sheriff said in unison.

AMELIA CALLED Mandy to see if she had left to go back to ZDV yet. Just when she thought she would have to leave a voicemail, Mandy answered.

"Hello," said Mandy.

"Hey, I was wondering if you had left to go to ZDV yet. I got to thinking and thought I might go with you."

"Really?" Mandy wondered about the change in her friend, but her excitement overrode any prolonged curiosity.

"Well, you know, I really am concerned about climate change. They are the only local group I know about where we can get actively involved," Amelia hoped she sounded convincing.

"Don't you have to work today?"

Amelia had thought of that. "I've had some time coming to me. I've been working so much overtime that the Sheriff suggested I take a day. So, I thought I would go with you if you hadn't left yet."

"No, I haven't. But I was planning on staying the entire day if possible."

Amelia hoped Mandy couldn't hear the eye roll. *Well, anything for work, right?* "Hey that's fine! It will help us get to know them better."

"I was planning on leaving here in about thirty minutes. Will that be okay with you?"

"Yep, I'll be ready."

Amelia hung up the phone and looked at Sheriff Markum to see if she had done well.

"I'm really concerned about this. It would be one thing if I was going into a situation armed, but I won't have a weapon with me."

"I have a pistol and ankle strap. I'll loan it to you. Let's hope that you won't need it, but just in case you do, you'll have it," said the sheriff.

"Do they have metal detectors?" Carrie asked.

Amelia hadn't thought of that. "We didn't have to walk through one last night, so I will assume, no."

"Then the ankle pistol might work. If they have a metal detector, then no." Carrie said.

"I hadn't thought of that. Hopefully, it will be fine. If they didn't make you go through one last night, then there probably won't be one today," said the sheriff.

"I need to go home and change. I don't want to show up in my uniform. I doubt that I would be well received in that case."

Carrie laughed. "No, I dare say you wouldn't!"

Within twenty minutes, the sheriff had gotten Amelia

the ankle holster, and she had quickly gone home and changed. Mandy was prompt and pulled up in front of Amelia's home in exactly thirty minutes.

"I'm glad the snow stopped again. I was concerned that it would keep snowing like it did Thursday," said Mandy.

"Well, it's still cold. I wish the wind would go away too," said Amelia.

"I'm surprised you reconsidered. I thought you had no desire to go back."

"I was just tired. I'd worked a long day yesterday and was really tired by the time we got there. Then sitting in those hard metal chairs for so long, took its toll."

"I can see that would be tough. I've worked from home a lot lately because of the snow, so I wasn't as tired. But honestly last night I just became more energized the more I heard Sharma speak.

"It's more than just a group, Amelia, it is a revered group of believers who revere creation the way it should be." Once again Mandy's face glowed.

Amelia watched her friend and was genuinely concerned. *She has definitely drank the kool-aid,* she thought. "It seems that way. I hope we learn more today."

The roads were much clearer than they had been the previous night so the trip seemed much shorter. In the daylight the compound was easier to see.

It appeared to have been some type of camp setup, on the edge of the lake. There was the large main building where they had met last night, with several smaller white frame cabin type structures. It reminded Amelia of the times she had gone to church camp in grade school.

There were only two other cars in the parking lot when they arrived, and no sign of anyone walking about. It seemed almost peaceful and serene.

Inside, Jacob greeted them. Amelia assessed that he was very high strung. He was a total contrast to Sharma who was the epitome of peace.

Jacob led them to a back room that was Sharma's office. He opened the door and ushered them in.

Sharma rose and greeted them both with grace and asked them to sit. Jacob stood at the back of the room by the door.

"Amelia, I'm surprised to see you today. I got the feeling that you had reservations about our group."

Amelia squirmed in her chair. "I was just tired last night. Once I got a good night's rest, I wanted to come back."

"We welcome you."

For the next hour Sharma talked once again about blessed creation and our duty to not just preserve it, but to bring it back to its perfect state of being. He discussed humankind's role in the process by making right moral choices. The purer humankind could be, the quicker creation would once again flourish.

Amelia thought she would choke. This was not just a normal everyday environmental group. This was a bunch of crazy people who worship creation. She would have to muster all her acting ability to appear as enthused as Mandy.

"I'm on board completely!" Mandy could barely contain her enthusiasm. "What do we do next?"

Jacob stepped forward. "We have written a series of

moral codes to help understand the boundaries. It seems that in this day and age of free thinking, many do not understand what true morality is."

Jacob handed a newly printed booklet to both Mandy and Amelia. "It's imperative that we make sure every choice we make is completely moral. There is no other way for creation to rise to perfection once again."

While Jacob continued to talk about moral codes, Amelia glanced at the booklet. Some items were understandable, but the list went into minute detail on many fronts. How on earth was she going to act as though this was all okay with her?

"Spend the day with us. We will show you around and introduce you to others. You can share a meal with us," said Sharma.

"We'd love too," said Mandy, who had yet to even glance through the booklet.

Amelia's skin crawled as they walked through the compound. There were eight cabins and Sharma had commented that about five were occupied. The residents seemed extremely happy.

They were all working at some task. It was a Saturday and most residents were there at the compound. Only a couple had Saturday jobs.

"Everyone is free to come and go as they please. Everyone has a job and contributes as they can. We don't have a large benefactor, so we do what we can to share and take care of each other."

"Honestly, we have found that those living here on the

compound have a much easier time with correct moral choices. The world is continually attempting to pull us down and force us to live immorally.

"Living here, we can pursue morality and also work towards perfecting creation." Sharma seemed to finally come to the end of his monolog. Mandy had hung on every word.

"How does one go about moving to the compound?" Mandy asked as Amelia's head jerked around to look at her. Seeing Jacob watching her out the corner of her eye, she realized she hadn't been quick enough to recover her look of shock.

Sharma smiled and ushered Mandy back into his office with his hand on her shoulder. Amelia stood dumfounded, not knowing what to do.

"ANY WORD from the search and rescue team on their progress?" Carrie asked.

"Yes, early this morning. They come back down the mountain each night and go back each morning. The snow stopped, and the sun helped them, but then it started snowing there last night. While we had an entire night of clear skies, they had more snow," said the sheriff.

Carrie sat listening, feeling disheartened. "What can we do? I've prayed and prayed, but I'll be honest, I'm losing hope that they will find her okay."

Sheriff Markum sat and thought. What could they do

from here? "Let's reconnect with the media to try and get the word out to area residents, TV stations, newspapers, bloggers. Maybe she is waiting it out in someone's cabin somewhere and has no working communication lines."

"That sounds good to me, but I can't imagine that there is no way for her to communicate with us. I can see her phone dying or something like that, but land lines are reliable, and there is the internet," said Carrie.

Sheriff Markum pulled her list of media contacts and prepared a media statement regarding Agent Tate's disappearance. With the list she had compiled in a group, it was easy to send them all the same media release at the same time. She expected their phone to ring in just seconds.

"Milford, I just cc'd you on a media release regarding Agent Tate. I'm sure the phone will ring soon."

"What specifically do you want me to say?" Milford asked.

"We need to find her. If anyone out there has seen her or has any idea where she might me, have them call us. She may be injured and staying with someone. We just need a lead to send to the search and rescue team."

"You got it."

Sheriff Markum found Carrie in the war room on the phone. "Thank you for speaking with me again. We have some new information that has come to light, and I wanted to ask you a couple of questions. First, have you ever heard of ZDV? It's a local environmental group. The letters stand for Zoroastrianism DeVito Variantia." Carrie waited for a response.

"Maybe you have seen their symbol. It is a large urn with flames of fire coming out of it."

Again waiting for a response.

"Thank you. Would you keep your eye out and if you see anything like that or hear of those letters or that name, would you please call me?"

Carrie hung up and marked a line through the name on her list.

"I'm calling all the people we've witnessed to see if they have seen or heard anything about ZDV. So far no luck."

Sheriff Markum stood looking at the white board once again. "I'm bothered by the inconsistencies. It is hard for me to see Beau Johnson concerned about the environment."

"What if he took the coin from someone or found the coin and just had it on him?"

"That could be possible. But if the killings are connected to the cult, why would they care anything about Beau?" The sheriff looked at Carrie.

Carrie sat down and wrote another email to Dr. Franz. Now that they knew the full length of the name, she wanted to reach out to him and see if he had any additional information. She knew school would be back in session, or maybe it was finals week, she didn't know. But whatever the case may be, she knew he probably could not get back to her quickly.

With the email to Dr. Franz sent, she Googled the entire name of the group. She put in the initials with various other terms such as Sardis Lake, environment, creation. The website to the group came up, and Carrie read every word.

"Look at this," Carrie said, moving aside so the sheriff could see the screen.

For the next thirty minutes the two of them sat perusing every photo and rereading every word. Once done, Carrie searched on the individuals mentioned on the website. Nothing came up.

"We need to run their names through our database. Maybe one of them has a criminal history and something, anything, we could pull them in for," said Carrie.

When the search came up empty, she leaned back, crossed her arms and huffed in frustration.

"I want to go out there, but I know Amelia is doing what she needs to do. I don't want to blow her cover. She'll get more than I would barreling in like a bull."

"I know. Have you finished making calls to everyone on the witness list?"

"No, I'll finish that and let you know."

Carrie got back to the mundane work that was what law enforcement usually was. She sometimes hated that she was so motion oriented. She had to continually resist the urge to be doing something, anything other than just sitting at a desk.

She had taken the victims in order and had worked through the list of contacts for Beau Johnson first, then Cory Stiles. She had made her way through two of Amanda Lee's friends, when she finally found someone who knew about the cult.

"So you went to a meeting with her?" Carrie asked Gracie McNash, Amanda's best friend.

Carrie opened the door to the war room and motioned for the sheriff to come listen in with her.

"Gracie, I'm going to put you on speaker so the sheriff can hear. Is that okay?"

"Yes."

"When did you two go to the first meeting?" Carrie asked.

"About two weeks ago. They have weekly meetings open to the public. They have other meetings through the week that only members go to."

"So it is a closed group that you must be a member of?"

"Mmmm, yes, I guess you could put it that way. They want to recruit huge numbers of people who care about the environment, but they are picky. Actually, they talk more about creation than they do the environment. To them, those words are interchangeable."

"So they want to get many people who are as passionate about creation as they are?"

"Yes."

"What are they so picky about?" This was all quite confusing to Carrie. If they wanted numbers to build a large group, then why were they so picky about who became part of it.

"Before I started going to ZDV, I looked at environmental issues as something simple like changing how I lived each day. Not using styrofoam, not wasting electricity, buying an electric car. You know, what I could do personally as an individual to help improve the environment.

"But they looked at it in a more spiritual sense. They felt that it was imperative that we all do those things, that if we made right moral choices in our daily lives as a form of worship, creation itself would rise up and begin to heal on its own.

"We've stolen the spirit of creation by living immoral lives. Then we've added insult to injury by being irresponsible in our use and waste." Gracie finally paused.

While Carrie was trying to formulate the perfect next question, she was also trying to decide if Gracie had bought into their hype.

"Gracie, this is Sheriff Markum. What is your honest opinion of this group? Was it something you wanted to be part of, or did you feel they had gotten a little off center?"

Exactly what Carrie had been trying to find the words to say.

"The more I listened to them, the more passionate about the environment I became. I firmly believe that we have to do more to protect our environment." Gracie paused. "But... I was never brought up to worship creation. I think we were made stewards of it and that we should be good stewards, but they literally worship creation."

"Did you and Amanda go back after that initial meeting?"

"We did. We joined that night after the first meeting. We were both so excited and ready to do whatever we needed to do. It was almost like an alter call at a church where they asked people who wanted to join their group to come forward after the meeting. Once the others had left, they had a little ceremony where we were joined to them."

"Can you tell us about the ceremony?" Carrie asked.

"Yes, well, we just stood and had to recite after Sharma a

creed of sorts. We each had to do it individually, not as a group. Once we had all said the creed, they gave us a silver coin to confirm our membership."

"Do you still have your coin?"

"I do."

"How many meetings did you two go to before Amanda disappeared?"

"We went every day. I guess there were about six meetings that we went to total."

"Have you been back since Amanda's death?"

"Yes. I wanted to share with the group. I thought they would grieve for her like I do."

"And did they?"

The line was silent while they waited for Gracie's response. "No. Honestly, they didn't seem to care at all." Gracie was choking back sobs in order to talk. "After that night, I never went back."

"Can you tell me about the last meeting you went to before Amanda's death? What night was it and everything you can think of about that meeting, no matter how small?"

"It was on Saturday before she disappeared. We had gone to the ZDV and worked printing and folding flyers."

"Her parents said she went to the movies with her boyfriend Matthew the night she disappeared. Did you see her at all the Sunday?"

"No."

"Tell us about that Saturday."

"It was normal, but honestly, she and I were getting a little tired of going out there every day. We had the job of folding the flyers. We sat at a large table and just talked and folded flyers for two hours."

"Were there other people around?"

"Yes, down at the other end of the table."

"What did you talk about while you folded flyers?"

Gracie was trying to think. It had been just another conversation with her best friend. "We were talking about Matthew. She thought she was in love." Gracie hesitated.

"Go head Gracie, tell us everything," the sheriff urged.

"She was telling me about their sex life."

"Okay, I can understand you not wanting to tell us specifics, but can you give us a general idea of how the conversation went?"

"She was giddy talking about it. She talked about his body and how it felt to lie close to him in bed."

"Could you tell if anyone else overheard you?"

"Yeah, we were getting looks from the others at the end of the table. I told Amanda to be quiet. But she didn't care. It was almost like she was bragging about it."

"So ZDV had a strong moral code, yet you and Amanda were sitting there talking about having sex. Did it occur to you that the others in the group might think you were violating the moral code?"

"Gracie?"

"No. I mean, it isn't wrong to have sex with someone you love is it?"

Sheriff Markum thought about how she should answer Gracie. She knew in her heart that morality was essential to living a good and godly life, but that a person couldn't do it on their own. They needed a relationship with God in order to live that moral life.

"What I believe isn't important Gracie. Did they ever tell you what their moral code was specifically?"

"No. I think they just assumed that we knew."

"Is there any place at all that they have the moral codes written down?" Sheriff Markum asked.

"Not that I know of. I'm still not sure what being moral has to do with reviving creation."

"Nothing Gracie. Nothing at all."

CHAPTER 17

Harley had made it in for a half day of work. He had to take it easy, but his ribs were healing nicely. He couldn't lift, but he could stand behind the counter and check people out. He also did other simple paperwork tasks and helped Claudia prepare invoices.

At twelve-thirty he was getting his coat to clock out and leave when River came through the front door. Immediately, the hair on the back of his neck stood up and his body tensed.

However, River didn't look the same. His walk was not the same, nor was the way he held himself. It also appeared he was hesitant to approach Harley.

"River," greeted Harley, standing tense waiting for confrontation.

River stood with his hands shoved in his jeans pockets as he looked down and to the side.

"I need to apologize to you. The sheriff has us coming

in, but I had to come tell you on my own how sorry I am. I knew if I waited until we got there, you wouldn't know for sure if I was apologizing because I meant it or because I had to."

It dumbfounded Harley. He remembered the roller-coaster of emotions he'd experience this week. First afraid of River, then furious, then worried that he was stranded in the blizzard. He wasn't sure what he was feeling at that moment.

"Thank you."

"I know I can't fix it. I could give you excuses, but what good are they? Anyway, I just wanted you to know, I'm sorry. I really am." River turned to leave and Harley called out.

"Hey, want to drive me to the sheriff's office? I was going to walk over there since it hurts so much to drive, but since you are here…" Harley smiled.

And River smiled. All was forgiven, if not forgotten. Harley wasn't sure he could just dive in and be buddies with River the way Blaine was. He and River had never had that kind of relationship. But it seemed there might be hope.

Blaine was waiting for Harley outside the sheriff's department when River pulled up with Harley in tow. With all three of them together for the first time in several days, the silence was awkward.

Suddenly they all three started to talk at the same time, then stopped and laughed. Their nervous laughter was disrupted when Milford opened the front door and yelled for them to come on in.

The sheriff's office was quiet. Milford was at the front

desk and Derek was at his computer. They could see the sheriff through her open door. There was no sign of the OSBI agents or Randy or Amelia.

The three stood unsure of what to do. They had kicked the snow off of their boots and stood in the puddles that were forming. Blaine had removed his hat and was spinning it slowly in his hands.

"Sheriff, you have visitors," yelled Milford.

The sheriff looked up and motioned for them to come on back.

The solemn trio walked into her office and stood waiting for reprimand. The sheriff stood and motioned for them to sit. Harley and Blaine took the chairs in front of her desk, and River waited while the sheriff pulled a folding chair from the other room.

"I'm surprised to see you all arrive at the same time. Did you car pool?" She joked.

"No ma'am, I rode with River. Blaine came in his truck," Harley said quite seriously. Sheriff Markum's eyebrow rose. They didn't even seem to think it was unusual for River to bring Harley to the station.

"We have a serious matter to discuss. River has admitted to the assault on Harley. He was armed with his rifle, evidenced by him shooting out the tire. By all rights, Harley you should press charges. However, this will go on River's record and he will do jail time, possibly serious jail time."

The three felt like someone had simultaneously hit them in the gut. River recovered first. "Sheriff, I've thought about it a lot this week, and it's the right thing to do. I know I committed a crime and I'll accept the punishment."

Harley was visibly disturbed. "No. No. No." He sat shaking his head.

"River I was so pissed at you. Man… I wanted to kill you. But, I would rather us start over and try to put this behind us. That is, if the sheriff thinks we can."

Sheriff Markum sat and looked at the three boys, men really, but she would never stop thinking of them as boys. River's remorse showed painfully on his face. Harley displayed an equal amount of sorrow and forgiveness. Blaine just sat quietly stone-faced, afraid of the potential outcome.

"I can't let an incident this serious go unpunished. I just can't. But I'm not sure that the judge would hand down an appropriate sentence either. River if you will agree to one hundred hours of community service, my choice, I'll re-address the situation at the completion of the hours. How does that sound to you?"

"Yes. That sounds fine. So that means, if I do my hours the right way, however you say to do them, then it will all be done?"

"Yes. But now I'm leaving myself some leeway here. If you don't do your hours or give me any grief before your hours are complete, then we will have to take this to the judge."

Relief washed over River. He was thankful. "Yes ma'am. Just tell me what to do and when to do it."

"Be back here Monday morning at nine a.m. We'll start then. Now go on and get out of here and stay out of trouble." Sheriff Markum was trying not to grin. Sometimes living in a small town where she knew the people, was well worth it. She knew these were good boys that had just stepped in a bucket of muck and she hoped it was behind them.

The three exited the sheriff's office much quicker than they had entered. Their moods were jovial and lighthearted.

"Hey it's Saturday. Let's go have some fun," said Blaine as they stepped outside.

"What should we do?" Harley asked.

"What if we go to the cabin and do it right this time? Let's go buy a ton of food and beer," River suggested.

"You ain't going to make us walk home again, are you," Harley asked.

River grinned and slapped Harley's back. "No, sir." Harley winced and River apologized. Blaine just laughed. It was good to have his friends back.

"So let's talk about this morality clause the ZDV has," said Carrie. She had watched the boys leave and headed into the sheriff's office.

"Okay. I have a feeling that is the motivating factor in all of this."

"I agree. What if, those two girls were getting in deeper and deeper? They were being watched and evaluated, but never knew it. When someone overheard Amanda talking about having sex with her boyfriend, they knew she had violated their moral code and that she must be dealt with." Carrie gauged the sheriff's reaction.

"Sounds plausible. However, you can't tell me that

everyone there adhere's to a strict moral code. And anyway, what was the code? If they never saw the code, how could they know they were violating it?"

"But maybe not everyone talks so blatantly about it. Amanda was sitting there in the group bragging about her indiscretion. Maybe it wasn't so much that she had been immoral, but that she was bragging about it."

The sheriff nodded her head while thinking. "So, Beau Johnson. Let's say he finds a lost coin. Think's he's found a gold mine, then he shoves it in his pocket. But someone from ZDV see's him, feels it is a sacred coin and kills him because he has violated some holy law. Then, Corey Stiles is a member of the group and does something like Amanda and they kill him for it."

"Culling the herd? Looking for purity?"

"Hmmm. Something's still off about it all. If that is the case, then they have strayed a long way from that ancient religion. I think it was wacky in the first place, but these people have taken it to a whole new level."

"Did you ask Gracie if she had ever seen Corey Stiles there?" Sheriff Markum asked.

"She didn't know Corey. He went to school at a little town east of here. I sent her a photo, but she couldn't remember, she thought maybe, but not sure," Carrie replied.

"Have you heard from Amelia?" Carrie couldn't help but feel a little concerned. Her last foray into undercover work with Lainey had nearly cost Lainey her life. Carrie still struggled with guilt over that case.

"No, not yet. I keep wanting to pick up the phone and

call her, or text her or something, but I don't want to do anything that would put her in jeopardy."

"Do we have anything actionable yet on ZDV?" Carrie knew they didn't, but thought she would ask, anyway.

"No, and we can't move too quickly or they will pack up and be gone to parts unknown before we can even get a warrant. No, we have to make this air tight."

"Where do we go from here? Just wait on Amelia?" Carrie asked.

"That's all I can think of for now. Did Dr. Franz ever get back to you?"

"I'll check."

"There has to be something somewhere that we're missing. You've only been here less than a week, but I've been dealing with this for almost four weeks. I don't want to find another body before we know more."

"Did you notice that the first three bodies were burned, killed on a Sunday evening?"

"That fact hadn't escape me, but I don't know what that means. And, if it was important, why did they deviate?"

"Does the cult have meetings on Sunday? Are those sacred days to them?"

"Another question for Gracie. I'll call her."

Carrie nodded and walked back to the war room. Where was Lainey? That one thought gnawed on her continually. Was she dead or alive? Carrie knew she had to prepare herself for the worst.

~

Jacob watched the two new girls. It was very clear that Mandy was completely on board and ready to do whatever was necessary to help creation rise to its glory once again. But that Amelia girl was simply a hanger on, and just by being here, she disrespected the group and their mission.

Sharma led Mandy back to his office and Amelia followed. Soon they were both seated and waiting for Sharma to discuss living on the compound, while Jacob stood in his usual spot in the back corner, watching Amelia.

Realizing she had nearly revealed her true feelings, she was determined to put those feelings aside and dive into the thick of it.

Sharma discussed what one needed to do to move to the compound. Amelia expressed excitement on purpose before Mandy could, surprising everyone.

They all turned and looked her way. "Sharma, the more you talk, the more excited I become. I'm ready to move to the next step too!" Then turning to Mandy, she said, "Mandy we can move here together. That would be wonderful, don't you think?"

It overcame Mandy with joy and she reached over pulling her best friend into a huge bear hug. "Yes Amelia, I do!"

Mandy released Amelia and turned to look at Sharma. "We're ready now. What do we do?"

Sharma smiled. "There is an induction ceremony that you need to go through. We usually do it at one of our members only meetings, but we don't have another planned until Monday." Sharma looked at Jacob. "Jacob, gather the residents and let's go ahead and have an induction ceremony right now. Then we can get Mandy and Amelia moved in."

Jacob nodded and turned to leave. He was completely against this. It was too soon, and he knew Amelia was not a true believer in her heart. But, he did as Sharma instructed and went from cabin to cabin requesting everyone's presence for the induction ceremony.

They were all very excited to have new members moving to the complex. The cabins were small, but could house up to four people. Sharma had decided that since there were empty cabins, they would allow Mandy and Amelia to room together in a cabin by themselves until they needed the space.

Jacob slipped into Sharma's office while the girls were in the main hall being prepared for the ceremony.

"Sharma, you know how I honor you, but there is something that I must say." Jacob was being careful to maintain a quiet and submissive voice with Sharma.

"Go ahead," said Sharma.

"I'm concerned about the new girl Amelia. I don't believe she is fully on board. I'm concerned that she is just joining and moving here because her friend is."

Sharma smiled and patted Jacob on the shoulder. "Jacob, don't worry. It will be fine. Since she will move here, it won't take long for her hesitations to subside."

"Sharma if I may make a suggestion. I think we should split them up and put each one in a cabin of long-term residents. I fear that if we leave them together, Amelia may spread her concerns to her friend. I fear it may do more damage than good."

Sharma considered what Jacob had just said. "No, I believe it is best we keep them together, however, I will do this... Let's put them in a cabin of residents and move two seasoned members out to a cabin by themselves. That way the friends will be together, but with two long-time members to help them."

"Yes, Sharma." Jacob still had his reservations about Amelia, but knew that Sharma's final decision should not be challenged. He turned to leave with a simple bow to Sharma.

Once back in the main hall, the residents were all seated and excitement rippled through the air. Mandy and Amelia sat on the front row, ready. Amelia's palms were sweaty. She didn't enjoy having to go through this, not knowing what it involved. She knew she was still struggling to pull off the act that she was on board.

Someone in the back sounded the gong, and Sharma entered. He welcomed the residents and apologized for the intrusion into their day. He then expressed his excitement over the two new recruits.

Soon, Mandy and Amelia found themselves standing on the stage repeating the creed, and holding shiny new silver coins. When Sharma placed the coin in Amelia's hand, she looked at it resting in her palm and a shiver went up her spine.

Marissa had laid in the dark closet for hours. No one had checked on her, fed her, or killed her.

She had shivered until she could shiver no more. The cold had made her sleepy, so she slept. When she was awake, her mind tormented her with all the wrong decisions and the prideful arrogance she had had. She thought she was too good to get caught. She thought she was impervious to danger. She thought she was smarter than the criminals.

All she could see was her greed for the story. Her need to get a career making story had been her only thought. Now she was not only in grave danger, but she had also put Brian, Mandy, and Doc in danger.

As she thought about Doc, tears fell on the blanket. She had fallen in love with him despite her best efforts. She had wanted to just play him and manipulate him to help her get her story. But, she hadn't expected him to be the man that he was. And he had fallen in love with her as well. And now she may never see him again.

Doc had been calling Marissa for hours, each time getting her voice mail. He was deeply concerned, knowing in his gut that they had caught her.

He drove to town and went to her hotel room. There was no sign of her and the desk attendant had not seen her either. He went to the newspaper, which was locked since it was Saturday.

Standing on the sidewalk outside of the newspaper office he shoved his hands deep in his jeans. He surveyed the mostly empty street, frowning. He knew searching all the usual places would yield nothing. Joe had found her and took her. He knew it.

Back in the warmth of his truck cab, he knew what he

had to do. He had to find Joe and rescue Marissa. He turned the key, and the heater blasted warm air at him.

He drove down an alley a street over from where Joe's warehouse was. He slowed to look between buildings, but could see nothing. Carefully, he wound through the surrounding streets and alleyways until he was where Marissa had parked the previous night. There was no sign of her jeep.

There was also no sign of any activity at the warehouse. He inched his way around to the back of Joe's warehouse. There, he saw a door he thought he could get into without raising suspicion. But once there, he realized it was firmly locked.

He was out of ideas. The thought to go to the sheriff crossed his mind, but he had no evidence that Joe had her and it would mean disclosing his involvement and wreck their entire plan. And it still wouldn't save Marissa.

The view from Riley's cafe was a good place to see who came and went through town. Doc went there, sat in a window booth and watched. It was two in the afternoon when he arrived and the diner was nearly empty.

Doc sat looking out the window of the diner nursing his coffee. He couldn't eat, but the coffee provided a small measure of comfort. Dirty snow was piled high in the gutters of the street where it had been graded to make way for the traffic. Cars were parked a little haphazard not wanting to pull into the snowdrifts.

The winter storm had kept most people inside. With few coming into town if they didn't have to, there was little activity for Doc to monitor.

He found his mind drifting to Marissa. He had dated when he went to college, but never allowed himself to become serious. He had a single-minded purpose, and that was to get his degree and get a job.

He had accomplished that goal. Once he was employed at the oil company, he'd felt some relief. But his desire to establish himself with his employer had seemed to take precedence over dating. There were several women he had taken out, but most drifted away, unable to compete with the hours he worked.

And honestly, he had never experienced the spark he had experienced with Marissa. In the city he had always been on guard when it came to dating and relationships. When he had come home, he had dropped his guard. Marissa had been a bright spot in his dark world. He wanted her back.

By five o'clock, he left to go back home. He stopped one more time by the hotel and was told once more that they had not seen her. His drive home was somber, as he feared the worse for her.

Marissa knew about none of Doc's searching. She had slept most of the day. Hypothermia was creeping in on her and she was at the point that she didn't even care.

SHERIFF MARKUM READ Amelia's text to Carrie.

"Mandy and I have been inducted into the group and have requested to live on the compound. We were each given a silver coin in the ceremony. It's just like what we found at the crime scene. We move into the compound Monday morning. In the meantime I am to pack and get things in order to move. I am back home and safe."

"I'm glad to hear she's safe," said Carrie. "Now, if we could just know that Lainey is safe too. Each day that there is no word, I grow more concerned."

"I know. But I also know that the search and rescue team are doing all that they can do. It's Saturday afternoon and there is nothing else we can do for now. I want you to come out to the ranch for tonight and tomorrow. You can come to church with us if you want to.

"Shep has been cooking again and he will be pleased to have someone else to cook for. I've complimented him for so long that he has started taking it in stride. A new fan will energize him."

Carrie thought that sounded good. "If you're sure. I don't want to intrude."

"You've seen our house. We built it for a large family and since the kids moved away from home, the rooms just sit empty. It's nice to have company." Sheriff Markum smiled at Carrie.

"I'll drive this time." Carrie smiled. "Let me go by the hotel and get a few things and tell the hotel staff that I'll be with you in case I'm needed."

By five p.m. Carrie was pulling into the drive of Sheriff Markum's sprawling log home. It could have easily sat on the side of a mountain in Montana. Carrie didn't normally like log cabins; she felt like a squirrel in a tree inside of them, but this one had expansive floor to ceiling windows that let in tons of light and the view of the forest.

They had also put sheetrock on the interior walls which were painted white. Only selective large beams spanned the high ceilings adding just the right amount of rustic charm.

Carrie parked in front and walked through the still deep snowdrifts to get to the portico and front door.

"You should have parked in the back," Sheriff Markum scolded as she opened the front door. "I never thought to tell you."

"I can't believe how much snow we still have."

"At least they are keeping the roads fairly clear now," replied the sheriff.

"Take the room you had before. I'll let Shep know you're here. I think dinner is almost ready."

Carrie took her bag to the upstairs room. She wished Lainey were there to enjoy the sheriff's hospitality. As much as she could have enjoyed the situation, she just couldn't completely do so Lainey still missing out in the cold.

She dumped her bag on the bed and stood before the window. The scene before her was of pine trees laden with snow. In the near distance rose the nearest mountain. Lainey was out there somewhere. *God, please find her safe and sound.*

Carrie's cell phone rang just then breaking into her thoughts. It was Randy.

"Hi," said Randy. It was good to hear his voice.

"Hi yourself." Carrie smiled.

"Any word on Lainey?" Randy asked.

"You know you would have been the first person I called had I heard anything at all."

"How's the case coming?"

"Well, only one more body since I came here. The clues are slow coming. It's pointing to a local cult that has its base in an ancient religion. But something doesn't ring true about it for me. The ancient religion fervently believes that cremation, or burning of bodies is sacrilege. If this new cult is patterning itself after them, then they would not burn bodies.

"Also, it confuses me. They worship creation, but particularly fire. They talk about sacrificing to fire, but they don't believe in burning bodies, so what it actually is they sacrifice to the fire, I don't know."

"Have you had any read-in from the academic world?"

"Yes, I emailed Dr. Franz at OU. He was very helpful. We've been emailing back and forth. Once we had some info on the name of the cult, I sent that to him, but he hasn't heard of it. It must be very small."

"I see. How are you?" Randy's voice held that familiar caring inquiry that Carrie had come to rely on when they were partners.

"I'm okay. I want to find Lainey, and I can't. I can't go get her. This wilderness is vast, and I have no idea where to look. I know the search and rescue team is out there looking and they are good and proficient at their job. I have to leave it up to them, and I can't stand it." Guilt rushed over Carrie. She still felt so responsible for the junior agent.

"You gave her to me to mentor, and now I've lost her in the worst blizzard this state has seen in years." Carrie wanted to say more, but what more was there to say?

"Carrie, you have done an excellent job. I made the right choice pairing her with you. Lainey is a good agent. She is making right decisions wherever she is. She knows the smart thing is to find a safe place and hole up there until they can rescue her."

"Yeah, you're right. I appreciate your confidence."

"Carrie, you know how good an agent you are. Don't second guess yourself or beat yourself up. Lainey will turn up and she will be okay."

Carrie appreciated Randy's words of encouragement. But they were only words that needed to be said, because what else could be said at this juncture? Randy and Carrie talked casually for the next fifteen minutes. Then, a knock on the door from Sheriff Markum announced that dinner was ready.

As Carrie walked into the dining room, the smells of another home-cooked meal welcomed her. She knew she didn't eat right, especially when she was in the middle of a challenging case like this one. She would forget to eat and then just grab something fast and consume it quickly.

"Welcome," said Shep beaming at Carrie.

"Oh, lasagne and homemade garlic bread. That looks awesome! Thanks Shep," Carrie was genuinely thankful.

The three sat, talked about other things besides work, and ate until they couldn't eat any more. Carrie watched how Shep and the sheriff interacted. She could tell from the look in his eyes when he looked at her, that he worshiped her. The sheriff was very respectful of Shep too. At work she was all take charge and in control, at home she seemed to appreciate having him to defer to.

It made Carrie long for something she hadn't let herself think about in years. She'd been about to be married to the love of her life when her parents had been killed. The trauma had changed her, and she had pushed Billy away. He had fought hard to stand by her, but Carrie had won out. Her meanness had finally pushed him away.

What if we had already been married when my parents had died? Would I have treated him the same or would I have clung to him for comfort? Her heart longed for that kind of intimacy again.

Carrie helped clean the table as Shep and the sheriff efficiently did the dishes. Once done, the three retired to the large living room where Shep threw another log on the fire. It seemed only right to lay conversation aside and enjoy the heat and comfort that only the fire could bring.

"Carrie, I think Shep and I will retire early. I'm beat and want to get some rest. Are you okay? Do you need anything?" Sheriff Markum asked.

"No. I'm good. May I stay down here for a while and enjoy the fire?"

"Of course. Feel free to make yourself some coffee, or tea, or whatever you can find. Make yourself at home."

The afghan was comforting as Carrie slid further down on the sofa and pulled it to her chin.

ONCE THE INDUCTION ceremony was over, Sharma gave instructions for Mandy and Amelia to go pack and bring their belongings back. He would allow them until Monday to pack and put their affairs in order. Monday would be the start of a brand new life for them.

It thrilled Amelia that they were being allowed to go back home. They had a tour of the cabin they would live in and had met their two cabin mates.

On the drive back to Wilburton, Mandy rattled on and on about a future where creation was perfect and humankind had taken its proper subservient place as caretaker of all creation.

Mandy was so lost in her dream world and telling Amelia her thoughts, that Amelia didn't have to be concerned whether she was saying the right thing. She couldn't have gotten a word in edge-wise if she had wanted to.

Mandy dropped Amelia off at her house at about six p.m. Amelia was starving, but wanted to make some serious plans. This undercover assignment was getting very real and dangerous.

Amelia thought about the victims. They had stripped each one of their outerwear, socks, and shoes. If this were to happen to her, she would want to have something that she could use as replacements.

She also knew she needed to be ready at any moment. She wasn't sure if her performance had sufficiently appeased Jacob. So, she wanted to be ready from this very moment on.

Being a size three and small-boned, she could put several layers on and still look average. She laid a tank top, t-shirt, button-up shirt, and a sweatshirt on the bed. As she stood and looked at them, she realized they wouldn't be the problem, even though if her coat was taken, these layers would definitely help.

She turned and began digging through her drawers. After a few minutes, she finally found an old pair of thick rubber bottomed socks she had been given in a hospital stay several years ago. She laid them on the bed and went to her pantry for a few supplies, returning with duct tape, baggies with zipper tops, and thin plastic shopping bags. Yes, they weren't environment friendly, but hopefully no one would ever know she had them.

Turning once again to her chest of drawers, she dug through another drawer. Finding what she had been searching for, a pair or cargo shorts, she threw them on the bed.

She folded the rubber-bottomed socks as flat and tidy as she could, putting one sock, a baggie, and a shopping bag in each pocket. She folded and refolded until she thought she had them laying as flat as possible in the cargo shorts pockets.

Time to try out her clothing plan, she first slid on a pair of tight ankle length athletic pants. Over that, the cargo shorts. She turned this way and that, looking in the mirror. Realizing the cargo shorts had other small pockets, she hurried to the spare bedroom and rummaged through a box of things her brother had left from when he lived with her.

Feeling like she had hit a gold mine, she pulled out a Swiss Army Knife, and a pair of nylon jogging pants. The knife slid perfectly into one of the smaller pockets. Digging further in the box she found another knife. A simple folding knife, slightly bigger than a regular pocket knife.

It slid into the other small pocket. Over it all, she pulled on her brothers nylon pants, pulled the drawstring tight, and returned to look in the mirror. Her brother was small like her and the pants fit well. There was only the slightest puffiness on her hips where the socks hid in her pockets.

She took two more pair of thick socks and laid them side by side on the bed, on top of another thin shopping bag. She laid each sock side by side, folded the bag over and taped it closed.

Taping the two ends of the package she had created, she wrapped it tightly around her waist and taped the ends together. She repeated that process with two pair of small stretchable gloves.

Placing those on the front, just above her abdomen, she taped that package to the first. *I'm getting plumper by the minute,* she laughed to herself.

Then on went the tank top, t-shirt, and button-up shirt. With the added padding the buttons hardly met and looked odd, so she pulled it off an opted for a long-sleeved t-shirt.

Another thought occurred to her, and she took two stocking caps and wrapped each one in a shopping bag and taped them around her calves, just below her knees. From the added layers and the effort she had been putting in, she was growing hot.

She had intended to not remove any of the hidden items regardless of how hot or uncomfortable it was. She would sleep in them and bathe around them until this was all over; she would have to figure out a way to endure the added heat. Although with the recent winter storms they had been having, that shouldn't be too difficult.

Over the long-sleeved t-shirt she added a hoodie, hoping her coat would still go over it all. Grabbing the ankle holster to re-attach it, she reconsidered. She wanted to play this out to catch the killer, but while hiding extra clothing was one thing, hiding a gun was another. At the last minute, she decided that she would leave it and rely on the two knives she had in her shorts.

Her furry Ugg's slid on well over the two pair of socks she had placed on her feet. Of course both pair would be stripped away if the killer wanted to bare her feet. Content with her reflection in the mirror, she decided she didn't look much larger than before.

Sharma had instructed them to pack light. Possessions were a hinderance to life and since they were sharing the cabin with two others, there was little room for unnecessary items.

She grabbed a duffle bag and threw in additional clothing items, the duct tape, and other random items that she thought she might could use in the event of a capture.

Throwing the duffle bag by the front door, she noticed a small can of pepper spray she'd taken from a pocket a few weeks ago and had thrown on the entry table. She quickly stuffed it into the pocket of her hoodie.

Now what? It was Saturday night, and she was hungry and tired of working so hard. She grabbed her purse, coat, and car keys and headed for the door. Buster's sounded good for a burger and a beer. Her stomach growled in anticipation as she locked the door behind her.

CHAPTER 18

Blaine, Harley, and River gathered everything they could think of to take to the cabin. They had each called their parents to tell them they were going camping. They each got an earful, but they were over twenty-one, even if just barely, so they did what they wanted.

An hour passed quickly in the grocery store. They kept thinking of all the things they wanted to eat, but then remembered there was little way to cook in the cabin.

High on reconciliation, Blaine suggested they buy a microwave, then Harley reminded him there was no electricity. Then River said, "We could get a toaster oven."

Blaine slapped the back of his head. "That takes electricity too, dummy." And they all broke out in laughter.

"We need to get pots and pans we can cook over the fire in the fireplace," said Harley. Both Blaine and River looked at him in awe, then laughed hysterically.

There was a portion of one aisle in the grocery that had pots and pans. "We need cast iron," said Harley. There were only two types, and they got one of each.

They bought steaks, and cans of beans. They bought boxed cereal and milk. They bought several kinds of chips and salsa, cookies, and donuts. When they checked out the cashier said, "That will be $165.37."

The three stood there wide eyed, then coming to their senses, they began pulling out their wallets. They split it pretty much three ways and headed to River's jeep. It was always the vehicle they took to go to the cabin. It had extra large rough terrain tires and could drive over a small car, although they had never tried.

The snow had melted back on most of the roads in the lower areas, but in the mountains where it was much colder and long shadows from the pines fell, it was still very deep.

The three didn't care though, the relief of their recent battles were quickly receding in the background. The challenge of driving up the mountain in the snow seemed like a great adventure to them.

It took about twice as long to get to the cabin as it normally did, but they did get there and immediately started unloading the food.

Blaine gathered kindling for the fire and worked on starting a fire in the fireplace. Harley squatted down beside him and just watched as the fire fought to come to life. So fragile and frail in its infancy, but a raging force once it found its footing.

The kindling took and Blaine sat a small dry log on the

fire. He would add to the pile as the fire took hold and grew.

The hunt and gather of food, the trip up the mountain, and the friendly banter during it all, helped to affirm a friendly bond. River had never been friendly with Harley. Harley had come into their fold after River's mood swing.

Now, it was as if they had all three been friends for years. They sat now staring at the raging fire drinking their beer and just enjoying the solitude of the forest.

As River sat, he thought about his uncle Joe and all that he had learned. Why had he never seen it before? Why had he had more reverence for him than his own father?

"Let's play cards," Blaine said finally tired of just sitting.

"Poker?" River asked.

"Sure, with toothpicks. I gave all my money for food," Blaine replied.

"Toothpicks it is!"

CARRIE COULDN'T SHAKE thoughts of Billy from her head since watching Shep and the sheriff. Redirecting her thoughts didn't work. She snuggled down into the afghan and closed her eyes.

Call him.

Where did that thought come from? I will not call him. Now I'm talking to myself about it.

Call him. You owe him an apology.

A knot formed in the pit of Carrie's stomach. She wanted to call him, but then again, she didn't. *What would she say after all this time? What would he say? Really, what would she say?*

She turned her wrist and looked at her watch. It was only 8 p.m. But, he'd gotten married and had a family by now. She couldn't disturb that.

Call him.

She looked at the black face of her phone. His number probably wasn't even the same anymore.

Call him.

I'm going to the nut-house for arguing with myself.

She scrolled through her contacts until she saw Billy's name. She tapped it and her phone started to dial. *Oh no!* She had just wanted to open the contact, not dial it. But before she could hit the big red button to end the call, a man's voice said, "Hello." It was Billy's voice.

She couldn't speak. Her chest had tightened, and she froze from head to toe.

"Carrie, is that you?" Billy asked.

"Yes," Carrie finally managed to say.

"Are you okay?" Billy asked. There was genuine concern in his voice.

"I'm sorry to bother you," Carrie began. "I just felt like I needed to call you."

"Are you okay?"

"Yes, I'm okay. There has just been a lot happen in my life and I wanted, well needed, to call you. Billy. I'm so terribly sorry for how I treated you. I broke when my parents died and I couldn't feel anything but a deep dark despair. I'm so very sorry you had to suffer because of it."

Carrie was now crying and her words had just tumbled

out. She had carried the burden of how she had treated Billy for months now and it felt good to tell him just how sorry she was.

Billy sat quietly and listened to her tearful apology. She had been the love of his life and when she had turned so viciously on him, it had stunned him. He had wanted to be there for her and help in whatever way she needed him to, but she just wanted to wallow in her anger.

When it seemed like she had said all that she had meant to say, Billy said, "I could sit here and tell you just how badly you hurt me, but you already seem to know that, so I won't. You were the love of my life Carrie. I would have done anything for you."

"I know." She could barely speak amid sobbing. "It's no excuse, but it destroyed me when they died. I don't want anything from you, I just felt that since so much has changed with me the last year, I needed to reach out to you and ask you to forgive me."

"I appreciate that."

"I carried that hardness for eight long years. I never got close to anyone that entire time, so it wasn't just you that suffered. I'd locked myself into the worst kind of emotional prison."

Billy sat quiet thinking about what Carrie had just said. Did he have the strength to prolong this conversation, he wondered. Then finally he said, "So, what changed?"

"I met someone who showed me it didn't honor my parents to lock myself away emotionally. Well, that was the first thing that happened. Then, I had an encounter with a lady who had a genuine relationship with God. She had

had a much harder life than I ever had, but she reached out to me in a loving way and taught me how much God loved me despite how horrible I'd been."

"I see."

"It seems that God has been filling my life with many people this last year to help me heal. And not just get better, but grow well beyond where I had been."

"That's good."

"Anyway, I don't want to disturb you any more. I know you're probably having family time. I just needed to say what I did."

"I'm not having family time."

"I thought you had gotten married."

"I did, but my marriage only lasted a year and we never had children."

"I'm sorry. I had heard you had gotten married. What happened?" Carrie asked genuinely concerned.

"She wasn't you."

Carrie sat silent.

"I came out of our relationship damaged too. You broke my heart, and I went into that next relationship damaged and angry. She paid the price for it."

"I'm so sorry," Carrie's voice was barely above a whisper.

"Well, that was several years ago."

"You never remarried after that?"

"No. I knew I needed to work on me, and I wasn't ready to endure the pain of another failed relationship." Billy snorted a laugh. "I actually wound up at church too. Do you remember Jack? Well, he kept hounding me to go to church with him. I wanted no part of it."

"But you finally gave in?"

"Yeah, I finally gave in. It grew on me and eventually I began to forgive you and the hurt started to go away, and one day I realized that God had healed my heart."

"So why have you not found someone?"

Billy was quiet. He didn't know what to say.

"I just haven't found the right someone."

BUSTER'S WAS CROWDED. There were few places to party around the small town of Wilburton, and with the snow and ice on the roads, Buster's was hopping.

There were no booths or tables available, so Amelia squeezed into the only vacant stool at the bar. "Hey Dan, can you get me a cheeseburger, and a beer? Whatever is on tap will be fine." Dan nodded agreement, and shouted the order to the back, over the din in the room.

The burger was great and so was the beer. She drank two of them before she turned around to survey the crowd. A group of her friends were playing pool, so she joined them. It was turning out to be a fun evening.

She'd arrived about eight and at eleven o'clock she was tired, and hot. "Hey, I'm going to step outside for a bit," Amelia said to the friend standing closest to her.

Craving the rush of cool air the outside would bring, she left her coat on the back of the chair she had been sitting on.

She felt like she was on the verge of a heat stroke and considered stripping off additional layers.

The icy air was just as refreshing as she had expected and she stood for several seconds just relishing the icy rush. She stood with her eyes closed, feeling her hot cheeks rapidly cool down.

Not looking forward to going back inside the hot bar, she decided to call it a night. She went back in, grabbed her coat and just simply waved goodbye to the crowd.

She only lived a few short blocks from Buster's, so in no time, she was pulling up in her driveway. She hopped out of her car and hit the key fob to lock the door. But before she made it to her front porch, she was grabbed from behind.

The perpetrator had her neck in a lock, with their other hand covering her mouth while also pinching her nose closed. Her feet slid in the snow as she tried to regain and hold her footing. Her gloved hands couldn't grip anything of substance as she groped and reached for something, anything to force her release.

Remembering the pepper spray in her hoodie pocket, she fought around her coat and into the hoodie pocket. Her gloved hands continued to hinder movement. When she could finally remove the spray from her pocket, it was too late.

Despite her attempts to fight back, blackness came, and she was drug back to her car. The killer had picked up her discarded key fob and unlocked her car door.

He had parked his car a few blocks over in a busy

parking lot and walked to Amelia's house and hid. An hour later, she had pulled up in her drive.

Working quickly before she woke, he pulled off her coat, boots, and both pair of socks. Then unceremoniously, dumped her into the backseat of her own car, placing her clothing items in the front seat next to him.

Each time he had taken action like this over that past few weeks, he'd felt a sense of accomplishment. Sharma hadn't understood the need to rid the earth of those who were antagonistic to their cause. Being indifferent was one thing, most were. But once presented with their cause with a passionate and succinct outpouring, how could they not eagerly come on board?

The worst though, was when they gave it lip service and joined their cause only to flaunt their disregard in the face of creation by purposely making immoral choices.

He'd been right about Amelia. She couldn't wait to get home and go to a bar, drinking and playing around all evening. He felt quite noble about pursuing and ridding their cause of the blackness set to destroy them from within.

Sharma was against violence, but this was his sacrifice to creation. As he drove, he chanted to creation…

Oh great creation, I bring to you another sacrifice, for you have said that one who sacrifices unto fire with fuel in his hand is given happiness.

Oh great creation, I bring to you another sacrifice, for you have said that one who sacrifices unto fire with fuel in his hand is given happiness.

Oh great creation, I bring to you another sacrifice, for you have said that one who sacrifices unto fire with fuel in his hand is given happiness.

From the backseat, Amelia moaned. Jacob quickly pulled over to the side of the road. He opened the rear passenger car door where Amelia's head rested. He took a white rag and shoved it into her mouth.

Turning her over, he bound her arms behind her with a long strip of cloth. Then he continued to wind a long wide cloth around her from her shoulders to her knees. This would protect her and make sure no marks were on his sacrifice while he was trying to control her. This would keep his sacrifice pure and undefiled.

By the time he had finished, Amelia was completely awake and struggling against her captor. But her full consciousness had come too late. Jacob had already fully bound her in such a way that she could not release herself.

Her mind raced as she lay in the back of her own car. Her shoes, and socks had been removed as well as her coat. She was thankful that she had planned ahead by bringing additional clothing items, but bound the way she was, there was no way to reach them.

Okay, she just had to play along and when the right time came, she would take her opportunity and escape.

Her car had not had time to warm from the short trip from Buster's to her home and the heater was now on low, as if the man wanted it to be cold in the car.

The glow of the dashboard shown on the silhouette of the man. It was Jacob! She inwardly chastised herself for not playing along better at the compound.

The moon was full, and she could see the tall pines

whipping quickly by as he drove. From her current vantage point, she could not determine where they were. Suddenly the car slowed, and the road changed. It was rougher than before. They had gone from a highway to a smaller, but still paved road.

Amelia was trying to determine how long and in what direction they were traveling, but it was difficult in her state of heightened distress.

Gravel crunched underneath the tires and the car came to a stop. Icy cold wind rushed in as Jacob exited the car. The door at her feet opened ushering in another icy blast as she felt herself being pulled out of the car.

Her bare feet landed on a gravel-covered area, still packed with snow. The gravel bruised her feet as it pushed through the icy barrier. She knew with her feet bare in the icy snow, frostbite would soon follow.

This is how he controlled them, by keeping them bound and their feet bare in the cold. He shut the door to the car and pulled her along. Bundled and bound in an almost mummy type fashion, she could only stumble along at best. Her feet were rapidly growing numb and soon the sharp rocks and sticks that broke through the snow were unnoticeable.

Tears began to fall from Amelia's eyes freezing to her now cold cheeks. The wind was harsh and caused the wind chill to plummet.

Amelia's numb toe hit a rock hard, and she stumbled forward, pulling Jacob down with her. The two of them tumbled for a few feet and then landed at the base of a tree.

They lay there face to face with Jacob's body pinning her

down. By the light of the moon, Amelia could see the face of a man so deranged, he was unrecognizable.

Standing quickly and jerking her back into a standing position, he hoisted her small frame up and over his shoulder. For the next mile or two, she bounced along as he held her tightly.

THE DOOR FLEW open to the dark closet and Marissa barely noticed. She was suffering from mild hypothermia and just wanted to sleep. She had had nothing to eat or drink since being taken captive and had become severely dehydrated.

When she didn't rouse at the opening of the door, a man stepped in and scooped her up into his arms to carry her to his Range Rover. Her head lolled to the side.

Earlier in the day, they had taken Marissa's jeep to an associate nearby who had a chop shop, and it was now in a thousand pieces, vin numbers gone. The other man opened the back, and he threw in Marissa. The entire time, she barely opened her eyes.

The Range Rover rumbled easily up the mountain where they had prepared a place to dispose of Marissa. The men laughed and joked the entire trip as if what they were about to do, was nothing at all.

An hour after retrieving Marissa from the warehouse, they pulled into a clearing. The driver got out and went to stand beside a rudimentary cross type structure they had put together.

"Get her out and I'll get the rope," the driver said.

Marissa was unceremoniously pulled from the vehicle and laid on the cross. Then men wound the rope tightly around each wrist and her ankles making sure that each was tied tightly and securely.

At the foot of the cross was a deep hole they had dug earlier with post hole diggers. As soon as they had secured Marissa to the cross, the men lifted the cross by the cross-beam, pushing the bottom post into the hole. As the cross dropped into the tight hole, it stood upright.

Marissa moaned slightly from all the agitation. It filled her mind with confusion but she could not arouse herself enough to realize why there was movement. Once the cross became still, she slipped back into slumber.

Earlier, the men had gathered kindling and small branches which they now lay at the foot of the cross.

"Ready?" One man said to the other. A nod affirmed that he was, and the fire was lit. The branches were damp from the snow, but the kindling soon caught. The men were content that the fire would soon rage and wanted to be long gone before it did.

Their doors slammed shut, and they followed the trail back down the mountain.

NIGHT WAS FALLING YET AGAIN, as were the snowflakes. The day had been bright and sunny and Lainey had enjoyed watching the birds flit from tree to tree through the small cabin window.

Her lethargy had increased, and she was feeling as

though she had a slight fever. When she had seen her broken leg, there had been no sign of broken skin that she could tell. The man had helped her move consistently which was very good.

However, the next time he came with some soup for her dinner, as he rolled her to her side, her breathing wheezed. She was getting pneumonia from being so stationary and breathing shallow for so long.

The man heard her labored breathing and cared for her. He fed her and turned her. Once he had her tucked in a new position, he said, “I’ll go soon.”

He had said that before, but then the weather had turned bad again. She assumed that he was waiting for clearer weather to go find help.

It was true the sun had shown brightly for most of the day today, but this afternoon the skies had turned gray again and the snow began to fall.

Lainey closed her eyes and drifted off to sleep once more.

As unconsciousness gave way to awareness, suddenly adrenaline surged through her body. Panic seized her as she realized flames were licking at her feet. She struggled to pull free, but heavy rope wound around each wrist and secured her tightly. She tried to draw up her feet up away from the fire, but they too, would not move.

How had she gotten to this place? This place of torment and fear? She was suspended on a large cross type structure, sturdy and solid. Surrounding the base of the structure was a circle of fire that was growing more ferocious by the moment.

The night was black and the only sound she could hear was the crackling of the fire. She screamed for help, but heard no response. There was no one there. There was no one to save her.

Sweat dripped into her eyes and stung as her body convulsed with wracking sobs. She jerked her hands and feet in an attempt to pull free from the tightly wound rope. Whoever had tied her had taken their time to ensure it securely anchored her to the post. The rope was thick and rough and gouged into her skin.

I have to think clearly. I have to calm down. I have to figure a way out of this. She took a deep breath, closed her eyes, and mentally offered a prayer of panicked desperation.

Almost immediately, she felt a soothing calm blanket her, but it was not a calming assurance that someone would rescue her, but one resigning her to her fate. She would die here today.

Just as resignation took hold, she heard voices and a rustling of the trees. Was it the men coming back to make sure the job was done? Should she scream for help?

"Help me. Help me, please."

The fire licked up and touched the bottoms of her feet. Marissa screamed out in agony, her eyes shut from the intensity of the pain.

Then the voices were closer. Someone was scattering the burning branches at the base of the cross.

She opened her eyes and looked down. Three young men were working feverishly to put out the fire.

"Are you okay?" Blaine asked Marissa.

All she could do was cry. Her chest heaved with sobs and she couldn't form words.

River pulled out his knife and began to cut her ankles loose from the cross. "Here, lift me up so I can cut her loose."

Blaine helped River climb onto his shoulders and he cut one arm loose. It dropped and dangled. River was trying to hold her while he cut the rope, not wanting her to drop and be hanging by only her wrist which could easily break from the weight.

Harley was also standing, holding her the best he could. When River cut the other wrist loose, she fell onto Harley and he staggered backwards.

"We need to get her warm, she's ice cold," said Harley panicked when he felt the icy coldness of her body resting on his shoulder.

Blaine stripped off his coat and helped to wrap her up in it. River had taken off his coat and wrapped it around her feet. Marissa laid lethargically in River's arms and let them care for her.

They had been playing cards at the table next to the window. The slamming doors of the Range Rover caused them to go still and watch. In just an instant, they could see the beginning of a fire and rushed out the door towards it, donning their coats as they ran.

The cabin was only about a hundred short yards from

where the fire had been started, but in these dense woods, one couldn't have seen the cabin from the fire.

Curiosity, as much as anything had driven the three to check out the fire. It wasn't the right time of year for a campfire, if someone was stranded then they would need help, but there was one other thing it could be. The sounds of the slamming doors and then catching site of the fire, brought one primary thing to mind — another killing.

Marissa was small and carrying her wasn't that difficult for Blaine. Harley had passed her off to him because of his ribs. As Blaine carried her, the other two kept her bundled in the coats.

Inside the cabin, they shoved furniture around and laid her next to the fire. "We don't want to get her too warm too fast. It could do more harm than good," said Harley. They knew he was right, so they scooted her from the fire and removed the coats. The air in the cabin was plenty warm.

The fire had startled Marissa out of the lethargy that hypothermia had drawn her into. Now she lay in excruciating pain from the burns on the bottom of her feet. She cried from the pain, unable to vocalize her trauma.

River looked at the bottoms of her feet. Large round blisters sat in a sea of dark soot. "We have to do something for her feet."

"We can't pop those blisters. That will be even worse," said Blaine.

For a few moments they tried to come up with a solution. They searched the cabin for something that would help. The cabin had been abandoned for years and no one except the three of them ever came there.

"Okay, let's do this," began Harley. "Let's take strips of fabric and dip them in water and wrap them gently around her feet. We can wash them off, then wrap them up. It won't help with the pain, but it may help keep them protected and keep the blisters from popping."

Blain stripped down and pulled off a white t-shirt he had on underneath his flannel shirt. The other two followed suit and soon they had several strips of white cloth and gently cleaned and wrapped her feet.

River went to the kitchen and pulled out a bottle of tequila he kept for those times when the thought of what his uncle had done overwhelmed him.

River knelt down by Marissa's head, poured the shot glass half full and helped Marissa drink it down. The straight tequila burned and Marissa pulled her head away.

Her crying had not subsided, and the boys were at a loss at what to do. River continued to urge her to drink. After four shots of tequila, one right after the other, Marissa's senses dulled. Her lips and face began to go numb, and she relaxed.

As she lay next to the fire with her rescuers sitting watchfully by, she attempted to reconstruct in her mind what had happened to her. So much was lost from the sleepiness and lethargy. It was difficult to build a solid timeline.

One thing she knew, she felt broken. Something was not the same within her. At that very moment, she didn't care if she wrote another story. She was thankful to the men who had rescued her, but that gratitude only did so much for her emotionally.

Cell phones did not work at the cabin, so no one even suggested that they try to call someone. No cell service had been one of the many attractive things about the remoteness.

"I think the best thing is for us to take care of her here tonight and take her into town in the morning. She doesn't need for us to get her back out in the cold tonight. It's also dangerous for us to try to drive down the mountain in the dark and snow," said River with the other two agreeing.

So they sat vigilantly by her through the night. None of them moving from her side, none of them sleeping, tending only to her needs until morning.

CHAPTER 19

SUNDAY

Amelia had no idea what time it was when they finally stopped walking. At the base of a rocky cliff, Jacob stopped and sat her on her feet. You'll have to walk the rest of the way.

She turned to look up and realized where they were; it was Robber's Cave. From where they stood it was a short climb up to the base and opening of the cave. She'd been here many times, but never in the dead of an icy and cold winter night.

She did her best to climb. She had never realized until then how much a person used their hands and arms to balance and adjust themselves when they walked. Jacob held onto her tightly so she would not fall and pull him down again.

The climb had been hard, and it exhausted Amelia. Before her, stood a large black oval gaping wound in the mountain's side. The site where many a villain had hidden out from whatever lawmen were after them, and today this villain had brought her there.

A screech in the night brought chills down her spine. The creatures of the night. *It is only a sound,* she told herself. *There are few predatory animals in Oklahoma. It was just a harmless bobcat.*

Jacob rubbed his hands together, also suffering from the cold. He had a pile of wood already gathered at the mouth of the cave and pulling a lighter from his pocket, quickly lit the kindling that rested on top.

Amelia hobbled toward the fire, but Jacob stopped her. "No, you don't. No warmth for you. We need to get you nice and cold so you just drift off into a sweet sleep. I can't have you fighting me while I get you ready for what I have planned for you."

Amelia felt like someone had punched her in the gut. Panic seized her and her mind raced to figure out what to do. They were so far away from any help, and the snow was still deep here in the mountains. If she tried to hobble away, she wouldn't make it very far.

Calm yourself down, Amelia. Keep a level head and think through this. He will make a mistake and you will be prepared. Then you can use the supplies you have bound to your body and you will get out of this, she encouraged herself.

She stood out of the warmth of the fire while Jacob squatted next to it warming his hands. Once warmed enough to carry on, he walked over to Amelia. We will not sacrifice to creation tonight. It will be tomorrow night, Sunday night.

I'm tired though, so I will need to tie you up out here so

you don't run away. He chuckled to himself as he thought how ludicrous it was, the thought of her running away.

He had a rope securely tied to a tree away from the fire. He dragged her there and tied the rope around her middle over her arms which were already pinned down with the long cloth wrapping. There was no way she could get her hands in a position to undo her prison.

Jacob checked everything twice before it satisfied him she wasn't going anywhere and retreated into the cave behind the fire. She could see by the light that he had a nice little cozy setup with a sleeping bag back there.

She had been working her tongue trying to get it in such a way that she could push the wadded cloth out of her mouth. The wad was sizable and filled her mouth pushing it almost fully open, making it difficult to shake loose.

Looking around, she hobbled over to the tree which the rope was tied to. She leaned towards it, pushing her mouth to the bark of the tree. She was hoping the protruding cloth would catch on the bark, snagging and then pull it loose.

It seemed simple in her mind, but by the time she had loosened it enough to push it out of her mouth. Her face was raw, but she could talk.

She didn't just talk; she yelled. "So you think you will leave me out here in the cold and sacrifice me tomorrow night! What a stupid idiot you are. I'll be dead by morning and your little plan will have been ruined. What an idiot!"

Amelia was that angry, but she also hoped to goad him into bringing her inside the cave for the night at least.

Perturbed, Jacob threw back the top of his sleeping bag and stormed over to her. He wanted to slap her but then she would be damaged. But wait, she already was. He could see the large scrapes across her lips and cheeks. *No!*

"What have you done?"

Amelia just glared at him in stoney defiance.

However, he knew she was right, so Jacob scrambled to untie the rope from the tree. Once done, he dragged her along to the cave, her feet stumbling to keep up. He pulled her deep inside to where there were several large boulders. He tied the end of the rope into a large loop, laid it on the cave floor and then tumbled the large rocks onto the center of the loop. Finally, with all his effort, he pushed the largest boulder that he could manage onto the pile.

"There, now you are inside until tomorrow." He said as he tugged the rope to make sure the rocks secured it.

It was only slightly warmer in the cave. There was no wind and with the fire at the opening of the cave, some heat worked its way toward her.

With the way he had her bound, she could only bend her knees fluidly, and slightly at her hips. Getting down on the cave floor to sleep would be another challenge. She got about six inches from the wall of the cave, fell backwards to it, and attempted to slide down the wall. As she slid, her legs pushed out in front of her.

Finally on the ground, she lay there awkwardly. Her feet were so cold and there was no way she could protect them. Exhaustion finally took her, and she drifted off to sleep. Her last thoughts were of planning how to not get burned alive.

But as she drifted away, still, no answer had come.

DOC DIDN'T SLEEP all night. He wrestled with his conscious. No matter what happened to him, he had to call the Sheriff and tell her about Marissa. It may be too late, even now.

He didn't want either of his brothers to hear his conversation, so he got in his truck and headed to town. He made the rounds once more to see if he could find Marissa, but there was no sign of her. There was also no activity at Joe's warehouse.

He went back to Riley's diner for breakfast and a hot cup of coffee. As soon as he ordered and received his coffee, he dialed the switchboard for the sheriff's office. A recording came on where he had to select his reason for calling.

Once through, he was speaking to Randy Turner who had switchboard duty for the weekend.

"I need to speak with Sheriff Markum," said Doc.

"She isn't in the office today. How can I help you?" Randy asked.

"I really, really need to speak with the sheriff." Doc had waited so long to call, that he didn't want to turn this over to a deputy and let it run its course. He wanted to talk to the sheriff now.

"If you will give me your name and number, and why you are calling, I'll get it to her asap."

Doc was trying to not lose his temper. He put his spare hand over his face and held his forehead. "You don't understand. It's urgent that I speak with the sheriff now!"

"Sir if you won't tell me the reason for your call, all I can do is take your name and number. I promise that I will get it to her." Randy was following protocol. The sheriff worked hard and if they put every little call through to her, then she would have no time to rest.

"Okay, okay." Doc conceded and gave Randy his name and cell phone. "It's about an abduction. But I don't want to say more until I talk to the sheriff."

"I'll call her now," Randy promised.

What have I done, Doc asked himself. I haven't helped my brothers by dragging them deeper into Joe's drug game and now Marissa is in dire danger, maybe even dead. And because I was trying to protect myself, I have waited until now to call the sheriff.

In just five short minutes, Doc's phone rang. It was the sheriff. Doc hurriedly explained to her the situation.

"Do you know for a fact that Joe has her? Did you see him take her?"

"No, but she isn't anywhere to be found. She was at Joe's warehouse where he does his exchanges. I haven't heard from her since."

"Okay, I will get a warrant to search the warehouse."

"I'll meet you there."

"No, you won't," warned the sheriff.

"Yes… sheriff, I will. I am responsible for her."

"I can't have you getting in the way."

"I'll stay out of the way. I just want to be there for Marissa, when we find her."

The sheriff conceded with her own demands. She and Carrie were ready quickly. She had made a call to the agent in charge at the DEA who promised to notify the FBI. They were to all meet there with a warrant in hand in thirty minutes.

Doc was already in town and he went back to the warehouse, keeping his distance. Soon unmarked black SUV's began to pull up and the Sheriff's and Agent Border's SUV's.

They had soon surrounded the warehouse and busted through the mechanics door next to the garage door.

Doc let them storm the building but when no one was found inside, he rushed in behind them. He searched frantically, looking for Marissa. Finally Sheriff Markum grabbed him by the shoulders and stopped him.

"Doc, she's not here." The sheriff held him until he made eye contact to her. "She's not here."

"Was she? In here, in the warehouse, I mean?" Doc asked.

"I can't tell. We'll have to get a forensics tech team in to run fingerprints, DNA, and scan for traces of drugs."

Doc sat down on an old chair and dropped his head in his hands. What was he going to do?

"Let's head back to my office so we can talk," said the sheriff as she placed her hand on Doc's shoulder, urging him up and along.

Heaviness weighed Doc down as he walked into the sheriff's station. His feet felt like lead and his body resisted all movement. He dropped like a rock into the chair offered him by the sheriff.

There was activity around him. The DEA and FBI were there and wanted to hear what he had to say. They were buzzing about in the bullpen, with activity of some sort, Doc didn't know what.

Sheriff Markum walked alone into the interview room

where Doc sat. She had encouraged the others to monitor from behind the two-way mirror. If she was unsuccessful at getting answers though, it wouldn't take them long to take over the interview.

She closed the door and sat a hot cup of coffee in front of Doc. The steam rose with an enticing smell and the promise of warmth, but he couldn't even lift his arm to bring it to his mouth.

"Let's start at the beginning," said the sheriff.

A tear rolled down Doc's cheek. Despite his best efforts, he was right where he had worked so hard to avoid. He took a deep breath and did his best to tell the sheriff the story of coming home when his momma had passed and how he wanted to only help his brothers.

His monologue included his fear of Joe, and how he wanted as far away from the drug business as possible. He told how he was trying to devise a plan to get him and his brothers out of it all.

"How did Marissa come into the picture?" Sheriff Markum asked.

Another tear rolled down. Doc told about what he had thought was a chance meeting and then realized she had been watching him to gain intel on her story about the drug trade in southeast Oklahoma.

He told the sheriff how they had fallen in love and of their plan to write the story as an exit strategy, hoping it would lead to Joe's incarceration without pointing the finger at Doc as the snitch.

They had learned of the warehouse from Brian who worked at the newspaper, a friend of Jessie Billings. Marissa was just going to do simple surveillance, take photos to include in the story.

When Doc had told the sheriff all that he could think of to tell her, he stopped and looked up at the window. "I wanted no part of the drug trade. Never! I left here to get an education and an honest job. I wanted to help my brothers get out without a death sentence from Joe. No one seemed interested in stopping him and I knew we were all dead men if we tried to leave."

"Thank you Joe," Sheriff Markum stood and left the room.

Carrie had been in the viewing room watching Doc's entire interview. She turned to the other agents in the room. "I know you guys always want the big fish. You think it's the best move in fighting the war on drugs.

"But I think you almost always forget the damage that is being done to those on the bottom rungs. They are real people, with real lives, that often get snared in something they can't get out of without the fear of death. We should be here for them, to fight for them too. Don't forget that."

With that last emphatic statement, she walked out of the room.

IN THE NIGHT, Marissa had found some relief and sleep. Her body temperature had risen to normal. At some point one of the three, she didn't know who, had placed a blanket on her, and she smiled.

They had kept the fire going and fed her tequila when it

seemed her pain had returned. By the first light of day, they were all three exhausted.

"I'm too old to stay up all night like this," joked Harley as he stood to go relieve himself out in the snow. His body felt stiff from sitting by the lady all night.

Blaine was in the makeshift kitchen sorting through the random foodstuffs they had brought. They had brought a lot of junk food, and very little real food that they would have to cook.

Knowing they would be here to eat breakfast they had bought cereal and milk, but also eggs and bacon. River came over to help Blaine. "Who do you think did that to her?" River whispered.

Blaine glanced over where Marissa lay, before whispering back, "I don't know. But there were two car doors that shut last night, so there were two killers and they don't know she's alive."

When Harley came back in, he went straight to Marissa to check on her. He sat back on the floor next to her, watching her.

Sensing his presence, Marissa rolled her head towards him, opened her eyes, and smiled.

"How are you this morning," Harley asked.

Marissa moved to try to sit up; Harley quickly moved to help her. She winced as the pain from her burned feet shot through her legs.

"I'm better. Thank you." Marissa was thoroughly humbled through her ordeal and entirely grateful to these young men.

"I need to call someone," Marissa said.

Harley started shaking his head before she had finished her sentence. "There's no cell service here. We'll take you back down the mountain soon. Harley and Blaine are getting some breakfast together and then we'll go. You need to eat, and we know we need to get you to the doctor."

They brought the cast-iron skillet to the fire, piled on more wood and sat it to rest on the fire, full of bacon.

Settling in to wait for it to cook, the three sat quietly again. They wanted to know what had happened to her, who had taken her and done this to her, but they sensed her frailty and sat quietly.

"My name is Marissa."

The three quickly gave her their names in return.

"I'm a journalist and I was writing a story on the drug cartel in this area. I was doing surveillance, taking pictures where they do their deals. They knocked me out and kept me in a closet. I don't know for how long."

River immediately tensed at her words, struggling to make sense of it. His uncle had done the same to him, but had let him go. His uncle tried to kill this woman. He suddenly stood up and walked out of the cabin.

Marissa looked up. "Did I say something wrong?" Her face had a woeful expression and her words were soft.

Harley shook his head and smiled at her. "No, it's okay."

LAINEY HAD SLEPT through the night, not even needing to relieve herself. She had been drinking water each time the man brought it to her, but she resisted it each time after a few sips.

She was eating less each time as well. All she wanted to do was sleep. Through the night she had dreamed and in the night she shivered from a feverish chill.

When she woke on Sunday morning, it was almost noon. Not even having the strength to open her eyes, she simply laid still listening for sounds. Only the birds could be heard.

Then she realized her fever had broken. The memory of the man sitting by her side through the night with a damp rag on her forehead rushed back to her. He had been there by her all night long.

She opened her eyes and turned her head looking for him. He should have brought her breakfast by now. But, she heard nothing. *Surely he wouldn't have gone without telling me,* thought Lainey.

The fire next to her was stoked and warm. She gave in to the urge to fall back asleep. *He'll be back again soon,* she assured herself.

As the door to the cabin scraped across the floor, Lainey's eyes flew open. It was the man. He was back. But the face looking down at her was not the man.

"Miss, are you Lainey Tate?"

"Yes, I am."

The man turned and confirmed to the other two men with him of her identity.

"Are you hurt?"

Lainey nodded. "I have a broken left leg, a sprained right ankle, and several broken ribs. Last night I thought I was coming down with pneumonia, but my fever broke in the night and I feel much better now."

The man pulled back the layers of blankets that had so carefully been tucked in beside her. "Who set your leg and wrapped your ribs?"

"The man who owns this cabin. He found me in the forest after I fell and brought me here. He has taken care of me this entire time. He cooked for me and helped turn me and relieve myself. He sat with me all night bathing my forehead with a rag. He made sure the fire never went out."

The search and rescue team just looked at her with confusion. Thc two that were standing looked around the cabin. There was no sign of anyone having lived there.

The one who had been kneeling next to her stood and conferred with the other two. Lainey couldn't hear what they were saying. Then he turned back to Lainey.

"Ma'am, there is no one living here. There is a thick layer of dust everywhere, and no sign of food, clothing, or anything else."

"He isn't here right now because he left to go get help for me."

The three men looked at each other, deciding it was best to not argue with her.

They had brought a stretcher basket to put her in and carefully worked to lift her and place her into the basket. As they lifted her into the basket, she could get a good look at the cabin for the first time. The men were right, there was no sign of life anywhere. Even the fire had died completely down.

It bewildered Lainey. Had she been completely delirious

the entire time? No, someone had brought her to the cabin, and had set her leg. They had fed her and taken care of her. They had kept the fire going for her, and last night had sat by her bed the entire time. She wasn't delirious, but she did not understand what had happened.

The three men carried Lainey out and through the forest. She told them the tale of having the wreck, getting lost trying to walk out then falling down the cliff face. She told how that man had found her and taken care of her, setting her leg and ribs, and keeping her warm and fed.

None of the three men said anything, they only listened.

AMELIA'S NIGHT WAS FITFUL. Each time she had awoke, she worked to wiggle her feet and toes to keep the circulation going. It was her greatest concern at the moment.

Birds chirping in greeting to the new day, eased into her dreams and she opened her eyes. It was a bright and sunny day. That was good. It would make escape much easier.

Sounds of Jacob scurrying about told her he was up and busy. His cheerful whistling was in dire contrast to her mood.

"Aww good, you're awake."

Amelia didn't respond initially, then, "I need to use the restroom."

He hadn't thought of that. He had captured all the others so late on Sunday before their sacrifice that hadn't been an issue.

"I have to go! If you don't help me, I'll spoil myself."

At the word spoil, Jacob jumped forward and reached for Amelia. He couldn't have her spoiled. Squatting down beside her, he began to shove up the wraps and jerk down her pants.

"Stop you fool! I need to do it myself!" She knew if he continued to pull her pants down he would uncover the shorts and added garments.

Jacob nervously looked about trying to decide what to do. "Okay, okay."

He helped her stand up and then began to shove the cloth wrap further up just enough to allow her to move her arms at the elbows, which also freed her hips. "Walk back into the cave and go there."

The rope wasn't long enough to walk very far, but Amelia took a few steps, turned her back to him, and smiled. She knew he was watching her closely so she would have to be sly. The first thing though was to relieve herself.

"Toss me the rag you had in my mouth."

While he scurried to find the rag, she slid her right hand into her cargo shorts and pulled out the knife with the folding blade. Fortunately, it was small enough she could palm it in her hand and he would never notice.

She hooked her thumbs into the waistband of the athletic pants and pulled all three items down at once, relieved herself, and used the rag, tossing it aside.

She stood and pulled all three pant layers back up again. Jacob was then immediately upon her, pushing her back to where she had slept.

"Please don't bind me up where I can't sit down." She looked at him with a pitiful look. "Where am I going to go barefoot? I can't even reach up high enough to undo the wraps."

Jacob didn't trust her, but then, she was right. He wobbled his head in a shaky nod, indicating for her to sit down as she was.

Relieved, she sat and pulled her frozen feet up to herself so she could massage them and hopefully warm them.

She wanted to get the socks she had bound to herself, but he would see her, take them away, and bind her back up.

Jacob sat by the fire eating from an open can of beans he had heated over the campfire. He never offered Amelia one bite.

Finished eating, he stood and walked out in front of the cave and looked around at the beauty of creation. He stood and raised his hands up and turned his face to the sun. Once again he began to chant…

Oh great creation, I bring to you another sacrifice, for you have said that one who sacrifices unto fire with fuel in his hand is given happiness.

Repeatedly, he chanted.

This is my chance, thought Amelia. She opened the blade on the knife and began to slice through the thick rope. Her knife was dull though, and she felt like she was sawing with a butter knife.

Sensing the movement in the cave, Jacob whirled around and ran toward Amelia. She in turn, whirled around from where she was sitting to stab at him with the knife.

He slapped her hand away, and the knife went skittering across the cave floor. "Stupid girl."

He attempted to hold her still while she struggled to resist him. He tugged and pulled and finally got the cloth binding back down below her elbows. She fought back, but was no match for his strength.

A few good kicks landed squarely on his legs, but with no shoes on, her blows had little impact.

He wanted to slap her, pound her, but he didn't dare damage the sacrifice. However, he shook her. Holding her by her arms he shook her violently and then thrust her to the ground.

She had damaged the rope where she had been gnawing on it with the knife, but he thought it was still formidable enough to hold her. *Where did she get the knife,* he wondered?

He reached his hands into the pockets of her brothers nylon athletic pants and groped around. Nothing. That must have been all she had.

He walked over to where it had landed, folded the blade and tucked it in his own pocket.

"Don't give me any more trouble. I mean it."

Amelia lay defeated on the cave floor. Sobs came rolling out. He would kill her and there was nothing she could do about it.

CHAPTER 20

The search and rescue team had been efficient in retrieving Lainey from the forest and bringing her down the mountain. She was swiftly transported to the hospital in McAlister. Sheriff Markum and Carrie had been notified and were waiting at the hospital for her arrival.

The sheriff was pacing the floor when her phone rang. It was Harley.

Harley, Blaine, and River were on their way to take Marissa to the hospital in McAlister, just as they had promised. Once they were back in cell service, they called Sheriff Markum.

"Aunt Wanda," Harley began.

"Yes, Harley? You know, I'm busy with something right now Harley." Sheriff Markum was feeling the pressure of so much going on. If there wasn't enough to handle, now she had Doc and that mess to deal with.

"I know, but we found a lady up in the mountains.

She'd been tied to a cross, and a fire started. We're taking her to the hospital now. I thought you would want to meet up there."

Sheriff Markum came to full alert, suddenly very interested in talking to Harley. "I'm at the hospital now. The missing OSBI agent was found and Search and Rescue are bringing her here as well."

Harley relayed the story of what had happened to Marissa. Her surveillance, her capture, how they had held her and then disposed of her. Harley continued with how they had been up at the cabin and had rescued her.

Sheriff Markum was dumbstruck. "I'm here in the emergency room now. I'll see you when you get here."

Just as she clicked off the call with Harley, the emergency room doors burst open and in came the search and rescue team pushing a gurney. It was Lainey.

Carrie rushed to her side and took her hand.

"Lainey, I'm so thankful you're here," Carrie spoke midst tears of joy.

"The man took care of me. I'm okay." Lainey smiled at Carrie.

"What man?" Carrie asked looking at the search and rescue team. They just looked confused and shrugged.

Carrie let them roll Lainey on into a room in the back to tend her and called Randy.

Not long after Lainey's arrival, Blaine, Harley, and River were carrying Marissa through the door. She was quickly deposited into a wheelchair and was rushed away to the back.

Once the rush of it all had settled down, Carrie and the

sheriff went to the cafeteria to get coffee and talk.

"So, was it the drug cartel doing the killing all along?" Carrie asked in disbelief.

It also confused Sheriff Markum. "I never thought that could be the case. This has just blindsided me. I never thought of this as an option."

"Once we see Lainey and Marissa again and get some answers from them, we need to go back to the station and lay this all out."

"Have you heard from Amelia today?" Carrie asked.

"No, too much else going on."

"Should we contact her to come back in?"

The sheriff thought about that for a moment. A check in her gut said no. "I just can't believe that the drug cartel has been solely to blame. I think the inconsistencies we've seen may have been that they tried to dispose of two people and used the burnings to make it look like it was the killer and not them."

Carrie nodded. "It would explain the inconsistencies."

It took two hours for them to get Lainey taken care of, her leg x-rayed and put in a proper cast and into a room.

Carrie and the sheriff sat as Lainey told the complete story of her wreck, getting lost, falling, and the man rescuing her.

"Lainey the search and rescue team said there was no man." Carrie was trying to present that to Lainey as comforting as she could.

"There was a man." Lainey told in great detail every movement, every detail of his face, hair, clothing, and his eyes.

"But the cabin was full of dust and there was no food or any sign of anyone. No one could have been there taking care of you and not disturbed the years of dust."

Sheriff Markum had been sitting quietly listening to the exchange. Lainey turned to look at the sheriff and asked, "Sheriff do you believe me?"

"I believe you Lainey." Carrie's head spun around to look at the sheriff.

"I believe you have experienced a miracle. I believe you were taken care of by an angel sent to minister to you until help could arrive."

As Lainey thought about what the sheriff had said, she began to smile. She thought back and could agree that he never talked about himself; he expressed no sign of worry or stress. And each time she needed something, he was just always mysteriously there by her side to provide.

So, they decided that Lainey had entertained an angel unaware. Their joyous discussion led Carrie to excitedly tell Lainey about the night she was at Sheriff Markum's when she received the baptism of the Holy Spirit.

She grew animated and excited and raved on and on about how it had made her feel and how she had prayed with the strange words and the comfort and peace it had brought.

Then, she told how she had always struggled to clearly understand a lot of what the bible was saying as she read and how that had suddenly opened up and her mind received it without restraint.

The more Carrie talked excitedly, the more Lainey

frowned. "You have to receive it too, Lainey, it will change your life!"

Lainey lay looking at Carrie. "No, I don't. I don't need it."

Carrie stood with her mouth hanging open. "What do you mean you don't need it? I know I need all of God I can get. How can you reject the Holy Spirit?"

"I have the Holy Spirit. I got it when I was born again."

"No, Lainey this is different. Yes, he is with you, but not in you."

"I'm fine without it."

"Fine? Fine? How can you be so arrogant and prideful, to reject the baptism of the Holy Spirit? How can you tell God you don't need his Spirit? How can you think you know more than God?

"Have you ever stopped to consider that the angel who was with you could have directly resulted from the sheriff praying for you in the Spirit? She has been praying in the Spirit for you ever since you first mentioned the darkness that was oppressing you.

"How can you say you don't need it? You won't always have the sheriff there praying for you in that way. The next time you may be on your own. Then you will wish you hadn't turned down the greatest gift God has ever given mankind. Yes, Jesus came to us to bring salvation, so - that - we - could - have - the - Holy Spirit."

Carrie's voice had grown louder. She was shocked and stunned that Lainey would reject something so incredibly wonderful. Why would anyone reject such a perfect and incredible and vitally necessary gift from God? How could she?

Sheriff Markum moved slightly in her chair and when Carrie looked over, she subtly nodded towards the door. Carrie shook her head and stormed out.

Once Carrie had left the room, the sheriff said, "She's been extremely concerned for you. She has wrestled continually with what to do and how to help you," said the sheriff.

Lainey looked sad. "I'm sure she has. I've heard that some churches believe that stuff about the Holy Spirit, but I was always taught that was over and done with back when the apostles all died."

"Yes, there are many churches who do teach that."

"But you don't believe it?"

"No Lainey, I don't. There are ample scriptures that talk about how we are all to be baptized in the Holy Spirit with the evidence of speaking in tongues. Jesus said that it was more beneficial that he go away so that the Holy Spirit could come and we could be baptized with the fire of the Spirit."

"But I have the Holy Spirit, don't I?"

"Yes, Lainey you do. After Jesus died and rose again, he met several times with the disciples. It is recorded at one meeting that he breathed on them and said receive the Holy Spirit. But then he also urged them to wait for the baptism of the Holy Spirit. It is two very separate things."

Lainey sat quietly. Her heart was burning, yearning to know more, but her mind kept wanting to resist it. "I want to know more, but not now."

Sheriff Markum smiled. "How about I do this... I'll write down some scriptures and some of my thoughts and give them to you. That way you will have them and can read them anytime you want."

Lainey smiled. "Thank you. I will. I promise."

AMELIA HAD LAID on the cave floor quietly in defeat the rest of the day. Every plan she schemed, she quickly discarded when she realized there were a dozen different ways why it wouldn't work.

The short winter day was ending, and it was growing darker in the cave. Jacob had spent most of his day just staring out from the cave, sitting cross-legged, still as a stone. She wasn't sure if he was in a trance or just staring. She thought at one point he had taken a drug of some sort, but she wasn't sure.

"You know I'm a cop, right?" Amelia spoke for the first time in hours.

Jacob whirled around to look at her, his mouth hanging open. "So?" Was his only retort.

"So... I'm working undercover to capture you. There will be other officers and law enforcement coming to find me." Jacob burst out laughing.

"Well, we saw how that worked for you, didn't we?" He doubled up laughing which just angered Amelia even more. "Who captured who?"

Wiping the tears of laughter from his face, he said, "It's time now for me to prepare."

Amelia's stomach knotted as Jacob walked away from the cave, and out of her site. She had to do something and do it now. Her mind and body was so tense, it felt as though her thoughts were just static on a radio.

She struggled between moments of clear thought and panic so strong that she thought it would stop her heart. She had pulled with her body as hard as she could against the rope to see if it would slip from under the rocks. It had not moved. She tried to wiggle in every way imaginable to see if she could loosen the wrap and rope that was tied around her. Nothing had worked, and it had all only increased her fatigue.

After several hours though, Jacob had not come back. Where had he gone?

Then she heard the crunch of snow underfoot and suddenly, there he was again. He rekindled the little campfire and sat to warm himself.

She almost asked him where he had gone, but then didn't want to hear the answer. It had been dark for sometime and had to be well into the night. He didn't speak as he sat squatting once again by the fire to warm himself.

Then she heard another screech. Another bobcat. But wait, no, it was different. She listened again, and there it was. It was not the high-pitched cry of a bobcat, but a more fierce guttural growl.

Oh no! It was a mountain lion. They had been nearly eradicated from this area decades ago, but in the last few years they had repopulated the mountains. Here she lay with no way to defend herself. She only hoped that it would just go away. She hoped she was far enough in the back of the cave that it wouldn't notice her, she hoped.

Jacob heard the cry as well and turned his head to look out into the dark, being very still. Then suddenly as fast as a flash, the lion was upon him. Amelia turned her head away and shut her eyes tight, trembling in fear.

She could hear the ripping and tearing of flesh as Jacob screamed. Was she to be next? Her entire body shook in terror.

Then finally, there were no more screams. She lay still hoping the lion wouldn't notice her further back in the cave.

Flesh still ripped and slopping noises ensued as the lion ate. Suddenly, a thought hit her that made her want to laugh deliriously, but she dare not.

Creation, Jacob's divine creation, had just consumed him.

BACK AT THE station Carrie and Sheriff Markum were busy at the white board.

Beau Johnson - coin-yes / cult-no /drugs-yes

Corey Stiles - coin-yes / cult-yes / drugs-no

Amanda Lee - coin-yes / cult-yes / drugs-no

Erin Jenkins - coin-no / cult-no / drugs-yes

"Beau and Erin both had an involvement with the drug cartel. I believe they were killed because the cartel wanted them dead, but disguised the kill as that of the serial killer. I believe Beau just happened to have a coin that he had found," Carrie said.

"And Corey and Amanda were part of the cult. Something went wrong there, and they were marked for an execution," said Sheriff Markum. "It might have taken us a lot longer to untangle this web if Marissa hadn't been rescued.

"What about the pentagram markings?" Carrie asked.

Sheriff Markum pulled out the crime scene photos again. "Let's take another look now that we have more information."

"I see what are remains of a pentagram at both Corey and Amanda's, and Beau's too. So, how could the drug cartel know about that? And wasn't Beau the first victim? He must be a cult killing and they tied him to the drug cartel by accident."

"He had a coin. Maybe that put him in the crosshairs of the cult. That coin is sacred to them," the sheriff said.

Carrie stood thinking and nodded. "We need more information from Amelia. Have you called her yet?"

"I'll do that now." Sheriff Markum dialed Amelia's phone and there was no answer. She left a voice mail for her to call the sheriff before she was to report back to the Sardis Lake compound.

"I know the answers are right in front of us, but I just can't see them yet," said Carrie.

"I'm sure we will soon, very soon."

AMELIA HAD LAID BARELY BREATHING for what seemed like hours. She had heard the lion eat and then lick to clean himself. Several times she thought he had gone, but then heard movement once again. He was guarding his kill.

Then without warning, the lion stood, took the carcass, what was left of it, in his powerful jaws, and walked away.

I'm alone. I'm all alone. I have to get out of here. Amelia began to try to roll violently away from the rocks that held the rope. She would wind herself up towards the rock and attempt to roll away with whatever force she could generate.

Nothing at all happened the first two times. She wanted to give up. Her body told her to give up. But, she knew she couldn't.

The third time a few of the rocks shifted. The fourth time she could feel the rope gain some slack. She rested then, to gain enough strength to give it one more good solid effort.

On the fifth time, she hurled herself the best she could with her arms and legs bound, away from the rocks. And, the rope sprang free.

Amelia rolled to a stop. Looking back towards the rocks, she saw they were all still in place. The rope had broken where she had cut on it earlier. The constant tugging had continued to weaken and fray the rope until it gave way.

But, she was free! Well, she was well on her way to being free.

Thinking once again to the next hurdle, unwrapping herself, she had a thought. It was a dangerous thought, but she had to try it. She deliberately rolled towards the campfire that Jacob had built. It had died down considerably, but there were still burning embers.

Could it be that the fire, the thing that had been meant to kill her, would now be her deliverer?

She rolled and pushed with her feet like they were rudders until she had the rope knot as close to the fire as she could get. It did nothing for a moment, then she heard a crackle. She poised herself to roll away quickly to smother any flame that grew too large.

Tiny little sparks gripped the hemp and traveled along the rope. None growing into large flames, just eating away like tiny glowing insects. Soon the glows subsided, and the rope was still intact.

She needed to get closer and maybe in a different spot. She could get burned, but she had to try.

Rolling in a different direction she scooted as close to the fire as she could. The fire caught the rope and flared to life. Amelia held her eyes closed and waited until she couldn't wait another second.

She felt the rope release and then immediately rolled away. The rope had caught fire but the several layers of clothing she wore had protected her skin. She lay panting from anxiety and relief.

Free. Now, she was free. The fire had riddled the swaddling of cloth and was easily removed in tattered strips. Amelia worked quickly to reach under her layers and undo the taped bundles she wore next to her skin.

Ripping them away, she felt a rush of cold next to her exposed skin. She made quick work of tearing open the packages. First she held her feet as close to the fire as she dared to warm them. Then she put on one pair of socks, then the zippered baggies.

Next, she put the second pair of socks on, then the trash bags. Over all those layers, she pulled on the rubber-bottomed socks. She wasn't sure the awkward getup would be easy to walk in, but at least it might keep her feet warm and dry.

She tugged on the two pair of warm gloves and stocking caps, zipped her hoodie up to her chin and pulled the drawstring tight down on her head. It was time to go.

The full moon had gone down quite a lot and now played peek-a-boo behind clouds. She was thankful that she was familiar with this area and the cave, because now she needed to rely on her memory to help get her out of there.

Reaching the bottom of the cliff, she suddenly stopped. Jacob had parked her car only about a mile or two away, but where were the keys? Had Jacob had them in his pocket?

She took a deep sigh, shut her eyes and climbed back up to the mouth of the cave. On her hands and knees she crawled over to where the lion had killed Jacob. Her stomach began to lurch and gave its best effort to release food she hadn't had.

Her body convulsed with dry heaves, but she had to look. Then the moon stepped back out into the night sky and the bloody remains lay before her. Strips of cloth that had once been khaki trousers lay strewn about.

Amelia reached out toward what looked like it might have been a pocket, with a short burst of whimpers escaping from her lips. Her hand shook as her gloved fingers clasped the bloody lump of fabric and she pulled it to her. She sat back in relief. She could feel the familiar shape of her car keys.

In one swift movement, she shoved them into her pocket, stood up, and climbed back down the rocky cliff.

THE DEA and FBI had spent the afternoon hammering out a deal with Doc. He had agreed to turn witness to all the cartel's and specifically Joe's dealings in exchange for being charged.

Hours after negotiations, agents brought both Bud and Jimmy into the station. They had seized and cordoned off the trailer where they cooked meth. Doc had been insistent that both his brothers receive the same deal they had offered him. He reasoned that they had been working with Joe much longer than he had, and therefore would have much more information to provide.

The fact that they had not willingly come forward hindered their willingness to make such a deal. Finally, when Doc refused to give them any information without the release of his brothers, the agencies caved, but with specific requirements.

Sheriff Markum had put her recommendation in as well, believing that it would be beneficial to have their information over the convictions.

Very late that evening, when Carrie and the sheriff were still trying to get the mountain of paperwork done, Amelia walked into the station.

She was a mess, and the sheriff ran quickly to her, helping her sit in the first chair they came to. She was rambling out a story but they could make no sense of it.

"Calm down Amelia. We are here. Take a deep breath and start from the beginning."

EPILOGUE

A week after Amelia came stumbling back into the Sheriff's Station, Carrie pulled out of Wilburton, heading north just before dusk. As she drove through the mountains, she pulled over to a scenic lookout and parked where she could see the mountains and the setting sun one last time.

Her heart was full of peace. It had been one of the most challenging periods of time in her life, but also would be remembered as one of the most wonderful.

So many threads had been woven together and then with persistence and God's help, they had unraveled them. They had extensively interviewed everyone involved with the cult, including Sharma who had been stunned and heartbroken by what Jacob had done.

Carrie just could not understand how anyone could worship an object, a created object. She would much rather worship the Creator, rather than his creation.

Much of why Jacob did what he did, would have been lost forever with his death had they not found his journals. He had written maniacally in journal after journal. He wrote every thought and compulsion in great detail.

Beau Johnson had taken a coin that a cult member had lost. Jacob retraced their movements and had found that Beau had taken the lost coin. He had been furious that Beau had so casually taken the coin as if it were just any other object. Their sacred coin. His anger had burned at Beau for his disrespect. When Ava had lost her coin, it rekindled his anger, because he knew someone else would find and dishonor it the way Beau had done.

Corey and Amanda had never taken the group seriously. They refused to move to the compound and continued to party, drink, and have sexual relations on a whim. Jacob felt he had to get rid of them, that he had to purge the non-believers, to maintain the purity of the whole.

The markings they had decided were pentagrams, were actually a strange derivative that Jacob drew over and over in his journals. They had the same star like shape, but were turned a different direction and all had a unique spiral in the center, and random dots placed at the intersecting lines. The doodling of a madman.

Jacob had driven the missing vehicles, which contained the victims shoes, socks, and coats into Sardis Lake which was within walking distance of the compound. Once back at the compound, it was easy to hitch a ride later back into town to his own vehicle. No one ever suspected a thing.

Erin Jenkins was the first killing of the cartel that they had tried to cover up by making it look like it was one of the others. It had not happened on a Sunday. The cartel had not been privy to the presence of the coin, so there hadn't been one placed in her pocket, had they even been able to get one.

They had heard through rumors of the murders that the victims had had their shoes, socks, and coats removed, so the cartel did the same.

They released the rest of the cult members. They could find no criminal activity which they could be charged with. A rogue mountain lion, a rare incident, had killed Jacob. So there would be no charges filed for the first three murders. His sentence and punishment had already been delivered.

The DEA and FBI were still strategizing over how they best wanted to handle the drug cartel, but they had released Doc and his brothers with the terms that they were to testify against the cartel when called upon. Bud did not want to move to the city, but as soon as it was possible, Doc and Jimmy settled into the apartment Doc had previously rented.

Sheriff Markum was pressing charges on the men who had taken Marissa and killed Erin. Marissa had overheard enough behind the closet door to convict.

Lainey and Marissa recovered nicely. Marissa's fervor to be an investigative journalist was somewhat subdued though. She still dreamed of being a famous investigative reporter, but thought she might venture out into less dangerous waters.

They had taken Lainey back to Oklahoma City the previous day and she was in the hospital there. So, now Carrie was traveling home on her own.

The sky lit up with beautiful gold, oranges, and reds. *Stunning,* Carrie thought. She smiled and thought about the last year of her life. What a change had taken place. Chaos had ensued with some of the most challenging cases she had ever experienced. And her life had been transformed during them all.

She thought of Billy. They had talked for hours the other night, neither one wanting to hang up. Her heart felt full, and she was excited to go home and see him again. Would it be the same, or maybe even better? Who knew? It might not even work out at all, but she was willing to try.

Her thoughts shifted to the deep spiritual changes that had occurred in her life, and they flooded her with thankfulness. She had been so lost. Bitterness and anger had been sending her spiraling down a deep and dark hole.

Her stomach knotted as she thought about her futile attempts to change her destructive behavior from the sheer force of her own will, and then how it had failed every time.

She thought about Pride's letter coming at the exact right time in her life, and the sacrifice that dear woman had made for her precious surrogate daughter, Jenny. Carrie felt such sorrow and yet thankfulness for her. She yearned for more than just the letter from Pride. Oh, how she would love to sit by her side and talk with her for hours on end.

And then there was Sheriff Markum. My, what a woman of God she was! She had such a quiet and godly confidence, amid deep humility. She was wise, and real, and genuine. A spiritual mother that God had sent to Carrie when she had needed her the most.

Then there was her introduction to the fire of the Holy

Ghost. She could have never dreamed her life could come alive any more than it already had, but it did.

Yes, this had been quite a year. Carrie smiled as she put her SUV in gear to drive back down the mountain. It had been her redemption year. The redemption of Carrie Border.

AUTHORS NOTE

My first novel, The Blood, was set in a completely fictitious town. With The Water and The Fire, I set the characters in real Oklahoma towns. The landmarks, streets, businesses, are almost completely genuine. I have however taken creative license with certain aspects. I meant no disrespect to those places and I hope that they will view my creative license as neutral and having no bearing on them whatsoever.

If you would like to read Sheriff Markum's scriptures and study notes to Lainey, go to The Fire page on my website and click the button 'Sheriff Markum's Letter to Lainey'. You will need the following password to access and read the letter.

1S2h3eri9ff

The characters in this book are all completely fictional.

The sheriff's department for Latimer County is in Wilburton, but I created this from my imagination only regarding how it might be, where it might be, and how it would be run.

The religion mentioned in the book, Zoroastrianism is an ancient religion predating the Muslim religion in the Middle East. It is still practiced by a few participants throughout the world, but is dwindling since they do not allow members from outside their familial circle to participate.

The offshoot was a cult that I made up and has no bearing whatsoever on that ancient religion.

Once again, let me say that I have no operational knowledge of how the various Oklahoma County Sheriff's departments, DEA, FBI, or the OSBI are run. I mean no disrespect to these outstanding agencies in my creative depiction of them and their officers. I hold law enforcement in the highest regard and I hope, should they read my books, that they can laugh at my creative portrayal and not take it as disrespectful.

ABOUT THE AUTHOR

Nancy's love of writing fiction began in the seventh grade in literature class.

Through the years she has written magazine articles, newspaper articles, countless blog posts, and both fiction and non-fiction books. Many of those books have made it to the Amazon best seller ranking as well.

Nancy resides in Oklahoma in the state she was born. Always a creative person, she has done more types of arts and crafts than you can imagine. Recently, she has found a love for watercolor painting in her spare time.

In recent years, she has been a professional silversmith and also did studio jewelry training for silversmithing. She was also a licensed Oklahoma state Realtor but is now spending the bulk of her time writing.

Nancy feels that writing fiction for the sheer sake of entertainment is not good enough. She has always desired for her novels to touch her readers' lives and to even change them for the better in some small way. The many emails, texts, messages, and reviews she has received is a testament to that.

facebook.com/NancyJacksonAuthor
x.com/NAJackson
instagram.com/najackson

ALSO BY NANCY JACKSON

Novels

The Redemption Series

The Blood - Book 1

The Water - Book 2

The Fire - Book 3

The Redemption Series Box Set

The Box, a Carrie Border Novella

Carrie Border, The Prequel - coming soon (summer 2024)

Choices Like Rivers

Business Enrichment

How to Go From Hobby to Business

How to Write Publish and Market Your Book

Social Media Marketing Blitz Workbook and Planner

Please review this book and any others that you have read.

It will help me more than you know!

www.ingramcontent.com/pod-product-compliance
Lightning Source LLC
Chambersburg PA
CBHW030812310726
48980CB00006B/475/J

* 9 7 8 0 5 7 8 5 6 2 8 4 1 *